THE GOOD BANKER

A FINANCIAL SUSPENSE

MICHAEL G.

This is a work of fiction. Names, characters, places, and incidents either are the product of the author's imagination or are used fictitiously. Any resemblance to actual persons, living or dead, events, or locales is entirely coincidental.

ISBN 978-1-7373648-0-1 (paperback)
ISBN 978-1-7373648-1-8 (ebook)
ISBN 978-1-7373648-2-5 (hardback)

Cover Design by 100Covers.com
Editing by Amy Pattee Colvin www.amycolvinwordsmith.com
Interior Design by FormattedBooks.com

DEDICATION

To those who lost their lives due to the COVID-19 pandemic.

PROLOGUE

A chill is in the air as I sit on a wooden balcony, enjoying my morning coffee. I drink in the scene below—a sapphire blue lake nestled at the bottom of a cliff; a sharp ridgeline warms with the glow of the rising sun. A million-dollar view is in front of me, and millions of dollars sit in my bank account.

I contemplate success. What does it really mean? How is it defined? For some, success means winning more of life's challenges than losing. For others, it's having a certain amount of zeros in their net worth. Does success mean performing well in your profession to earn various awards? Is it having a loving family? Is it being a well-respected member of your community or having a large circle of friends? Perhaps it means having the freedom to do what you want at any given point in time.

I've often struggled to define success for myself, which is why I need to tell my story for the greater good of society and for the "little guys" working within behemoth corporations.

In this quiet morning light, I enjoy the sunrise and ponder the meaning of success while looking over this surreal body of water. I am reminded of the first day of my banking career, July 15th, 2004. I walked into the 41st floor of One Brickell Tower in Miami, Florida.

ONE

"Welcome to DMNC Bank USA, Jacob Gilbert," said a woman in her mid-forties with a short bob cut. She wore a conservative dark grey pants suit with a white blouse. My eyes went directly to her right lapel, where I saw a bright white name tag stating *Alexandra McGuire* and *DMNC Bank USA.*

I turned towards the lady and hesitantly smiled, "Thank you, Alexandra; it's a pleasure to be here today." A quick gaze to the left lapel highlighted a small circular golden-colored pin proudly displaying *15 years of service.* My initial impression was that Alexandra took great pride as a loyal corporate employee. Within the first couple of minutes of meeting her, I realized she ensured her trainees were well provided for and that she took personal accountability for how well they performed and grew within the organization.

"Please call me Alex; we have coffee and bagels in the corner. Feel free to grab some as we have a big day ahead. We will start in about fifteen minutes, and I've asked all the new hires to introduce yourselves to each other in the meantime."

I responded with a half-baked nervous smile and felt my stomach sink a little bit further as I walked through the doors of our training room. As far back as I could remember, I've had severe social anxiety whenever entering a new place with many unknown people—whether competing in a sport, going to a party, attending the first day of school, going on a first date, any first really—my weak stomach always showed its ugly head to take control over my entire body. Although I was a Division I athlete, I never could entirely control my nerves in these situations, so I'd clam up and not perform my best.

I took a deep breath and closed my eyes for a second longer than normal. Then I walked through the doorway into the training room. Five people stood in front of the twenty-five-foot continuous window lining the left side of the room. A whiteboard with a projector perched at the front of the room, and five rows of long tables filled the rest of the room. Each table had four seats, and in front of each chair was a book, a company pen, a box, a bag, and a notepad—all of them were placed perfectly with great precision.

My eyes drew directly to the view. The sight of the Biscayne Bay from downtown Miami is a sight best seen in person. You see three causeway bridges that connect the City of Miami to Miami Beach. You see the port with gigantic cruise ships filled with bright-eyed tourists waiting for their next adventure, and as your gaze reaches further into the distance, you view private islands in the bay adorned with mansions owned by celebrities. You see private boats on the bay and bigger yachts in the ocean on the other side of Miami Beach. A look to your left, towards the downtown area, reveals over twenty cranes working on high-rise condos; you see Bayfront Park and the Miami Heat area's perimeter hitting right against the water. Then you look to the right and realize you are smack in the middle of other high-rise office buildings that line the Brickell Avenue area.

A friendly voice interrupted my visual tour. "Hi, I'm Tim. What is your name? Did you find the place okay?"

I tried to peel my eyes from the beautiful sights that compete with the Manhattan skyline. I glanced to my left, the direction from which the greeting came, and viewed my first coworker in the banker training program. He was a rather short Asian fellow, in decent shape, who spoke in perfect English. He looked younger than twenty, as his hair was thick and gelled to professional perfection. I wished I had hair like that. He was clean-shaven; although, I doubt he'd be able to grow a full beard even if he tried. His clothes looked a bit rumpled and not as crisp as I would expect a new bank trainee to wear. Yet, he seemed comfortable in them.

"Hi Tim, I'm Jacob—first days always make me a little nervous. What college did you go to?" My anxiety showed through my higher-than-normal vocal tone.

"I went to Florida International University. But I graduated five years ago. Where did you go? Is this your first job?" Tim asked with genuine interest.

"Yes, it is," I responded with a less than confident smile. "I actually just moved down here yesterday, and yes, I found the place okay. The view is tremendous. I don't know how we are going to concentrate with *that* right there." I gestured to the window. "I just graduated college two months ago from Boston College. Where did you work the past five years?"

"I was working at a different bank. Have you met with Harry? He was my old manager, and he moved here to DMNC last year as the Florida Market President. He recruited me. He told me I could make more money here, and that was the catalyst for me making the move."

"Cool. Well, if it's okay, can we sit together?" I asked as I eyed the breakfast spread in the back of the room.

"Sure, but I sit in the front row to portray that I am a diligent employee." He offered a slight wink.

I half chuckled, placed my binder at the front table, and walked to the breakfast station thinking about my intense interview with Harry a month earlier. I gave myself an imaginary pat on the back by connecting with Harry's protégé immediately.

I was juggling a coffee in one hand and picking a cinnamon raisin bagel in the other when I heard a frat-like, boisterous, and embarrassing, "JOOOOEEEEEY!"

I snapped around to see Dann Frazier—two n's because one is just not enough for Mr. Frazier—walk through the door. Though I found his entrance unseemly, I briskly walked over to him.

A broad, fake grin plastered his face as he strutted into the room wearing a new bespoke black pinstriped suit with black pebbled leather Italian designer buckle shoes. Dann loved to be the center of attention. He continued his loud and lively greeting with a faux New Yorker accent, "What UP? We are finally here! This place is awesome, bro; look at dat view! Why didn't you call me last night? I went with these chicks to The Grove; it was hella time! Then I was going back to my place with—"

Wishing the floor could swallow me and worrying about first impressions with other coworkers, I cut him off, saying, "Well, I arrived pretty late yesterday afternoon and wanted to get a good night rest as we had to be here before eight this morning and I wasn't sure about traffic."

As my voice trailed, Dann picked right up, "I told you this move is going to be amazeballs for you."

My eyes drifted across the large rectangular-shaped room to see who else from our training class had arrived. I noticed at least eight other people talking to each other, mostly one-on-one conversations. I glanced back at Dann, "Oh, hey, don't call me Joey. Use my real name, please."

Dann energetically replied in a voice too loud for the room, "Why? You are such a Joey. That name is way cooler than your real one."

From behind me came a monotone question, "Who is Joey?"

I turned and saw the familiar face of the Florida Market President, Harold Goldman—the man who interviewed and hired me.

Dann calmed his tone slightly and responded, "Oh, this is Jacob, but we call him Joey. Doesn't he look like a Joey?"

Harry proceeded, "Well, I don't care what anyone looks like; I just want everyone to be excited starting at this firm, and I wish much success to all. This training class had many applicants. You all should feel honored to be selected. There are only fifteen of you, and I expect each one of you to make us proud. Now, if you'll excuse me, I need some coffee to start my day."

We watched our big boss making his way to the coffee and food table, confidently carrying his small and round stature in an understated designer suit.

Dann turned back to me, "We can pick up our apartment keys Saturday morning! So excited to be moving into the Camden; it's supposed to be one of the best buildings for young professionals in all of downtown. Can you say 'livin' da bachelor life'?"

"Oh wow, I don't even have a bed to sleep in," I replied as my eyes peered around the room.

"You better get on that."

"Can't tonight; Jen is driving down from Jacksonville for my birthday."

"Oh right, happy birthday! You gonna hit that at your hotel?"

"Um, you know it's not like that."

"That's right, Jen won't let you into her pussy cat. Meow!" Dann laughed at his lewd joke.

"Shhhhh. Not the place. Okay?" My irritated tone came through.

Wanting to get out of this conversation, I scanned the room for someone to save me from my discomfort, then Dann nonchalantly mentioned, "I will make reservations for three at Prime 112 at 7 pm. We can sing happy birthday to our big boy."

Can he just invite himself like that? Well, he is my future roommate and friends with Jen as well; it'll be fun, I hope.

A confident voice entered from my left, "Hi fellas, my name is Steve, and this is Don. Nice to meet you. Are you excited for the first day?" Dann and I slightly turned towards two gentlemen in their late 20s to early 30s.

Steve had jet black hair, six feet tall, and it appeared he enjoyed the gym based on his V-shaped torso visible through the cut of his suit. He also seemed to enjoy flashy watches as my eyes immediately locked onto an enormous hunk of junk timepiece that adorned his right wrist.

His sidekick, Don, was probably five and a half feet tall and not-too-skinny but not-too-fat. His auburn hair was so carefully styled it must have taken him thirty minutes at least, but most noticeable was his teeth. It was evident his front teeth were fake—they looked like chicklet gum and were so white that the morning sun glistening off the Biscayne Bay seemed dull after a peek at his grill.

Dann greeted them with an oversized phony smile, "Greetings, gentlemen, it is quite a privilege to be starting at this fine financial institution. You know Joey and I go way back, so it's nice to meet others we will be working with. What were you doing previously?"

Before I heard their answers, my mind drifted again; *I've known Dann for ten months, that's not "way back" to me. I wonder what "ages" means to Dann?* With effort, I redirected my mind and rejoined the conversation.

Don scrambled forward to Dann like a puppy running to a bowl of fresh puppy chow. "Well, thank you for asking. Steve and I just spent the past four years at Smith Barney. We had some outstanding years but felt the culture wasn't quite right for us, so we made a move in tandem. I think it's great you two are seasoned friends as it really helps during the transition period of changing firms. Also, it helps us to carpool as we live up in Palm Beach County!"

Outstanding years? Not right culture? Move in tandem? My mind bounced around like a ping pong ball—another sign of my anxiety. All these questions flowed through my brain, but it wasn't the right time to ask them. I dreaded that this training program might be an overly gelled hair, fancy suit, designer shoe, flashy watch wearing one-upmanship contest.

As Dann was about to gloat about another asinine thing, trying to impress the Palm Beach boys, we were saved by the bell, for now.

"GOOD MORNING ALL. I ask you all to take a seat." Shouted Alex as she made her way to the front of the room.

I walked towards the front of the room with my lukewarm coffee in hand and couldn't help but think, *all that chatter happened in only fifteen minutes? I have all this discomfort trembling throughout my body. How much longer before training is over? At least, I have an awesome birthday dinner to look forward to.*

"Jacob, up here." Tim motioned to the seat next to him, right in the front row. The other thirteen new hires filed into the other seats in the room, and Harry took a stance right in front of the vast window to the left.

Once everyone was seated and the chit-chat slowed to an end, Alex looked out the window and announced, "Isn't this a great view, ladies and gentlemen?"

Ladies? We have ladies? I was probably the only one not looking out the window as I scanned the room for the ladies. *Ah, there's one, and there is another, and what a beauty she is.*

The beauty's eyes moved from the window back to the front of the room, and she couldn't help see my big noggin swiveled to the back of the room. We made eye contact, and she politely smiled. I made it seem I was looking around the room and quickly turned toward Tim, noticing he still didn't have a jacket on.

Alex then looked at Harry, "I really hate to be the party pooper, but we are going to have to close the blinds."

What? No!

"Team members tend not to follow instructions when they stare out the window." We all looked at Alex as if we'd dropped our ice cream cone on the ground.

Alex noticed the discontent in the room, "Okay, we can leave the blinds open for now. But once mid-afternoon comes along, I'll close them as that is when the classroom fatigue definitely sets in."

Phew, I still have a view. At least for a while.

"The first thing I'd like to do is go around the room and request everyone stand up, introduce themselves, and share one fun fact about yourself that you think will surprise the group. I like to do this because in six months, when we are—fingers crossed—graduating from this banker trainee program, I will ask you to do the same, and you will all be tremendously better at this."

Alex paused for a moment. "I will go first. My name is Alexandra McGuire, but please call me Alex. I have been a DMNC Bank employee for seventeen years, and I love coming to work and putting my name tag on every day. It lights me up to have two new trainee classes each year. I love seeing you on day one like this and take great pleasure seeing you years later making a difference at the bank and hopefully moving up the ranks.

"I grew up in New York State, came down here for college, and never left. As you can see from the view out the window, this place is paradise. But make no mistake, you need to come to work every day and put forth the effort required to be successful. One thing that most people wouldn't know about me is that I am also a ballroom dance instructor."

Everyone's mild demeanor perked up as we unexpectedly learned Alex liked to grace the dance floor, adding another layer to the person who held our fragile careers in her hands.

"Harry, why don't you go next." Alex looked over to Harry, leaning against the window with a cup of coffee in hand.

Harry walked towards the front middle of the room. He stopped about two feet from me, giving me a direct view of his pleated crotch. In a complete monotone, he said, "Yeah, thanks, Alex. As all of you should already know, my name is Harry Goldman, the Florida Market President for DMNC. My office is on the top floor of this building. Some of the people in the window offices on my floor sat in your seats only a few years ago. Let me tell you, the view on that floor trumps this!" He chuckled at his flat joke.

Then his face became more serious. "I took over this market about eighteen months ago. DMNC is a subsidiary of a very large German Bank conglomerate with the most attention given to the New York and California markets. They think of Florida as this sleepy retirement village that attracts a lot of foreigners. Just look at the skyline of cranes; if that doesn't signal growth, I don't know what does. Let me tell you there are tons of opportunities here, and all of you were hand-picked to harvest all the possibilities in this market."

As Harry adjusted his coke bottle glasses, Alex inched towards him and whispered, "Introduction, please."

"Oh. Haha. See, class? Alex will always keep us on track. I grew up in Ocala. How many native Floridians do we have here?" Two hands went up. "Yeah, that's what I expected. I graduated from the University of Florida and immediately moved to Miami and started my banking career, just like a few of you recent graduates we have here today. You'd never know it by my current rotund shape, but I went to college on a wrestling scholarship. However, by junior year I was more interested in touching women than men, so I quit."

A roar of laughter emerged from the frat-boy clan in the rear, and I tried to get a pulse on how the cutie behind me took the comment. I laughed along with the rest, being one of the sheep Harry wanted us to be. Tim gave me a peculiar look, which I didn't understand.

Alex walked back to the front of the room, faking a smile.

I bet she's cringing inside at Harry's comment. I would be if I were her.

"Okay then. Thank you, Harry."

"My pleasure. Don't mind me; I'm going to camp out in the back and listen to y'all introduce yourselves, then I'll make my way to my office."

Returning the room to a professional tone, Alex continued, "I always find it interesting how people choose their seats. As you noticed, I let you all pick your seats. Is it true the ones in the front are the most attentive and eager to learn?" As she glanced my way and I looked to my left at Tim. He gave me an ever-so-slight nod of the head, and I smirked.

I think I like this guy.

She continued, "Those of you in the back, wake up; you're going next."

Dann shot up like someone called tequila shots. "Hi everyone. My name is Dann. Yeah, just Dann but with a double N. You know, because two is always better than one."

I sunk into my seat as I want to escape this overly coy smugness that I am friends with. *How did I end up with this guy as my friend? He's loud; he's sloppy; he's crass—basically, everything I'm not. But I shouldn't be so hard on him; if it weren't for him, I'd probably be selling cars now.*

"I grew up on Long Island." *No, you didn't.* "I just graduated from the University of Miami. Go Canes!"

He turned to Harry and continued, "You know we got robbed last year. Should've been six National Championships." He turned back to the front of the room, "And something you wouldn't guess about me. Well, I was an all-state lacrosse player and was recruited to play in college but decided to focus on my grades instead."

I swiveled my neck to look back at Dann. His grandiose belly strained against the lower buttons of his white shirt, spilling slightly over his brass Ferragamo belt buckle. I couldn't help rolling my eyes. *Yeah, I was on the ATP Tour and quit to focus on my grades too.*

Suddenly I felt like I'd been gut-punched as the coffee and bagel were burning my stomach. *What am I going to say at my turn? I have to sound confident and say something impressive and unique.*

While I was worrying about what to say, Dann sat down, and the person next to him stood up, flashing his oversized white front teeth. "Hi everyone, my name is Donald Deeds, but please call me Don. I grew up in Jacksonville. Y'all might think we're all rednecks from Jax, but we are not! I have been blessed in life to come from a prominent family in my home area and attended Clemson University, obtaining a bachelor's degree in finance. Although my family was in the restaurant business, I always had aspirations of starting a career in finance. I did just that, starting my career at Smith Barney, where I was one of the top rookie Financial Advisors in Florida a few years back. But after speaking to Harry and others, I realized this institution offers tremendous growth opportunities, which is why Steve and I decided to make the move." Don rested his hand on Steve's shoulder.

They look like they're about to pose for engagement pictures.

Steve got up and belted out a high pitched, "YAOOOOOOOO." The entire room erupted in laughter and cat-call.

I immediately glanced at Alex. The painful smirk frozen on her face blatantly stated, "Who did we just hire?"

Since Harry was in the back of the room, I couldn't get a good read on his reaction.

Steve swayed back and forth, and a nervous tick caused his right shoulder to rise whenever he was about to start talking. "My name is Steve Arnold. I grew up on Long Island. New York in da house!" He smiled and pointed to Dann with a playful gun-like hand gesture. "I moved to Florida to attend the University of Central Florida, then moved to the Palm Beach area five years ago where I met Don at our previous firm. I look forward to learning and becoming a better all-around banker. So, the surprising thing about me is that this physique is all-natural; no steroids used here! Anyways, let's do this!" He pounded his hand on the table as he sat back down.

My eyes brightened. *What a couple of characters we have in this room.*

"Next up," said Alex.

I don't even think I took in the next person's name as their voice bored the crap out of me, and I was still stressing about what I would say for my introduction. The introductions droned on.

"Hi, my name is Pierre St. Paul. I grew up in Haiti; I played college football at the University of South Florida..."

"Hi, I'm Naomi Peters; I come from Jamaica, the land of three little birds…"

A lean, expressionless, tall white guy stands up—he must have been six foot seven inches tall. "Hi, I'm Ward Riggins. Believe it or not, I'm one of the few that actually grew up in South Florida, and yes, I'm aware, I'm tall. Some even call me Tall Ward."

Why does waiting my turn give me such anxiety? My attention drifted and became engulfed in that stunning view. Another five people droned on—nothing exciting or worth remembering. Then it's her turn.

A young, vivacious woman stood up. She adjusted her snug navy blue suit jacket and ran her hands down the front of her tight pencil skirt that just showed how curvalicious she was. Her slim body couldn't have been much more than five feet tall. She appeared to have DD breasts and a sexy rear-end any guy would notice from a football field away. As she stood, she swayed her body subtly and enticingly.

With a big smile, she introduced herself. "Hi, my name is Rosanna Perez. But my friends and family call me Rosie because I make everyone see things through rose-colored lenses."

Everyone chuckled.

Beautiful and funny; Hello, Rosie!

"I was born in the D.R.—Dominican Republic for those who aren't familiar. But I grew up down here and graduated from Florida Atlantic University two years ago. I worked as a wine distributor for the past few years but have always had a passion for helping people financially. Umm, something surprising about me...umm…I don't know." She started to blush.

I felt the heat of her discomfort wash over me. *Say something!*

"It's okay, Rosie, take your time," Alex said soothingly.

Rosie nervously chuckled, "It's so hard to compete with all of you in this impressive class, but I'll assume you wouldn't guess that I was valedictorian of my high school." She then blushed to an even deeper tone of red, made eye contact with no one, and quickly sat back down.

I glanced at her one last time, but she was still embarrassed and looked at the table. *We have someone smart and humble here. Fellas in the back—take notes!*

Alex's voice piped up, "That is some accomplishment, Rosie. Please be more confident! Okay, now only two more left, Tim, you're up!"

"Hi everyone, I'm Tim Chen, well Timothy, but please don't call me that because I'll tense up thinking I'm in trouble."

I locked eyes with him and gave him a slight chuckle.

"Although you may think I came here on a boat, I was born and raised in Seattle. My parents are from Korea. I moved to Florida in high school and also went to FAU." He looked directly at Rosie. "But I was not as intelligent as Rosie to be valedictorian!"

Rosie blushed again and seemed like she wanted to sink further into her seat.

"Believe it or not, I'm married. *His name is…*" Tim promptly stopped speaking—you could hear a pin drop as we all remained quiet and still. Just as the awkward moment started to pass, Tim broke into fervent laughter. Everyone was dumbfounded.

"I'm just kidding! Well, I really am married—to a woman. Her name is Sharyn."

The class has a good round of laughs. As he sat down, my eyes locked with Tim's, and I whispered, "Good one!"

How am I going to compete with the comedian and valedictorian?

Alex chirped to Tim, "Well, your wife should have reminded you to wear your jacket to work."

Tim sat further back in his chair and softly responded, "Oh, I left it in my car."

"Okay, class, last but not least, Jacob, you're up."

Oh shit, what am I gonna say?

TWO

My mind drifted back to fifteen months prior. It was the spring of 2003.

"What is going on, Jac! Your first serve is 70 miles per hour?" Concern bled through the voice of my college tennis coach, Davis.

"I don't know. I have this feeling like a knife is stabbing me in my shoulder blade," I nervously responded.

"Do you want to get it checked out by a doctor?"

"No, let's continue. Might be because it's freakin' 45 degrees out." *Dammit!*

"That one was 65."

After the serve, I pulled up and grabbed the back of my shoulder.

Coach Davis noticed and decided to change things up, "Let's stop serving and practice cross-court forehand."

As I moved from center baseline to my right, every step felt like the knife was getting deeper. Topspin forehand smash. Again and again and again.

We both walked to the bench and sat right in front of the net pole. Coach Davis noticed that my mind was elsewhere and solemnly declared, "I can't see you like this, Jac, something is wrong."

Ignoring my pain and reality, I responded, "I think I've just been sleeping wrong. My neck is stiff and affecting my shoulder."

Coach started massaging my shoulder. I screamed so loudly that all the players on the court stopped playing. "Oh my God, oh my God! It feels like someone is taking a chainsaw to my right shoulder." Tears of pain filled my eyes, and I gave the nod to the coach that I needed to get checked out.

"Well, we have some bad news." The orthopedist bluntly stated as he walked over to the bright board where he displayed my spinal MRI.

Is this what we all look like from within?

"You have a compacted cervical spinal disc. This means that the more you use your right arm, the worse it is going to get, which means you may need surgery."

Surgery!?!?! I still have eight matches left this season.

Coach Davis hesitantly asked the doctor, "How long will it take to recover?"

"Oh no, we cannot have that mentality here. Unfortunately, this is a long-term possible lingering injury. Jacob will not be able to return to action for at least eight weeks and will need to have a healthy dose of physical rehabilitation to dislodge the spinal discs to where they need to be for him to have a normal pain-free life."

I was brought up not to show my emotions, but I felt a sense of shame and embarrassment that I couldn't contain. I sat there motionless as tears welled in my eyes. As they ran down my face, Coach Davis put his arm around me and told me everything would be okay. We would just be patient and follow the doctor's orders.

I felt devastated. Thousands of hours of cardio and swings on the tennis court over the past ten years. Oh, and the scholarship. *What happens to that if I can't compete at a high level anymore?*

My mind was racing, and all I wanted to do was go back to my dorm and mope. And that is what I did the rest of that day and the next and the next. It wasn't until the third day when my father called me and gave me some tough love.

"Son, I understand you are very upset and disappointed. But life knocks us all down at times; this is one of those times for you. However, you still want to be successful. That means picking yourself up, going to rehab, and getting better."

I sat still, staring at the phone with nothing to say.

To fill the blank space, my old man continued, "You know, when you come home next month, I have a nice internship at the dealership for you. You can go to your rehab early in the morning and come to work afterward—it will look great on your resume for next year."

What?! Does he really think I'm going from D-I athlete to selling freaking cars?

"Um, yeah, I don't know, you know I'm not good with people." I hardly articulated the sentence.

"Go to rehab. Get it done. Talk soon, son. Mom sends her love."

"Okay, bye." Click.

Our father-son relationship was pretty superficial. If the old man weren't my father, I wouldn't have much to do with him. We were very different.

My father was the showman's man. He loved talking and connecting with people at work, in the community, and at church. He always gauged his success by how many people knew his name or how many stupid plaques he had in his office for success-in-excellence at the dealership. He loved showing off his plaques, and it was as if his success didn't exist if he didn't have the wall-hangings to prove it. He hated handing out trophies to people he didn't believe deserved them.

He liked to say, "Why are we giving awards to below-average players for just showing up? There's no success in being ordinary. The trophies are for being extraordinary."

I didn't care about trophies—maybe it was a passive-aggressive response to my dad. As I won trophy after trophy in youth tennis leagues, I just tossed them in my closet to collect dust. Then one day, my father came to my room and built shelves in two corners. He then went into my closet, dusted off the half dozen tournament trophies I won, and proudly displayed them in a space where only he, my mom, and I would see them. I couldn't have cared less, but I let him do what he needed to do.

After the shelves were up, he gestured to the trophies, "Now that's what I call success."

Is a plastic trophy a success? Is the meaning of life's success based on how much junk we can win with our name on it?

After selling cars for years and receiving success plaques nearly every year, he became finance manager—the hours were better, and he could regularly get home at a reasonable hour for dinner. New job, same attitude; it was all about displaying how great he was.

I can still hear it, "You know we have the special friends and family discount, and if they are your friends or family, they are mine too! Please send them my way." Or "You must be due for a new car soon; how about you come my way, and I get you a new ride at a great price."

My stomach sank every time I'd hear that, which meant my stomach sank a lot, and I'd get super anxious awaiting the person's response. If it wasn't an emphatic yes or agreement with my father's statement, I had to mentally remove myself from the conversation.

My old man thrived on the salesman challenge. He thought he was playing a sport where a "no" was a point for the other team. In turn, he'd dig deep in his ninth-grade vocabulary bank to find the right zinger to win a point for his side. I always thought points were meant to be won on the court, field, or rink.

After conversations with community members where I sat silent the entire time, he'd always try to talk with me on the ride home. "You know, son, you can speak up and tell people how good you are in tennis. It will impress them and induce them to make more conversation with you."

Never wanting to be defensive or create an uncomfortable atmosphere, I'd usually just not respond or write it off with a "Yeah, but I wasn't interested in engaging."

My mother had not had a job in twenty years and was happy being a housewife and an usher at our church. She tried for years to convince me to be an altar boy, but I never succumbed—it was bad enough I had to attend Catholic school from age five through college.

All those years of Catholic brainwash, and I still couldn't recite anything from the bible—sex and drugs are bad; repentance and the Lord are good. Be a model citizen. *Who is this model citizen?* Maybe, my mother; she was a good person. My father, sometimes, when he wasn't trying to make gains for his personal use.

After the phone call with my old man, I decided to show my face to society again. I went to class and attended my first physical therapy session. While waiting in the lounge of the PT office, I noticed a flyer about studying abroad in Italy. I used to see signs like this all over campus, but being an athlete made studying abroad impossible.

I was always intrigued by the idea of travel abroad. In contrast, my father did not see much value in it. I could hear him saying, "Why would I want to leave the best country in the world to walk on dirty streets, not have ice or air conditioning?"

For that reason, our family vacations were relatively local—renting a bungalow on the Jersey Shore or driving up to a cabin in Maine. Being an only child made those vacations, well, un-vacation-like. Dad incessantly babbled about his success at work. Mom stayed quiet for the most part but stood up for herself when need be. I spent ninety-nine percent of my time daydreaming about friends that I could connect with.

I always felt lonely. I never had much of a social life due to my tennis schedule and wasn't comfortable opening up to classmates. I was the tall, slender, athletic kid with a bad complexion and low confidence and was probably an enigma to everyone. I was always chosen first in physical education class, but once that was over, my popularity waned through the rest of the school day.

I was usually terrible at making my own decisions. I generally went along with whatever the most persuasive person suggested I do. This is why I followed my parents' suggestion to attend Catholic school my whole life. I listened to them tell me to work as hard as possible to succeed in tennis—which generated the trophies collecting dust on the shelves in my room.

But, as I held the brochure for study abroad in my hand, I knew for once, I would make my own decision. No one was going to talk me out of it. At this point—for maybe the first time in my life—I put myself in my parents' place to see how I could convince them to pay for a year of college abroad.

What do I say? How do I say it? When do I say it? What exactly is the power of persuasion, and how do I use it?

As quickly as I decided to go to Italy, the pain returned as the PT worked my neck and shoulder. "I don't want to be negative, but this is going to be a tough injury to come back from in a short period of time. You are going to need to take months off from playing tennis."

As much as my shoulder physically hurt, the pain of abandoning tennis competition emotionally hurt. Without a real support system of good friends at Boston College, I knew I didn't want to go back if I couldn't play tennis with my teammates.

One night after class, I gave my old man a ring. "Hi, Dad. It's me. I received some bad news today. The PT thinks my injury is worse than the doctor stated. He thinks I should take the whole summer off, and I have to come to terms that my collegiate tennis career might be over."

For the first time I could remember, my father was speechless. I heard heavy breathing coming through the other end. "Jac. Ugh. Jac—listen, things are going to be fine. Just keep—"

Surprisingly, I cut him off. "I know it sucks, but I have a plan."

"Oh?" My old man was surprised.

"I don't want to risk further injury, which could lead to surgery, so I'm taking the summer off. I know you've wanted me to intern at your dealership for years. So why don't I work for you this summer and, uh, I saw a new opportunity today too."

"Opportunity?"

"Yes, there is an international business school that is accepting American students. In Florence, Italy."

"Italy? What? When?" He was a mix of surprised and baffled.

"Well, it would be for the next academic semester starting in September. I really want to do it." My confidence shone through.

He took a lower, slower tone, "Look, Jac, I know you've been through a lot this past week or so. Maybe you should think—"

I had instant courage to cut my old man off, "Nope, I've done all the thinking I need. I want to intern with you this summer and go to Italy after."

"Okay, son, I'll talk to your mother."

"Thanks, Dad." A smirk spread across my face. I unexpectedly convinced my old man of something I wanted—finally.

"Take care, Jac."

The next few weeks went by very quickly with physical therapy and preparing for finals. It was a little hard saying goodbye to Coach Davis and my teammates from the past three years. But honestly, I felt relieved—no more pre-match stomach issues, no more performance anxiety, and no more freezing my ass off in the New England winters! As I hit I-95 south, I felt at ease for the first time in years.

New Jersey, here I come, then before I know it—ITALIA!

That ease I felt driving back home didn't last more than a couple of days, and I began kicking myself for actually agreeing to work for my father. What in the hell was I thinking? *Oh, yeah, ten weeks of pain for ten months of pleasure in Italy. I just need to remember that!*

THREE

My reverie was broken as Alex called my name again. "Jacob, introduce yourself."

As I stood up from my chair, my muscular legs wobbled, and I had to use my hands to push on the table to get up. I fixed my brand new off-the-rack black pinstriped suit jacket and tucked my striped black/white/pink tie inside. I turned to the rest of the class, "Hi, I'm Jacob Gilbert. I grew up in New Jersey and just graduated from Boston College. Something you might be surprised by is that Dann and I spent part of this past year studying abroad in Italy, and I can speak a little Italian."

As I looked back to make eye contact with Dann, he shined the salesman's smile. He proceeded to fill the dead air with, "Jacob forgot to mention that it's his birthday today, and we are celebrating at dinner tonight!"

The entire room erupted with birthday wishes.

Harry looked up from his blackberry, "Happy birthday, Jacob! Lunch is on me today! And let's bring your tablemate, Tim, too. I think I owe him a lunch from his employment at our previous firm."

Multiple emotions raged through me. I felt a nervous shake from standing up in front of the group, horror in response to Dann announcing to the whole room that it was my birthday, and bewilderment about Harry's lunch invitation. I took slight comfort in knowing my new pal Tim would accompany me.

The rest of the morning was a blur. I know we learned about the history of DMNC dating back a century in Germany, but I couldn't tell you anything else discussed. All I could think about was the impending lunch with Harry and Tim.

What were we going to talk about?

I think Tim noticed my extreme nervousness as my leg didn't stop bouncing, and our shared table was probably vibrating. During one of the breaks, Tim said, "Don't be nervous about lunch; just follow my lead. You'll be fine."

I sighed a quick breath of relief, but before we knew it, a few hours flew by, and it was noon.

During the elevator ride and the short walk over to Brickell City Center, I didn't say much besides a few one-word answers in response to Harry and Tim's small talk questions.

"How about lunch at P.F. Chang's?" Harry asked us both.

"You know I eat other food besides Asian." Tim playfully responded with a laugh.

I chuckled.

Harry, maintaining a serious face, proceeded, "Well, it is Jacob's birthday; let's have him choose."

"Oh, I am new here. I don't have a preference. P.F. Chang's sounds fine to me." I stated in a super-serious tone.

Tim and I sat on one side of the booth as Harry began his monotone spiel, "You know, this is the first trainee class since I've been here that I am excited about. I think we made a lot of great hires, and my expectations are very high for you all. Jacob, I know you are intelligent, but the banking business is a different animal than the collegiate system you're used to. Tim was a valuable asset to our previous bank, and that is why he is sitting in that seat today. You will have a formal mentor in your branch; however, I expect you two to create an informal mentor-mentee relationship. So Tim, please take some time whenever you can to show Jacob the tools of our trade. I think it's important."

"I sure will," Tim promptly responded.

"One thing I know Tim will agree with me on is, I expect one-hundred-ten percent effort and no excuses for missing production goals. I made sure everyone that is sitting in that class has a fire in their belly to become successful at DMNC."

As he continued in monotone, my mind wandered. *What does successful mean to Harry? To Tim? To my old man? To me? Making money at all costs? Wearing the right clothes? Doing the right thing even if it doesn't generate the biggest sale?*

"Enough with the business talk. So, Jacob, I know we spoke in our interview but tell me more about your personal life that we didn't get to then." Harry picked up his unsweetened ice tea.

As I looked up from my plate, I saw Harry's intimidating emotionless face. I truly noticed how thick his coke bottle glasses were—they almost made his eyes look distorted. *Okay, stop critiquing the man, and think, respond, speak!*

"Um, ah, well, you know—"

Harry cut me off, "Tim, we are going to have to get Jacob better at speaking off the cuff."

At the challenge, I jumped right in, "I think I mentioned how I played tennis at BC during the interview. I spent the past ten years of my life on the court, and I'm now ready to compete and win in the corporate space." It felt slick as it rolled off my tongue, but I also felt it was disingenuous and canned—something that my old man would've said. I cringed a little after I shut my mouth.

"You know, that was one of the primary reasons I hired you. I know the dedication it takes to be a D-I athlete; as I mentioned, I was one too. Also, Dann gave you a glowing recommendation. Even though I usually don't take recommendations from other candidates, I could tell Dann has what it takes to succeed here. If he went out on a limb to recommend you, you'd have to have the proper qualities yourself.

"I like that you played tennis as it's almost like wrestling at the collegiate level. You compete independently, so you are the only one to blame if the match doesn't go your way. But at the end of the day, you and your teammates come together to beat the real opponent, the other university team.

"I like to think of banking as the same. I want all of you trainees to compete with each other for who can produce the most; then, I want you to beat the tenured bankers. Eventually, we can bring Florida to number one across the bank and increase our market share to the point where we start beating up on the other banks in the region. That is competition, and I want fighters. I want people who will do what is necessary to win. And when we win, everyone's bank accounts will be full of cash to do with what you want."

As our food came, all I could think of was winning, filling my bank account, and proving Harry right for hiring me. From that meal on, my mind was laser-focused on learning all I could to launch a successful banking career.

As Harry signed the bill, he looked up at both of us, "I trust Tim will teach you much of the banking knowledge he has learned. There will be no excuses if Florida is not the number one region within DMNC bank within two years."

It was clear, Harry's version of success was to win—and win at all costs. Unfortunately, at the ripe age of twenty-two, I didn't know what those costs might be.

The rest of the first day passed quickly. The highlight for me was locking eyes with Rosie a few times. She even gave me a slight hint of a smile. I felt the decision to move to Miami was awesome while starting my corporate career in paradise.

After my inspirational lunch with Harry and Tim, I looked at Dann a bit differently. *Maybe he didn't always have his own interests in mind. Maybe he did care about others, like me. I wouldn't be here if it wasn't for Dann. Maybe I should be less critical of him?*

Alex wrapped up the day, "Okay, class, great first day. Look forward to starting tomorrow at eight sharp. Please make sure you get a good night's rest. And again, happy birthday to Jacob!"

Dann walked up to my table. "I'll pick you up from your hotel at 6:30 this evening. See ya later."

Tim and I took the elevator down together to our cars. I liked Tim, and I could see he took his responsibility to be my non-official mentor seriously. Our conversation covered college, women, sports, and how Harry sounds exactly like Ben Stein.

"Okay, bro, see you tomorrow!" yelled Tim as he jumped in his Honda Pilot. As I walked to my 1994 hunter-green Ford Mustang, I saw Harry roll by in his black BMW 745. He waved, and I mentally calculated how long it would take for me to be riding in that car.

The hardest decision of my night was figuring out what to wear for my first time out as a Miami resident. I decided to go with a trusted pair of stone-washed jeans and a hot pink polo. Nothing shows you fit in South Florida like a fluorescent collared shirt!

Dann, late, as usual, screeched to a halt in front of the hotel in his silver new-ish BMW 3 series, pumping some 50 Cent. "Are you ready!" he shouted from the car as I made my way to the door.

I turned my head to the side to see if anyone noticed, rolled my eyes, and hopped in the passenger door.

He continued, "Are you ready for the best steak you've ever had in your life?" He then took a double look at my outfit and asked, "What's with the hot pink? You actually expect to get some pink tonight?" He laughed at his crude joke.

I let the question go and told him Jen was running a little late driving down from Jacksonville and would meet us at the restaurant.

We drove over the 395 causeway and headed to the southern tip of South Beach, where we valeted at Prime 112. The hostess led us to the back of the restaurant, and we waited for Jen to arrive. She came about twenty minutes later and gave us both big hugs.

As we all sat down, she proudly exclaimed, "I know we are celebrating Joey's birthday tonight, but I have some exciting news of my own. You are looking at a future lawyer! My LSAT score was good enough for the University of Florida, and I will be going to law school there starting next semester!"

We both congratulated her, and Dann gave her a locker-room high-five across the table.

Dann leaned back, showing his girthy mid-section, "Now this night is really something to celebrate; Joey's birthday, our first day at the bank, and your admission to law school! Let's get some shots!"

I looked up reluctantly, "Shots? We have to be at work tomorrow at eight!"

Dann using his best power of persuasion, countered my skepticism, "C'mon Joey! Life is about enjoying and having fun, you know. Plus, we are sitting in class all day. Hell, we are in training for the next six months! I think we can handle some good times."

"I'm down for shots." Jen declared enthusiastically.

"Where you sleeping, by the way?" Dann asked Jen as his eyes scanned the restaurant for our waiter to place our drink order.

"Umm, in Joey's bed. I hope you have a king in your room." Jen playfully responded.

I smirked with semi-blushed cheeks.

In an overly loud voice, Dann crowed, "Oh? Is the big birthday boy getting lucky tonight?"

Patrons at other tables turned in our direction.

Jen quickly rebuffed, "Oh no, Dann. You know we're just friends. Joey and I agree that our friendship is as strong as it is because we have not been intimate, nor do we plan to be. Right, Joey?" Jen looked over to me, showing pearly white teeth through thin lips and bright light blue eyes.

"Uh, um, yeah, I agree," I mumbled, then looked down at the menu.

Dann slightly shook his head, "I don't know how I could sleep with a hot blonde and not want to jump her bones. Just sayin'. I hope Joey uses his dick more down here than he did in Italy!" Dann became noticeably agitated about not yet placing our shot order.

In a faux New York accent, Dann yelled at the first waiter that glanced in our direction, "Three shots of your finest tequila!"

We haven't even received our first paycheck, and I can't imagine what this tab will be. Dann does come from a successful real estate family up north. Why didn't he want to work with them?

The shots arrived, and we all raised our glasses. Jen said, "Can you believe that less than a year ago we all met in Italy and now we are eating at the best steakhouse in South Beach? This is awesome, buddies! Cheers!" We knocked 'em back and ordered another round. The meal was excellent; my belly was full of filet mignon and tequila.

Due to the alcohol taking over Jen's small frame, I ended up clutching the steering wheel of Jen's old Toyota SUV, driving us safely to my hotel for the night. When I opened my door, Jen plopped on my bed, fully clothed and passed out moments later. I made my way to the bathroom to get undressed and found myself feeling empty. I gazed into the mirror, scrutinizing what stared back at me. My mind drifted back to the day the three of us met last year.

FOUR

In 2003, September in Rome offered spectacular fall weather. During the four days of study abroad orientation, the adage "Do as the Romans do" rang true. Apparently, we American college students needed to be taught the way of the land and the dos and don'ts of living abroad for the first time.

Drinking was tolerated for all ages, but it was unacceptable to become the clumsy loud drunk ugly American. Smoking in public was just fine—actually the norm. Asking for condiments, do you want to offend the restaurant? Oh dear, vino, make sure you drink the very last drop and enjoy! And soccer, or calcio, is life. Period.

What I remember most from the first day was the jetlag—I'd never flown more than four hours at one time in my life. I also felt like the odd man out in my room, as I was assigned to share with two surfer dudes from Cali whose conversations were seemingly endless loops of, "Bro, what kind of surfboard do you have? What kind of chop do you like to ride?" I decided to be anti-social with headphones on and stuck my nose in a book.

The next day was your typical tourist day in Rome. We visited the Coliseum, Fontana di Trevi, Spanish Steps, Vatican City. My most vivid memory was towards the late afternoon in the Pantheon, where the light and shadows highlighted the fantastic architecture.

I was tired of all the small talk among our group of thirty. "Where are you from? Where do you go to college? What do you like to drink?" I wandered off, and as I made my way to the edge of the Pantheon, I saw a familiar face. I was confident it was one of ours in the group. I slowly walked towards her and noticed her eyes were downcast, and she looked somber. She was petite, had shoulder-length blonde hair, and charmingly timid blue eyes. I noticed they were filled with tears.

"Hey, what's going on?" I said in a concerned tone.

"Oh, don't mind me; I'm a mess," she replied, giving me quick eye contact, then looked down and away.

I put the palms of my hands up with a slight shoulder shrug, "A mess? We are in one of the most amazing places in the world. This should be a magical time for us."

She wiped her eyes dry with her sleeve, then brought her chin up and looked me in the eye, "It's just so hard seeing him all day like this. And I have to spend the next four months with him!"

Him, who's him and what?

She continued, "How shitty is it for him to dump me in the Miami airport? Yeah, the fuckin' airport while we were waiting to board an eight-hour flight where we had to sit together! What. The. Fuck. He thinks everything is great. Well, it sucks. Studying abroad together was my idea!"

She carried on bitching about this guy that apparently was in our group. I drifted away from listening to her words and peered back to the group, wondering who the guy was. I never was good at pep talks. I never was captain of any of my tennis teams, maybe because I never knew what to say at the proper times. But I had a pretty girl who was crying in my presence, and I knew I had to cheer her up.

"Well, he's an idiot!" I firmly stated, cutting her off mid-sentence.

She turned quiet, noticeably startled by my tone.

I continued, "Yeah, any guy who does something like that is a fool, and you should be happy he showed his true colors sooner than later. You have two more days in this introductory group with him, and then you can separate yourself from him when we get to campus. He wants to see you cry because he knows as long as you're crying, he maintains power over you. So tell him to fuck off by smiling and having the best time you can!"

An air of calmness poured over her as she locked eyes with me, and I swear I was in love at first sight or lust, or whatever, but I felt something, a feeling that had previously eluded me. I felt like I meant something to the opposite sex for the first time.

She smiled, stretched up on her tippy toes, and gave me a huge hug, and said, "Thank you for that." She pulled away from the hug, saying, "I'm Jen." Then nervously chuckled.

"Hi Jen, I'm Jacob," I said, grinning from ear to ear.

"You know what? Fuck him! You want to go out tonight, Jacob?"

"Of course!"

I dropped by Jen's room, and we made our way through Rome to find a bite to eat. Much of the evening was hazy—I don't remember what I ate or drank—but I clearly remember feeling like I belonged. We got to know each other as one can only do in a foreign place, eating unfamiliar food and trusting each other to get back to our hotel safely. You have to stick together in new places, and being the tall and broadly-built man, Jen stuck close to my side.

We eventually found a *birreria* where the tables were removed to create a makeshift dance floor with a DJ in the back next to the bar. We threaded our way through the crowded floor of people dancing and arrived at the bar. Jen shouted to the bartender, "Two shots of tequila!"

My stomach clenched, but I clinked glasses with Jen, "Salute! To new friends and new beginnings!" We poured the fiery liquid down our hatches. Jen looked at me, smirked, grabbed my hand, and dragged me to the dance floor.

Above the booming music, I yelled into her ear, "I can't dance."

"Oh, Jacob, just go with the flow." Her eyelids drooped, and she smiled sweetly, swaying her hips back and forth with mini jumps in between.

I looked at her "flow" and thought, *I can do that!*

As the DJ played Nelly's "Hot in Herre," I could tell I was getting quite hot, though it might have been a combination of the alcohol and the jam-packed dance floor filled with Europeans who tend not to think of personal space as a right but a luxury.

Yep, I was feeling *hot in therre*! Then I started to grind on Jen. She kept her eyes closed in this sort of dreamy state as I crouched down to her level. I put my hands on her lower back to bring her towards me.

Yes, I think this is the time; I think I'm reading this situation properly; I think—no, I know it is time for a kiss.

I held my nerve, closed my eyes, and planted my lips right on Jens. She opened her big blue eyes centimeters from mine and pulled away. She shook her head, hugged me, stretched up, and whispered in my ear, "Let's just dance."

Huh, what did I read wrong? She was giving me all the signs that she wanted me. But I must have gotten them wrong. I should cut her some slack; she was just crying earlier today. She had an emotional day; let's just enjoy it.

The rest of the night, we drank and danced, and we eventually stumbled our way through the confusing maze of Rome's side streets back to our hotel, singing together in discord—we didn't sing too loudly, of course, as I made sure we were not the ugly drunk Americans! We had a great night, and I knew Jen and I would be long-time friends.

The next couple of days passed in a flash. Before I knew it, I was sitting next to Jen on the train ride from Rome to the International School of Florence. Little did I know at the time how much of my future and identity would change from that day forward.

The train cars had double seats facing another set of double seats with a small table in between. Jen and I boarded quickly and sat on one side. Jen called out to Dann and invited him to sit across from us.

I'd met Dann briefly over the past couple of days, and my initial impression was that he was a narcissistic douche. I wasn't at all excited about staring at this pear-shaped guy for the next couple of hours. Oh well.

One of our conversation topics landed on Catholicism in Rome. I mentioned that I attended Catholic school my whole life, and this would be my first academic year away from a Catholic school. Tongue in cheek, I asked if attending school in a very Catholic country counts as attending Catholic school. Jen said she came from a Catholic family in Jacksonville, and she was proud of her upbringing. Dann told us he didn't really give a damn about religion and that it mostly was "horse shit."

The conversation transmuted from religion to sex—apparently, this was the natural conversational progression of college students. Jen alluded to losing her virginity in high school but didn't feel comfortable with sex until being with her ex-boyfriend—who sat a few rows behind us.

Dann boasted about all the women he "took down" at the University of Miami. He even acknowledged that learning a little Spanish helped him with the coeds. My stomach did a flip, and I turned beet red when Jen casually asked, "So, Jacob, what's your story? What about you?"

"Well, you know, I went to Catholic school my whole life, and I was always focused on playing tennis up until recently." I tried to remain calm.

Dann barely let me finish, "Are you a fuckin' virgin?"

"No, of course not." I nervously started playing with the hair on the back of my head—a habit that began in grade school when I needed to explain something in front of someone else.

With false machismo, Dann gloated, "Oh man, are you sure? Like the Virgin Mary we just saw hundreds of paintings of? It's okay; you met me. And I will be the one to help you lose your V-card! By the way, who was the husband of Mary?"

"Joseph." Jen quickly responded.

"Oh my Gawd, he totally looks like a Joey!" Dann smacked the table in front of us with open palms, making the passengers around us jump.

Jen and Dann both laughed, and Jen announced, "You are so a Joey. You're even from New Jersey; how could it be more fitting."

As if there aren't guys named Joey in the other 49 states.

Hence the nickname was born. From that day forward, in Italy and elsewhere, I was introduced as Joey to everyone we met.

FIVE

From: Steven.Arnold@DMNCbankusa.com
To: Dann.Frazier@DMNCbankusa.com; Timothy.Chen@DMNCbankusa.com; Donald.Deeds@DMNCbankusa.com; Jacob.Gilbert@DMNCbankusa.com; Pierre.StPaul@DMNCbankusa.com; Ward.Riggins@DMNCbankusa.com
Date: Aug 13, 2004; 11:32 AM
Subject: Friday Happy Hour

YAOOO! Bankers...
Today marks one month since the start of our training program. Don and I have our monthly guys-only happy hour scheduled for tonight. 6pm at the Ale House on Brickell.
Let's do this!

Steve

I *'m actually being invited out with the guys—not everyone has been included. Maybe I'm part of the gang now!*

The last time I went to a guys-only happy hour was the previous summer, and it was a bunch of middle-aged guys sitting around a table talking about car sales, problematic clients, and their families. For some reason, I had a feeling this happy hour would take on a whole new meaning.

The email came during the first week that we were in our respective branches and did not have any direct contact with each other. I knew it would be a good time for us to come together to share what we learned.

The previous four weeks in Miami flew by while moving into the apartment with Dann. I filled my time with working, furniture shopping, figuring out my way around town, and it felt like Dann and I went to dinner with some of his UM buddies every night. It was nice to hit the beach on the weekends, but I didn't have any friends around besides Dann, and I quickly realized I did not want to rely on him to be my source of all social entertainment.

That Friday, I left work in the late afternoon and headed home for a quick change of clothes. I entered the Ale House right at six o'clock. I noticed tables around the interior's edge and a big rectangular bar squatted in the center with a few pool tables on one side.

As I made my way around the room to find my new banker buddies, I heard a familiar "YAOOO JOEEEEEY, ova heere!"

I looked over and saw a disheveled Steve playing pool with a cute woman. It was obvious he came right from the office—the top button of his pastel blue dress shirt was undone, his tie flopped over his shoulder, and his cuffs were unbuttoned and folded so many times that his sleeves barely made it down to his elbow.

Steve noticed my perplexed look that asked, *why are you here alone with a woman, and where is everyone?*

He began to explain, "Don and Pierre will be here in a few minutes. Did Tim and Dann say they were coming?"

"Yes, they are on their way from their branches. I snuck out a few minutes early to head home and change." I looked down at my casual outfit that looked better than Steve's shaggy business attire.

"Oh, this is my girlfriend, Amy. Don't worry; she'll be leaving in a few. She knows the rules; guys happy hour once a month." Steve belted out a shout like he was Usher and knew that night was going to be epic. He must have known something I did not at the time as my energy level was pretty low from having a very hectic previous month.

I tried my best to make small talk with his girlfriend. She took a liking to me and began chatting with me more than him. I asked her about their agreed monthly separate happy hours. She explained that she needed time with her girlfriends, and she knew that time apart made time together more special. Since I never had an official girlfriend in my life, I thought it was interesting to learn her perspective about the different intricacies of the male and female relationship during the dating cycle.

After a few minutes of talking to Amy and Steve while kicking back my first drink of the night, I saw Tim strolling in with his white collared shirt, low hanging orange tie, and black suit pants. His hair was still in perfect place even after an eight-hour workday.

Tim made his way towards us and was greeted boisterously by Steve, who introduced him to Amy. I walked over to the bar with Tim asking how his first week in the branch was.

"I have some good news for you, Jac!" Before I could inquire about the good news, he interjected, "Oh shit, I forgot my pill!"

"What pill?"

"It's kind of embarrassing, but some of us Asians can't really drink alcohol, and literally, if I have one drink, my face turns bright red." He looked down to see what he pulled out of his pockets—phone, wallet, multiple receipts. He realized he didn't have his almighty pill. "Hey, I'm going to run to the store and get some Pepcid AC."

Curious about the good news he was about to share, I said, "Okay, I'll take a walk with you."

We turned to Steve from across the bar and motioned to him that we will be right back. We then exited the Ale House and began walking down the street.

"So wait, your face really gets red? I gotta see this one day!"

"Honestly, it is something no one wants to see. A freakin' tomato face scares away the chicks." He laughed.

"What do you care? You're already married."

"And she would run away!" His tone became more serious. "Speaking of women, this super cute chick works in my branch. She's the customer service representative. I got talking to her today."

"Oh, yeah?" My head was running circles, trying to figure out where he was going with this.

"I showed her my wedding ring, and she became more relaxed around me. I wasn't like all the other men in the office trying to flirt with her, and she started opening up to me."

He continued, "She said she's working full time and is in college as well, so she hasn't had time to find a quality man to date. Mariana is her name, and she is from Colombia; she is very pretty."

My face brightened. "I like Colombians," I spouted out as I opened the door to CVS. Tim walked in and then realized I might never have even seen a Colombian woman.

Tim nodded his head in agreement, then continued, "Cool, I think I can set you two up, and you guys would make a really cute couple."

I started to play with my hair as my anxiety set in. "You really think so?"

"Definitely! I'll set it up next week. Don't worry, just call her when I tell you to, don't say anything stupid, and you're in."

Walking back to the Ale House from CVS, I felt a sense of exuberance that I hadn't felt for a while. I had a group of guys that actually wanted to spend time with me, and I met a guy a month ago that is actively trying to set me up with a beautiful young woman. On top of being in a highly coveted banker training, living with an old college buddy, the move was turning out to be a great decision.

We re-entered the Ale House and noticed Pierre and Don had arrived. Tim and I made our way back to the pool table as Steve belted out for the whole place to hear, "YAOOOOO, what are your CD rates? Now, I want some haaaard rates for a twelve-month certificate of deposit!"

Tim, Pierre, and I all looked at each other with puzzled faces then burst into laughter while shaking our heads. We shared our first week's stories working in the branch with our new coworkers and the experiences of dealing with the general public, which in some locations could be dramatic at times. We found out that Steve's CD rant came from him overhearing a fellow banker getting pressed on CD rates, and we all could relate to hearing an overly demanding client walking into the branch determined to obtain what they wanted from the bank.

We all knocked back two or three drinks over the next hour or so while playing pool and getting to know each other on a more personal level. Steve was a true wild card, and I tried to better understand his demeanor and personality as more alcohol flowed through our systems.

For the first time, I chatted with Pierre outside of training. I never felt physically small in my life, but standing next to the six-and-a-half-foot massive framed former lineman, I noticed my eyes going higher and higher. Pierre's hairline, midway back on his head, gave him the illusion of looking older than he actually was. He took great pride in his appearance and was arguably the sharpest dresser in our class—a navy pinstriped suit with a matching vest was his staple. A white shirt and pink tie perfectly placed in the center of his collar completed his image. He might have worked eight hours that day as well, but he was as crisp as if he was showing up for morning duty—something no one could say about Steve.

Pierre had an unforgettable handshake. He had enormous paws; it was like shaking hands with someone wearing boxing gloves. We talked a lot about sports, and I picked up that this guy was a ferocious competitor. He fought his ass off playing football on the field. It was obvious no one gave this guy anything in life as a young immigrant; everything he earned was through hard work. I respected that a lot. It also was apparent he had a thirst for learning, maybe more than I did. He asked many questions and was truly sincere.

"You know people will think that I was hired to fill the Little Haiti branch role because I speak Creole. That just fuels my fire. Same thing happened in college when I received a football scholarship. My classmates felt I shouldn't have been there. But you watch, Jac, I'm gonna prove them all wrong and be successful!"

In that conversation, I realized that I needed more hunger. For most of my life in the classroom or even on the tennis court, I mostly succeeded with natural talent. My greatest concern wasn't with my performance but about fitting in socially. The conversation with Pierre made me think deeply about whether I was putting in my best effort. *If I was indeed holding back, then why?*

Before I completed the mental analysis of my previous efforts, Dann showed up. "Heyyyy gentlemen, are you ready for this shit-show tonight?"

Can't this guy ever show up on time? Can he ever enter a room without calling attention to himself? Sometimes I can't believe we're roommates. Ugh.

I looked around the Ale House to see who noticed our ruckus. The others were talking about where to go next.

Dann hollered out in a too-loud voice, "Joey, I hope you didn't drive here because we are going to get shitfaced! We are going to finally show you what a night out in Miami really means. Let's take this party on the road and hit up the beach. The Delano Hotel has an awesome vibe this time of the evening."

Tim rolled his eyes and said, "Okay, you single men, have fun tonight. I am going to get back to the wife before I get myself into trouble."

As he shook my hand, he went to my ear and let me know that he'd hook me up with Mariana the following week. I felt a warm sensation overcome my face, which I quickly realized must have been the alcohol. *But was it more than that?*

The five of us squeezed into Don's VW sedan. As we rode over the 395 bridge, I noticed the mansions on Star Island to my left and the gigantic cruise ships to my right. I'd never been on a cruise ship. *How do those monstrosities float?*

We made our way to Collins Avenue, then north up to 17th Street—the heart of Miami Beach.

"Here we are, boys, the historic Delano Hotel and pool," Don exclaimed as we waited for the valet to welcome us.

We entered the hotel and gazed upward toward the vast vaulted ceiling of the lobby. Walking toward the rear doors, we passed a couple of restaurants. Exiting the rear doors, Dann turned back to us, "Oh, wait until you see this pool."

The sun went down an hour ago, but the pool emitted green light from the edges, and the moon was rising above the ocean in the background. We made our way down some stairs towards the glowing rectangular pool. Beautiful women in short cocktail dresses showed off their toned legs and cleavage. Fit men looked casual in jeans and button-down shirts. One section of the pool had tables in it—yes, tables in the water! The water was four inches deep; people stood at tables with shoes off, and some of the women danced and splashed to the deep house music the DJ played.

"Isn't this fuckin' awesome?" Don asked.

I looked over at Don, who was significantly shorter than I, and I noticed his burnt orange hair was still gelled in place. *If I smack the top of his head, would he feel it, or would his hair act like a helmet defending him from any onslaught?*

"Guys, over here, this lovely lady is going to take care of us this evening." Steve motioned us over to a table towards the back of the pool, near the DJ. "Let's get a round of shots!"

So it began; the slow drift of what was left of my sobriety quickly morphed into a state of drunken bliss. The DJ moved from deep house to the latest dance songs. The area around the pool filled in, and conversation wound down as Don, Steve, and Dann tried to start dancing with random women. Pierre and I stood taller than most of the crowd and gave each other a look whenever a beautiful woman came towards us. My hips swayed to the music—at least I thought—and a slight grin parked on my face. I felt no pain or worry whatsoever.

Late evening approached quickly, and the five of us reconvened. "Let's get outta here. Who wants to let it all out at Club Space?" Don asked us.

With my glazed eyes, I gave a befuddled look that asked, *What is Club Space?*

Dann shouted, "Hell yeah, what a way to end the night, plus it's kind of on our way home." He gestured toward me.

We shuffled back to the hotel lobby in a single file line as people danced elbow-to-elbow on the pool deck.

While we waited for the valet to bring the car, Pierre called a cab to get back home. He said he wasn't much of a clubber. When the car arrived, the rest of us piled in, and we made our way back over the 395 causeway back to downtown.

Club Space sits in a less than desirable neighborhood, and Don parked his VW in an adjacent lot. As we walked the block and a half to the club, we passed a homeless encampment that must have had twenty bums laying down, spewing a sour scent of urine.

We approached the entrance and joined the line, but time passed quickly as time typically does under the influence of alcohol.

"The cover is forty dollars," said the bouncer. *What? Forty dollars to enter a club in the middle of homeless people? How good can this place be?*

I shot Dann a perplexed look. Were we really about to pay that amount of money just to enter a building that looked like a dilapidated warehouse in a sea of dirty concrete? He responded with a curt nod.

After paying our cover charge at the window, Don took us all to the side, "Okay guys, this club has three distinct rooms. We have house-lounge, hip hop, or electronic dance music."

Steve shouted, "EDM for sure!"

I didn't have a preference, so I followed the group up the dimly lit black staircase that led us to the dance room. *Good choice.*

Beautiful women filled the room—just like the Delano pool deck. At this place, though, it was clear they wanted to dance and not schmooze. Not sure if it was the music, the open-air roof, or the hot women, but I started to sweat as we made our way through the room to the bar.

The music was pumping, DJ playing the latest electronic dance songs, and I was in awe of my first experience in a Miami nightclub.

In time, I found myself waiting in the bathroom line. I heard a "YAOOOOO, Joey!"

I looked back through a couple of people and saw Steve waiting as well. "Joey, get a toilet stall."

Does he really want to do number-two right now?

A few minutes later, Steve and I crammed into a bathroom stall. As I took a piss, I heard him fumbling in his pockets. He was starting to get giddy. "You ever try this before?" As he shows me a one-inch clear mini-Ziplock baggie with a white powder that looked like baking soda.

I shook my head no.

"Oh, you are in for a treat tonight, buddy!"

Normally I would have balked at trying a drug since I've never done anything like that before. But in the wee hours of the morning, sharing a bathroom stall in a Miami club with a new coworker, everything seemed like it was fine in my altered state of mind. "Sure, let's try it."

"Ok, just hold one of your nostrils down and sniff in as hard as you can with the other." He presented me his credit card with a thin line of powder on it.

I inhaled deeply, and I immediately felt pins and needles at the top of my nasal passage, followed by a rush of pressure in my brain. As I let the feeling take control of me, I saw Steve snort what seemed to be quadruple the amount I took.

We both left the bathroom, feeling our chests were as large as concrete blocks. The energy and euphoria I experienced were something I'd never felt before. The music sounded terrific as my legs gained more bounce with every step I took.

Steve led the way. I could see he was headed toward something specific, but I didn't know what. I merely followed. He slowed down, and I noticed a practically naked and exceedingly sexy woman lying on a table on the side of the room.

Her body and face were painted, chocolates were scattered across her, and she seemed only to be wearing a bikini bottom.

Must be abstract human art.

Then, to my surprise, Steve started walking around her table like a dog waiting for his next meal. He shouted to me that she looked hot and delicious. He took a piece of chocolate off of her body and then moved toward her feet. Suddenly, Steve grasped her ankles, pulled them apart, and put his mouth and nose directly into the woman's crotch. He rapidly rocked his head side to side on her bikini-covered vaginal area.

Shocked and infuriated, the woman screeched and popped her head and upper body off the table. The chocolates, once nestled on her breasts and arms, flew across the room. The bouncer, who was only a few feet away, saw the commotion, and the woman pointed at Steve.

Steve tried to get away but got yanked from behind, almost falling to the ground. He was brusquely escorted out of the club while making some inaudible sounds. I quickly sidestepped the whole situation and scurried to the adjacent hip-hop room. I stared around blankly and shook my head with a smirk.

That couldn't have happened. Yeah, I'm super fucked up. That had to be in my imagination. I need to go find Steve.

Unexpectedly the drug mixture in my body took over, and the euphoria I felt was incredible. Nothing mattered, and everyone looked like they moved in slow motion. I was never much of a dancer, but my footwork would've given MC Hammer a run for their money. I was living in a dopamine rush world.

After what seemed like hours, I realized I had been sweating uncontrollably and made my way to the bathroom again. I stared at the mirror for a few seconds and noticed my eyes seemed alert, and my bottom jaw wouldn't stop moving side to side.

I felt a hand on my shoulder. "Joey, where the fuck have you been?"

I look back, and Dann's standing there.

Forgetting my vocabulary, I shrug like a bug-eyed sweat-drenched zombie.

Then Dann asked, "Where the fuck is Steve?"

I shrugged again, and for the first time in what seemed like hours, I remembered what Steve did!

Dann continued, "C'mon, let's get out of here."

My zombie-self followed Dann out of the bathroom, and he turned back towards me, "Damn Joey, you are fucked up! What the hell happened?"

My vocabulary returned, and I started babbling, "Steve got crazy. He got kicked out. He gave me some cocaine." I finally felt a slight feeling of shame.

"Cocaine? Stay away from that shit, man! What did Steve do? Have you seen Don?" Dann was trying to get a grasp of the situation and round up the troops to go home.

"You see the girl on the table with the chocolates on her?" I asked in the quickest possible way.

Dann nodded with a grin.

"Well, Steve thought he was superman and decided to climb the table and lick her pussy!" I exclaimed, noticing I kept talking faster and faster.

"Get the fuck out!" Dann shouted at me as he noticed Don walking our way. "Don, you gotta hear what Steve just did," Dann yelled over to Don, but he couldn't hear us as the music was blasting.

"Oh, I was just with Steve outside. He was thrown out of the club by a bouncer! I put him in a cab to meet up with his girlfriend." Don calmly reported.

The three of us proceeded to exit the club; I looked down at my watch—it was four in the morning. Wow, that was a crazy ten hours, and I was crashing big time. I don't remember the ride home, but I do remember the ringing and pounding that jackhammered in my head for most of that Saturday.

Just what type of people did this bank hire?

I spent the weekend nursing the worst hangover of my life, and I barely dragged myself out of bed down to the pool. I couldn't wait for the following work week to start. Well, what I was truly excited about was that Tim was supposed to connect me with the Colombian cutie from his branch.

The DMNC Bank branch I worked in was in a good neighborhood, composed of primarily middle-class retiree clientele. Jeff Winder was my branch mentor. He was in his mid-thirties, living the traditional family life, and made it known right away that he received no compensation for training me. Every Friday, he asked me whether I'd be sitting behind him or if I would be in banker training class the following week.

Jeff's office resembled the swamp in Gainesville. An abundance of Florida Gator swag decorated his office—coffee mugs, plaques, magazines, and a business card holder in the shape of a Gator head. Initially, I thought all that stuff was kind of cluttery and unprofessional until I witnessed an interaction with a customer.

I don't remember why the bank customer was upset, but he came in noticeably miffed. While Jeff was looking at his computer screen, trying to work out the issues, the customer randomly asked, "How do you think the Gators are going to do this season?"

Jeff immediately stopped looking at his computer screen. He engaged the customer in football talk and opened up the season preview magazine going over all the new recruits. A few minutes later, the client's attitude totally changed, and the interaction ended in a friendly tone, all from a simple question about football.

That interaction taught me that just because something starts badly doesn't mean it has to end that way. The quicker you can find common ground and establish rapport with customers, the better the interaction.

The branch manager, Salvatore O'Connor, was in his mid to late forties—just imagine the odd combination of lasagna and corned beef. Sal had a distinct brown goatee and a wheezing laugh you could hear from across the branch. He was a customer favorite, though.

Sal liked to stand at the four-foot-high desk to the left of the front door and greeted more than half of the branch clientele by name when they walked in. If he weren't busy, he would walk the teller line to engage waiting customers in small talk about their business or personal life. He'd get a kick if he could make the customer laugh. It was like a personal game of his; if he got a chuckle out of them, he'd give himself an imaginary point, though I'm not sure who kept score.

I can picture it now, Sal swaying side to side, his hands hanging down in front of his body while engaging bank customers in conversation. Once the customer would chuckle, Sal laughed with a smoker's wheeze, then lightly patted the customer on the back or the shoulder. It was a sight to see him work the room. You would think he loved people the way customers felt at ease being in his company.

One of the first regular customers I met in the branch was Ms. Li. Almost daily, she'd come in, carrying a couple of plastic bags full of who knows what. She'd hand the bags right over to Sal. Ms. Li hardly ever engaged in conversation with anyone else in the branch, and her appearance indicated she might be semi-homeless. Her poker-straight hair was always a mess. Her clothes were usually stained. Her pants were too long, and the bottom of them was ragged from dragging across the ground. Her shoes tended to have holes or a broken strap.

Sal explained that looks could be deceiving. Ms. Li was a good customer of the bank, and although she always kept a few hundred thousand dollars on deposit, he mentioned how she had a vast real estate rental portfolio—her net worth was north of ten million.

According to Sal, she volunteered in the soup kitchen each morning. She'd then pick up multiple shopping bags of expired food from Publix or other local restaurants, take some items for herself, and give the rest to others, like her favorite bank branch manager. Basically, everyday loaves of stale bread and boxes of expired snacks showed up on our break room table. Once the staff truly understood what was going on, the food was never touched by anyone other than maybe the cleaning staff. Sal just didn't have it in his big heart to tell her not to give us the soup kitchen food.

One day I scolded Sal, saying that the food was really for the people who couldn't afford it. I told him about the times during high school when I volunteered at the soup kitchen in the low-income section of our diocese. Sal was undeterred.

Later in the week, when Sal ran the soup kitchen food back to our break room, he grabbed some papers off the fax machine. He handed them to me and asked me to give them to my mentor, Jeff.

I glanced at them and noticed it was a complete and signed credit application. At the time, I didn't think much of it. I handed it to Jeff, and I noticed he immediately placed it face down on the side of his desk without explanation.

Overall, the branch was a stable environment. We had a few women that spent way too much time in stagnant roles. I could imagine the carpet growing through their feet as they stood at their places year after year. One teller complained about everything, and we knew it was best to avoid that person at all times.

It was apparent Sal was the glue that kept us all together. He'd spent more than twenty-five years at the bank. He proudly told his story; he started as a part-time teller at eighteen and worked his way up the ranks to become branch manager about a decade later.

The highlight of that week was receiving a call from Tim. Some life events are vividly etched in our minds, and to this day, I remember exactly where I was when I received that call. I was driving home on Biscayne Boulevard when my mobile phone rang. I flipped open the phone and pulled up the antenna.

"Yo, Jacob, it's Tim. For some reason, my co-worker Mariana doesn't believe I'm actually married."

I replied with an "uh-huh."

He continued, "So she finally asked to see a picture of my spouse, and I showed her a picture of you."

I've never been good with pithy responses, and I was dead silent for the next ten seconds; it felt like ten minutes.

Tim broke the silence with laughter. "I'm just kidding, bro! Jacob, say hello to Mariana! She's standing right next to me, and you're on speakerphone."

Taken aback, I sighed and responded, "Hi, Mariana. I see that you fell for Tim's antics. Don't worry; he had the whole class tricked for a hot minute on our first day in training."

Mariana leaned into Tim's phone, "Yes, Tim is a really funny guy. You're lucky to have him as a friend. He told me you are tall, handsome, athletic, and I need to meet you."

Tim cut her off by continuing, "Jacob, I'm going to get her phone number and give it to you. She said she's free this Saturday night. I know you are too, so I expect you to set something up with her."

Before either of us could say anything else, Tim said goodbye and hung up. I just kept replaying Mariana's voice in my mind. She sounded cute with that thick Spanish accent.

After the call, I couldn't stop thinking of the hours upon hours I spent last year with Rodrigo as he coached me through how to speak with women.

SIX

The first two months at the International School of Florence went by in a flash. Each day after class, Dann, Jen, and I would meet up at one of our dorm rooms. We would either hang out with other Americans, or stay with our own trio, then go to the cafeteria for dinner. We had already taken two full weeks off from class, one in each month. The first week, the three of us traveled all over Italy—from Florence to Milan, to Venice, to Amalfi Coast. We created lots of memories and laughs. In the second week off, we flew to Spain and visited a few highlights.

The school had less than a thousand students. About two-thirds were international students, most of which came from the USA. The final third were Italians. The school had a tradition of friendly semester-long soccer tournaments that pitted the international students against the Italians. I stopped playing soccer when I was ten, but I decided to play since I wasn't playing tennis anymore. We practiced at least once a week, and it was the first time in a long time that I genuinely enjoyed playing sports for fun again.

In a passing conversation during practice, I mentioned that I was a washed-up tennis player. Another player on our international team overheard me and responded that he was one too. He was a Brazilian national named Rodrigo Gosta. "You played competitive tennis?" He asked me in his slight Portuguese accent.

I told him I played three years in college but got injured earlier in the year and needed months of rehab. He shared his story about moving to a prestigious tennis academy in Florida during high school then joining the ATP junior tour at the age of twenty. He told me about playing with top players a few years back.

"Elbow tendonitis," he said as he kicked the ball back to me during warmup. "Sucks, man. Ruined my career, and I had to give up the junior tour. I enrolled in college in Iowa and got bored living in rural America, so I came here." He looked up from kicking and asked, "Did you bring your racquet here?"

"Yeah, but I haven't hit a ball in seven months. I'll be super rusty."

"Don't worry about it. I haven't played in months as well. Let's play tomorrow after class. Courts are just under the bridge over there." He stopped kicking the ball and pointed in the direction of the courts.

Twice per week, we smacked the yellow felt off the balls. It felt good to get back on the court. My neck didn't hurt anymore, but I definitely developed a little muscle atrophy which made my serves and forehands less powerful. Rodrigo was a beast on the court; you wouldn't know it by looking at him. He was probably an inch or two taller than me, but he was super lean with long, gangly arms and legs—built like a real tennis player.

He told me he spent six hours a day on the court at the Florida tennis academy. He practiced with such precision that he'd have to hit a certain percentage of cross-court forehands in a one-foot box before his coach would allow him to leave the court. The next day, he told me, he'd have to have a certain percentage of serves going to the area of the court the coach wanted. Rodrigo usually won our matches. I competed well, but his training and skill level were on another level. We had awesome rallies, but on almost every crossover, we would engage in spirited conversation.

Clearly, Rodrigo was a ladies man. His height, bronze skin, confidence, and genuine extroversion made him naturally engaging with the opposite sex. I wasn't quite the opposite, but my pale white complexion mixed with acne scars always made my confidence level teeter with women. Not to mention carrying around life-long social anxiety combined with severe introversion.

During the couple-minute breaks during each match, he gave me real-life pointers and examples of how he would open up a conversation with women. He told me it should be easy for me to talk to women on campus because there was a guaranteed chance to see them again if the conversation didn't go anywhere the initial time.

After a month of playing tennis together, it was the beginning of December, and finals were already upon us. I was considering going back to Boston College for my final semester, but Rodrigo told me he was staying for the spring semester and suggested I do the same. After getting my parents' buy-in, I stayed as well. The Tuscan winter was mild, and we continued playing tennis.

During one of our matches, Rodrigo casually suggested, "Hey, let's go to Amsterdam for Christmas. We can stop in Switzerland on the way back." I offered no objection.

A few days before Christmas, the fall semester ended. It was hard to say goodbye to Jen and Dann. For the first time in my life, I felt like I was part of a friend group where my attendance mattered. I sensed our little friendship family was falling apart. Although Rodrigo was mostly a reserved member of our family, I wasn't sure what to expect over the holidays as we'd never traveled alone together, and he always marched to the beat of his internal drummer.

"I never thought I'd be ordering legal marijuana and buying legal prostitutes on the streets in my life! Amsterdam is awesome!" Rodrigo exclaimed as we walked down a short flight of stairs into a dimly lit coffee shop.

The "coffee shop," known to be legal marijuana establishments in Amsterdam, are unlike most coffee shops Americans would recognize. We walked in, and from behind a U-shaped bar, a quirky Dutch barista happily greeted us. He was incredibly knowledgeable about the menu he handed us—the menu didn't list any coffee drinks at all. Instead, options included Greenhouse Special, Silver Haze, Northern Lights, White Widow, Skunk Haze, and the list went on. I looked at the menu as if it was written in a foreign language instead of English.

"So which one you gonna get?" Rodrigo looked up from the menu at me. I gave him a perplexed look followed by a nervous smile. "Have you ever smoked before?" He asked me with a suspicious look as his eyebrows furrowed closer to his eyes.

"Nope. Never. No idea what I'm ordering."

Rodrigo took control and ordered two pre-rolled joints for us. Greenhouse Special it was.

We received them, moved towards the back of the coffee shop, and settled on oversized chartreuse sofa chairs. "Okay, I'm going to light the end of the joint. You need to suck in and inhale for a few seconds, then exhale."

A few seconds later, I started coughing uncontrollably, almost hacking up one of my lungs. "What the...hell....man?"

"Oh hellz yeah, you are getting hiiiiiigh. Just relax." Rodrigo slouched further back on the sofa. A dozen other people sprawled on different couches; it was a very mellow place, and people kept to themselves. The distinct smell of Mary Jane made its way to every square inch of the establishment.

"Can you believe you can choose a hooker as you would a can of soda through a vending machine window? This place is fucking awesome. Merry fucking Christmas to us!" Rodrigo was coming alive.

At this point, I slumped back into the sofa next to him and stared at the ceiling. All kinds of thoughts zipped through my mind. Some went by too fast to analyze, others moved slowly, and I understood their meanings but then quickly forgot. "Yeah, I've never touched a prostitute and would never," I said with a childish giggle after admitting my purity.

"You know what you are, Joey? You're a *Bubble Boy*!" Rodrigo raised his voice for all of the coffee shop patrons to hear.

"Bubble Boy?" I repeat back in confusion.

"Yes, you've never smoked pot, you don't have sex, and your nickname is after Joseph from the Bible! You got to live and enjoy life. These next few months, I will make sure we enjoy life." He paused and looked around the room, "Starting today!"

The marijuana disconnected my overly analytical mind, and words did not flow easily for me. The opposite was true for Rodrigo. The guy who, at times, didn't say a word wouldn't shut up. He went on and on about every subject he could think of—tennis, life in Brazil, having random sex with women, to why he wanted to stop in Switzerland on the way back to Florence.

"Swiss banks are the most secure for funds. They have strict banking restrictions that allow people to have protected accounts. It is illegal for banks to reveal the accounts' true owners unless they receive a court order. I grew up in São Paulo, where corruption runs rampant. When I go back to Brazil, I will have to siphon some of my funds to another country in order to feel safe. So I thought, what better idea than to stop in Switzerland and open up two accounts, one for me and one for you."

I was still staring into the ceiling of the coffee shop avoiding eye contact, "But I don't have any money for that."

"But we will in the future; that's what you need to think about."

I couldn't think strategically at that moment, so I let him continue to talk. Who knows how much time passed as he rambled.

Finally, I opened my mouth again, "I'm hungry."

The rest of that night was a blur. I remember waking up feeling rested—the most relaxed I've felt in months.

Rodrigo was already up in the bed next to me in our hotel room. "You know, I'm gonna help you get laid this next semester. I don't want you going back to the States a Bubble Boy no more."

The sentence rolled off his tongue eloquently as I rubbed the sleep out of my eyes.

"I think you should go after the Italian women on campus. People always want a taste of what's different. Did you know they put beets on Big Macs in Australia? I went to McDonald's solely to eat a Big Mac with beets when I was there for a tennis tourney a few years back."

I must have given him the most confused look ever as he felt he needed to go deeper into his thoughts. *Why is he talking about freaking beets on a Big Mac?*

"American women can have guys like you anytime they want back home. They are coming to study abroad to experience different cultures, different food, and probably different men. So why compete with other American men going after the same women?"

For some odd reason, it seemed like his primary goal was to find me a woman. I don't know why; I never told him I needed one. Maybe he thought I needed to have more romantic relationships to realize something significant about myself.

"What you need to do is learn more Italian. I'm going to find you an Italian tutor. The more Italian you learn, the more confident you will be. When I moved to Florida, I was sixteen. I spoke little English, and taking classes in English forced me out of my comfort zone. It was hard, but was necessary for me to grow and feel comfortable in the U.S."

He had a point. I spent the first four months in Italy just hanging around other Americans speaking English. I didn't venture out and get to know any international students besides him.

The rest of the Amsterdam week was spent in a hazy blur in and out of coffee shops and restaurants—we must have gained over five pounds. "When we get back to campus, we are hitting the courts hard," I said multiple times as the food tasted better than anything I ever tasted in my life.

At the end of our Christmas break, We hopped on a quick flight to Zurich, where we spent New Year's eve 2004. We both left Switzerland with the most expensive bank account I'd ever opened, costing roughly $50 per month. Rodrigo's look implied that I'd be thanking him someday.

How is he so persuasive?

SEVEN

After Christmas break, back on campus, Rodrigo and I suited up in our spandex leotards as the winter weather prevailed in the rolling hill-filled Tuscany region. One day, during our three-minute end-of-set break, Rodrigo hit me with a question that I was not ready for, "What are you going to do when this semester is over?"

I looked at him as if he asked me how the earth was created. I gave him my trademark shrug and mumbled, "Probably work with my father until I can find a job in New York City."

"Is that what you want?"

"No! But I don't know what I want."

"This is why you are a Bubble Boy. You need to see what is out there and make the best decisions for yourself."

"Why? What are you going to do?" I asked him, thinking I had turned the tables on him.

But Rodrigo played conversations like he played a tennis point, well planned out and executed to receive a weak ball mid-court which he could put away easily. "My father has connections with a couple guys that work for PetroBrasil, the government-run oil company. It's one of the largest industries we have in Brazil. However, they want me to start working in China. Not looking forward to living there." He looked down at the strings on his racquet.

"To China?" I was surprised, to say the least.

"Yeah, but it better not be for more than a year. I went there once for a tennis tournament, and those people live like savages. Not for me. But I know this will give me the experience and connections I need to become successful in my country."

"So you're not planning on living in the U.S.?" I asked.

"I would need an employer to grant me a work visa. I don't want to deal with that. Unless Jen wants to marry me." He chuckled at his joke as he walked to his side of the court. He then turned around and walked back towards me. "I went to the student office and scheduled an Italian tutor session for us. Tomorrow after class. Oh yeah, Bubble Boy, now you will have no excuse not to talk to an Italiana!"

I rolled my eyes, hit the balls back to him, and we continued our match.

"*Ciao, ragazzi! Mi chiamo Valeria.*" The next day we were greeted by a slender young woman with an olive complexion and black kinky hair. I responded, "*Piacere, mi chiamo* Jacob and this is my friend, Rodrigo."

"Oh, I was expecting one student. We really don't structure our learning for one teacher and two students. Rodrigo, can I bring my friend to tutor you?" Her professional tone made Valeria seem much more mature than I initially perceived.

I interjected as Valeria was about to leave the room, "Rodrigo practically speaks Italian already as his native tongue is Portuguese and speaks fluent Spanish as well."

Rodrigo chimed in, "Is your friend as beautiful as you?"

Valeria blushed, smiled, and looked down. She and I started to giggle, but Rodrigo's face was set in stone

"Uh, let me see what I can do. How often do you want lessons?" She quickly reverted to seriousness after she noticed Rodrigo meant what he asked about finding a pretty female tutor.

Rodrigo responded, laying it on thick, "Whatever it takes to be able to have simple conversations with nice ladies like yourself."

"I think if we meet three times per week for an hour with the current fluency Jacob has, he should be able to speak nicely within two to three months."

"Great!" I responded as enthusiastically as possible.

Then I thought about our schedules, "Will this affect our tennis training?" I asked Rodrigo.

Valeria asked, "Oh, are you the two that play tennis late afternoons after class?"

I nodded.

"You guys are amazing. I sometimes watch from the parking lot; I've never seen live tennis like that before."

Realizing I had some latitude, I decided to try and make a deal, "Well, how about we have a tennis lesson on the court each week. You still teach me Italian, and I will teach you how to properly strike a tennis ball."

"Deal," she happily responded.

"Dang, Bubble Boy, you aren't as bad as I thought." Rodrigo winked at me.

Valeria looked at me funny, wondering about Rodrigo's response, and again, I shrugged. She chuckled. "Well, Jacob, let's take a seat and begin."

"*Va bene.*" And our session began.

Shortly after, a cute young Italiana greeted Rodrigo, and he gave me a big smile as he walked to the other end of the library.

The second semester in Florence was far different than the first. I didn't create the same strong friendships I did previously, but it hardly bothered me. Rodrigo and I were practically joined at the hip, eating almost every meal together and playing tennis three times per week after class.

When the designated travel weeks came, we stayed close to Florence, taking weekend or daily train rides to the towns and cities close by—mainly because both of us were going broke from taking many trips the first semester.

I did save a few thousand dollars while working last summer, and I didn't feel comfortable asking my parents for money while I was galivanting around Europe. Instead of traveling, I ended up playing tennis nearly five days a week as Valeria genuinely wanted to learn the game. On the court, she was teaching me Italian, and at the same time, I corrected her English grammar.

We also spent a lot of time together, probably the most time I ever spent with a woman before. She was three years younger than me, and I knew I wasn't going to stay in Italy beyond May, but sometimes you just can't help the feelings you get for someone. You may put up a wall to avoid romantic feelings, but getting to know someone you connect with does something to erode that wall. Before you know it, you have a special place in your heart for that person.

That's what happened to me with Valeria. She eroded my walls and let me open up for the first time to someone of the opposite sex in an intimate way. Those next three to four months were some of the most stable and amazing times I'd had in my life. For the first time, I felt like I had a true friend and a companion—someone with whom I could be completely myself—no more trying to impress coaches, other players, classmates, or random people at college parties.

One weekend Valeria and I took an hour train ride to Vicenza, the home of the clothing manufacturer Diesel. While browsing the gigantic three-story factory store, I came across a sweater with the word "SUCCESSFUL" arched along the chest. *That damn word again. What is that shirt supposed to mean?*

I held it against my chest, looking in the mirror, trying to imagine it on me. Valeria sidled up next to me and said, "That shirt fits you perfectly."

I gave her a double-take, then quickly tried to decipher if she meant that the size fits me or if it fit my personality and persona.

"You need to get that sweater. Hang it in the front of your closet, and it will always remind you that you *are* successful no matter what kind of day you are having," she said in an uplifting tone.

I smiled and gave her a peck on the lips. She grabbed my hips and brought me towards her, and we made out right between the clothing rack and the changing room—Italian romance at its finest.

To: Jacob.Gilbert@aol.com
From: DannThaMann@aol.com
Date: May 1, 2004; 10:42 AM
Subject: Get your ass down to Florida

JOEY,
How the hell you been? Just trying to finish this damn school year and bang a couple more coeds, but what else is new. More importantly, I just finished my second interview with DMNC Bank in Miami. Actually met the Florida market president in the second interview. Well we were talking and your name came to me as someone that would also be good for the role. The bank is hiring 15 trainees. It's a 6-month training program! That's like another semester in college, but we get paid to party! Anyways, when are you getting back to the states to get your ass to Miami so you can interview? Hit me back.
Dann

I re-read Dann's terrible grammatical email a few times and stared at the computer screen. I turned to Rodrigo and told him about the email. "Dann seems to be looking out for me. He may have found me a job."

"One thing to know is, Dann only looks out for Dann." He calmly replied as he typed his own email as we sat next to each other in the computer lab on campus. He then stopped typing and asked me, "Well, is it a good opportunity?"

"Not sure, seems pretty selective as they are hiring only fifteen people for a training program within a large bank." I gave a one-shoulder shrug to Rodrigo.

"Go for it; what's the worst that could happen?"

Planning for the worst is something that never resonated with me, so without really considering Rodrigo's comment, I focused on getting to Miami after the semester ended.

The next few weeks flew by, just like any other good times in life. Since emotions had been a foreign language to me most of my life, it was hard to understand my feelings about picking up my entire life to move, this time for an undetermined future.

Seeing Valeria's puffy, tear-ridden face on the top of the steps on campus is an image burned through my memory. Although I knew our relationship wouldn't last due to living in separate countries, it was still a painful goodbye. I wish it were a "See you sometime," but we both knew it was a firm goodbye.

She was a fabulous tutor; by the end of our lessons, she'd taught me how to hold a basic conversation in Italian. However, she was not just an awesome tutor, but Valeria was probably my first true love. We never discussed being together in the future, but we had a deep understanding of each other, and I would always cherish the moments we spent together. Whenever I had some free time, and my mind would wander, I thought of her and wondered, "What if?"

Saying goodbye to Rodrigo was hard but easier than Valeria—as I knew it was going to be an "Until we see each other again." He was off to tour Eastern Europe for a month and then would make his way to China to start his career with PetroBrasil.

It was a long and lonely flight back to the States. But my mood improved as I was excited to start the next phase of my life.

EIGHT

"Welcome back, class; I hope you all had a wonderful long Labor Day weekend. I also hope you all behaved, because if you didn't, you know, I will find out. I tend to hear things for some reason." Alex McGuire stood in front of our training class as she did six weeks ago, but this time she had a sly grin on her face.

Today was the first time I'd seen Steve since the face-in-crotch incident. He nodded when he walked in, but something told me the story got out somehow. *But how? Did Alex know that we had an all-guys happy hour a couple weeks back? She's been in this job a long time, class after class; surely, she'd pick up on the subtle cues of each group.*

As my mind drifted towards how much Alex knew about us, another woman walked into the classroom.

"Class, this week we are going into sales and communications training. We all have the pleasure of spending this week with an impressive woman that has helped many of our training classes. I'd like to introduce Lucy Snailing. Lucy runs a consulting firm specializing in training professionals in all industries—helping people with their communication and sales techniques. She has traveled from Michigan to be with us today! Previous classes have told us this was one of the most important weeks of the training program because of what they learned. I ask you to give her your respect and undivided attention. So without further ado, Lucy."

Alex grinned from ear to ear as she greeted Lucy, seemingly handing over the judge's gavel for the week.

"Hello CLASSSSSSSSS," Lucy roared to wake us all up.

We responded with a less enthused, "Hello."

Lucy gave us a creepy look that seemed to lock eyes with all fifteen of us at once. "NO! That is not good enough, people! You need enthusiasm! People need to feel the enthusiasm come out from you! So let's do this again!" she demanded.

We all responded, "HELLO LUCY!" Through all the shouting, I heard Steve's voice coming in loudest from the back of the room.

"Okay, that's better. You know the best way to remove a band-aid, right? Of course you do—you rip it right off!" Lucy was a high-energy hand talker, and her ripping motion came awfully close to my face as I sat directly in front of her.

"I would like a volunteer to stand up and be interviewed by me." She moved around the room like a squirrel hunting for its next nut.

Steve offered to go first. *Shocking.*

He stood up and gave his patented, although shorted, "YAO!" A few of us chuckled.

She looked at him sternly and asked him where he learned that. I noticed my hands start to shake a little, and sweat started to emerge from my armpits. *Good thing I learned early on to wear an undershirt in Florida.*

Lucy walked to the back of the room and stopped about two feet from Steve. She firmly shook his hand and took a long time to let go. "So Steve, very nice to meet you here. What do you do?"

Steve looked completely dumbfounded but recovered quickly. "I'm a personal banker." He then looked around the room with a smug look, thinking he was slick and quick on his feet.

Lucy responded, "Tell me more."

Flustered, Steve came up short, "Uh, I, well, it's more complicated than that—"

She cut him off, "Than what?"

He quickly gained control of himself, "I help people with banking needs."

"Oh, okay." Lucy drifted to the side of the room in front of the giant window. We all turned to look at her, and from our angle, the sight gave us the optical illusion she was walking on water.

"So, would any of you now know what Steve does if you didn't know him from this training class?"

Pretty much everyone shook their head no.

She continued, "Steve was brave going first, but just because you're brave doesn't mean that you know what the hell you're doing! On Friday, we will go around this room, and I'm going to ask you all what you do. I want a well-thought-out, precise value proposition from each of you. This is also known as an elevator pitch. The name comes from the scenario that you are on an elevator with a stranger, and you have a limited time to pique their interest in what you do for a living. Not the best term, I know, but I didn't make it up."

I knew I'd feel horrific anxiety for the entire week because, at any point, Lucy could put any one of us on the spot where we had to stand up in front of our peers, and sometimes Harry. We had to be ready at all times, no daydreaming until lunchtime.

Lunchtime came that Monday, and I felt like I needed a nap. Tim stood up next to me, motioning to go, and mumbled, "Where you wanna go?"

As we left the room to catch the elevator with others, Rosie and the other woman in our class, Naomi, approached us, asking if the two of us wanted to join them. I looked at Tim, and he responded, "Sure, but I have a lot of junk in my backseat, so we will have to take two cars."

Rosie quickly looked at me and said, "Okay, fine, I'll ride with Jacob."

Whoa, this hot chick wants to ride with me? Fantastic!

My heart might have skipped a beat, and I became a bit flushed, but we were walking out to 95-degree weather, so I used the heat for my benefit as I unbuttoned the top of my shirt and lowered my tie a little.

"I have the green Mustang over there."

"Oh my God. I love Mustangs!" She sounded as excited as if I was going to give her a ride in a Ferrari.

"Well, it's a 1994, and it's showing its age."

She looked at me with a smile.

We hopped in, and I followed Tim to the restaurant. Rosie became very talkative, something she was not in class.

"So, are you happy you accepted this job?" she asked.

"Yes, I think this training is a very good experience, and I've been lucky to connect with a handful of guys in the class. How about you?" I tried to glance at her but thought twice. *Better keep my eyes on the road.*

"I'm pleased with it as well. This is an excellent bank to work for, and I heard we can make a lot of money with commissions if we perform well."

At a red light, I was finally able to look over at her—petite, toned legs crossed in a tight black pencil skirt that sat well above her knee. The seatbelt lying between her breasts made it easy for me to look down at her bra; turquoise it was.

It was a good color for her. Were her panties turquoise too? Stop thinking like that; she has an engagement ring on.

She noticed that I saw her ring and asked, "So, do you have a girlfriend?"

"No, I do not, but I just started talking to this girl that Tim introduced me to. She works at his branch as a customer service representative."

"That's awesome that you and Tim became close so fast." I nodded, and we arrived at our lunch destination. We got out of the car and met Tim and Naomi inside the restaurant.

"Wow, an hour goes quick when you don't want it to end, huh?" Rosie flatly stated as I pulled my Mustang back into the parking lot at our building.

I nodded with a shrug this time.

We both opened our doors and started walking back into our building. Rosie stopped and turned toward me, "We should do happy hour after class one day."

Uh, I'd love to, but you're engaged. What's this about?

I looked down as we walked towards the entrance doors and mumbled, "Yeah."

"Ooookaaaay, guess not!" she said defensively.

I stopped for a second and looked directly at her as I was about to grab the door for her. She stopped too, and we locked eyes. I noticed her seductive brown eyes for the first time.

I started to giggle like an embarrassed schoolboy and tried to muster as much excitement as I could, "I would like to go to happy hour with you!"

A big smile emerged on Rosie's face. "Sweet! What's your phone number?"

Each day for the rest of the week became a little less uncomfortable as the training taught us how to develop compelling elevator pitches. I felt like I'd be ready to go by Friday.

The big day arrived, and Lucy looked directly at me, "So, Mr. Gilbert, please stand. Hi, I'm Lucy. What do you do?"

I stood up, maintained good body posture with my hands at my side, and tried not to sway side to side—something I often did at the beginning of the week.

"Hi Lucy, I am Jacob Gilbert. I'm a personal banker with DMNC Bank. I'm responsible for growing and servicing our bank clientele from simple deposit accounts to lending, to investment management, among other services." I exhaled noticeably.

Lucy's face brightened. "Bravo, Jacob! That gives a great quick idea of what you do, and an interested party can then ask a follow-up question if they choose to do so. How did that feel?"

"Felt good. Is it the weekend yet?" I joked.

Everyone chuckled, but of course, Dann needed the last word as I heard a soft after-the-fact comment from the back of the room, "Yeah, that's 'cause he's got a hot date this weekend!"

Can't that guy ever shut up and mind his own business?

I rarely looked forward to specific events as anticipation always created feelings of anxiety rather than excitement. Still, that Saturday night after communication training week was something that I looked forward to without realizing it. It was the night I was going to meet Mariana!

I called Tim on Saturday afternoon, letting him know the plan. He was super excited for me. Dann even got creative and made a paper Colombian flag and put it on the desk in my room with a handwritten "*mucho gusto*" written on the back.

I wore my best jeans, a nice button-down, my black leather slip-on Kenneth Cole shoes; I gelled my hair carefully for the first time in months.

I hopped in my Mustang and drove twenty minutes to Mariana's place in North Miami. She lived in an apartment complex that wasn't of the nicest caliber. She texted me not to ring the doorbell, so I called her from my car when I was in front of her building.

A petite woman with straight jet-black hair, a round face, and a fantastic body sauntered down the stairs toward me. She wore a tight light blue sleeveless V-neck top that met her jeans at the right place—you could see just a smidgen of her flat stomach if she moved in certain ways. Tight jeans showed off her nice toned butt, and white platform open-toed shoes completed the look. She opened my car door and gave me a luminous smile. I must have been grinning ear to ear and blushing.

"So nice to meet you, Jacob. Thank you for picking me up. I know you probably wanted to meet me at the door, but I live with a family, and I don't want them all in my business all the time. I hope you understand." She turned to her right, grabbing the seat belt.

"No problem, I'm just happy we could finally meet!" I replied with newfound enthusiasm learned this past week from Lucy. Getting up in front of the class yesterday gave me more confidence in my communication; I felt the confidence in my voice as Mariana and I conversed on the way to Bayfront Park.

We walked around the park most of the night—looking in shops and people-watching at some of the restaurants and bars. A live performance took place in the middle of the park. I know we went to the Hard Rock Cafe, but Mari so enthralled me, I don't remember what I ate or drank. It felt like the time was going so fast, and so many things were to be asked and discussed. Too soon, the time to take her home arrived; I guess that's the true sign of a good first date!

As long as I live, I will never forget her face the moment I dropped her back at her apartment. She gave me a hug, a peck on the lips, and as she moved to open her door, she looked back, head tilted, showing her perfect pearly white teeth. Then, just like that, she was gone.

Feeling like I was top of the world, I put on some R. Kelly "Ignition Remix" and sang at the top of my lungs while driving home, "It's the freakin' weekend; baby, I'm about to have me some fun."

Over the next few weeks, life finally slowed down a bit, and I could get more into a groove. Depending on the week, our training was either in the branch or in the training center. During training center days, I nearly always ate lunch with Tim and maybe a few other trainees.

I had dinner or drinks with Dann most nights, and I spent weekend nights with Mari.

About a month after I met Mari, I noticed that Dann was annoyed by how much time I spent with her. I didn't feel guilty at all because he had a bunch of college friends that he could hang out with.

At the same time, Dann upped his drinking. He'd drink to excess four to five nights per week. He'd be out at the local pub with his college buddies until the wee hours of the morning most Thursdays, and he'd go out clubbing Friday and Saturday nights. I'd go with him on occasion, but I certainly couldn't keep up with him.

Often I'd get home around midnight if I'd gone on a date with Mari; then, Dann's drunken careening around the apartment at two or three in the morning would wake me up. A few times, he brought home random girls he'd met at the bar and thought it would be funny to have them enter my bedroom while I was sleeping. One girl—and I have no idea what she looked like or who she was—decided she was too drunk to go home, so she got in bed with me. After a few gentle prods, I directed her to sleep on the couch.

How much longer could I stand living with Dann?

The next training week I vividly remember was "credit week." I knew nothing about credit before this week. When we received our training agenda for the year, I specifically circled this week. I wanted to be alert for all of it as I knew it was essential to understand the basics as soon as possible to become successful as a personal banker.

Alex, wearing another perfectly tailored pantsuit, greeted us with the same smile as she always did. This time she introduced another woman. This one was in her late thirties or early forties. She had a chunky build and incredibly blonde hair—too blonde, which meant she must have been bleaching it for years. I noticed she had a large Chanel bag, a gold Rolex, diamonds in her ears and around her neck.

Was this her way of showing her success to her peers? But who was I to judge? What did I know anyway?

"Hello class, I am super excited to be here. I love teaching new hires and banking rookies. My name is Sarah Stanley. I am the regional credit consultant for the Florida District. I am responsible for helping all the bankers originate credit applications. I'll teach you everything you need to know—helping you with sales techniques, assisting you with the underwriting, and walking you through the closing process."

I looked around the room. It was apparent that those who previously worked in banks understood the terms, and the banking rookies had bewildered looks on our faces.

Sarah continued, "The bank trusts me so much that I have a one million dollar credit authority. What does that mean, you might ask? It means that any credit application for personal or business use that originated out of our region's bank branches, I, and I alone can approve the loan if I deem it necessary. Up to one million dollars."

She walked around the room. Some people seemed impressed with her spiel, and they corrected their body language by sitting more upright. No one made a sound as Sarah transitioned her way from right in front of me to the window, then around the back of the room. She stopped in the back right corner where Dann sat.

Sarah looked at Dann's nametag and called him by name. Dann perked his head up, and she asked him, "How would you explain what I do to someone who doesn't know me?"

I looked down at my DMNC pen. *Not communications week again!*

Dann shot up; his big apple-shaped bottom rocked his chair with the sudden movement, and it almost fell over. "Well, Sarah, I would say we have this great woman who is our regional credit consultant, and she is responsible for assisting us bankers learn how to originate and close loans!"

"I am impressed, Dann. Most of the people I ask to do what you did, were not able to." She almost touched him on the shoulder to say, "Good job."

I kept my eyes glued to Sarah and Dann's body language as they seemed to lock eyes after that exchange. It was subtle, and most of the class didn't notice. But I knew Dann, and I knew how he flirted.

He definitely was flirting with our credit consultant! Who the hell does he think he is? But I also flirted with Rosie, and she flirted with me. I wonder what Rosie is doing for lunch.

A few hours later, I found myself at lunch with Rosie. Alone. For the first time.

"Dann was totally flirting with Sarah this morning," I blurted out like a tattler kid.

Rosie looked up from the menu and looked directly into my eyes, "No way, she's like twenty years older than him. And her boobs are ginormous. How could he be attracted to her?'"

"I don't know, but I saw it, and I know Dann. And by the way, he likes women with huge boobs. It's his thing," I replied.

"Oh, so you know Dann's type, huh?" She playfully responded.

"I mean, I've spent a lot of time with him in different situations, so yeah, I do." In my matter-of-fact-banker-tone.

"So, what is your type, Jacob Gilbert?" Rosie asked and quickly looked back into the menu.

"Jacob Gilbert? So proper we are today, huh? Umm, my type, well I like dark features—you know, dark hair, olive complexion—oh, and a great smile." I then looked down at the menu.

"Uh-huh…." Rosie wanted more.

"Okay, I like petite women, but not skinny. I like a nice handful of breast and a great ass that is way more than a handful. Nice toned legs and stomach. Is that asking too much?" I winked at her.

Am I really flirting with an engaged coworker?

"Not completely, but you know you just basically described me. Just wanted to let you know that." She winked back, and our banter was interrupted by the waiter.

I decided it was best to change the subject after we ordered, so I blurted out, "You know Don Deeds practices his elevator pitch in front of the mirror?"

Why do I keep acting like a ten-year-old girl with the class gossip? I've never been a gossiper before, so why now? Am I nervous? I do have a beautiful woman sitting with me, just the two of us. What would Mari think of this?

With Rosie's full attention on me now, she responded, "Definitely doesn't shock me. Don is a total narcissist. Do you see the way he dresses? From the chicklet front teeth to his porcelain-like gelled hair. And the pocket kerchief. He wears a different one each day. Who does that?"

At that point, I realized that Rosie's façade in class was super deceptive. She had a lot more emotional intelligence than she showed. She had a pulse on everyone and everything in that room. *What was her pulse on me? Time to go back to quiet, non-gossiper Jacob.*

She noticed I didn't bite on the Don trash talk. "You know who he looks like?" She started laughing uncontrollably. "Syndrome, the supervillain in *The Incredibles.*"

I started cracking up and joined her in laughter. It seemed we stopped at the exact same time and shared an awkward look. She moved her eyes from mine to the left and casually asked, "When are we going on that happy hour, Jacob Gilbert?"

"Thursday?" I immediately responded and then felt a rush of blood to my face.

"Thursday after work it is!" She smiled and started eating as lunch had just arrived.

On Thursday, Sarah opened class with the following question, "Why do cars come with spare tires?"

Dann shouted out from the back of the room with an overt New York accent, "Because flat tires happen."

"Exactly, Dann. Flat tires happen. Would we drive around with a spare tire all the time if we knew when the flat would happen? Of course not, but there are many unknowns in life, and we carry the spare around for convenience when we need it. That is how I want you to think of a revolving line of credit and how to present it to our bank clients. The number one reason for a solid bank customer to decline a line of credit is because they do not have an immediate need for it.

Our job is to explain that we offer lines of credit for those who might not have an immediate need. Think of the spare tire analogy. Okay, who wants to role play with me?"

My hand hid beneath the table. But slick-haired chicklet-teeth, Don Deeds was happy to play.

He must have practiced this last night in front of the mirror. Am I really going to happy hour with Rosie this evening?

"A million dollars is a lot to trust someone with, don't you think?" I asked Rosie as we walked into the Ale House bar to officially start our happy hour.

She replied in a businesslike tone, "I heard it was Harry's underhanded way for us to close more credit in Florida." Then her facial expression brightened, and she turned towards me, "Why are we talking about work when we were just at work all day? Let's relax and have fun!"

She had a good point, but what else am I supposed to talk about with an engaged co-worker? Her engagement?

"So I've noticed that ring on your left hand. When is the wedding?" I raised my gaze from her ring to her big brown eyes.

"Just because I have a ring on doesn't mean I have a wedding planned. My fiancé and I have been together since high school, and although he bought me a ring that shows he wants to marry me, I am not ready to get married. I'm only twenty-four. I want to have my own life too."

"I understand. I can't picture myself getting married anytime in the near future."

"What is going on with that girl Tim hooked you up with?"

"We see each other once or twice a week. I know what you mean about wanting to have our own time too outside of dating someone. I mean, she's in school and works, so she doesn't have a ton of free time at this point." I badly wanted to change the subject. "What do you do for fun?"

"I like to stay active. I run, and I like to dance salsa at the bars or clubs as well. Do you know how to dance?" She smiled, and her eyes opened wider with her question.

"I don't know how to salsa. I barely can dance at a regular club." I glanced down at my vodka soda.

"Well, you seem to be super athletic, so I am sure it won't be too hard for you. Do you want to go dancing after this?"

"Sure, why not."

Our conversation flowed from topic to topic—work, significant others, and life. None of it was dull, for me at least. Eventually, after a few drinks, our conversation turned into a total flirt-fest. Before I knew it, we were driving to a Latin club.

Rosie taught me the basic salsa moves, and I had a couple more drinks to boost my confidence. On the dance floor, the music took over, and I felt my hands wandering slightly down her lower back. She noticed and didn't move them, so I inched further down. She moved one of her hands from my shoulder to the side of my face. I crouched down to her level for a second, and before I knew it, we were kissing voraciously on the dance floor. The mixture of the alcohol, the music, and the feeling of her butt in my hands was exquisite and time froze for that moment.

Oh my God, this is incredible! Rosie is so hot! I can't believe I'm out with a woman this gorgeous!

Around midnight, I drove her back to her car, and we made out a little longer. To my surprise and entirely out of character, I suggested we have dessert and a nightcap back at my place. The only problem was that I didn't have any dessert in my quasi-frat apartment. I only could assume she knew what I meant by dessert.

And yes, she did. As I made my way onto Biscayne Boulevard, I noticed Rosie was creeping towards my driver's side of the car. She whispered in my ear, "Dinner and dancing were really yummy. Do you mind if I continue to have something yummy?"

I could've given myself whiplash with the amount of velocity I moved my head back into the headrest! "Um, sure, what would you like?" I asked as I kept my eyes glued to the road.

Rosie grabbed my crotch, and I noticed the blood flowing towards that area immediately. "I want to feast on this yumminess," Rosie said as she unzipped my pants.

Rosie might have been with the same guy since high school, but she sure knew what she was doing. Between her head in my crotch and the few drinks I had, that was the most difficult ten-minute drive of my life!

We quickly made it up to my room without running into Dann, ripped off each other's clothes, and our hands and mouths went all over each other's bodies. After it was over, Rosie went to my bathroom to clean up and get dressed again. Laying alone naked on my bed, I realized I let my second head get the best of me. Not sure if I was more worried about Dann finding out or feeling guilty for Mari.

I was never raised to be a cheater. Am I a cheater? I didn't do anything for this to happen. I was just there, and it happened to me! And it felt so good. Oh, I need to call Mari! How do I call her when Rosie is here? What will Rosie tell her fiancé?

When Rosie came out of the bathroom, I told her it was late. I suggested it was best she spent the night with me, and I'd drive her back to her car super early so she could get ready for training class. She obliged and smiled, undressed again to her panties, and lay next to me as we watched TV until we both passed out.

My alarm jolted us up at six o'clock. I took a quick shower and got ready in record time as Rosie was waiting for me. I opened my bedroom door quietly, trying not to make a sound. As we tip-toed past Dann's room, I looked toward the living room, and he spotted us.

Dann was sitting on the couch, shirtless, in his boxers, drinking a Coke and eating a Pop-Tart. His hairy chest and big belly drooping over the waistband of his boxers didn't help the slight hangover and anxiety-filled morning.

SHIT!

"Heyyy boys and girls. Did you two have a good time last night at happy hour?" Dann leered at me. His look expressed his power over the situation, a power he thrived on. He was power-driven, always wanting control in the driver's seat. Neither of us answered his first question, so he asked another, "What are you doing up so early?"

My eyes didn't quite meet his as I gazed out the sliding glass door adjacent to the couch. "I, uh, well, Rosie and I went dancing, and I didn't want her driving home too late." I felt my heart rate rising and noticed some beads of sweat forming on my forehead.

"Oh, it's all good. Rosie is cool. She's welcome here whenever. I like her better than Mari." He smiled as he looked Rosie up and down.

I turned towards the front door with my hand on the knob, "Okay, well, I'm going to drive her back to her car. Then we'll head to training separately."

"Wait a minute! Why don't you let Rosie take your 'stang, and I'll drive you to training?"

Rosie was clearly uncomfortable, and I could see from her face she wanted to break free from the apartment immediately.

I chose the path of least resistance. "Okay, Rosie, here are my keys. Take my car. We'll figure out how to get your car back later." I dropped my key in her open palm, opened the door for her, and walked her a few feet into the hallway.

I gave her a quick goodbye hug and came back into the apartment, where I saw Dann's chin in the air gulping from his Coke can. "No kiss goodbye?"

I looked down and shook my head.

"Joey, that is one hot piece of ass. You should be proud of taking that down." He got up, walked to his bedroom, and looked back. "Don't worry; I won't tell Mari. I'll be ready in fifteen minutes."

I took a deep breath, flopped on the couch, and stared at the ceiling. *What have I done?*

As I waited for Dann, I flipped open my phone to see that I had missed three calls from Mariana. I immediately called her and addressed her initial worry and disappointment that I didn't answer my phone last night. I told her that I was with Dann and his college buddies in Coconut Grove, and the music was loud, and I couldn't hear my phone. And of course, I didn't want to wake her by calling too late at night! She seemed to accept this explanation.

I felt totally different while walking into the training class that Friday morning. Usually, I'd enjoy having the sun hit my face as I walked from my car to the building. That day, my eyes barely wanted to open, and I had a pounding headache. Everything was a bit fuzzy. Plus, I was elated and horrified by the fact that I'd had unexpected steamy sex with a colleague. Not how I liked to start my day.

"Happy Friday, class! Thank you for being on time. Today is the last day of credit training, and you will all be in your branches for the next couple of weeks. So let's make it a fabulous day of learning!" Alex said with her hands clasped together like she was a sixth-grader at show-and-tell.

I tried not to make eye contact with anyone. But Dann got my attention and wiggled his eyebrows at me. My eyes must have been in a dead stare because I felt Tim bump my arm as he leaned over, asking, "Bro, you alright? You don't look that hot."

"Yeah, I'll be fine, must have had a few too many last night," I replied.

I looked back, and Rosie was in conversation with another classmate. I gave her a questioning look, which she returned. Although it was never blatantly discussed, we both knew not to speak of last night to our classmates and her look that morning made her wishes clear.

Before I knew it, lunch was upon us. As class broke up, Dann quickly came to my desk and said, "Joey, come to lunch with us. I'll meet you downstairs."

Before I could ask who "us" was, Dann scurried out the door to the elevator.

As I made my way down the elevator to the parking lot, Dann had his car out waiting for me. I noticed our credit consultant, Sarah, occupied the front seat, so I opened the back door on the passenger side and hopped in.

"Where the heck were you last night, Joey?" Dann asked me in a semi-playful voice.

I don't want our credit consultant to know my personal business. Why is he asking me these questions in front of her? And wait, why are we going to lunch with her in the first place? So many things to analyze in such a short time, on top of nursing a hangover.

"Uhh, I, uh, oh went dancing with Mari," I stuttered.

"Doesn't she have school on Thursday nights?"

"She didn't have it last night." *Stop asking me questions, Dann!*

Before Dann could ask another question, I thought as fast as I could of something to say to redirect the conversation, "So Sarah, what do you think of our class this week?"

What kind of question was that, Jac? So trivial.

Sarah pulled her skirt down a bit and tried to turn back towards me, "I think your class is going to be incredibly successful! You have a lot of talent in there, and part of my job is getting that talent to produce; well, on the credit side of the bank at least."

After a short pause, she continued. "After spending some time with Dann this week, he gave me a little color around the new bankers in the room. As you may know, I worked in the role for seven years before Harry promoted me to this role at the beginning of this year."

Wait, Dann and Sarah have been spending time together this week? When? Where? How? My head had been so far up Rosie's ass in class that I must have missed something.

We sat down for the lunch special, and I casually asked, "So you two have gone to lunch before this week?"

They both looked at each other and nodded their heads yes.

"I see. So I'm sure Dann told you that we were study-abroad college friends, but what about you? I'd like to know more." I sat forward on my seat while unbuttoning my top button and pulling down my tie—like it makes a difference for the forty-five minutes at lunch.

"Well, I'm a Florida girl born and bred, as I mentioned in class. I even went to Tallahassee for school at Florida State and moved back here afterward. My mother was a banker, so she got me into banking right out of college, and I stayed in it for...well, if I tell you how long, you'll guess my age, and a true lady never tells her age."

Dann let out a chuckle. I smiled as professionally as I could.

Sarah continued, "I did the married thing as well. I have two kids. Let me tell you, it's not as glamorous as they show in the movies."

"Oh yeah?" My eyes perked up.

Dann butted in, "Joey has got a little girlfriend of his own these days." Now both of their eyes were on me from across the table.

My face turned ruby red, and I said, "It's super early, you know."

Dann turned to Sarah, "Aren't you in a real relationship when you spend every weekend night together and speak via phone every night?"

Sarah chuckled a little, "Yeah, I agree. You got yourself a real girlfriend, Jacob!"

I let out a sigh, knowing I needed to change the conversation again, "So Sarah, can you provide us some pointers to be successful in this role?"

That adjective kept finding its way into my vocabulary.

"I was telling Dann last night that Harry has a plan. He plans to grow this market like never before. Harry believes if he can do this, he will take over the National Banking Director role, which he's made no secret he is after. Many bankers who have been in the role for years just sit back and wait for customers and business to fall in their lap. You may hit your sales numbers this way, but you will not be a top producer or make the kind of money you want. I know you both didn't take this job to make fifty grand a year. What you have to do is find centers of influence that will provide you business."

You talked to Dann last night? Where?

"Centers of influence?" I asked. I tried to prevent my wandering eyes from staring at her DD breasts hanging out of her white blouse, nearly on the table edge right across from me.

"Yes, the acronym is COI. These are other professionals in the area that deal with similar clients that will need banking services. So think of attorneys, accountants, realtors, business consultants—"

I interrupted, "Business consultants?"

"Yes, these are people who help small businesses or even individuals to find financing, among other services. Some people are very busy with their business operation, and they prefer to hire someone to find and coordinate the type of services they are looking for."

My eyebrows rose, and I noticed my headache subsiding.

Sarah continued, "To be honest, finding a high-quality business consultant to work with is part of the reason I am in my current role. A lot of loan business referrals came my way for a while. I was always on top of the stack rankings for credit. Harry quickly noticed that, and he created my current position—I was hand-picked for it."

"That's awesome!" Dann put his chopsticks down and looked like he was about to give applause, but he quickly realized where he was and caught himself.

For the remainder of lunch, I was thinking about and trying to understand the idea of centers of influence. I was also watching the subtle gestures between Sarah and Dann. My mind was still a bit fuzzy, so all I yearned for was to lay down on my bed. Then I remembered I had a date that night with Mariana, not just any date, but *the* date. The date where we both agreed to take our relationship to the next level.

For the rest of the afternoon, my body was in class, but my head was in the clouds thinking about taking my relationship with Mariana to the next level and feeling guilty about spending the previous night with Rosie.

Tim noticed I was more of a space cadet than usual. I must have looked at him with my anxious face. He tilted his head and gave me a look, wondering with his eyes about what was going on. I actually wanted to get his opinion but didn't want Rosie to overhear.

At the next 10-minute break, I motioned to the elevator. As we made our way to the street for a walk, I told him I had some anxiety about my big date with Mari. I knew Tim was very happy for me because he thought it had been many months since I was intimate with a woman.

"You know, it's normal to be nervous. I've had performance anxiety myself at times." We both looked down at the sidewalk as our black dress shoes hit the concrete in unison.

"Actually, it isn't performance anxiety. I'm in a little bit of a pickle. Last night I went out to happy hour with Rosie, and we ended up at a Latin dance club and started making out on the dance floor and in the car a little. Well, okay, more than a little in the car, and she came home with me and spent the night."

Tim's eyes lit up. He momentarily put his hands in front of his face in mock shock. He lowered his hands, revealing a huge grin, and said, "Bro! Rosie is smoking hot! I mean, Mari is hot too, but *Rosie*?"

He couldn't believe I scored the forbidden fruit of our class. I kind of couldn't believe it either.

"Wait! She's engaged! What. The. Fuck?"

"I know, I know, it's bad. But it gets a teeeeeny-bit worse. Dann knows."

Tim became super giddy, enjoying living vicariously through me. But then it hit him, Dann knew. If Dann knew, before long, the whole class would know.

I continued, "The crazy thing is I've done nothing to show her I'm interested. I've put no effort into this situation."

"*Women*! They want what they can't have. The more you ignore Rosie, the more she wants you! But you're still getting together with Mari tonight?"

"Yes."

After a pause, Tim nudged me in the ribs, "How was she?"

"I don't kiss and tell—but I will tell you, she's spectacular. And that ass. You can bounce dimes off of it."

"*Stop*! I can't take it anymore. This is awesome, bro! I'm going to fantasize about her when I masturbate tonight!"

"Too much info, Timmy! Wait, what about your wife?"

"Oh, when you get married, you'll see. Sex? It's an uncommon occurrence. Like it needs to be planned 'n shit." Tim shrugged.

Did he get that from me?

"Okay, so let's go back to your date with Mari tonight."

"I'm not really nervous about performing. I just don't want to force her or for it to be awkward."

Tim stopped. Then I stopped a step ahead and turned back. He started to walk, and this time he put his right hand on my shoulder. "Ohh, I get it. You're not sure she's ready even though she told you she was."

I semi-rolled my eyes and gave a slight nod in embarrassment.

"Look, I don't care what anyone says; it's hard to get a good girl in the sack. I mean what, Mari, she's hot, and she goes to church regularly, right?"

I nodded more confidently now.

"Okay, so this is what you do. You call her and tell her you're going to pick her up. Tell her that you are going to a nice restaurant on South Beach. You show up with roses—wait—yes, bring roses. Dress nice, maybe wear what you have on now. But before you leave your apartment, take a couple of roses out of the bunch and pull the petals off them. Create a heart shape from the rose petals on your bed in your room. Then when dinner is over, don't ask what she wants to do; take her to your place. And for God's sake, if you have time, put on clean sheets before your date."

Facing each other, Tim then put his other hands on my shoulder as mine were still in my pockets. He looked directly into my eyes, although a little closer than I'd like him to be at this point. "You're going to have to tell her you love her."

My eyes grew wide. His right hand nudged my cheek, and he burst out in a uniquely-Tim laugh, bringing his hand to his mouth to cover it. I took it all in, not laughing, but with a forced smile.

After he stopped laughing, he continued, "Seriously, bro, if you want to get it on with Mari, follow that advice, and you'll be calling me tomorrow telling me all about it. C'mon, let's get back to class."

We turned back to walk back to our building; I stopped and spoke louder than usual, "I don't know if I love her."

He stopped again, looked back at me, and said with dead seriousness, "Who knows what love is. But if she *thinks* you love her, your life will be a whole helluva lot easier. I know it is for me!"

Tim's advice worked like a charm. Who knew he was so wise? From that point on, I used him as my newly found confidant. We spoke to each other multiple times per week over the phone, and our trust in each other grew. I found myself telling Tim things I'd never told anyone else. Our relationship grew, as did my relationship with Mari. Though Rosie was hot and gave a good ride, I knew she'd be a one-night stand. Living with Dann, although sometimes overwhelming, was going just fine. My new life in Florida was moving along smoothly, and I was excited for what the future held.

NINE

As the hot, humid weather became less humid and cooler, I realized we were just weeks away from the holiday season. In less than a month and a half, the year would become 2005, and we'd all be done with training and in our banker roles full time.

I noticed my pants were getting a little tighter, and my face was looking puffier, but I didn't mind because I was happy. I had very little stress, a promising job, new friends, a new girlfriend, and life was good.

Back at the branch, things were heating up. The snowbirds were starting to arrive from up north, and foot traffic increased weekly. My mentor, Jeff, saw customer after customer; sometimes, he was so busy he didn't have time to drink his coffee or take a lunch break. Sal was all over the place. He must have put in 15,000 steps per workday as he was never one to sit down.

One day, as I walked across the lobby, Sal summoned me to his desk. I walked over and noticed he was engaged with an older gentleman that I had not seen before.

Sal waved his hand towards the gentlemen, "Mr. Vacca, this is Jacob. He is my new banker hire. He is just finishing up the new training program that they revamped this year."

"Nice to meet you, Jacob. I wish you lots of luck here; don't worry, *you'll need it.*" Mr. Vacca proclaimed.

Sal burst into his wheezing laugh and swayed side to side a little bit faster. I faked a smile as I didn't quite understand what Mr. Vacca was trying to say.

Sal stopped swaying, "Mr. Vacca was a branch manager up north for over thirty years. He had a vacation house down here, so we'd talk about managerial issues from time to time. But he recently retired, so we will be seeing a lot more of him as a customer."

I realized that even though I stood up straight, Mr. Vacca was still a good inch or so taller than me. Mr. Vacca slightly looked down into my eyes and lightly grabbed my right tricep. In a surprisingly serious tone, he said, "Don't let these sonz-a-bitches bully you around. You hear me? You seem like a nice kid. Don't let them corrupt you."

He let go of my tricep and turned toward Sal with a light-hearted voice, "Hey, Sal, what kind of sales campaign you got goin' on now?"

Sal rolled his eyes, started to sway again, and sighed, "Please! We gotta sell these damn credit cards like they're hotcakes!"

"Those sonz-a-bitches! So glad I'm retired, or my eye would start twitching, thinking of how I was going to hit those sales goals! Hey kid, you have one of the best managers here; make sure you follow his direction. Don't get caught up in all the nonsense. I've seen way too many bankers come and go because they got caught up in the bull-shit. Don't let it happen to you!" He gave me a slight wink and then motioned he was on his way to the teller line to make his transaction.

What the heck is he talking about? I know there had to be some sort of subtext there; I just wasn't following.

I gave Sal a look that asked, "What is he talking about?"

Sal gave me an eye, and I followed him back to the break room for a minute. "He's a riot, huh? Don't worry about what Mr. Vacca says. He's just a guy that worked here for way too long and got bitter.

Or maybe he's always been bitter. He has a good heart but sometimes a little misdirected. But he did say one correct thing—stick by me, and you'll be fine."

"I had lunch with Sarah Stanley the other week. She advised us to use centers of influence. She mentioned that she used business consultants to originate more loans than any other banker." My tone rose as I ended the sentence to make it seem like I was asking a question when, in fact, I was making a comment. However, I knew Sal would pick up on this.

"Oh please! Sarah Stanley is the last person I want you taking advice from."

The break room door opened; a teller was looking for Sal to get into the vault for more cash. "We will pick this conversation up again," he said as he fumbled around for his keys in his pocket while walking towards the cash vault.

Before I had time to analyze what Sal was trying to say, Jeff hollered out to me to grab another fax off the machine. When I handed the fax to him, he quickly placed them face down on his desk to the side of his computer.

"Shall we have some lunch?" Jeff asked.

I shrugged and looked around, "I think we can go now."

Jeff stood up and took off his jacket to put on the back of his chair, "Listen to me, Jac, *we* run this place. Sal is *the* manager, but not *your* manager. We bankers are the ones that keep the lights on in this place. Remember that, and things will run smoothly for us."

Although Sal was the branch manager and the tellers and service representatives directly reported to him, the bankers were responsible for the sales. Harry wanted a direct pulse on us, making sure he was our direct manager, with a dotted line reporting to our branch manager.

Basically, if the branch manager and Harry disagreed on how to handle a specific situation with a banker, Harry was the one that determined the outcome. It was just another way Harry subtly let everyone know he was in charge—and it was his way or the I-95 highway.

Jeff and I let the staff know we were leaving for lunch and made our way to my Mustang. He pulled a mini-gadget from his front suit pants pocket. It was a new Samsung flip phone. It was probably less than two inches long and about a half-inch thick. "Wow, that is small," I said.

"That is *not* what she said," Jeff playfully responded.

I let out a big laugh.

"You know what this can do? Text message. So you don't have to talk to people over the phone. Look, you hit the 8 button once for the letter T, then number 4 two times for letter H, and letter 3 twice for letter E. Try it!" He was excited, like a kid showing you how to use a new toy.

"Eh, why would anyone want to waste all that time to write words when you can just pick up the phone and call someone."

"This is the way of the future!"

My phone started to vibrate in my pocket. I flipped it open and saw it was Rosie. *What did she want?!*

"Hi, Rosie, what's up?" I answered.

"Heeyyyy. How's your day going? I've been so busy but just been thinking about you. I know we haven't seen each other in two weeks, and I miss you." Her voice was so soft, so sexy, and so smooth on the other line.

My eyes scanned the area and drifted to Jeff, who was preoccupied texting at a pace of one word per minute. "Aw, that's sweet. Yes, it's been too long since we have caught up. But, um, I, uh, actually this isn't a good time. Sal isn't keen on talking on the cell phone during work hours." I felt proud that I could think so quickly on my feet.

"Oh, I thought you'd be at lunch; that's why I called. But no problem. Can we go for happy hour again next week?" She asked so sweetly it was nearly impossible to say no.

"Uhh, next week, uhh." I paused and noticed that Jeff was paying attention to my conversation as it seemed he got frustrated in his texting. "Ummm. No. I can't. Gotta go." I hung up quickly.

God, she's so hot, so sweet. But I'm dating Mari. I can't believe two smokin' women want me at once. Is this really my life?

After closing my phone, I put my car in reverse. Jeff looked towards me, "You just said no to your girl?"

"Uh, yeah..." I trail off. I didn't want to explain.

Jeff seemed to accept my answer and changed subjects, "So what was Sal telling you back in the break room right before we left?"

I shrugged and said he told me a funny story about Mr. Vacca and made sure I changed the subject towards Gator football, which was like catnip for Jeff.

That Saturday night, Dann's frat crew invited me to my first Miami Hurricanes football game at the Orange Bowl. I invited Mari as my guest but didn't tell Dann until right before the game. I'm not sure if I felt uneasy by being around drunk, obnoxious frat dudes all night or sitting four hours in the dumpy Orange Bowl stadium. Maybe I felt guilty for blowing off Rosie. Either way, I was grumpy. Mari noticed it. Dann noticed it. But I didn't care. I was feeling just fine in my grumpiness.

Mari slept over that night for the first time. I woke up in the early hours and went to the kitchen for a drink of water. Frat dudes littered the living room. One slept on each couch, a couple were on the floor, and two chicks sprawled out in Dann's room. I was super annoyed that the place was trashed, and six people I didn't know crashed at our place.

Later I could tell Dann was annoyed that Mari was in the kitchen using it like she owned the place. He said nothing, but knowing Dann as well as I did, nothing had to be said. He rallied his troops and went out for brunch while Mari and I spent the rest of the morning cleaning up the mess. I drove Mari to her place in the afternoon and shifted my focus to the coming week.

On Tuesday, I rose earlier than usual and noticed Dann sitting in the living room in his boxers. He said, "Hey Jac, I'm up early because Sarah set up a breakfast for me to meet her business consultant friend. Why don't you come with me then I will drop you at your branch?"

I didn't have anything else scheduled for the morning, and I always liked to watch the interaction between Dann and Sarah, so I agreed. The drive to breakfast was quiet. We both just listened to the crap music Dann had on; normally, I'd be mentally preparing for meeting a new person, but I just kept thinking, wondering about what was going on between Dann and Sarah.

Dann and I showed up first, and we sat in a booth in the corner. "Should we same side it or sit across?"

I gave him my patented shrug as if it didn't really matter. Same side boothers it was. While we both were perusing the menu, a gentleman showed up at our table. "Dann Frazier?"

"Yes." Dann's head popped up from the menu.

"Jerry Stein, Miami Business Consultants. I wasn't sure if it was you, but what other stuffed suits are sitting next to each other in here?" He let out a boisterous laugh. I tried to hide my eye roll as best as I could.

"Where is Sarah? I thought she was going to be here." Jerry slid into the empty side of the booth and waited for a response. He had on slip-on blue suede shoes, overly-trying-to-be-trendy jeans, and an untucked collared shirt that probably needed ironing. He was in his mid to late forties, but his greyish receding hairline didn't help him look his age.

"Sarah had an emergency with her son, but she didn't want to cancel. I brought along my colleague, Jacob Gilbert. We are bankers focused on small business lending. We work out of some of the local branches in the area. Sarah thought it would be great if we could put a name with a face and see if business can be had for all," Dann said.

Some people are made for the spotlight, and those people tend to rise to the occasion. Dann loved the spotlight, and he definitely knew how to talk a good game. He spoke confidently and unequivocally among strangers, something that always eluded me, especially in business dealings!

Jerry proceeded, "I am glad Sarah set this up today. I am not sure how much she has told you about me, but we did a good amount of business together. However, I understand she isn't in a producer role any longer, and I've asked her who I can work with moving forward. I guess she took her time to introduce the next person because she wanted to be confident that you will do a good job. So, please tell me a little about yourself."

Dann's eyes lit up like New York City's New Year's ball. He sat on the edge of the booth seat with both hands firmly on the table. This was what he was waiting for, and now it was his show to steal.

"I was recruited to DMNC Bank right out of college. Senior management liked my experience working in the finance side of the real estate industry with my family and my business studies at 'The U'." Dann made the "U" hand gesture to show he is one of "them."

Jerry interrupted, "I attended 'The U' too!"

Dann dropped his stiff business tone and puts a smile into his voice, "That's awesome, great university, I must say!" He looked over at me and gestured in my direction. "We are excited that Jacob was able to join the bank as well through my recommendation to management. Also, he is an outstanding tennis player, so don't mess with him!" Another insincere laugh bubbled out of Dann.

What? Wait a minute. Is Dann trying to imply that he was the reason I was hired and that I was his underling? Really?

The three of us managed to make small talk as we ate our pancakes. Of course, I was mostly quiet. During the semi-awkward breakfast, I knew enough to see that Jerry was sizing us up and weighing our competence and trustworthiness. After more mindless chatter from Dann, it was time to leave.

"I'll be in touch with some referrals. Meanwhile, let's plan a time you can come to my office, and I'll introduce you to the staff. Probably after the new year would be best. Take care." Jerry walked off in the parking lot to his midnight blue Maserati.

"We are going to drive that kind of car soon," Dann exclaimed as he hit the back of my arm and unlocked his Beamer. Then we were on the way to our respective branches.

Another week in the branch passed. Our training group had one more week of classroom training; then, we had the last two weeks of the year off. I booked a flight back home for Christmas and was actually looking forward to seeing my family for the first time since July.

For the last happy hour of the year, The Banker Gang, what our training group decided to call ourselves, agreed to meet in Las Olas in Fort Lauderdale. I left the branch around five o'clock that Friday and called Mari as I approached I-95 north.

"Hi, babe." I greeted her in an overly sweet voice.

"Hi Jacob, I've missed you. It's been a long week. I can't wait to see you."

"Uh, um, well, I'm on my way to Fort Lauderdale. You know, it's the last happy hour of the year to see the guys."

"What? Why are you going to happy hour?"

"Well, ah, you know, I only moved here a few months ago, and these guys have become my new friends. I think it's positive to grow those relationships. Also, when we are together, we talk about what we are learning on the job as well." I felt the white lies as if they were cicadas burrowing tiny holes in my stomach.

"I still don't understand why you are *choosing* to go to happy hour." Mari paused, but I let her keep going. "If I had the choice of being with you or with my friends, I'd *always* choose you!"

The air felt smashed out of my lungs. I felt I couldn't breathe. I was already on the highway and couldn't make sense of what was exactly happening. Dead air echoed through the phone.

"Hello? Jacob?"

"Yes, I'm here. Uh, I guess I'll turn around and pick you up later," I mumbled in disappointment.

"Okay, I'm leaving the office at six, see you later. I love you," Mari cheerfully stated.

"Love you too." Another mumble.

Without properly analyzing the situation, I found myself turning around and putting my head in the sand. I didn't call anyone to let them know I wasn't making it. When I returned to my apartment, Dann wasn't there, and I changed into clothes for meeting Mari.

Why was Mariana so adamant about seeing me? Or did she not want me seeing my friends?

I couldn't place my finger on what was going on. For the first time, I wasn't genuinely excited about seeing her. But once we were in each other's company and she rocked my world in bed, all those questions sort of went away, at least, for the time being.

I spent that weekend entirely with Mariana. I don't even know if I saw Dann more than to say good morning. Suddenly it was Monday morning, December 15th, the start of the last week of training.

Getting ready that morning was bittersweet. The past five months went by like a flash. I reminisced about all that I learned in the classroom, at the branch, from my coworkers, and, for some reason, Rosie's smile in my car. Speaking of Rosie, she'd been mostly quiet the last few weeks, and we barely had any interaction. I felt a little anxious, especially about seeing Rosie that morning.

I barely even noticed that Mari was still at my place that morning, getting ready by my side. Part of me felt like the weekend had been too much of a good thing. My mind was elsewhere, and not sure she noticed. Mari took my car to her office, and I hopped in with Dann to get to the DMNC tower on Brickell. In the car, I asked Dann about his weekend and if he went to the happy hour.

Dann usually didn't like to talk much in the morning, but without much provocation, he opened up, "I had a date. She was a hot piece of ass. Took her to the Faena Hotel, and we had a good time!" Dann proceeded to tell me details, but my mind wandered. He could've said a lot of things, but they just didn't register. My focus was on the training week ahead and Rosie.

We entered the building to the elevator on our way to the 41st floor, just like any other classroom morning. I sat down next to Tim in the front row as always. We had our usual morning chat, catching up on each other's lives. As Tim told me a story about his wife, I noticed

Rosie coming in to take her regular seat behind me. I made eye contact and gave her a big smile. She tilted her head and gave me a wink.

It was going to be a good week. But wait a minute, why am I so focused on Rosie? So we had a one-night-stand, and I tasted the forbidden fruit, but why aren't I thinking of Mari? Mari was very possessive this weekend. She talked me out of going to the last happy hour of the year with the guys. Rosie is so hot, and so easy to talk to, and so not possessive...

Before I knew it, Steve and Don approached. "Where the hell were you Friday? Your 'stang broke down on 95 or something?" Don let out a laugh through his chicklet teeth.

Tim looked at me for my response, and I quickly looked over at Rosie to see if she was listening, but she was talking to Pierre. I paused and pursed my lips. "Yeah, I know; I should've called to tell you I couldn't make it. It was Mari and my three-month anniversary. So I had to take her out." *Good fib.*

All three of them gave me the look of acceptance as it seems any guy gets a pass with an excuse like that. Don launched into a story of how legendary the night was, and it was a shame I missed it. All I could think of was Steve's face in the crotch of the model at the nightclub and thought, I've already had a legendary night with The Banker Gang; what more could there be?

Right as we had a break in the conversation, Alex walked to the front of the class and asked us to take our seats. "Welcome class for your last week of training. It is always a proud week for me. I love to see the growth and knowledge you all have obtained over the past five months. I know each and every one of you will flourish in your banker roles.

"This week might be the most important for some of you. No, we are not learning about sales or any products. However, this week is all about compliance. I'll teach you how to analyze and understand bank compliance and why you need to abide by these oh-so-important regulations. Compliance helps keep our bank out of regulatory trouble and keeps people from being terminated."

I looked around the room, and almost everyone's ears perked up when we heard the word "terminated."

Alex continued, "I have to admit, some people that were in those seats in prior years did not abide by some of these regulations and standards. Because of that, they are no longer with our firm. So I would like to stress that all of you take this week seriously. I know this is our last week before the holidays, and a lot of you are thinking of your travels and plans, but please listen. This information is critical to your success and the bank's success."

I knew that Alex's plea fell on many deaf ears. In the branches, all our managers treated compliance like it was bullshit. The message we received was to clear account stipulations as fast as possible. Compliance was not discussed in our team meetings at all. Instead, all we heard was sales, sales, sales—morning, noon, and evening. We received training on how to hit our sales goal for that day, week, and month. Compliance was an afterthought—until Alex drove home the pillars of it.

"You're going to hear these acronyms often: KYC, CIP, AML, BSA, HMDA, Reg. B & E. Has anyone heard of any of these?"

A few hands went up—the hands of those who had previously worked in other banks. As I looked behind me, a familiar face that usually sat in the back corner of the room next to the window was missing. Harry was not present.

That's interesting and weird. Harry is always here for training—especially Monday morning; I wonder why he isn't today. Maybe he's already gone on vacation.

Alex pulled up the compliance slides from the projector. "Know your customer and customer identification procedures—KYC and CIP respectively—are identity verification procedures for individual and business customers. These procedures are *essential.* You need to verify that the people asking for loans are who they say they are. If you don't verify, you could end up funding a fraudulent loan. Each of you is in a critical customer-facing role. You open accounts and take loan applications. Signing your name to the form guarantees that you verified these people's identities."

Typically Monday morning training sessions were rowdy, most of the chaos stemming from the back row of guys. But today was a sleepy morning for sure. My mind was in the clouds. I couldn't wait for the first break to talk to Rosie. I kept trying to play the conversation in my head. *Do I ask her how she's been? Do I tell her I want to see her again?* Every time I played a different scenario in my head, I became more anxious, and the less I paid attention to Alex.

The morning break came and went so fast, Pierre had my ear about the Dolphins. I couldn't care less but wanted to be respectful, so I kept up with his nonsensical jabber about how the Dolphins still needed to find Dan Marino's replacement. I did make eye contact with Rosie, though. Lunch came and went; before I had a choice, I was pulled into the car with Dann, Steve, and Don. I actually thought of calling Rosie during lunch break but then thought better of it. How would we both talk with co-workers around?

Man, I've gotta stop thinking about Rosie. I'm with Mari. Rosie is engaged.

The afternoon session started with the projector slide reading Anti-Money Laundering and Bank Secrecy Act. I looked back, and Harry was still not there.

My head was still thinking about Rosie, but then I started to replay last Friday. *Was I becoming whipped by Mari? I know I've stopped calling my friends as much. I can't believe I skipped a guy's happy hour. Was she now keeping me from forming friendships with my other classmates?*

I had so much to think about it was impossible to listen to why Anti-Money Laundering was essential to my job. I mean, who puts money through a laundry machine anyways? I sat through the class, but I don't think I could tell you one thing about the subject.

Finally, class was over, and I caught up with Rosie in the parking lot. I nonchalantly sidled up next to her and put my hand on her waist. I accidentally scared her a little. I let out a big laugh, she laughed, and my anxiety vanished.

"Heyyyyy," she greeted me in a very flirtatious voice, lowering her shoulder into my chest. I almost got an erection just by her doing that.

"I missed you," I said with a big smile.

"You have? I haven't received any calls from you."

"Yeah, I know. I'm sorry. It's just been—"

Rosie cut me off, "Look, I totally understand. What happened a few weeks ago probably shouldn't have happened."

Noooooo! That night was amazing, and I don't want her to regret it.

"What do you mean? I had a great time with you!" I said in a slightly sad puppy dog-eyed face.

"I had a great time too, but you know my situation, and I heard that you skipped happy hour because you are getting serious with your girlfriend."

Who the hell told her that?!

After an awkward eye-locked silence, she said, "I've got to go, Jac. I'll see you tomorrow." She got in her car, started the engine, and pulled away.

I just stood there and watched her leave. *If only things were different.*

The rest of the week passed quickly. I continued to fantasize about Rosie anytime I had a spare moment. We gave each other flirtatious looks the rest of the week, but I knew we were going nowhere.

Is this what they mean by being emotionally involved with someone? The fantasies are fun, but the reality sucks.

Before I knew it, Friday arrived—the last day of formal training. I looked to the back of the room, and Harry was still missing. He'd been gone every day this week. Tim made a private comment to Alex about Harry being missing. Alex just rolled her eyes and shrugged. I butted in and asked if Harry was on vacation. She quickly replied that he wasn't big on compliance training week.

What wasn't said was that she and Harry had disagreements about how banker training should proceed. Alex seemed more stressed than usual, but it didn't seem that anyone other than me noticed or was concerned. Everyone was looking forward to two weeks off, and thoughts drifted to starting our positions full-time at the beginning of the new year. If compliance training were truly important, they shouldn't have scheduled it for the last week of class.

The day passed in a daze, and Alex continued to drone on about different regulations. The blinds were closed to block the afternoon sun, and we all were pretty sleepy. I know I was struggling to keep my eyes open, and when they drifted shut, images of Rosie danced in my head.

"Reg. B is about the process of giving a loan customer communication regarding their application status. Now, Steve, if a customer comes in and sits down at your desk and states that they want to obtain a home equity line of credit and asks you about bank interest rates. Is this a formal request for a loan application?"

At this point, Steve, practically laying his head on his forearms on this desk, perked up a little. It seemed he dozed off for a bit as he had a big red mark on his forehead where he was laying his head, "Umm. YAO. Uh, I think that's a request."

Alex's face crumpled, then with a furrowed brow, she walked to the back of the room toward Steve, Don, and Dann. "No! That is wrong. You people are not paying attention to important details. The bank can get into a lot of regulatory trouble if you don't learn these regulations or if you improperly apply them or at the wrong times."

Alex kept harping on. We weren't learning these crucial banking terms in the manner she wanted. As Alex paused mid-tirade for a breath, we all heard a soft-spoken, "Who cares?"

Alex stopped speaking and looked like someone had slapped her across the face. She stared around the room and, in a venomous tone we'd never heard from her, asked, "WHO CARES!?! Who cares? Who said that?"

Alex's eyes were big and wide, her cheeks flushed. Always prim and proper, she was coming undone right before our eyes. Stress splashed across her face. Tim and I sat still staring forward and down at our desk. I didn't look behind me and made sure not to make eye contact with Tim or anyone else as I knew I would've cracked a smile.

Alex was pacing and canvassing the back row. She stopped, bent over, and got right in Dann's face, "Did YOU say that?"

Dann had a big shit-eating grin on his face, "No, Ma'am, wasn't me."

Alex didn't buy it. "Don't give me that shit, Dann! I had to put up with all your narcissistic shit talk these past five months. FUCK!!!!" Alex screamed so loud the boaters on Biscayne Bay may have heard her.

Tim and I were like porcelain statues. I felt my heart beating hard and sweat forming under my armpits. Although Dann was a wise-ass most of the training, I was pretty sure he wasn't the one that made the comment. To me, it sounded like it came from Chicklet Don, but I couldn't be sure.

Alex stormed out of the room. We all looked around blankly. I stared wide-eyed directly behind me at Rosie. She was hiding a smile. I looked at Pierre; he was slightly shaking his head as he couldn't believe what he saw. I looked at others and mainly saw shrugs. It was probably the first time we all were together, without an instructor and completely silent.

Our leader, who had it all together, who directed us harmoniously in person, via email, and via phone, completely lost her shit. It was one comment. Was it at the wrong time? Possibly. Was it correct? Maybe. But one thing is for sure, something was going on with Alex, and it surely surprised every single one of us in that dimly lit room as the sun tried its hardest to shine through the little space between the shade slats.

A few silent minutes went by, and people started whispering. Dann broke the whispers by stating to the whole class, "It wasn't me, guys."

Pierre, who was mostly quiet and for the most part spoke only when spoken to, stood up, and everyone lasered in on him. "Guys, it doesn't matter who said it. I don't think any of us should throw anyone under the bus. We are a team, I consider you all my friends, and we are in this together. It looks like Alex is stressed for some reason. Maybe something is going on with her personal life; we don't know. One more thing, I've never felt a connection with coworkers like I have from this class. I hope we are all able to help each other to become successful starting in January."

All of us erupted with cheers, whistles, and claps. I think all of us expected Alex to come back once she heard our roar. She didn't.

Then we each took turns standing up and stating our thoughts. Don got up next. "I am not admitting it was me who said that comment but, I really appreciate all of you for sticking together. Not just today. Sometimes things have happened at our happy hours that are better left unsaid. I know people kept their mouths shut for the good of the group. I just want to let you know how proud I am of all of you, and if I can be of assistance to anyone moving forward, I am just a call away."

It seemed that everyone felt like making some sort of closing speech.

Thirty minutes passed as most of the class stood up and reiterated mostly the same thing. I then stood up. "Do you think we should call Alex? I mean, it is very unlike her to do this."

Rosie raised from her chair and gestured that she would call her. About a minute later, she reported the call went to voicemail.

I continued. "Class dismissed!"

Another roar came, mainly from the back of the class. Everyone stood up. I shook Tim's hand and told him I was really glad we became friends from this class, and he brought me close for a hug. We then all went around the group shaking hands or giving hugs.

It was a surreal feeling. I felt we gained more trust with each other because of Alex's blow-up than would've happened with a manager present. For the entire training period, I felt underlying anxiety generated by a false need to perform well against the people in that room. However, at that moment, I felt we all were a team fighting for the same thing—success in our new role. Every single one of us walked over to the Ale House, and the shots began, which was also the beginning of not remembering much else that evening.

Early the next day, Mari drove me to the Miami Airport for my flight to Newark. She was a little choked up, saying goodbye. This would be the longest time we'd been apart since we started dating, and it was over a major holiday. I was ready for a break, but it seemed she wasn't. She kept asking me if I was going to see my female friends from home. I said no, even though I wasn't sure that was going to be true. I had a lot to think about on that flight.

How does success look like in my new role? How do I feel about Mari? Why do I think about Rosie so much? How will I explain my first five months in Florida to my family?

After I landed and turned on my cell phone, I noticed I had a voicemail. I listened to it, and it was from Alex. I couldn't have been more surprised. Her brief message asked me to call her back, so I did as I waited for my father to pick me up.

Alex promptly answered. "Hi Jacob, thank you so much for returning my call. I would like to give my sincere apologies to you for what happened yesterday. It was totally out of line, and there is no excuse I can give to justify it. It was completely unprofessional, and all of you deserve so much better. I hope you accept my apology."

I felt Alex's regret come out of my phone. "Of course, Alex, I accept your apology. We all have bad days, and someone mentioned you might have been dealing with something in your personal life—"

Alex cut me off, "Nope. My personal life is fine. I told my husband what I did, and he couldn't believe it because it is not something I would ever do. I don't know what is going to happen to me regarding my bank position, especially if someone reports my actions to human resources."

I quickly responded, "I would never report you for that. I don't think anyone in our class would either. After you left, we actually took turns going around the room, making statements about our time during training. Then we all gave each other hugs and proceeded to get drunk at the Ale House!" I chuckled.

"Jacob, you are an outstanding individual. It was my pleasure to be your manager these months, and just remember to do the right thing. I can't say much more than that. Listen to what Harry says, and then use your own moral compass to decide how you will respond. Unfortunately, I can't give you any more details than that. Just remember to use the integrity you already have!"

"I appreciate the kind words. And I thank you for all the knowledge and assistance you have given the rest of the class and me. I hope this all works out."

"Yeah, me too, okay, let me continue calling all of your classmates to apologize. Happy Holidays!" I finally felt Alex's chipper attitude come through again.

Right as I hung up the phone, I saw my father, along with my mother, in the car pulling up to the arrival gate. They both jumped out to give me big hugs. I looked around, slightly embarrassed. They treated me like I was a twelve-year-old taking my first solo flight, asking me if everything went well, and so on. I didn't answer them; I mean, I made it. What does it matter now?

My father barely waited for me to buckle into the front seat. "So, how's the big-time banker doing? Do you like the job?" he asked.

"It's been good so far. We just finished training yesterday. I officially start the position in January. But I like it. I met a few friends from the training class."

My mother leaned forward to my passenger seat and said, "We have missed you so much, Jac! I'm so happy you're home for Christmas this year! But what about your personal life? Are you seeing a lucky lady in Florida?"

She had to go there already? Only thirty seconds into the car and my mother goes right for the jugular. I knew I needed to practice my response to this, but my hangover headache didn't allow it.

I managed an, "Uh, yeah."

My mother got closer to me—almost in my headspace—she giddily asked, "Really? Who is she? How did you meet?"

Every fiber of my body wanted to pretend like I didn't hear, but I couldn't pull that off. I pursed my lips and groaned slightly.

My father gave me a look that said I needed to answer my mother. "Her name is Mariana. A new coworker introduced me to her. She also works at the bank, but a different branch location."

"Mariana. I like that name. It sounds ethnic. Is she American?" My mother slid back into her seat.

"She's from Colombia. She's also in college, Florida International University." I responded curtly, hoping the questions would stop.

"Oh, I see. Well, that's nice, dear."

My father sensed I didn't want to go into more detail. To make small talk, he pointed out some new building construction on the way back home. Although I knew my parents wanted more information on my new life, I felt at ease for the first time in weeks. I was looking forward to the Christmas festivities.

TEN

To: All Florida Bankers
From: Harold.Goldman@DMNCbankUSA.com
Date: Tuesday, January 4, 2005; 7:06 AM
Subject: Jumping into January

Hello Team,
First, I would like to wish all of you a very happy new year. Second, please welcome the new training class to their new roles today. We have these new bankers in different branches spread throughout the South Florida market. I ask all of you to make them feel welcome. Third, as you know, new year, new sales goals. I expect all of you to come out with a fast start on new accounts and new loan applications. The first call night of the year will be tomorrow, Wednesday, January 5th at our main Brickell building from 5-7 pm. Please bring a printed sheet with customer names and phone numbers to be ready to start dialing at 5 pm.

Best,
Harry

That was the first email I read after being officially a DMNC retail branch banker. The thought of having to cold-call people during dinner time made the hair on the back of my neck stand and gave me a burning feeling at the bottom of my stomach.

Maybe it was the two cups of coffee I gulped on an empty stomach during our Monday morning branch huddle. However, if I were honest, I'd have to say my body's response was from anxiety I felt as I officially returned after taking the two weeks off.

My body felt like it did so often while working in the car dealership with my father before leaving for Italy.

ELEVEN

"Jacob, this is Al Martin; he will be your boss this summer. Al is one of our top salespeople at the dealership and has been for years. He has been excited to have a summer intern for a while now. I told him how well you have done in school, and I am sure you both can teach each other things."

After my father introduced me to my new summer pal, he walked to the corner of the large Ford dealership where his office had been for fifteen years or so. I had visited my father at work many times, but this time it felt different. I knew it wasn't going to be a quick visit. I knew I was in for eight to ten hours of grueling work, and with my neck and shoulder still in some pain, I was almost regretting the whole deal I made with my old man as I walked into Al's office.

Al stood up, shook my hand, and directed me to a seat across from him. His office was nicely decorated, typical family pics, drawings and artwork his kids made for him, and of course, plaques on the wall showing his sales excellence month after month, year after year.

I guess prospective buyers look around his office and think, "This is a good man. Look at his nice family and all those awards—how could he earn all those awards if he isn't good at his job?"

Al sat back in his chair and looked directly at me, "Your father is a great finance manager, and it has been a pleasure working with him all these years. Seeing you grow up to become the fine young man you are has been exciting for me as well. Your father has kept all of us abreast of your tennis and academic accomplishments; I think that's all great. Ever since he told me you'd be working with me this summer, I took time to think about how we both can make this the best summer for both of us. I don't want you sitting around bored. So have you thought about what you gain to learn from working here this summer?"

I pull myself up from my semi-slouch, "Well, uh, um, I really haven't had a formal job before, so I haven't put a lot of thought into what I should be learning."

Maybe because I have not thought about working at a car dealership at all—I wish I'd never made the deal. I want these ten weeks to fly by.

Al raised a brow, "I see. Well, you have been successful in other competitions, so let's see how we can apply some of that success into the business side of life."

I nodded my head, even though I was dumbfounded by that answer.

Al started to shuffle around some papers on his desk. "Ah, here it is. This is a list of prospective buyers that have either visited our dealership in the past or called in for information. Some of these people have already purchased a car, but there are probably others that have not and might need a nice nudge to get back here to discuss their vehicle needs."

I sat at the edge of the seat and saw a list of names, dates, addresses, and phone numbers. Sweat formed in my armpits. *I really should've worn an undershirt. Well, at least this is a white polo.*

Al then handed me the papers. "So, I think the first order of business is for you to go through this list and see how many appointments you can set."

I must have blushed or looked scared.

Al continued, "Have you ever called people you don't know before?"

Mutely, I semi-nodded yes.

"Ok, good, so you know how to introduce yourself and the proper way to start the conversation." Al ended the sentence with more of a statement than a question. I mutely nodded yes again, as if I knew what the hell he was talking about. My eyes glazed over like a deer staring at oncoming headlights.

Al got up and motioned for me to follow him. He walked me out to the showroom floor, then over to an empty cubicle on the side of the floor where some of the associates or receptionists sat.

"Here is a good one. There is a phone for you; don't worry about a computer or schedules. Just try to get these people in the door for a test drive or further negotiations on a vehicle they were discussing. I'll come check on you in an hour or so. As you know, from previous visits, water, coffee, and donuts are in the waiting area; feel free to grab some."

My stomach was roiling, and I couldn't think about eating anything. Slowly I sat down on the seat. I looked through the papers he gave me—name after name, page after page. I looked at the phone and saw a loaded gun pointed at me. I then thought it would be a good idea to use the bathroom. I hand motioned to Al that's where I was headed. Alone in the bathroom, I splashed water on my face and stared at myself in the mirror.

I started mumbling a full-on conversation with the person staring right back at me. *What the fuck did you get yourself into? Who the hell wants to be cold calling these people? I can't do this! You can't do this! Think. Think fast. How do you get yourself out of this mess?*

As I was finishing my monologue with the mirror, another sales associate entered and possibly heard me. He introduced himself and stated the whole team was excited to have me as a summer intern; they'd heard many positive things about me. After that comment, I knew there was no way out but through.

I made a trip to the coffee station and nervously smiled at the cute receptionist. I wanted to plead for her help, but I couldn't muster a word. My throat closed up.

I walked back to my cubicle. I looked at the list again. And again. Then the phone. I opened my cell phone; no missed calls; it was just after eight in the morning. I knew my father usually didn't leave the office on a Monday until after six-thirty in the evening, or later depending on if he was working on a specific financing deal.

Was I going to have to make cold calls for the next ten hours?

My leg started to shake, bouncing my knee up and down. It shook so much that the cubicle next to me was in motion. It was so quiet at that time in the morning that everyone could hear the awkward conversations I'd have. A complete anxiety meltdown coursed throughout my body.

I needed to take a walk. I snuck out the side door to the new car lot outside. I paced along the long lines of new cars. I started looking at the prices and different models and started memorizing those facts. This eased my mind a bit from the calls I was going to have to make. I was probably out there for thirty minutes, but it seemed like much less.

When I felt calmer, I made my way back into the dealership. I saw Al outside of his office, and I quickly made my way to my cubicle. Al came over to me and leaned on my cubicle, "Jac, I've been looking for you, just checking in to see how the calls are going?"

I popped my head up with a look of fear. Al asked, "Everything okay?"

Without thinking, I said, "Well, not sure if my father told you, but I had a pretty serious injury this past semester, and I was on the phone with my new physical therapist, and he was following up on me to see what I have been doing and wants to see me three times a week. I know I'm supposed to work long hours here, and I want to put them in, but at the same time, I really want to get my neck and shoulder better."

Wow, that was ingenious; maybe I can think on my feet when needed.

Al straightened up, which highlighted his large belly—*a basketball could fit snugly under that Ford white polo.* His lower body was slim—*there must be a lot of pressure on those poor knees.*

"Oh man, yes, your father mentioned that's why you're working here, because of your injury. I am sorry to hear that. Although it might not seem like it from looking at me, I know how important physical health is, especially for someone young like you. I know I'm supposed to report how you are doing to your father, but between you and me, if you do what you need to, you can come and go to your physical therapy as you please. If you feel you need to go every day, that is fine; just communicate with me about it. I'm going to give you my cell number so you can call me if you are coming in late or need to let me know your schedule. I want you to be successful in life."

"I really appreciate that, Al." I paused and then continued, "Can I be honest with you?"

"Of course, Jac!"

"I've never cold-called before and have no idea what I am doing." I pulled a forced smile across my teeth as a little kid would if caught doing something naughty.

Al let out a loud chuckle. I closed my lips. "Jac, cold-calling is one of the hardest things to do. No one truly enjoys it. And if they did, well, there is probably something wrong with them!" Al grabbed a chair from an empty cubicle and took a seat next to me. "Did your father tell you how you're going to get compensated this summer?"

I shook my head no.

"Well, that helps me understand your confusion. We agreed that if you make appointments, take people on test drives and leave the rest to another sales associate or me, and if those people purchase a vehicle, you will earn a commission on that sale."

My eyes lit up. "Really?"

"Yes! We could be talking a couple hundred or maybe up to a thousand dollars depending on the car they purchase! There is some nice money to be made for you, just for making some phone calls and setting up appointments. And if you are interested in learning the business, you can sit behind me with these customers as I go through negotiation. You can see how I establish rapport and begin to understand what motivates these people to buy."

Al paused. I smiled and nodded in agreement.

Al continued, "I apologize for not explaining this better an hour ago. I honestly thought your old man explained this to you."

I shook my head no. "My father and I have limited conversation. Maybe because I am difficult to talk to."

"You've never seemed difficult to talk to when I've seen you in the past. I think we just need to build up your confidence. Confidence is the true ticket to sales. Take a look at that phone. What is the worst that can happen to you from that phone?"

I stared at the black handset and number keypad next to it. The cord was tightly raveled and sitting nicely on the desk. I shrugged.

"Don't shrug. You're a smart kid. What is the worst that can happen to you from that phone?" he asked again.

I mumble, "Nothing, I guess."

Al cracked a smile, "Now, I don't know about you, but I have never heard of anyone coming through the phone and punching someone."

I laughed.

"Honestly, Jac, the worst that can happen is your feelings get hurt because someone is having a bad day and takes it out on you. Someone you have never met and don't know is mean to you. That *is* the worst thing that can happen." Al placed his hand on my shoulder. "Jac, have any of your previous competitors been unsportsmanlike or mean to you?"

"Of course, just the nature of the beast," I responded.

"Okay, I want you to think of it as a game. Let's call it a numbers game. A certain percentage of people will be genuinely nice and either make an appointment with you or tell you they are not interested anymore. Those calls will most likely go pleasantly, and you will feel good after hanging up the phone no matter the outcome.

"Then there will be the avoiders. Those are the people who most likely avoid everything in their life, including buying a car and whoever else calls them wanting them to make a decision. They will be respectful but never commit to anything. You could call them every week, and they will tell you they are busy no matter what time you suggest and never want to make an appointment. The longer you make these calls, the easier they will be to recognize and move on from.

"Then there are the total jerks. They will talk to you without respect and condescend. I want to be the first one to tell you this—if you feel a person is doing this to you, tell them to have a nice day and that if they want to come in, they know where we are. Two things will happen. They will either become more agitated because you won't take their crap, or they'll realize they are being rude and calm down, and you will be able to determine if they are interested in coming in or not.

"So there it is! It took me years to learn what I just summed up for you in three minutes!"

My eyes grew wide, and my nerves started to settle down. "Al, that is tremendous. I was so nervous and had no idea—"

Al cut me off, "I want you to have a good summer here. I don't want you to dread coming in every morning. So this is what I'm going to do; I'm going to write a situational-based script for you. This will help you the first few days or weeks to feel comfortable and not let your emotions dictate the conversation. Today I'm just going to have you follow me and maybe some of the associates around to see and learn more, so you feel confident in what we do around here. How does that sound?"

"Great!"

The next few days, I shadowed Al and a few other associates and learned a lot about the cars and the sales process. I also started driving to work separately from my old man so I could go to physical therapy in the morning or afternoon and either go home or go back to the dealership.

At the end of the first week, Al handed me a typed-out telephone script. It had a situational-based tree and talking points to use based on the customers' responses. I sat down at the cubicle with the list given to me on my first day. I took a deep breath, picked up the handheld receiver, and dialed the first number. I read from my script, "Hello Mister ____, my name is Jacob Gilbert, and I am calling from Tri-State

Ford. You inquired about a new Ford Explorer a few weeks ago and wanted to find out if you are still in the market for this vehicle?"

"Yes, I am," the voice responded from the other end of the line.

"That's great, sir! We are running Memorial Day and summer specials now. When is a good time for you to come in, take another test drive, and see the Explorer you are interested in?"

"This weekend is good. How about Saturday at noon?"

"Perfect. I'll put you on the calendar."

I hung up the phone grinning. I pinched myself to check if that was a real conversation or an illusion in my mind. I went straight to Al's office to let him know I set an appointment for Saturday. He then told me he didn't work most Saturdays. I looked at him with confusion.

Al explained, "My family is my number one priority. Of course, I try to do my best at this dealership, but I am not like other sales guys that put in sixty-hour weeks. I believe work-life balance is essential. I know your father doesn't seem to quite have that balance down. Jac, moving forward, I want you to realize how important this balance is.

"However, I have an agreement with a couple other sales guys here; if the customer is brought in the door by one of us and the other closes it, we split the commission fifty-fifty. So we are going to give this customer to another salesman, and it will be fine. See, it's all about working smarter, not harder. A lot of weekends, I'm making commissions, and I'm not even working!"

As I walked back to my cubicle, his talk resonated with me. My father had been working fifty- to sixty-hour weeks for as long as I could remember. He was hardly around on the weekends, never joined my mother in church on Sundays. We rarely took weekend trips as a family. Yes, my father might have been considered successful by some, but was he really if he was always at work and not doing what he wanted on many days? Al seemed to make sense of life in general and motivated me to be as efficient as possible on the phone.

I went back to my cubicle for call number two. "Hi, my name is Jacob, and I'm calling from—"

"I'm busy. Call me back another time." Click.

Okay, well, that didn't go as well.

Call number three's response, "You must be the fifth person to call me from your crappy dealership! Take me off your damn list!" Click.

Al wasn't kidding when he told me it was a numbers game.

Al walked by and asked, "How are the other calls going?"

"Got hung up on twice." I looked away.

Al chuckled, "You know it would be more fun for you if you didn't take what anyone says personally and play it like a game. You know, some points you win, some you get beat, and some you lose. Let's try to keep the ones you lose at a minimum. And by lose, I mean the ones you fumble the conversation and talk the person out of the appointment."

After making several calls that first couple of weeks, I realized Al was incredibly wise. The less I emotionally invested in each call, the easier the job was on my psyche. I started compiling the statistics of which calls fit into the three categories Al taught me—the respectful, the avoiders, and the two types of jerks. Once I finished the first list, I created an excel spreadsheet and presented it to Al.

He was surprised that I'd compiled the list and by the percentages. He took the printed spreadsheet and sat back in his chair, looking it over and grinning, nodding his head vigorously.

Then he put the paper down and looked at me, "Jac, this is gold! Although I knew that most people fit in these categories, I never really took the time to figure out the percentages. You know, with a list, we can figure out how many people will buy a car and estimate how much revenue the dealership will earn. Now we can put a revenue estimate on lists!"

I'd taken a statistics class the previous year. Knowing that data could be skewed if there wasn't enough, I said, "Well, Al, since this is just one list, I suggest I continue these statistics throughout my time here so you can properly gauge the actual percentages. A data sample this small could be skewed."

Al looked at me as if I was telling him the secret Life of Pi. He smiled and said, "I'm going to show this to your old man. He'll love it!

Keep doing what you're doing. In no time, you'll be cashing in some nice commission checks!"

So I continued the calls. I made sure I was as persistent yet personable as I could be. I made a dramatic shift from being scared of the phone to a calling machine. Al's script helped me immensely, and I never deviated from it. That piece of paper was like my security blanket. I never went to work without it.

During the appointments I scheduled, I would sit in with Al and observe how he greeted the clients, started the conversation, and negotiated. Al was a seasoned veteran in all aspects of car sales. Although speaking to unknown people always gave me anxiety, Al was smooth with establishing rapport and connecting with people.

I learned a lot that summer, and maybe I taught him a little too. I probably put in forty-five to fifty hours per week for the whole summer. I brought in over sixty people for vehicle appointments during August—an enigma since most families are on vacation that month. I earned commission on thirty vehicle sales in August alone, and I saw my savings account approach nearly five digits for the first time in my life—just in time for my study abroad.

TWELVE

The first day of being a personal banker passed in a blur as I saw customer after customer. Mainly, I resolved service issues, and most of that time, I had no idea what I was doing. I'd try to go to Sal for help, but he and Jeff were busy as well. Sal advised me to call the banker helpline 800-number. Nothing lowers the customer's confidence more than when the banker across from them is calling the internal SOS line! But I continued to learn with every interaction.

Wednesday was cold-calling night, and I wanted to create a script like I had at the dealership. Sal printed out a list for me to call from the branch for our call night. Jeff seemed not to be concerned.

I showed up at the Brickell headquarters right at five o'clock. About thirty of us bankers filed into our old training room. I found it fascinating to watch the body language of the rookie bankers from my training class versus industry veterans. My training class gang were more outgoing, friendly, and had better posture. In contrast, some women in their fifties struggled to smile, and the dread of the next two hours was etched on their faces.

I took a seat in the second row next to Tim and Pierre, and we made small talk discussing our time off and first two days in the role. I saw Dann walk into the room with Sarah, which piqued my interest. I scanned the room for Rosie but did not see her.

Harry made his way to the front of the room and asked us to be seated. I finally saw Rosie scurry in the door, taking a seat in the back row. I tried to make eye contact with her, but she didn't see me.

Sarah joined Harry in the front of the room, which was much darker than the other days we were in there as the sun was already setting to the west. Harry began, "Welcome to 2005! Are you ready to leap into January?"

I think he was expecting an enthusiastic response, but he only received a few grunts. Harry wasn't one for rah-rah anyways.

He got straight to business. "This is a super important month for all of us. This month dictates how all of us start the first quarter and the year. It is hard to catch up to hitting our goals if we fall behind in January. For that reason, all our goals are skewed higher for this month and the beginning of the year. I expect all of you to be hitting the phones and pounding the pavement soliciting good, sound business for our bank."

Pounding the pavement?

Harry began pacing at the front of the room. "I know all of you sitting in these chairs have the competence to succeed in this role. If you didn't, you wouldn't be sitting in this beautiful room. But you need to prove to me that you have the *desire* required to be successful in this role. Desire cannot be taught, and it needs to come from within all of you. Each. And. Every. Single. Day."

The room went silent.

Sarah stepped forward out of the shadows of the room, "Please know that Harry and I want you all to be successful. I am a resource for all of you to use in any credit situation you may come across. My cell phone is attached to my hip; please call me any time to discuss scenarios or issues you may have. Additionally, we could schedule one-on-one role-playing."

Harry surprisingly broke from his monotone speaking style and interjected, "That is a *fabulous* idea, Sarah! As the adage goes, 'Practice makes perfect.' When I was a wrestler, practice was the way everyone got better. I am going to incorporate role-playing in these meetings moving forward. I will take suggestions on what scenarios we can play, email me privately.

"Okay, team, you all should have a list of names and phone numbers to call now. I don't want anyone logging on to a computer and fumbling around to find information. That's a big-time waster! Don't ever put down the phone receiver, and your fingers should be working that dial-pad like a six-string guitar. Tonight's goal is for each of you to schedule four in-person appointments."

Everyone raised their head forward as that was universally considered a tough goal to meet.

Harry continued, "I know, I know. You think that is an unattainable goal. Well, it's only unattainable if you tell yourself that! Normally we have a fifty to sixty percent show rate on appointments. So if you set four, realistically only two, maybe three will show. Before you leave, each of you will hand in a call log that lists the number of dials you made, the number of people you actually spoke to, appointments made, and callbacks you will make if the person was busy or asked you to call back another time. I will personally be looking at these lists. No one will leave until you set your four appointments."

I looked over to Tim and shook my head slightly. He sighed and said, "We just need to get this over with. Do you have a list? Because I forgot mine."

I open my eyes wider, "You forgot yours? Harry is going to go crazy on you! My branch manager, Sal, printed out a list for me before I left. I didn't get a chance to really look at it since we have been so busy."

"Ah, Harry will be fine. I'll sneak into an admin office to get a computer and find people to call from there." Tim sounded confident enough. "Well, I'm going to get going, so I get a good office to call from!"

The last thing Harry told us before letting us out of the room was that we could use any available phone on this floor or the top floor where all the executives sat. "Find a phone and start dialing!"

Before I started searching for a phone, I wanted to find Rosie, but she seemed to be the first one out of the training room. I wandered around the cubicles on the other side of the floor but couldn't find her. A few people filtered into the offices surrounding the floor, but I decided to take a middle cubicle—just like last summer at the dealership.

I sat down, put the list out in front of me. Again, I had that overly anxious feeling as I did that first day of my summer internship. I pulled my cell phone from my pocket; no missed calls.

I felt parched, so as everyone was getting settled, I made my way to the break room to find the water cooler. Harry was in there talking to Pierre. I overheard him congratulating him on taking two loan applications on his first day on the job.

How the hell was he able to take two loan applications already?

As I sipped my water, Harry looked over at me, saying, "Jac, I am expecting big things out of you too. Go get 'em, tiger!"

I nodded my head in agreement and scurried back to my cubicle.

I looked down at the list again and then the phone receiver. I stared at the dial-pad and the cord. The cord was tangled, and I felt the need to untangle it for the next three minutes. I tried to remember what Al taught me; no one can physically hurt you through the phone.

What is there to be afraid of?

Then I realized I didn't have my security blanket—my script! The office, which was always freezing, became overly warm, and I proceeded to unbutton my top button and took my jacket off.

What was I going to say to these people? Why was I calling? At the dealership, the goal was simple—get them into the place to buy a new car. What exactly was my goal here? To introduce myself?

I started to analyze, then over-analyze, to the point of paralyzation. I physically couldn't move. My eyes scanned the room to see if anyone was watching or walking around, all clear. I looked down at my watch, 5:35 pm.

Another hour and twenty-five minutes of this? I wonder who Dann is calling, and Rosie, and, well, everyone. What were they all saying? You know, it's rude that I didn't say hello to Rosie. I should find her and say hi.

I stood up and put my jacket back on. I saw Harry making his way around the floor. He approached me and asked, "Everything okay, Jac?"

"Yeah, Harry, I, uh, need to use the restroom," I replied.

"Okay, be quick. How are your calls going?"

"Fine. Okay, I'll be quick," I mumbled as I quickly walked away.

Five minutes later, I found myself in the same cubicle again, looking at the same list and the same phone. I checked my cell again, no missed calls. *Doesn't anyone need me right now?*

I picked up the phone receiver and started to dial the phone number next to the first name on Sal's list. My heart pounded so intensely I could imagine it ripping out of my shirt. I tried to tell myself this is just like cold calling from the car dealership. But who was I kidding, this was different, and I didn't have the leadership of someone like Al to help me through this.

The phone started ringing—ring, ring, ring, voicemail. I vacillated on whether or not to leave a voicemail. By the time I heard the beep, I froze then hung up quickly.

I wonder if they were going to call back.

On to number two on the list. Ring, ring, "Hello?" I heard on the other end of the line.

"Hi, uh, this is Jacob Gilbert. I, uh, sorry to bother you, but I was wondering if you had some time to discuss your banking needs." *What am I saying?*

"Who? Do I know you? Where are you calling from?"

I hit my forehead with my open right hand since my left hand held the phone. "I apologize; I am calling from DMNC Bank, here in Miami. Do you have time to come into the branch this week?"

"You know I wasn't going to answer the phone. Why are you calling me from an 800 number if you're in Miami?"

"Uh, I am?" I asked nervously.

"Yes, you are. Figure out what the hell you are doing before calling me again." Click.

What the hell is this person talking about? I go right back to the dial pad and dial my cell number. My caller ID has the number coming from an 800 number! What the fuck? Who the hell is going to answer a phone on a Wednesday at dinner time from an 800 number?

I go to another cubicle and call my cell again—a different 800 number. I then call the 800 number back with my cell to see if the phone rings. No ring. IT goes to an automated phone system of DMNC Bank.

How are people going to reach us?

I thought I needed to tell Harry about this problem. I went to his office. His feet were on his desk, and he gazed out his window at the pinkish-blue sunset.

"Hey Jac, I hope you're here with good news." He took his feet off his desk.

"Well, Harry, I'm here with more of a concern. I noticed that the caller ID on some of these phones shows an 800 number. And for one, that makes people automatically suspicious of the call, and I know many won't answer the phone. And two, if they wanted to call back quickly after a missed call, it has them calling an automated number." I end with my patented one-shoulder shrug.

"Yeah, I know that. We've been trying to work with corporate technology and our telephone provider, but that hasn't stopped anyone else from making appointments. Get back down there and make me proud! I know you have it in you. You told me during our interview how great a cold-caller you were during your summer internship. This is no different."

Um, but it is!

"Okay, Harry, I'll do my best."

I turned to exit his office and noticed Rosie sitting in a cubicle to the right corner of the floor. I made my way over to her, but she was on the phone. She held up her index finger, indicating for me not to speak. I waved and gave her a big smile. She ignored me, and I chalked it up to her being in a conversation.

Again, I made my way downstairs to the same cubicle. This time I took the extra second to see who was making calls. I must have passed five or six other bankers that weren't on the phone and didn't seem to be in the middle of dialing or picking up the phone either.

What were they actually doing?

For the next hour, I overcame my anxiety and just started dialing. I must have made 50 calls. Ninety percent of them went to voicemail.

Shocking! Considering these calls are coming from a freaking 800 number.

The people that did pick up the phone were so old that they probably didn't have caller ID, or their eyesight so poor they couldn't see the numbers. The average age of the person I spoke to was over eighty, and a few had a hard time hearing me.

Zero appointments. That is how I ended the call night. Harry started to gather up the troops to get us back to the training room to report our results.

Do I lie? Do I tell the truth? Maybe if I wait to the end of the line, I could see the numbers from my peers and put in a number that sounds realistic. Bingo!

I took my time going back to the training room. People looked like they were going to a wake and had to greet the grieving family members at the door. Everyone was somber and docile. It was seven o'clock, and most of us hadn't eaten since lunch—that may have affected the mood. But no one made small talk, not even Don, who looked impatient as he waited to report his results. As I shuffled my way to the back of the line, I saw Dann walking from the elevator doors with Sarah. He made his way over to me.

"Joeyyyyy, how'd you do, big boy?" A wide smile emerged from his face.

"Eh, not much traction." I shrugged and looked away. Then I looked back and asked, "And you?"

"I made a couple of calls with Sarah. Remember the guy Jerry we met with a few months ago? Sarah and I made a joint call, and he has three business clients he wants to introduce me to. Isn't that sweet?" His grin grew, and he patted me on the back as if to imply he wanted a pat on his back instead.

"Yeah, that's awesome." I mustered up some fake excitement.

"You know, Joey, it's not how many calls you make; it's the outcome of the calls. But you already know that, cold-calling king of your internship! C'mon, let's log our numbers and get the hell outta here."

My log showed fifty-five calls, seven contacts, and two appointments. So I made a white lie, big deal.

On my short drive home, I dialed Rosie. "Happy New Year, Rosita! I know we didn't get to speak to each other tonight. How was your dialing?"

"Oh my God, I absolutely hate cold-calling. It terrifies me! But I spoke to a few nice elderly ladies and convinced three of them to make an appointment with me. So we'll see how that goes. How was your dialing for dollars?"

"Honestly? Terrible! Did you know that our outgoing number shows as an 800 telemarketing call? I hardly got anyone to pick up the phone. And when I did, I felt that they were born in 1910."

Rosie started laughing, "I didn't know about the 800 number; that's peculiar."

A weird silence entered the conversation. Usually, Rosie always knew what to say to get me going, but I could tell she was holding something back.

"Something wrong?" I asked.

"No, all good here." Rosie paused and then, in a tone she didn't usually use, said, "I have some news that I have been slow in telling you. My fiancé and I made our wedding plans over Christmas break. We are officially getting married in June."

I tried my hardest to drum up excitement for her and said, "That's awesome! I'm happy for you." An awkward silence settled in again.

She continued, "I meant to call you during the holidays but just didn't find the right time. Look, I don't want you to think I've regretted our flirtatiousness and the time we spent together because I haven't. I've had a really good time with you, and you're a great guy."

My stomach started to sink again.

"But it has finally hit me that I am getting married, and I need to be one-hundred percent committed to my fiancé. I think it's best we don't see each other outside of work settings anymore." Silence again.

I felt like I'd been punched in the gut. "I get it, and I understand."

Rosie's tone became lighter, "Oh Jac, I am so happy to hear that. I have been stressing out about having this conversation with you. I really want to continue our friendship. We can talk on the phone and talk to each other during these shitty call sessions. I know you have been dating Mari for a few months now and, not that I want to tell you what to do, but you should use your energy to make her happy and do well at work. That is what I am doing. I hope it all works out in the end."

I felt kind of sick. Although I had not eaten in the past seven hours, my appetite was gone. I ended the conversation, "I wish you the best of luck with your marriage, and we can still be friends. However, I just got home and need to talk to Dann about dinner because I'm starving. Have a nice night."

"Bye-bye, Jacob."

I sat in my car and stared out the windshield. I couldn't even tell you what I was staring at, but I realized Rosie was correct.

I should be giving one-hundred percent to Mari and not use any of my emotional energy on Rosie. But why does this conversation hurt so much?

I knew it was a fling from the beginning, I didn't even put much effort into the time with Rosie, but it still stung. I pulled myself together and entered my apartment, where Dann greeted me dressed in comfortable clothes. "What the hell took you so long, you take the bus? I'm starving; what you wanna eat?"

The next day, one of my two phantom appointments actually showed up. Sal walked a newly retired couple into my office. We introduced ourselves to each other, and as they took a seat across my desk, the husband nonchalantly plopped a $400,000 check on my desk.

"We just sold our home up north and recently retired. I was going to deposit the check into my checking account, but Sal suggested we speak to you and see if there were better options for us," the husband explained.

This moment was the first time I realized the power of the personal banker role. People of all ages and economic backgrounds come to you for advice about their personal wealth, and it is the banker's responsibility to advise the best thing for them. By definition, that would be taking a fiduciary responsibility. However, sometimes peculiar things in business occur—for example, the bank's interests usually don't align with the customer's interests—and we bankers are like sitting ducks trying to make both interests meet for the ultimate goal of serving ourselves!

I picked up the check. It was the first time I'd seen so many zeros on a check.

The customer must have noticed my facial expression as he continued, "Yeah, we were surprised too. The real estate market is on fire now. We had four offers within a weekend, and our house became the subject of a bidding war. We got over $50,000 more than we were asking!"

"Wow! That is amazing! I am happy for you. So my job here is to make sure you are offered all your options for these funds and assist you with your decision. What is your risk tolerance on these funds?" I felt so professional and astute; I must have been grinning hard.

"Zero. We have never been risk-takers, and we do not plan to start taking risks at this point in our life."

"Okay, understood, let me pull up our current bank rates, give me a minute, please."

I calmly turned towards my computer, but inside I was freaking out. Part of the excitement was because this was my first real client interaction of this magnitude, and part of it was due to the nervousness of trying to remember where the rates were listed on our internal system. The last thing I wanted to do was call the banker helpline and ask for interest rates! I could've told them our system is acting up, but what confidence would they place in our system or me if I did that?

"Okay, here we go. If you put that in your checking account, we would only be paying a 0.10% annual percentage yield. So I would say Sal gave you good advice to look at other options. That being said, the federal funds rate, which determines short-term bank rates, has been rising and is currently around 2.75%, so a savings account would be in that range as well. How do you feel about locking it up for a while in a vehicle like a certificate of deposit, also known as a CD?"

They both look at each other in agreement. The wife said, "That is fine with us."

"For you to get any type of rate that you could earn decent interest on, we would need to look at either a six-month or one-year term. The six-month term is paying 3.50%, and the one-year term is 4.00%." I picked up my trusty Sharp financial calculator and started making calculations. "If you put this check into a one-year CD, you'd earn $16,000 this coming year in interest with zero risk to the principle."

They look at each other again and start whispering. The husband breaks the silence, "We really wanted to obtain a higher rate, but if risk is involved with a higher rate, then we'll settle for the one-year CD."

I quickly responded, speaking faster because of my excitement, "Yes, I totally understand, and yes, you are correct; if you wanted other options, there would be inherent risk, and you made that clear right upfront. I am not sure about your income situation, but $16,000 per year sounds nice."

The husband sat forward in his chair and placed his arms on my desk, almost trying to look at my computer screen, "Okay, let's do it!"

"Great! Excuse me for a moment."

I walked out of my office and tried to get Sal's attention, but he was conversing with another customer. I walked to Jeff's office, and he had a couple sitting across from him. He noticed me lurking at his doorway and gave me the index finger, signaling to wait a minute. I paced back and forth for what seemed to be ten minutes which in reality was one. He excused himself from his customer and pulled me to the back corner of the lobby, "What's up, Jac?" Jeff asked.

"I just sold a CD, but now what do I do?" I started to play with the hair on the back of my head. Nervous habits die hard.

"Uh, Jac, what are you talking about! You sat behind me for weeks seeing how to open the different accounts. You build their profiles or make sure they are updated if we have them in the system already. Then you pull them together in the product section in the bank system. You click the CD they want, and it should get you to you the printing section."

He noticed I was extra nervous. "You did a great job getting them to commit to a CD, don't be nervous. You know what you're doing. Just calm down and make conversation with them, so they don't notice that you are nervous. Remember, that always works, just ask them some questions and let them talk while you figure it out. Okay, I gotta go. And the last resort is calling the banker helpline." Jeff patted me on the shoulder, then turned and walked back into his office.

I took a few deep breaths and returned to my office, "Sorry about that, folks, just needed to pick up something behind the teller line. So where up north did you live, and what jobs did you recently retire from?"

That opened a can of worms. They didn't shut up about their town, their jobs, their family, local restaurants; you name it, they were talking about it. It didn't matter how long it took me to figure out the system. The deal got done, and after they signed for it, they sat in my office another ten minutes. Jeff was right about getting the customers to talk. When they talk, they forget how long things take!

I walked the couple out of my office and opened the front door for them. Sal looked at me with raised eyebrows, and I gave him a thumbs-up. He smiled and nodded. As the couple exited, Mr. Vacca entered.

I greeted him right away, "Good morning Mr. Vacca."

"Good morning, young man. Happy new year to you and Sal over there."

I started walking next to him as he entered the teller line. "Mr. Vacca, did you know you can receive 4.00% on our one-year CD?" I asked with a smile.

"Those sonz-a-bitches got to you already? You'll be selling credit cards to me next week. You just wait, kid." He turned away, making it known he was there for one and one reason only.

I chuckled and walked to Sal's desk. I informed Sal of my customer interaction, and he let out a little wheeze laugh and patted me on the shoulder for a job well done. He said, "It's nice that we got you on the board for a new account, but we need to find you a loan application somehow. How was the list I gave you for the call session?"

I shrugged and slightly shook my head with a scrunched face.

"Yeah, that's what I was afraid of. I have an idea, though. I have been reading that the Fed will continue to raise the prime lending rate for the rest of this year. It might be a good idea for me to compile a list of home equity lines of credit we have on the books and see if they want to refinance into a fixed-rate mortgage before rates rise." He gives me a wink and turns back to his computer. I walked back to my office feeling accomplished.

A couple of weeks later, I received a call from Tim as I entered my branch for the day. I closed my office door and flipped open my cell.

"Yo Jac, I got bad news about Mari. All of us in the branch just received notification that her employment with the bank has been terminated."

I was flabbergasted and didn't know what to say, "What! Why?"

"Honestly, I don't know why. I tried calling her cell, and it went to voicemail. Maybe you should try calling her to see what is going on? Just wanted to give you a heads up. If you want to play dumb and not call, that is your prerogative."

"Ok, thanks for letting me know; I know what I'll do. Talk to you later."

I immediately tried calling Mari on her cell to no avail. Then the pace at work picked up—one customer after another, practically all day. Finally, towards the end of the day, Mari called me. Her tone was somber, and she told me she would come to my branch parking lot to tell me what was going on.

She showed up about an hour later and parked her car next to my Mustang in the side parking lot where no one inside the branch could see us. I greeted her more empathetically than usual, "Hi babe, I hope all is okay."

She forced a smile, but her eyes were puffy, and it was apparent she had been crying most of the day. She wore a t-shirt and jean shorts with sandals, clearly not work attire. "I wish I could say everything is okay, but it's not. I don't have a job anymore, and I am unsure of how to get one at this point."

I gave her a confused look and tilted my head to the side.

"My employment authorization expired, and due to bank rules, I was automatically terminated." She spoke flatly without emotion.

I had so many questions to ask, but at the same time, I wanted to comfort her, so I hugged her. She hugged me back tighter than ever, and my heart sank. Tears almost filled my eyes. "This is bullshit. Why did your employment authorization expire? And why does the bank terminate right as it expires?"

Mari tried to hold back her tears to explain, "When I came to the United States four years ago, my brother thought it would be best to apply for political asylum."

Political what? Guerrilla warfare, huh? I gave her a perplexed look.

She responded to my non-verbal question, "Political asylum states that it is unsafe to live in my home country for risk of persecution."

"Why would you apply for that when your parents and other siblings still live in Colombia?"

"Jacob, I was sixteen years old and didn't know anything. I listened to my brother, who had been living here for a while. I trusted him. He got me this attorney through the church. The jerk didn't show up to one of my court dates this past year, and the judge got angry. My attorney said he was going to make it right, but obviously, he didn't. I was supposed to have my new employment authorization by the end of last year, and it never came in the mail."

Still hugging each other, I pulled my head down towards her and asked, "Are you going to confront this attorney?"

"Yes, he works in his office on Sunday. It's in Doral. Want to take a ride with me?"

What attorney has office hours on a Sunday?

Without thinking, I immediately responded, "Of course."

Mari genuinely smiled for the first time in that exchange.

I continued, "And I'm going to email Harry to see if he can make an exception for you to work at the bank still."

Her smile grew bigger, and she pulled me down to her level for a big juicy kiss.

I found it challenging to focus on work the rest of the week. I kept thinking of Mari's attorney meeting on Sunday. I'd never heard of attorneys working on Sunday.

Mari picked me up from my Brickell apartment, and we made our way west to the Dolphin Expressway to Doral. We entered what seemed to be an industrial section of town. Many of the buildings' windows were protected by wrought iron bars. Almost all of the signage on buildings and billboards was written in Spanish. I felt like during that short drive, I left the States and entered South America.

We walked up the stairs of a sketchy two-story commercial building. I saw a door marked Immigration Attorney, and we entered. The office smelled like a combination of booze, disinfectant, and cigar smoke. Crushed paper coffee cups and empty soda cans littered every surface. The waiting area couch was riddled with holes, and all the magazines for clients were in Spanish. The receptionist's desk was unattended, and various papers were scattered across the top.

I looked at Mari with an unspoken, "Where are we?"

She walked to the back of the office and knocked on a door. A hefty Latin man greeted us with a fake smile and asked us to take a seat. As we sat, I noticed he must have had over a hundred manila folders piled on his desk.

This guy is drowning in clients. I wonder if he's really good or completely incompetent.

Mari started speaking to him in English, asking about her employment authorization. He responded in Spanish, and Mari then followed suit. Knowing a bit of the language, I picked up some things but missed the most important elements of what was actually happening.

During a break in the conversation, I gave Mari a quizzical look and shrugged my shoulders with my palms up.

She turned towards me and said, "My attorney tells me that the judge ruled against me in the political asylum case I filed four years ago. Since I do not have an active case with U.S. immigration, my employment authorization was not renewed."

Then I poked the lion with a stick and asked, "If your attorney was present at your hearing last year, would that have made a difference?"

At last, her attorney decided to speak English. With a Latin fire spewing from his eyes, he roared at me, "That has nothing to do with Mari's case! The evidence was already presented to the judge. We can ask to re-open the case, but a very, very small percentage of cases get reopened."

I looked at Mari as to what her decision was going to be.

She was always a fiery woman, never backing down, especially not in disagreements with me. But she looked feeble, beaten down, and lost. Mari turned her attention from me to the attorney glaring over the manila folder pile.

How many other "Mari type" cases were in that massive pile with no regard from him, as in this case?

"Sure, let's petition to re-open my case. Will I receive employment authorization with this petition?" she asked.

Her attorney said, "Unfortunately, only if the case is reopened. Otherwise, I don't have anything else to tell you. But I will make sure my office sends the petition in, and I will be in touch."

I could tell Mari didn't want to get out of that chair, but she eventually pulled herself up, put a fake smile on her face, and shook the man's hand as we were on our way out the door.

The afternoon sunlight hit our faces—a wonderful reprieve after being in that dingy, dimly lit office for the past twenty minutes. However, I noticed that Mari wasn't herself. I tried to think of ways to cheer her up, but all that came out of my mouth was, "How about a ride to the beach?"

She looked at me and nodded, and we were on our way back east.

My email to Harry about Mari's employment fell on deaf ears. He and Sarah always spoke about exception this, exception that, but in this case, there were no exceptions. I guess when the federal government issues a mandate, exceptions get erased from the vocabulary. However, what that email did was verify for Harry the fact that I was with Mari, and as I look back, his knowledge of this did not help my cause.

That week Mari called me at work to tell me she found a new immigration attorney that would meet her within the week, but he was in Fort Lauderdale, and she asked if I would come along for the ride.

In the city of immigrants, she finds the immigration attorney thirty minutes away.

Mari picked me up from my branch at four in the afternoon, and we were heading northbound on I-95 in no time. The ride was tense and quiet. His office was in an old residential home converted into professional office space. The sign on the door read, Immigration Attorney, and was in English. We entered, and the lobby was tiny with a couple of chairs in the waiting area and, of course, magazines, mainly in Spanish. A tall, skinny guy in his fifties with glasses greeted us. He had on jeans and a button-down shirt and didn't look like an attorney.

We walked into his spacious office. His desk was in the back, and in the front was a couch facing a black leather captain's chair. This is where the attorney liked to sit for his client meetings. One entire wall was a vast bookshelf. I perused some of the titles and noted almost all the books were about immigration law.

This guy's library suggests he might know what he's doing. The real question is, has he read any of the books.

Mari started explaining her situation, and I learned details of political asylum that I'd never thought of. She finished her explanation with the fact she no longer had employment authorization.

The attorney took a deep breath and said, "Your situation isn't ideal. Political asylum is a tough one. I work with many immigrants just like you who applied for political asylum because it seemed to be the easiest path. Immigration allows you to file it, then automatically gives you a work permit. However, then it's the immigrant's responsibility to prove the case in front of the judge that he or she is a true political refugee. Political asylum is like getting caught in a giant spider web. Once you're in, you're in, and there is no way to get out."

I looked over to Mari. Her head was down, and she used a tissue to wipe away tears. My heart was breaking inside, but I didn't want to admit to myself that her situation was futile.

The attorney continued, "Now Canada has a much more relaxed policy towards immigrants in your case. You could move there for a couple of years and try to re-apply for residency here."

Mari brought her head up and shook it no. Then she looked at me with a sad puppy dog look.

Then the attorney said, "You didn't hear this from me, but you always can find a stupid American to marry. That is almost the most ironclad way to gain residency here. But I am *not* telling you to marry a stupid American!"

All three of us gave a little chuckle, as if the idea was a joke, and got up from our chairs. As we walked out the door, the attorney poked his head out of his office and stated, "That'll be a hundred and fifty dollars; I take cash or check."

I give Mari a look of disgust.

She shrugged and said, "They're all the same, I swear."

We didn't say a word as we made our way south on I-95. She held back her tears, and I felt heavy-hearted. She was an immigrant who left her parents and family at sixteen to come to the States for a better life. She graduated high school, was attending college, and worked full time to pay for her life here. It seemed so unfair. Being born in another country shouldn't determine how she was treated or if she could make it on her own in the States. Her situation bothered me, and compassion welled up within me.

About fifteen minutes into the ride, Mari finally broke the silence. "Jac, I love you, and you should know that. But I don't know what is going to happen to me. For that reason, I think it's best we go our separate ways."

What, wait, no! I finally met a great woman that I professed my love to for the first time in my life, and a measly three months later, she breaks up with me? I know immigration is a hassle, but we'll sort it out. I just got pseudo-dumped by Rosie a few weeks ago, and now I'm officially getting dumped again? No, I cannot accept this! I need to do something. But what can I do? Ah, I can be that "stupid American." But, gosh, that is some commitment on my part. But it's either that or losing the only woman that I have loved. Think, think…

I broke my silence. It was tough to talk because an elephant was standing on my lungs. "I don't want to end our relationship. You are the most amazing woman that I have ever met." I took a deep breath, "What if we got married? I mean, purely for immigration reasons, and we would continue our relationship as if we are still dating."

My hands poured sweat, and I kept rubbing them on my navy suit pants.

Mari's face lit up, and she briefly took her eyes off the road to look at me, "You'd really do that for me?"

Before thinking, I blurted, "Of course! I know you'd do the same for me if the situation were reversed!"

Mari flashed a huge smile and started crying as she navigated driving on the highway. "Oh my God, Jacob, I LOVE YOU!" She wiped the tears from her eyes. "I don't want this to affect our relationship, though, and I don't think anyone should know, not even our family. I think this should be extremely private, and we will continue our relationship as we are not legally married. I mean, it's just a piece of paper after all, right?"

All I could do was stare to the left at the I-95 divider—concrete block after concrete block slid by. "Yeah, uh-huh, sure."

What the hell did I just get myself into?

About a week later, we went to the Miami-Dade County Courthouse to apply for a marriage license and needed to wait the mandatory three-day "cold feet" period. We decided to get married on Valentine's Day 2005, so it would look more "real" to immigration.

The night of the thirteenth, I went over to Mari's apartment. She ushered me right to her bedroom as she didn't want the family she lived with to know what was going on. I brought my dark grey suit with a royal blue shirt and a purple and blue tie to wear for the next day. We watched a movie, but I couldn't follow the plot, my mind was in the clouds. I don't remember having any negative feelings, but we both were tense. We both had a tough night's sleep.

We set the alarm for six-thirty to have time to get dressed and ready before our eight o'clock appointment with the Justice of the Peace. We drove in our separate cars as I had to get into the branch right after the ceremony. We took the short staircase outside the courthouse and were directed to the matrimony room.

The room couldn't have been larger than fifty square feet and held about ten chairs. We requested that the court have two representatives sit in to sign as our witnesses as we didn't invite or inform any of our friends or family.

During the vows, I made sure to cross my fingers, you know, so that the vows didn't ring true. I also crossed my toes in my shoes, then thought, *if I cross fingers and toes, do they cancel each other out?* I was so enthralled with the superstition of the crossings that I didn't even know what happened during the ceremony and couldn't even tell you what Mari was wearing.

A signature and a few pictures later, we were legally married and on our way out the door. We didn't say a word as we walked to our cars. I went to Mari's car and opened her door for her. She put her hands around my shoulders and caressed the back of my head with her hands, and looked up at me, saying, "Thank you so much, Jacob. You have no idea what this means to me." She pulled me in for a passionate kiss as we stood between her open door and her car.

After our kiss was over, I pulled away, looking at my watch, 8:35 am. "Shit, I need to get to work. I'll tell Sal I had some car trouble on the way. Hopefully, he understands."

Mari called to me as I jogged to my car, "Jac...uh,"

I turned around, asking, "Yeah, what is it?"

"I feel bad asking you, but I got three overdrafts this past week due to not having a job anymore. Ninety dollars is a lot of money for me, considering I had to pay that attorney and the marriage fees."

As her voice trailed off, I said, "Yeah, uh, don't worry about it. I'll take care of it for you."

A bright smile spread across her face. "You are the best hubby I could ask for! I look forward to our Valentine's date tonight!"

She ran over to give me another hug and kiss. Then I jumped in my car, and all I could think about was what I just did—I needed to repent.

Am I going to hell for betraying the sacrament of marriage?

But before I could adequately analyze that deep question, I had to call Sal to come up with some excuse to let him know I was running late.

THIRTEEN

A month passed without any drama on the work-front or with Mari. Unexpectedly my parents decided to visit. I was reluctant to have them, but I knew I couldn't stop them.

"Welcome to Miami, *e Bienvenidos a Miami*." That was the sign Mari made, thinking it would be a proper way to welcome my parents on their maiden voyage to the MIA. My mother looked surprised when she saw us waiting for them as they pulled their luggage through the airport, each waving one hand at us with smiles plastered on their faces. Mari ran up to give them both big hugs, which I thought was odd as I never properly introduced them before.

"Hello, Mr. and Mrs. Gilbert! It is so nice to meet you finally. How was your flight?" Mari exuded pure excitement as if she was meeting her in-laws for the first time—or something like that.

My mother responded first, "So nice to meet you as well, Mari. The flight was fine, and we're excited to see Jacob's new life down here finally."

My father nodded to Mari in a very businesslike way with a half-smile. He liked attention, but I'm not so sure he liked the welcome sign type of attention. On the way to the parking garage, he started walking next to me and steered us to gain distance from the ladies.

"How's the gig, Jac?"

And how did I know that was going to be his first question of what could've been a hundred different questions to open with.

I was looking all around, forward, side to side, trying to remember exactly where I parked. Without putting much thought into my answer, I responded with a simple, "It's going well."

"Great, glad to hear it. Your mother and I just want the best for you."

To fill some of the dead space, I told my father how integral Al's instruction on cold-calling was for my current position. "Yeah, believe it or not, we have cold-calling sessions every month. We all get together at the main office, and we break out into different cubicles and offices and just call through a list of individuals. I have to say Al taught me a lot about cold-calling, and it made me feel a little more comfortable. Although calling prospects to purchase cars versus calling them for financial product sales is quite different, but nonetheless, Al's guidance still helped me a lot. I keep meaning to email him to let him know how much he assisted my development. Maybe, you can pass on my thanks?"

"Jac, that is fabulous. I definitely will let Al know when I get back. I bet he'll feel good about it."

I smiled at him and then looked behind us where Mari had my mother's ear about who knows what. I pointed to the next row of cars, saying, "And here we are."

My father took a look at the now 11-year-old 'stang, "Jac, I think it's time we find you a car that matches your career. What do you say?"

I looked at Mari, her face brightened, and I looked back at my old man as I popped the trunk open and realized this coupe might be tight with their luggage and four rear ends that needed to fit inside. "Yeah, you may have a good point. But I hate to break it to you, Pops, no more Fords!"

He pulled his upper body back and brought his palms up. I laughed and continued, "Didn't you say I needed a car that fit my job?"

We got into the car, and Mari told us of her plans for the visit. "I hope you are all ready for an action-planned weekend. I looked up restaurants, museums, different beaches, and all types of activities we can do."

My mother curtly responded, "I understand it is spring break time, but please know we are not in our twenties anymore."

We all forced a chuckle, and I drove the crammed coupe to my apartment.

That day Mari and I gave my parents the "tourist" tour. We visited downtown, the Vizcaya Museum, Key Biscayne, and a restaurant in South Beach right on Ocean Boulevard that Mari found. Like all of those restaurants on the main strip, it was overpriced, and the food was below average. However, it is a must for any tourist to experience the authentic South Beach vibe.

We all sat down at the outdoor table; Mari and I sat on one side facing my folks. I was a little uneasy about where the conversation would go knowing they like to ask questions, and we hadn't had time since they landed for direct questions. I could tell my mother wanted to be respectful, but she was burning to know what was going on between us as this was the first woman I introduced them to as my formal girlfriend.

I need a drink, hell, I need shots, but my parents do not drink. Good thing they don't have any idea how much I've been drinking the past eight months. Mari is a wildcard when she drinks.

We ended up ordering four glasses of water. As the small talk from earlier in the day subsided, my mother opened up the conversation. "Wow, I always think of the bright lights of New York, but these fluorescent lights down here really get you in the spirit, huh. Mari, is that what drew you to Miami?"

Mari glanced over at me, and I gave her the nod to tell her story—obviously, the truncated version.

"Yes, I love it here, but actually, my brother moved here in the early '90s. I would visit him every so often, and after Christmas break four years ago, I decided to move here permanently."

My mother responded, "I find that fascinating. It must have been difficult to leave your parents, I assume. I say that because Jacob left us after high school, and I was devastated. But looking back, it was a great decision for him as I am proud of the young man he has become over the past four years. Jacob doesn't tell me a lot of information, but I got the tidbit you two met at the bank? I think that is so sweet! How do you like working there?"

Mari, now a little less sure of her answer, started to teeter. "Yeah, uh, Jacob is a driven man, and I love that about him. Did he tell you how well he is doing? He landed a big new account last month, and he took his first mortgage application this week! But more importantly, he was such a gentleman when we first started to date, and I realized that he must have come from a good family." Mari looked down at her water glass, grabbed it to take a nice long sip, then returned the glass to the table.

My mother asked, "Do you like working at the bank, Mari?"

Mari nervously looked around; I gently gave her a nudge under the table, encouraging her to answer. "Actually, it's unfortunate that I am not able to work at the bank anymore. I thought Jacob told you, but my employment authorization expired, and I am working on getting it renewed." She looked at me and continued, "Yeah, Jac, I forgot to tell you, I might have a new job soon. But let's not count our chickens before they hatch." She shrugged.

She must have picked that up from me.

I could just imagine the thoughts running through my parents' minds when she said that. Sometimes what's not said is louder than what is said. Within moments, our food was served, and I felt saved by the bell. I tried to change the conversation direction—I asked them about their food, talked about what else was on Ocean Drive, and mentioned that we should walk over to Collins Avenue and the

Lincoln Road Mall. Fortunately, that seemed to take their minds off of Mari's employment issue for the moment.

After our tourist walk around South Beach, I drove Mari back to her apartment. I fibbed and told my parents she still lived with her brother; she didn't, but I didn't want to get into more drama with Mari and her family issues.

When we arrived back at my place, I gave them my room, and I slept in Dann's as he was out of town for the weekend. My mind kept going back and forth between reflecting on chicks he banged on the bed I was laying on versus what my parents were thinking. It was extremely unusual for my old man to stay quiet the whole day; he always had someone's ear about some nonsense. No nonsense from the old man meant he was taking it all in.

What exactly was he taking in?

Before I could form proper thoughts about either, I was fast asleep. In my clothes. On top of Dann's comforter. Probably the best decision.

The next day, I intended to do something alone with my folks. I planned to take them to breakfast and then to a Key Biscayne beach. However, Mari called me—like she did multiple times a day; she really needed to get a job. She asked what we were up to and basically invited herself to the beach with us.

I met her in the parking lot and told her to deflect any more questions regarding her employment situation and our relationship. She pouted at me, but I think she understood where I was coming from. From the beach, my mother then invited Mari to dinner and then to brunch on Sunday. The parents' visit was more like a weekend double date.

The next time I had pure alone time with my parents was on the relatively short ride to the airport Sunday afternoon. I find it fascinating that some things in life are remembered so vividly. That trip to the airport was one of those moments for me.

My father sat in the front seat, and we waited at the red light before entering the Dolphin Expressway. My father spoke directly for the first time all weekend. "Mari seems like a nice girl, but some things don't add up for me regarding her employment and family situations."

I looked through my rearview mirror to see if my mother was paying attention; she didn't seem to be as her face was buried in her book like it was most of the time on the beach and during my driving.

Dad continued, "I don't know much about immigration laws, but son, listen to me."

I took my eye off the red light and looked to my right, but I didn't have the guts to face the old man eye-to-eye, so I glanced at the side of his head.

He pointed his index finger at me and said, "Don't do anything stupid...like marry her."

I cannot be sure of my exact facial expression, but I know I froze.

The light turned green, and the impatient South Florida drivers honked at me, which got me all frazzled. I hit the gas pedal heavier than I should've; we all jolted back into our seats as we entered the highway.

I mumbled, "Yeah, of course not."

He smirked and looked out the window at the flights taking off. I counted down the minutes to when they would be on one of those flights.

On the drive home, I got lost in thought. *Did he know what we had done? Was it father's intuition? Was he right about not marrying Mari?*

After I arrived home, I tried to block his words from my mind and get ready for the coming week. I visualized closing my first mortgage.

On the second monthly call night in February, I felt like I was in a groove. It was like I was back in the dealership. Sal compiled a list of customers who had a balance on a home equity line of credit account—accounts that acted like a credit card while using your home as collateral. The rate was based on the Wall Street Prime Rate, which had been rising for the past year. The belief was the rate would continue to rise as the economy was overheating and the Fed needed to tighten the money supply.

These calls were easier for me than the previous months as I started off each conversation by asking if their monthly payments had increased. The obvious answer was yes. Then I invited them into the branch for a meeting to discuss options.

I made a couple of confirmed appointments from this; however, only one resulted in a mortgage application. This couple had about $150,000 outstanding on their home equity line of credit account, and I convinced them to refinance it into a traditional mortgage with a fixed rate. I took the application during the meeting and waited a few days for the underwriting department to let me know what documents the borrowers needed to produce and how to order an appraisal on the home. A few weeks later, it was finally time to invite them back in to sign the new loan documents. I went through the documents to make sure I understood what I needed to explain, and I made a note of where each of them needed to sign.

They came in, and I even surprised myself with how fluently the technical credit terminology flowed from my tongue. With every one of the fifteen-plus signatures, I felt more confident in my explanation. It was also helpful that the customers were not credit educated, so why wouldn't they trust my explanations?

Towards the end of the typical crazy day of back-to-back-to-back-to-back customers at my desk, I finally had the proper time to review the loan documents before sending them to our back office for booking. I then noticed I missed a signature! I uttered a few choice words under my breath and walked to Jeff's office before realizing that he left early that day. I went back to my office and called my non-official mentor, Tim.

"Hey Tim, I screwed up, and I'm in a pickle."

"What's the problem, Jac?"

"I closed my first mortgage, and I missed a signature from the customer." I paced through my office like a caged hamster. "I can't believe it! The worst part is that this is a notarized document, and I either have to get them back in here tomorrow and lie about the date, or I have to get underwriting to produce a whole new document set and get the customers back into the branch tomorrow. I'll look like such an idiot!"

Tim calmly replied, "Relax, Jac. I'm finishing up here, don't do anything or tell anyone, I'll be there shortly, and we can figure it out."

"Ok. Thanks." I closed my cell and tried not to stress too much.

Tim showed up after we closed the branch doors for the day. I walked him over to my office and shut the door. I showed him the documents and pointed out the lines without signatures. He pointed to signatures on other pages of the loan package, then back to the empty lines, "So you need these two signatures over here?"

"Yep."

"Ok, wait here. I'll be right back." I watched Tim walk behind the teller line to the back room. He was gone for about ten minutes, and I spent the time sulking about the mess-up in my office.

Tim was chipper and said, "You're all set!"

He proudly handed me the whole loan package. I went through it and noticed the missing signatures magically appeared. I gave him a surprised but doubtful look. I then realized his artistic masterpiece.

I smiled more and let out a laugh. "You are a piece of work! But aren't they going to notice it was photocopied?"

"You fax these in, so how is anybody going to know?"

I gave him a look of pure admiration.

He continued, "I mean, it's not like they weren't going to sign it if you told them to, so I don't see a problem. Plus, it helps everyone. You won't look like a moron, and the customers won't have to come back tomorrow. Now go fax that shit in! And congratulations on your first loan!"

I started laughing and shaking my head simultaneously and ran behind the teller line to fax the documents to the loan closing team. I noticed another fax came in with attention to Jeff. This time I actually took time to look at it as he wasn't in the office.

It was a loan application printed on Miami Business Consultants letterhead and signed by someone. I didn't pay too much attention to it as I was just relieved to close my first loan and dropped it on Jeff's desk.

I came back to my office, and Tim, grinning, patted me on the back, "I'm so proud we popped your loan cherry! This calls for a happy hour celebration!"

"Let's do it!" I said, relief oozing out of my pores.

About fifteen minutes later, Tim and I found ourselves at our favorite happy hour spot, the Ale House bar. Tim was more talkative than usual, "Are you still hooking up with Rosie?"

"Nope, I told you she dumped me!"

"I know, but women always change their minds. Mine is such a pain in my ass. And don't get me started how lazy she is. I work all day, she works maybe a half-day doing nails, but she expects me to do all the shopping and cleaning. Ensure Mari knows your expectations of what a true partnership is before you commit to her for life. I've learned my fucking lesson!"

Do I tell Tim we are married? Nope, Mari and I promised each other no one will know unless absolutely necessary.

"Sorry to hear that, Timmy. I know women can be a pain in the ass. My parents were just here for the weekend, and Mari invited herself to practically everything we did. It was hard to tell her no, but at the same time, it was good for my parents to spend some time with her."

"Has she found another job yet?"

"No. Right now, she's technically illegal."

Tim chuckled, "Not that you would, but don't marry her, Jac!"

I looked down at my vodka soda, "Yeah, of course not. Her attorney is working on getting her employment authorization renewed." Trying to change the subject, I asked, "Do you know how everyone is doing regarding performance as bankers?"

Tim semi-shrugged and said, "I don't pay attention to others too much. I know Pierre is a loan application machine. Harry makes sure everyone knows that. The Palm Beach Boys are doing pretty well, I hear. Harry mentioned that he is working on having daily reports, so everyone knows how they are doing daily."

"Daily! Isn't that excessive?"

"Yeah, but he's the boss, so whatever he says goes. Just try to do your best, and that means trying your best to sell more deposit and loan accounts!"

We each finished a couple more drinks, and I headed home. I received a call from Mari. She sounded excited for the first time since I agreed to marry her. "Jacob, I have some good news! One of my friends connected me to a family friend who owns a restaurant. It's in Hialeah, but at least I will be able to start working soon. I think it's a Cuban place, which stinks as I won't be able to practice my English at work, but I'm just relieved that I will have some money going back into my account again."

"That's great! When are you going to be working?"

"I start this weekend. It's going to be mostly nights as that is when they are busy. So I assume I will be working weekend nights. I know that will cut into our time together." She sounded disappointed.

I tried to sound sad, but instead, I was relieved. Already my mind drifted to hanging out with Dann and the guys more—my weekends had been engulfed with Mari the past few months. "Oh, I see. Well, at least you have a job for now. I guess I'll have to find weekend plans."

"Are you going to miss me? You better miss me, Jac!" Her voice switched into an adamant and severe tone as she said, "I don't want you drinking with Dann and his friends all weekend. I know what those guys are up to. You're not like them!"

"Yeah, I know, but I still am trying to meet guy friends here, and that is what I have at this point in time. Don't forget I spend a lot of time with Tim; you like him. Oh, and guess what, I closed my first loan today. Tim and I just had a few drinks to celebrate."

"Yes, I noticed from your voice that you'd had a few drinks. On a Tuesday? Jac, you should start cutting back on your drinking."

I replied overly sarcastically, "Yes, Mom."

Mari screeched, "Don't call me Mom! You don't fuck your mother, so don't call me that. Gotta go. Bye!"

A couple of days later, Dann mentioned how his buddies were renting a limo to go to Club Mansion in South Beach on Saturday. He asked if I wanted to join them. I told him Mari was now working weekends at a restaurant and to count me in.

He became giddy and did a belly-shaking dance. "Yeahhhh, boyyyy. Joeyyyy, we are gonna get you fucked up and show you what the Miami party scene is about!"

I was happy to see him so excited. I replied, "Yeah, yeah. Oh, by the way, I closed my first mortgage this week, $150,000." I finally felt proud at work.

Always playing the one-upmanship game, Dann responded, "That's nothing. Come to me when you're doing big boy loans like me. I've closed over $1 million this quarter already."

I slyly responded, "Must be nice to have Sarah in your back pocket!"

FOURTEEN

The first quarter flew by. It could've been the immigration mess with Mari, or figuring out my new job, or trying to juggle my employment, relationship, and friends. Whatever it was, those first three months were a blur. But with a new quarter comes a quarterly review with your boss.

Harry invited me to his top-floor office in the main downtown building at the beginning of April. I didn't know what to expect as this was my first formal review. I knew I was trying to learn the job as fast as I could. My branch was mostly a retiree branch, so opportunities for new large accounts or loans were pretty slim due to the demographics of the customer base. But I knew I had a couple of solid accounts, and Sal didn't seem to have any complaints about me.

I walked into Harry's office and felt my heart rate rise. Things were so tense with him at certain times. Check that—things were *always* tense with him. I walked in; he had on his thick circular glasses as usual but had his jacket off. I'd always been hypnotized by the amazing view from his office, which sometimes made it difficult to pay close attention to what he said until I pinched myself to come back to reality.

Harry motioned for me to have a seat and asked, "So, how do you think you performed in your first official quarter of production?"

Honestly, how does one respond to that question?

I answered with what I thought Harry would like to hear. "Every day, I feel more comfortable in the role. I think I've had some successes, but there is always room for improvement."

Nailed it!

Harry paused for a few moments, which felt like minutes, "You think you had some successes? Interesting, please let me know what you think they were."

Okay, here goes.

"Well, I closed my first mortgage a couple weeks back. That was for $150,000. I have opened several small accounts and one big one too. I am learning the system and all the different service requests as well."

Harry looked at a piece of paper and said, "This report shows the mortgage, but I see your deposit balances are below $100,000. Where is the big account you referenced?" He showed me the paper. It was a tabular grid of all the accounts I opened, the amount of deposits from each, loan applications, loans closed, and so on.

I took a quick look, "There must be a mistake; I opened a $400,000 account. It doesn't show in the balances."

Harry made direct eye contact, not a pleasant feeling from him for some reason. He replied, "Oh really? I have not had any issues with this report from any of your peers. What kind of account was it?"

"A CD."

Harry sits back in his seat with a semi-smirk, "Ah Jac, those are not considered in your deposit balances because we earn so little on those accounts. For example, if you put that $400,000 in a checking account, we would have earned about four percent a year on it in revenue. A CD, and you most likely opened a promo rate CD, well, I don't even think we earn a quarter of one percent. You know what, here, take this calculator, we are going to do an exercise."

I took his calculator and started listening to his direction, "Plug in 400,000, then multiply it by 0.25 percent. What is that?"

"One thousand."

"Now times that by 0.10 percent."

"One hundred."

Harry sat forward, hovering over his desk. "Jac, that is the amount of revenue that goes to your grid. As you can see, your revenue threshold is two thousand. So you'd need twenty of those accounts to hit your threshold."

I felt as though he pierced a hole in my balloon, and my feeling of elation fizzled to the floor. I had a massive lump in my throat.

"Just think of this as a tennis match. You dropped the first three games. You need to efficiently work your service game and smash a few aces right now to win a game. I don't accept excuses from any of my bankers, and I will not accept any from you.

"Pierre has taken over fifty loan applications this quarter—you have taken two. Steve has opened over one-hundred-fifty accounts—you have opened twenty, that's barely more than one per week. Remember, the goal is to open two new DDAs per day. And about the mortgage you closed, you need about seven more to get to your goal.

"As I said before, it's still early, but I need an action plan from you. What are you going to do to get your numbers where they need to be? Sitting in your office waiting for people to walk through the door is not going to cut it. That business is gravy which should be considered a topping; we need you to find your base business, the business that will get you paid out in incentive. Some of my bankers make $20,000 in quarterly bonuses. I want you to be one of them. Unfortunately, this performance isn't going to get you anything for a bonus, and I am going to be closely monitoring you moving forward."

I was stunned. I knew I didn't light the world on fire, but I didn't realize that my job would be closely monitored so soon. I sat quietly.

Harry paused a few moments, then continued, saying, "I am going to start a daily sales report with distribution to all bankers and managers. Everyone will know their production from the previous day and their cumulative quarterly totals. I believe this will create friendly competition and motivation to produce more. You're an athlete, you must like competition, and I think this is a good replication."

I walked out of his office completely embarrassed.

I really want to tell Tim and Sal about this. Maybe they could give me a different perspective to make me feel better. But what was I to do? Quit? Never. I had to make it work. Somehow.

The following day, I was one of the first people into the branch. I made sure to get time with Jeff before the day started. I sulked at him about my quarterly review with Harry.

"Just part of the job," Jeff responded. "Don't think you're the only person that received that kind of review. I've had a couple of them."

"What did you do?"

"Jac, you see the customers that come through this door. Some of them wear diapers, and they aren't babies! The business doesn't walk through that door as it may in other branches. I had to find other sources to send me business."

"Is that how you get loan applications faxed to you?"

"Oh, you noticed that, huh? Yes, that is an example of what I'm talking about. An outside contact sends me prospects looking for loans. If I'm able to provide the loan, I make sure to open them a new account, so we capture their deposits as well. It's been a reliable source of business, and it ensures I hit my goals."

"I see. Yeah, I know that Sarah Stanley had a contact within the Miami Business Consultants company."

"Exactly, actually, she was the one that set me up with my contact." Jeff started to get a little jittery, playing around with his mouse and keyboard. He looked up, "Keep your head down in the branch but make sure you go out to find your own business. That is your sure-fire way to find success in this role."

From: Rgosta@hotmail.com
To: Jacob.Gilbert@aol.com; DannThaMann@aol.com
Date: May 7, 2005; 11:39 PM
Subject: Come to Brazil

Yo punks,
I'll be out of shithole China next month. Plan to get your asses down to Brazil in July or August! Let me know when you book your trip.
Later,

Rodrigo

FIFTEEN

"Joeyyyy! You book your flight to São Paulo?" Dann yelled at me as I walked through the apartment front door on a hot June Friday after work.

"Gonna do that this weekend; send me your flight details, so I book the same one." I walked out of my room to sit next to him on the couch. As I sat down, Dann got up to go to the fridge. He opened two Coors Lights and gave me one.

"What are you doing tonight, Joey? Oh, wait, what is Mari having you do tonight?"

"She doesn't make me do anything, man." I took a sip of the beer.

"You don't have to lie to me. We are friends. I know you married her for her Green Card." He smiled, then pulled his head back and started to chug his beer.

What?! Is he testing me for my response? Stay cool, calm, and collected.

"What are you talking about?" I calmly responded in a monotone voice.

"I know you married her. You need to start being a man and taking control of that situation. She has you by the balls!"

"How do you know?"

"It's public record, you idiot!"

"Why would you even look?"

"Because mail with her name started coming in. And it looked like official letterhead. So I searched Dade County public records. I understand why you did it, but you need to show her who is boss! She is pussywhipping you around. That's not cool."

Shit, fuck, shit. Ahhhhh.

"Okay, yeah. I did it to help her out. Please keep this between us. My parents don't even know." I started chugging as well.

Dann let out a laugh, shook his head again, looked down at the top of his beer can, saying, "You idiot. I didn't realize I had to teach you everything, Altar Boy!"

I got up as I needed another drink.

Dann yelled at me, "Get me another, Joey. Oh, we are going out tomorrow night; you gonna come?"

"How can you afford to party this much? That limo night set me back weeks. I barely have a few hundred dollars in my account each month after all my expenses."

Dann grinned large and said, "Because I'm closing business like a boss! I told you I closed over a million dollars in loans and made a few thousand in incentive pay for the first quarter." He took another large gulp. "Steve and Don are coming out tomorrow too; you should come."

"Yeah, let me talk to Mari about it, but I should be okay to go. She's working tonight. I said I'd wait for her until she gets out to do something."

"Where did she get a job without papers? Working under the table, I assume!"

"She got a job as a waitress in some Cuban place in Hialeah."

Dann looked out the sliding glass door. "Fuck that shit. Good luck with that headache!"

I shrugged, then I stayed in my room until Mari called.

Mari came over to my place around eleven o'clock, and we went right to bed. The next day, I hopped on my computer to look up flights to São Paulo, Brazil. Mari asked me what I was doing, and I told her that our friend from study abroad invited us down to visit in August.

I was sitting at my desk in front of my computer, and Mari was lying belly down on my bed facing my chair. "I don't know why you want to go to Brazil. I hear they have a lot of STDs there."

"What are you talking about? We aren't going there to have sex!"

Jesus, what is she thinking?

She rolled over and faced the wall. "All I know is Brasileiras are big whores. I trust you, but I don't trust them! I really don't want you going there."

"This is a reunion trip. I haven't seen Rodrigo in over a year, and I want to go."

Mari rolled her eyes and sighed. "If you must. But I want you to call me a lot when you're there."

"Of course, I'll try to call daily."

Mari brought herself up to her knees on my bed, faced me, then put her hands on my shoulders. Looking into my eyes, she said, "No, Jacob. You will call me at least three times per day. I need to know what you are doing there."

I looked into her eyes, and I saw she wanted sex, so I did what every other young heterosexual male would do, "Sure, I will call you three times per day."

We started kissing passionately, and our clothes ended up on my bedroom floor.

After it was over, Mari's head was on my chest. "What are you doing tonight? I probably will have to work till the restaurant closes."

I looked up at my ceiling fan going round and round, "Um, well, some of the guys from work are getting together, so I was thinking of joining."

Mari picked her head up, then brought her body up to straddle mine. She looked down at my face and asked, "Is Dann going?"

"Uh, I'm not sure."

She put her hands on my cheeks, "I don't want you to go if he's going. I don't trust him."

"So now you are telling me who I can and can't hang out with?"

"If you told me you didn't want me to see someone you thought was bad for me, I'd listen to you."

"I don't think you should tell me what I can and can't do in my free time."

"Your free time? I was planning on coming over after work, so you should be here waiting for me. You don't want to spend the night with me?" Mari turned her head slightly in a flirtatious way.

"I do want you to spend the night here. However, you won't be here until midnight, and am I supposed to spend the whole evening here by myself?"

"I just don't want you going out with those guys."

"I'll be home by midnight."

"So you're going out with them?"

"Yes, I don't see the problem."

"Fuck that, Jacob! That is so disrespectful to me!" Mari started searching the floor for her panties, pants, shirt, and shoes.

I kept trying to think of what to say, but all I could do is follow closely behind her like a little puppy dog.

Mari grabbed her phone and bag from my desk, "Jacob, you need to figure out what is important to you. I'm leaving, so you have your free time to do whatever the fuck you want to do!"

"Mari, wait! Mari, c'mon, this is ridiculous," I begged.

"Yes, ridiculous how rude you are!"

I blew a fuse. "Rude? Yeah, I'm rude. You're the fucking bitch! I fucking married you like an asshole! I sacrificed so much for you, and this is what you do?"

Fire exploded out of my ears.

Mari stormed towards my bedroom door and turned back before she hit the hallway, saying, "Go fuck yourself, Jacob! Have fun with your friends."

I ran towards her.

"Don't touch me! Get away! You really need to think about what you want!"

Mari stomped out the front door and was gone. I was so mad that I took my phone, chucked it at the wall, and it smashed to pieces.

Damn, now I need a new phone! Ugh! Mari is so manipulative. It's like she doesn't want me to have any friends of my own. I can't believe I let her treat me like this. Maybe Dann is right; maybe I am pussywhipped.

I headed out the door and to the mall. It was good to get my mind off Mari for a little bit as I drove to get one of those new Motorola Razr phones. After cooling off, I arrived back at my apartment, where Dann was a blob on the couch. I realized that he probably heard our fight as he was a notoriously long sleeper who didn't get out of bed until noon on weekends.

"Everything okay, Joey?"

"I assume you heard that fight this morning?"

"I heard some yelling. I'm proud of you for sticking up for yourself!" He looked at my hands. "You got the new Razr? Nice! I need to get one of those. They are sweet! Now you need to get a new car to match the new phone, ha!"

I looked down at my shiny new silver Razr. "You know what, fuck it, I'm gonna get a new car. Wanna go car shopping with me today?"

Dann laughed, then he stopped when he realized I was serious. "Sure, you let me handle the negotiations, little boy! You're gonna get a sweet deal today! Let me get dressed. I think you should get a Beamer."

I smiled and shook my head, "I don't want to be like you. We are going to Infiniti!"

"Alright, let's do it."

Dann and I drove out in my 1994 Ford Mustang and drove back to our apartment building in a 2003 Infiniti G35 coupe, black on black. Boy, was I excited! I almost forgot about the fight I had with Mari that morning. Retail therapy truly is effective, at least for the short term.

That night, Dann, YAO Steve, Chicklet Don, Tall Ward, and I drank and partied our faces off in South Beach. Of course, the night didn't happen without drama.

Don and his chicklet teeth greeted me by saying, "Congratulations!"

I looked at him with a confused face; he then said that Dann told him I married Mari. I almost spit my drink out. I then went over to Steve and Ward and asked them if Dann had recently told them anything about me. They said Dann told them I was married, but they both dismissed it as a Dann story.

While Dann ordered our round of drinks at the bar, I confronted him about telling The Banker Gang about my secret marriage. He looked me straight in the eyes and realized I was pissed.

He gave me his trademark fake salesman smile and put his hand on my shoulder to imply, "We are all friends; it's no big deal."

You. Are. Not. My. Friend. Right. Now. I can't believe you. You're such an ass!

I punched him in his big blubbery gut. I yelled at the top of my lungs, "IT WAS NOT COOL, DANN!"

I definitely caught Dann by surprise. It wasn't a hard punch, but he retreated a few steps and keeled over a bit. I walked toward him, grasped his hair, pulled him upright, and venomously whispered, "Dann, I asked you to keep my shit private; I don't appreciate you telling anyone. Can you promise me you won't tell anyone else?"

He gave me a half of a nod, which I knew was as good as I would get from him. At that point, all I wanted to do was get black-out drunk and forget about the day's two fights.

I woke up around ten the next morning, went straight to the fridge, chugged a whole bottle of water, and popped two Tylenols. Through my ringing head, I knew I had to see Mari.

I put on a pair of tennis shorts and a t-shirt, drove to her apartment in my new ride, and walked up to her door. She opened it wearing a tank top and short shorts.

I greeted her. "Hello Mari, my name is Jacob; nice to meet you." I extended my right hand for a greeting shake.

Initially, she leaned back, suspicious of my intentions. I stood still. Eventually, she smiled. "Hi, Jacob. Very nice to meet you. Now come over here and kiss me!"

After we kissed, I pulled back, saying, "I'm sorry for yesterday."

Mari looked up at me with her big dark brown eyes. "Me too." Then she dramatically moved her head around, sniffing, and said, "Jac, what the hell have you been doing? You smell like shit."

SIXTEEN

The first half of the year was over, so what did that mean? A mid-year DMNC Bank meeting that reviewed results from the first two quarters and provided updates on what to expect next. I was not excited about the meeting.

Tim and I decided to ride together. He helped me calm my nerves. "Bro, there's going to be a couple hundred people there, Jac, don't worry. No one will get singled out. Yeah, there may be a list of the top performers, but it's just a dog and pony show. Just relax and stare at Rosie, like I do."

We both let out a big laugh, and I shook my head in slight frustration about how that whole situation played out. Tim noticed my reaction and said, "Okay, okay. Sorry about pouring salt on that open wound, but the real question is, why is that wound still open? You have a younger hot woman that I set up for you. What more could you ask for?"

Um, I don't know Tim, maybe that she is a U.S. citizen!

"Yeah, you're right. Mari is a great girl. And man, she knows how to work her body. She is actually doing fine going to school and working at the restaurant. Her hours are mostly on the weekends, so it gives me the freedom I need to party with the guys." I gave him a raised eyebrow.

Tim shook his head and gave me a big grin, "You mean getting drunk with crazy Dann."

I shrugged.

As we exited the 41st-floor elevator, we were greeted by a sign that read, "Welcome to DMNC Bank 2005 Mid-Year Meeting." The training room looked much different this time. The desks were replaced by individual chairs packed in like sardines. Bankers and managers who rarely see each other chatted with each other in small clumps around the room. I was never one for small talk, so I stuck next to Tim until some of our training gang arrived.

It was time to begin, and Harry asked that we all take a seat. This time, Tim thought it was best to sit in the middle of the room, you know, "to blend in better." Sal came in right on time and found a seat on the other side of me. Sarah joined Harry at the front of the room, and we all expected Alex, but she never showed up.

Harry loved the eyeballs of his underlings on him. He didn't live for the spotlight, he thrived in it. He began, "Hello all, can you believe we are more than halfway through 2005?"

He looked around the room, and I heard a faint "YAOOO" coming from the back.

"Overall, the Florida market is doing pretty well, but I know we can do better. Today, I wanted to congregate so everyone understands where they stand in regards to performance reporting and what to expect moving forward into the second half of this year and beyond."

Harry paused to walk across the front of the room, and it looked like he wanted to walk towards the back of the room, but the room was so packed he wouldn't have made it.

Boy, it's like an oven in here! I'm really glad I didn't wear my gray wool suit. I wonder how long this meeting will last. I can't wait to get out of here.

Harry continued, "I am going to pass around a couple of papers. While I do that, I am going to put the stack rankings on the projector. I hope you all can see. Let's start with the bankers and then go to the overall branch production for the managers."

He gazed around the room to gain the pulse of who was paying attention and who wasn't. He adjusted his glasses multiple times and kept running his hands through his non-existent hair.

"Ah, here we go. As you can see, some of our bankers had a phenomenal start to the year. I want to give a shout out to two of our rookie bankers—Pierre, please stand, and Steve Arnold, please stand as well.

Pierre looked around, standing tall but seeming timid in the spotlight. He showed an unsure smile. Steve jumped up and started pointing out his banker buds from training and his branch. I pointed right back at him. He gave me a slight wink.

As they both sat back down, Harry continued, "As you can see, around the middle point of the stack rankings is where the drop-off in production hits our team negatively. I will not point out specific names, but those at the bottom, please take notice and know you need to pick up your production if you want to make it here. I really don't want to be as blunt as that, but it is what it is."

I scanned the bottom of the projected banker stack ranking and noticed my name listed as 57 out of 59 bankers. I metaphorically felt as though Dann just punched me in the stomach. I became woozy and couldn't move. I directed my eyes to the carpeted floor.

Sal noticed my discontent and lightly patted my thigh, "Don't worry about this, Jac, it's still early. I think you will get to where you need to be. You know we have a tough branch for the new business that Harry wants."

As I looked up at Sal, my eyes welled up.

A complete embarrassment. I am a complete embarrassment, and every one of my peers now knows this.

Only two people were below me—one of them was on maternity leave for three months that year, and the other had been at the bank forever, and he was retiring at the end of the year. So, in reality, I was in a class of my own, the very bottom!

Sarah began to talk about credit metrics, and I saw Pierre and Steve's names up there again for loan applications and whatever else she was reporting. I couldn't stop thinking about how embarrassed I was.

I've competed at a very high level my entire life, and I don't ever remember having this feeling of shame. What did I need to do? What did I need to change? And how do I accomplish that?

I appreciated working with Sal and his kind words, but unless something changed and changed fast, I would be in the basement of the stack rankings the rest of the year. I was truly lost. Lost in my profession that I took so much pride in, lost in an immigration marriage, lost living with a guy I realized I couldn't trust.

What was I doing with my life? How did the last twelve months lead me to this?

Harry then took back control of the meeting, which brought me back from my maudlin introspection. He thanked Sarah for her credit update and proceeded to show everyone the branch stack rankings. Sal's branch was in the middle of the pack, primarily due to Jeff's first-half results. Sal didn't seem thrilled nor distraught.

The last part of the meeting received the greatest uproar from the bank staff. Harry brought up both arms, extended them wide with all fingers out, "Okay, now for the changes I've been working on with the national team for the past few months. We will now send daily productivity reports. These reports will encompass previous workday activity and rank you on your quarter-to-date and year-to-date results. They will rank the bankers and the branches in the Florida market. I will have a conference call every afternoon at four, and the branch managers can call in, so that day's results can be obtained and reported for the next day."

A huge group groan came in, mostly from the managers, as they saw this as a new way to micromanage them. Sal just kept shaking his head in disbelief. He murmured, "These sonz-a-bitches."

I looked at him with one brow raised where he just kept shaking his head in disgust. I looked over at Tim. He took a deep breath, had a surprised yet not surprised expression, and gave me a look that asked, "'When is this meeting over?'"

As fast as the meeting adjourned, I motioned to Tim that we needed to jet. The ride back with Tim was docile. It felt like we were driving back from one of the tennis matches that I lost, and I didn't want to discuss what happened. I didn't want to sit and chat with anyone; I didn't want to have a drink either. I wanted to go home and sulk alone, which is precisely what I did, eating ice cream, watching reruns of Seinfeld.

Was I the George Costanza of our banking group?

One random day after work, a couple of weeks after the mid-year meeting, Dann and I ordered some Chinese food for dinner. At the dining table in our apartment, Dann was bragging, as usual, about all the new accounts and loans he was bringing into the bank. He made a sly comment about me being at the bottom of the stack rankings. "You know I have been in regular contact with Jerry from the Miami Business Consultants, and he stated he hired a number of new guys to find new business. I think it would be good for you to go in there one morning and teach the new guys how you can help them with new clients. You know, go over the different types of loan accounts we offer and some of the deposit products as well. Go in there with some Dunkin' Donuts, some printed bank fact sheets, and some DMNC pens, you know."

My eyes opened, and my brows rose.

"Jac, we gotta get your numbers up like mine. Sarah told me that Harry has no qualms about writing anyone up if he feels they are not performing. So, you want me to set this meeting up for you? I think you should go in there before we leave for Brazil."

"Yeah, sure, thanks, Dann," I rapidly responded between forkfuls.

"No prob kid! That's what friends are for. Dang, this orange chicken is some good shit."

I ran the idea of me going into the Miami Business Consultants office by Sal the next day. I framed it as Dann's idea. I was a bit skeptical since the whole concept seemed a little shady to me—the business consultants were acting as middlemen between clients and the bank.

Sal reassured me that I was simply being introduced to prospective customers. As long as I followed the compliance protocol of know your customer, I'd be fine. I vaguely remembered the compliance information Alex tried to teach us before her meltdown.

The importance of meeting your customer face-to-face, or knowing your customer, was to help reduce or prevent fraudulent loans. Banking regulations required bankers to obtain proper documentation from clients in person. Meeting prospective clients through Miami Business Consultants was no different than meeting clients walking through the branch doors. As long as I followed the rules, I'd be doing nothing wrong.

Sal then reminded me I needed to do something to bring my sales numbers up, which meant—at least in my mind—I didn't have much of a choice. Due to my bank branch being highly seasonal, the dog days of summer only brought tumbleweeds through the door.

I emailed Dann and asked him to set up the consultants' meeting for a few days later. He offered to go with me, but I politely declined as I knew he would take over the meeting, brag about himself, and probably would suggest I was his underling, which I wasn't and didn't want them to think so.

For the next three days, all Dann talked about was how to position various loans and accounts to the new guys. "Jac, you need to let them know you are their partner. You are on the same team as them. Give them enough information about our underwriting, but don't tell them all the details."

Yada, yada, yada.

I yessed him to death. I should've just recorded, "Yes, uh-huh, sure, great, got it," and replayed it every time he tried to give me a new pointer.

The meeting was scheduled for a Friday morning. I had trouble sleeping the night before as I was anxious about my presentation. Multiple consultants would be present, all expecting me to provide pertinent information. Meeting new people, in general, always made me nervous, but getting up and presenting in front of the consultants was a whole new ballgame, especially while trying to project confidence in a subject I was still trying to learn.

I woke up super early, put on my best navy suit, matched with a white shirt and a red and blue striped tie. Nothing shows power like a navy suit and white shirt; well, that's what I told myself anyway. I hopped in my G35, made a quick stop at Dunkin' Donuts, and proceeded to their office.

I arrived right at eight o'clock, and it seemed that many of the staff hadn't arrived yet. The office was in a strip mall, with Miami Business Consultants written on the front door. I knocked, and Jerry noticed me through the glass door. He welcomed me in, saying, "Jacob, thank you so much for coming today. It's been a while. How have you been doing?"

I forced a big fake smile, "Good morning Jerry, uh, yeah, it's been a while. Things are going well. I look forward to meeting your new guys, and hopefully, we can create synergy."

I even used lingo I learned in business school. That had to give me immediate credibility, right?

Jerry's eyes brightened, "Synergy, I like that. I like that a lot; I think I'm going to incorporate that in my vocabulary. Don't worry; I'll give you credit for it."

He put his arm around my shoulder, and we both chuckled. Jerry continued, "Look, Jacob, some of these guys are young like you, and others have previously worked in other finance companies. Although I hired them, I am still trying to see if they will be a good fit here. So,

I'll attend your presentation as well. Don't be nervous; I am going to ask the questions they should be asking, so this is kind of training for all of us." He stopped, turned, and faced me before we entered the main conference room, "Please, just speak to us like you would your peers; no need to be nervous."

I smiled and said, "Okay. Thanks a lot, Jerry." We walked by a bunch of offices and a large back room that had blacked-out windows.

Hmmm, that's peculiar. I wonder what that's about.

Jerry opened a door. In front of us was a large table, and on the far wall was a whiteboard with names and numbers of loans in process from his employees. I guess it was his own type of stack rankings. Twelve oversized black leather captain-like chairs faced the table.

Jerry pointed at the head of the table. "There, please take a seat. I am going to round up the troops, and we can start."

"Ok great." I took my place at the head.

After the greetings and introductions, I found myself presenting in front of five new consultants plus Jerry. As Dann suggested, I started by discussing the different loan products offered at DMNC. I passed around some bank-produced fact sheets regarding our mortgage products, home equity line of credit accounts, auto loans, small business lending, and so on.

Jerry honed in on the small business lending products, especially the unsecured lines of credit we offered. It was apparent he knew our basic underwriting guidelines, but he tried to mask exactly how much he knew. He said, "So team, as you can see, DMNC has a robust small business unsecured product. The prospective business needs to be at least two years old, and the owner or owners need to have a 700 or higher personal credit score. Jac, can you share with the team what documentation is needed and how you verify how long the company is in business?"

Scrambling to remember the details, as I had not taken a small business application to this point, I tried to buy some time for my answer. "Uh, I um, well, we look it up."

Jerry was trying to help me at this point, "Oh, I assume you mean looking at Sunbiz.org, right?"

"Yes, that's correct, Jerry."

"So team, as long as Sunbiz's date of business incorporation is at least two years old, we are okay. Now, Jac, at what loan amount does this become a full application versus a fast underwrite for lower loan amounts."

I looked down at my small business printout from the bank, "Well, uh, here it shows that up to $100,000, we do not ask for financials on the business. So, it looks like all we need for loans under that amount is a one-page signed application from the owner, a personal credit pull, and verification from Sunbiz. Oh, and I would need to meet with the business owner to verify their identity. That just means them showing me an ID, such as a driver's license."

Jerry leaned back in his chair, seemingly surprised, "Oh, so you have to meet them physically? You won't take a signed application on their behalf?"

At that moment, the subtext dawned on me. Now I understood all those faxes Jeff received—the ones he didn't want me looking at closely.

Oh, shit. Jeff and the other bankers working with this group aren't performing the proper KYC compliance processes. This is some sketchy stuff. If the clients receive loans they can't pay back, they could create issues for the bank.

Uncomfortably, I reiterated, "Per our bank guidelines, we have to meet the customer face-to-face and positively identify them."

Jerry stood up, walked over to my side, and faced the five sitting at the table. He said, "Okay, guys, that's not a bad thing. We should be meeting with these people face to face anyways. Meeting in person creates credibility and a better chance of closing the business. I mean, we normally meet them to sign the final loan documents anyways, so I don't see this as an impediment to our course of business. Oh, one more thing, did you bring some paper applications from your bank so my new guys can see exactly what information is needed from the business owners?"

"Uh, I didn't. Usually, I enter the application on our computer."

Jerry promptly responded, "Yeah, that's if the customer goes into the branch. But I am talking about when bankers take applications off branch sites like ours. We don't have access to your computers, so we need to write the required information on something."

"I can print some out and bring them in to you guys. Here is my business card with my contact information." I walked around the table, handing them out.

Jerry shook my hand, indicating the training was over, and said, "Jacob, this has been very informative. Thank you so much for coming. Guys, I ask for you to get Jacob in front of a business customer that needs a line of credit. Jacob, expect a call from one of us soon."

Jerry thanked me again and walked me out the door. I opened my car door, but I looked back at the Miami Business Consultants before I got in. Something just didn't sit right with me. I had this weird gut feeling on the ride back to the branch.

Sal asked me how everything went. I told him something was "off." However, because I couldn't explain it or give details, he just waved his hand and reiterated that I wasn't doing anything wrong if I followed bank policy. Lastly, before he walked away, he reminded me I needed to pick up my production—fast.

I gave Mari a ring about my Miami Business Consultants presentation experience. She didn't have much to say but did express concern about my production levels. And, of course, towards the end of the conversation, she asked me to refund a couple more overdrafts she created in her DMNC checking account.

I then called Tim to explain what happened during my presentation. He wasn't too surprised or bothered by it, saying, "Bro, do you think fifty people a month go into Pierre's branch in Little Haiti and ask for a new account? Of course not; he creates a need for them. He seems to be really good at it. I mean, those people don't have much money. But at your branch? There's a lot of wealth there. I bet most of your customers would easily qualify for a loan. You need to match the proper products to the type of customer you are dealing with. During customer interactions, probably when I should be listening to them more closely, I am always strategizing in my head how I can get them to open a new account or take a loan application. Most of the time, it doesn't happen, but if I have twenty interactions in a day and two to five take my sales pitch, I hit my goal for the day. It's a numbers game. Now that I think of it, we should take Pierre to lunch or something and see how he does it."

Tim was only six years older than me, but he had this robust wisdom. He also had a great way of putting major things, such as work and female situations, in proper perspective. I always felt better after talking to Tim, which is why I spoke to him so much—possibly more than Mari!

About a week before leaving for Brazil, I mentioned to Dann that one of the new guys from the Miami Business Consultants office called me and had a carpentry business in South Miami interested in an unsecured line of credit. Dann pretty much invited himself to the meeting that the consultant set up, which was supposed to be at the carpentry business's main office location.

However, the consultant called me on the day of the meeting and explained that the customer had a job he needed to get to in the afternoon and asked if we could meet him at a Wendy's down south, near Kendall. I picked Dann up at his office, and we went to meet the owner, Pedro, who was in his forties and spoke basic but broken English.

I felt completely out of place as Dann and I, in full suits, crammed next to each other on the same side of a Wendy's booth—the things you do to gain business. As I expected, Dann took control of the conversation. I could see Pedro had a hard time following Dann's fast speech and fake New York accent.

Dann obviously didn't remember Lucy's number one rule from communication class; know your audience! And by the way, didn't Dann brag about picking up women speaking Spanish in college? Yet another Dann story.

I translated Dann's fast-talking New York accent to a slow, over-pronounced wording so Pedro could understand.

Maybe if I use some Italian words that I know are similar to Spanish words, Pedro will understand us better.

Pedro took to what I had to say and began to ignore Dann. I asked Pedro how long he'd been in business and if he had been making a profit.

Pedro responded, "*Seis* month in business. No profit. I need loan for profit."

I tried to frame the question differently but received the same response. To my surprise, Pedro abruptly stood up to leave, saying that the consultant had all of his information and that he looked forward to hearing from me.

We noticed that he hopped into a white commercial caravan. It was strange though, a business name should've been painted on the side of the van. However, all we saw was residue from the previous business name. Nothing reflected the name of the company Pedro owned and was on the loan application.

I pointed that fact out to Dann. He shrugged and continued chowing down on his Double Baconator. He washed it down with a huge slurp of his chocolate Frosty and burped. Yes, the dude chose a Frosty as his primary beverage.

The new consultant called me that afternoon, and I shared my concerns about his client—Pedro directly told us he'd been in business under two years and didn't turn a profit. I also mentioned the peculiar lack of messaging on his work van.

The consultant tried to explain away all of it, using the excuse that Pedro spoke limited English and maybe we misunderstood. He said he would send me the Sunbiz link to prove Pedro's business had been incorporated for a few years. However, I stood my ground and politely declined to take the application. Besides, I couldn't be bothered with a new loan application since I was leaving soon for vacation! The consultant was not happy with my decision and made it known he'd discuss the situation with Jerry.

I dedicated the weekend before Brazil to Mari. She'd been drooling over my new Razr phone, so I surprised her with a pink Razr for herself. She was ecstatic that we had matching phones and raised her mood even though she made it known she was not happy I was leaving her for ten days to go to Brazil.

I had to promise her multiple times that I'd call her when I landed. I'd call her no less than three times per day—when I woke up, sometime in the middle of the day, and at night before I went to bed. I wasn't sure how I was going to do that, but I promised it no less.

Mari drove Dann and me to the airport in my G35, and I left her with my car, house keys, and phone. I had an inkling she was going to use all of them while I was away.

SEVENTEEN

Apparently, Dann and I missed the message that Brazil is in the Southern Hemisphere, which meant our Miami scorching summer heat was the total opposite of São Paulo. Neither of us packed a jacket, and we each only had one long-sleeve shirt. Adding insult to injury, Rodrigo's house did not have central heat or insulated windows.

Oh, the chills we both felt that entire week, but at least Dann had more than a few layers of fat to insulate him. And unfortunately, I gained a layer or two of insulation myself since moving to Florida.

"Welcome to Brazil, you punks!" Rodrigo greeted us with a big smile flashing his brilliant white teeth against his natural tan complexion.

"Damn, Joey, you got fat. What the fuck? You eating too much fatty pussy in Miami?" He let out a raucous laugh, and I looked at my spare-tire-covered abs.

"And Dann, well, you always looked like a fucking pear, so nice to see that hasn't changed!"

I laughed at that one. Dann was good at transforming any insult into something positive for himself. "Yeah, well, this body is one of the top producers at the bank these days. So there's that!"

I rolled my eyes. Rodrigo noticed and smiled with a slight head jerk to make it known that Dann is Dann, and nothing had changed in the year and a half since the two had seen each other.

As we entered Rodrigo's car, which was comparable to the size of a Smart Car, I started to stress; I needed to find a phone and call Mari.

With excitement in his voice, Rodrigo said, "I hope you brought your balls this week because we are going to have some fun. Oh yeah!"

I cut off his fun and asked, "Hey, how can I call back home?"

"Joey, you just got here. What, are you closing some big piece of business these days?"

Dann butted in, saying, "Oh, Joey's got himself a woman these days. A Colombian who owns his balls."

They both had a good laugh at my expense as I looked out the passenger side window.

After the laughter subsided, Rodrigo turned to me, asking, "Really, Joey? You found a way to get over Valeria and meet someone? Is she a hottie?"

Before I could answer, Dann leaned his girthy body forward in between the two front seats, "Yeah, she's pretty hot, but no way I could deal with all the drama she puts the poor kid through. I mean, I prefer just banging random puss these days. I have to say I've been doing pretty well in that category as well." Dann chuckled and slid his big ass back into the back seat.

"I am proud of Joey. When I met him, he would almost piss his pants when a hot woman walked by. Now he's getting some action. Nice job, bro!"

Dann chimed in again, "Yes, he has made quite the progress since the first days in Italy. Damn, it's freezing here. I thought Brazil was hot. How am I going to see Brazilian ass in thongs in this weather? What the fuck, man?"

Rodrigo turned his head back for a moment and said, "Don't worry, my friend, we'll see plenty when we go to Rio de Janeiro in a couple of days. But for now, I hope you can go for a nice welcome massage. Oh yeah!"

After being panic-stricken due to the crazy traffic and the even crazier way Rodrigo drove, we arrived at his house and dropped off our luggage. Then we found ourselves back in his little car, driving on the shitty São Paulo roads like he was racing in Le Mans, France.

Dann, who usually doesn't get rattled easily, was getting a little scared by Rodrigo's driving—weaving in and out of traffic and even driving on the wrong side of the road to pass who he thought were incompetent drivers. "These muthafuckers don't know how to drive; they are assholes!"

Trying to think of something to discuss to take Rodrigo's mind off of driving like a maniac, I decided to ask him how his year in China was.

"China? Fuck that place, man. I will never go back there; they are savages! The worst year of my life. You know the women don't even shave their pussy! Disgusting. So basically, I went to work and watched porn. I even found out the hard way I was eating rat meat instead of chicken for my first few months! So gross! I'm so happy to be back. I get boners just by seeing these Brasileiras walking by in the streets."

"Have you played any tennis?"

"Nope. Sucks man. Did you bring your racquet? We need to play this week, but you might even beat me. I'm so rusty!"

"Actually, I've hardly played this year. So you're still going to beat me, but let's definitely play this week."

Dann chimed in yet again, asking, "What the fuck am I going to do then?"

Rodrigo looked in the rearview mirror at Dann, and yelled, "Masturbate, my friend!"

Rodrigo wasn't kidding when he mentioned having "welcome massages." He took us to this place where attractive women greeted us, and we selected our masseuse out of a lineup. I took the entire hour for my private full-body massage. When I returned to the lobby area, Rodrigo and Dann seemed to have been waiting for some time.

Rodrigo said, "Damn, Joey, you take a long time!"

"What do you mean? I thought we were all getting an hour massage?"

Dann and Rodrigo both looked at each other and started laughing. Rodrigo blurted out, "Joey, you are a freakin' Bubble Boy."

I finally realized why they were laughing and grinned. "Ohhhh, yeah. You got that kind of massage? I should've guessed."

Dann said, "Yeah, he's straight-edged at work too!"

As we headed out the door, I asked, "Hey, can we stop by a payphone, please?"

With a bubbly voice, Mari answered the phone. "Hello, Jacob! I miss you so much! How was your flight? What are you doing?"

"Everything has been good. It actually is pretty chilly here. Rodrigo is giving us the tour. We are going to Rio in a couple days, so that should be fun."

"Are you guys partying? I don't want you clubbing there. You know I don't trust those Brasileira whores. Oh, and I want you to call me Princess from now on because you are my Prince!"

"Uh, Princess? Um, Okay. Well, we are getting going now. I'll call you later. Love you."

Mari huffed, "Jacob, I want you to call me Princess!"

"Okay, I miss and love you, Princess. I'll talk to you later."

"I want you to call me before you go to bed tonight! I love you. Oh, call your phone number from now on, I am running low on minutes on my phone, so I have been using yours."

Dann overheard part of the conversation. "Damn, Joey, she really does have you by the balls! Princess?" He let out a snort, then Rodrigo joined the laugh.

Glad they're enjoying themselves at my expense. Sheesh, even I can barely believe I just called Mari Princess. I've gotta nip this in the bud.

After having way too many caipirinhas the night before, Rodrigo took us to the top of the city of São Paulo, the Edifício Itália building. Growing up in New York's shadows, I thought I knew what a large city was like, but São Paulo was vast. High-rises sprouted up in every direction. Though I'd seen some amazing sights and architecture in the past, viewing this city from this height, put me into a trance. I kept thinking about how all these people lived in this tiny patch of earth.

But before I could get fully lost in my thoughts, I had to find a payphone to call Mari. I also knew I'd be the butt of another off-color remark from either Rodrigo or Dann—it's like they took turns mocking me, and it was a friendly competition among those two.

A couple of days later, we found ourselves on beautiful beaches and basking in Rio de Janeiro's warm weather. Contrasting the natural beauty was aching poverty. I didn't understand what poverty was until I visited the heavily populated favelas that adorn the big mountain on the backside of the beach.

Ignoring the poverty, Rodrigo either wanted to show us a really good time, or he truly missed living in Brazil over the past year and wanted to indulge in his cultural vices—gorging on unlimited food at Brazilian steakhouses and clubbing nightly until three in the morning.

This clubbing is getting stressful! I have to set my alarm each morning to make my promised call to Mari, but I'm barely awake. Always checking in with her has become an anchor. Other guys don't check in with their girlfriends three times a day while on vacation, do they? If this is what a successful relationship looks like, I'm not sure I want one.

By this point, the guys just accepted those calls as a necessity of my travels, but I knew it still annoyed the crap out of them.

On the last day in Rio, Rodrigo wanted to go hang gliding off the mountain and land on Ipanema Beach. It hadn't occurred to me before, but at that point, I realized Dann had a serious fear of heights.

Dann said, "No thanks, I don't want to do that shit. Not trying to die in Brazil. I'll hit up a massage parlor while you guys try not to crash into the mountain."

With travel time, the hang-gliding experience took over three hours and was the first extended time that Rodrigo and I were together without Dann.

Unsurprisingly, Rodrigo started to complain about Dann. "Does that guy ever stop bragging? I mean, he's a fatty. Maybe we need to buy the rose-colored glasses that guy wears!"

I chuckled and said, "Tell me about it. I live with the dude. Every day he has to let me know what he does and how great he is. He is actually doing better than me at the bank we work for, which still boggles my mind. He became buddies with one of the senior women in our Florida District, and I think she has been helping him out."

"Which bank you guys work for again?"

"DMNC. They have some locations here."

"Oh yeah, I know that bank. Some of the guys I work with use that bank."

"How is PetroBrasil?"

"I was a bitch in China. But my father is introducing me to some of the senior people within the organization locally. They all have solid relationships with the government. There is so much fucking corruption here. I know these guys are getting massive kickbacks on contracts and sending it to their private Switzerland bank accounts. I've been thinking; maybe we can make some money and have them send some of that money to the U.S.? But I am one person. How do I stop the corruption? I don't. So I am going to play the game to my advantage."

"Yeah, I hear you. I feel like I am in a similar situation. I get pressure from management to perform no matter what. All they care about is quantity and not quality. It's hard to push back on the machine if you are just one person. Everyone plays the game, or they get off the ride and does who knows what next."

"You know what, Jac, I always thought of you as someone I would partner with and do business together. I believe you are an honest person, and we all need a few close, honest people we can trust in this world. I consider you one of them for me."

I smiled at him genuinely and replied, "*Grazie, Rodrigo*!"

"Here, it's *obrigado*. But I'll think of ways we can work together. Don't tell Dann. I don't trust that pear ass!"

"*Obrigado*! Now wish me luck so I won't die on this ride flying down to the beach!"

"You can't die, man! Who else is going to call Mari three times a day? You sucker!"

Fifteen minutes later, after an incredible flight down eight hundred meters weaving back and forth in front of the mountain, we landed right on Ipanema Beach.

True to form, afterward I found a payphone. It was my twenty-third call to Mari during this trip, and the calls weren't cheap.

EIGHTEEN

A couple of days later, Dann and I landed in Miami, and my anxiety about work production renewed. The rest of August and September were pretty barren for me—customer traffic at the branch came to a crawl, no more referrals from Jerry's new consultants crossed my desk, and my bank balance was abysmal.

I felt guilty for leaving Mari when I went to Brazil, so I bought her a gold necklace that set me back quite a bit, and after all the trip costs, I realized I needed to cut back on partying and spending.

On top of that, Mari barely kept her financial head above water waiting tables a few nights a week while still going to school, so she "borrowed" my credit card. She always gave me the card back; however, the balance on the credit account kept rising.

I was burning out. I had performance calls in the morning, at the end of the day, call nights every week at this point, and my numbers were still low enough for me to stay in the basement of the stack rankings.

Sal saw my discouragement through my body language and always tried to cheer me up. He'd tell me he'd been in this business for almost thirty years, and it was a rollercoaster. I just need to keep my head up, and things would work out. His support was genuinely helpful, and I felt the most peace while at the branch.

Hearing Dann brag about his success, and hearing Mari bitch about her job and cry about her immigration paperwork was taking a toll on my psyche.

When October rolled around, I had something to look forward to. I'd attend Financial Securities training for a week in Fort Lauderdale, staying at the W Hotel right on the main beach road. The training was broken into a few sessions so that banker staffing wasn't interrupted in the district's branches.

Eight bankers were in my week's training, and to my dismay, Tim wasn't one of them. Of course, Dann was in my session along with Tall Ward and Naomi from our training class. The other folks were bankers from prior training classes, and I didn't know them outside of the Harry meetings or call nights.

The week mostly prepared us on how to pass the FINRA Series 6 and 63 exams so we could sell mutual funds and annuities in our job. Every day a section of class was dedicated to how to propose these products to bank deposit customers. "Oh, Mr. Jones, I noticed you have $XXX in your account, earning a small interest rate. Would you like to discuss non-bank options to earn a higher interest rate?"

I didn't speak too much to Ward during our initial training months, but since he was one of the few people I knew in this week-long training, I started chatting him up.

He was quiet and humble. He attended the University of Florida on a volleyball scholarship, and I don't think anyone in our class knew that. I learned he played tennis in high school and wanted to hit the ball around after class to get some exercise.

Ward, unlike myself at the time, worked out regularly and maintained his strong physical shape from his competitive playing days.

Although he wasn't as quick as I was, his long gangly arms covered the court as well as many players I played against. Playing with him made me realize how much I missed the friendly competition of tennis—maybe because it was something I knew how to win, when lose seemed like all I was doing over the past year.

On the Thursday of that training week, Mari called after class. She made it known she wasn't happy—I wasn't calling her enough, she was broke and bored during the day, and immigration was taking too long with her paperwork so that she couldn't work legally at a decent job or get a driver's license. I didn't pay close attention to the conversation as I was trying to change quickly and meet Ward on the tennis court. As I approached the court, Ward was practicing his serve, waiting for me. I gave him a wave and let him know I'd be off the phone in a minute, trying to end the conversation.

I said to Mari, "I know you are having a tough week, and things haven't been going your way, but I will be home tomorrow afternoon, and we can have a nice weekend together; however, I gotta go. Ward is waiting for me to play a tennis match before we have a team dinner."

Mari became agitated, "Fuck that, Jacob! What is more important, your stupid tennis game or me? We have hardly spoken all week because of your damn training and lunch with this person, dinner with that person! You need to give me attention too! It's not all about what you are doing!"

"Hold on, hold on. Are you getting angry that I want to play tennis with a co-worker for an hour before we have to get ready for dinner? What, do you want me to talk to you for the next hour until dinner?"

"Yes, yes I do. You owe it to me. I mean, you didn't even ask how my day or week has been. It's all about you!"

I saw Ward taking notice of my now heated conversation, so I exited the court and headed to the parking lot. "Mari, my friend is waiting for me to play tennis. I gotta go. I am hanging up now."

"If you hang up on me, we are fucking done!"

"What? You're a crazy fucking bitch. I'm going."

"Don't call me again, you fucking jerk!"

I walked back into the tennis court, shaking my head. Ward asked, "All okay in lovers' paradise?"

"Some women are fucking crazy! I think we just broke up," I said, frowning.

"Shit, man. If you need to go makeup, we can play another time, you know." He started walking in my direction, extending his condolences.

I motioned him off. "No, she can't get her way all the time. We are playing, and I hate to break it to you, but I see blood in the water, and you are probably going to get your ass kicked today!"

And he did. I don't think he won a game against me; I was an animal on the court, and it felt amazing. I felt determined for the first time in months!

I didn't call Mari that night or the next morning. Our training class was over right before lunch, and Ward, Naomi, Dann, and I had lunch in the hotel before heading back to our homes. After eating, I hung around at the table, an uncommon behavior for me since I typically went outside to call Mari.

Dann asked me why I wasn't following my invisible leash and calling Mari.

I said, "We broke up last night."

Dann didn't believe me at first, but Ward spoke up and confirmed it, saying he was around for the ill-fated conversation yesterday afternoon.

Dann asked, "So what are you doing this weekend then if you're not obeying your keeper?"

I shrugged.

Dann smacked the table with both palms, "How about an impromptu trip to the Keys? My parents have a vacation home in the Lower Keys near Key West. We can relax in the sunshine by day and party our faces off on Duval Street at night!"

He scanned the table for reactions. My eyebrows popped up, and I looked at Ward and Naomi.

Ward bluntly stated, "I'm single and have no plans."

Naomi seemed surprised that Ward was single and said, "I am newly single as well and would love to spend the weekend with you guys."

I gave Naomi an eyebrow raise and asked, "Are you sure you're okay spending the whole weekend with three single guys? Full warning—I know some of us can be crude at times, and we don't want to offend you."

"Please, Jac, I grew up in Jamaica with many older brothers. I am fully aware of how crude you boys can be!"

A couple of hours later, Ward and Naomi met Dann and me at our apartment, and we were on our way to Summerland Key for the weekend. Dann and I took a weekend trip to his parent's place one of the first weekends I moved in with him, but I hadn't been there since I hooked up with Mari. She didn't want me going without her, and Dann made it known Mari wasn't invited.

That weekend was a breath of fresh air, literally and figuratively. As much as Dann gloats and talks shit when he is your friend, he makes sure you are taken care of and always asks people what they preferred to do or eat.

Once I told Dann that Mari and I broke up, he treated me completely differently. He stopped making fun of me for not having a set of balls and seemed to express compassion toward me as I was on an emotional rollercoaster that weekend. It's weird to say, but I felt like our friendship was re-established and grew stronger. He also seemed to be concerned with my work production and that I had grown apart from Jen.

Apparently, due to the excessive drinking on Friday night, Naomi and Ward ended up in the same bed. Dann and I were pretty surprised. All the months we were in training together, neither of us picked up any flirtation between those two, maybe because they were in other relationships? They seemed to want to go at their leisurely pace that Saturday morning, and who were we to get in the way of that? Dann suggested we take a ride to Bahia Honda beach for a bit of relaxation.

We plopped down in two chairs and soaked up the sun to cure our hangovers. Dann turned to me and said, "You know, Jen is really upset that you don't call or talk to her anymore. When was the last time you spoke to her?"

I took a deep breath and sighed, "Yeah, I know. I feel bad about it too. Just that it was always hard to call her around Mari, and if I called Jen and she didn't answer, there was a good chance she'd call me back during times I was with Mari, and well, Mari would just explode in anger or jealousy, and it would cause friction between us. So it was just easier to stop talking to Jen rather than get into another bickering match with Mari."

Dann pulled out his black Razr and flipped it open. "I'm gonna call her now, and we are going to get you two back together—in whatever weird non-sexual sleeping together fucked up relationship you two had before."

As he raised the phone to his ear to call Jen, anxiety returned. I knew Jen would bark at me like a high-strung chihuahua.

"Here, Joey, she's on the phone." Dann hands me his Razr, and I hesitantly accepted it like it was potentially an explosive device.

"Hi, Jen. How are you?"

Just as I expected, Jen barked into the phone, "How am I? What the fuck, Joey? I call you, and you don't answer, and you never call me back. When was the last time we spoke?"

She stopped talking, and dead space surrounded us. I stammered, "Uh, um, well, yeah, it's been a while. Look, I'm sorry."

"I thought we were friends! You totally disappointed me. This year has been tough in law school, and I wanted to invite you up here for a weekend to party. I have a friend that I wanted to set you up with too." Jen's voice slowly calmed down with each word.

I looked at Dann. He stared aimlessly into the water. I got up and started walking along the edge of the water with his phone to my ear. I said, "Mari and I broke up the other day. She didn't want me talking to you. I tried to explain you were just a friend, but she didn't believe me. She said you called me as much as someone who would be more than a friend. Trust me. I have missed you too. I feel horrible about abandoning our friendship like I've done. I hope you forgive me."

"You need to stick up for yourself, Jacob! Dann tells me all the shit she has you doing. It seems she ran your life. I don't know the details of your break-up, but maybe it's for the best. Honestly, I worry about you. I know..." She trailed off.

Did Dann tell her? Did that lying pear-shaped piece of shit tell her I am married? After I pleaded with him not to tell anyone?

She continued, "I worry about you because I feel like she is taking your identity away, and I also worry that you are going to get back with her, so I'm not going to say anything else regarding her. But on a more positive note, um, does this mean I am invited to come visit?" I could feel Jen's smile growing wider through the phone.

I chuckled, "Yes, you are always invited. Hold on, let me get Dann's attention."

I walked back to our beach chairs and put the phone on speaker. I said, "Jen wants to plan a Miami visit."

Dann's eyes which were previously sunken with dark circles, brightened, "Yeah, Jenny! Wait, let's plan an Italy reunion and invite Rodrigo too! Will be just like old times!"

"Yayyyy, my friends! I finish my semester at the beginning of December, so the second weekend would work perfectly. Oh, this will be so much fun! I'm going to put together a group email. Let's make this happen!"

Dann and I ended the call agreeing with Jen's timing and told her we looked forward to her visit. I handed Dann's phone back to him, and he looked up at me, "Welcome back to the party of life, big boy!"

Everyone who has been in a failed romantic relationship knows the break-up steps—denial, anger, depression, resentment, acceptance. Each stage is a monster in itself, but sometimes the emotional roller-coaster takes over, and all you want it to do is stop and put your feet on sturdy ground again. Sometimes, the option is to stop the rollercoaster and exit the ride in the same spot where you started, such as back in the same relationship.

I tried to stay mentally strong in the days and weeks after the weekend trip to the Keys. My intention was to be done with Mari, but one day she showed up at my door. Dann wasn't home to help me keep my shield up, and I let her inside.

She told me she was there to pick up some things she kept at my place, but I knew she was there for another reason. Talking led to more talking, which led to crying, which led to hugs, which led to kissing, which led to undressing each other, which led to lying in bed naked. Which ultimately led to getting back together.

I tried to sneak around for a few days without giving Dann an indication of our reunion, but he found out. I don't think he was surprised, but I do remember that he advised me, "Don't let her control your entire life this time. Put your foot down when you need to."

It was obvious he was disappointed; my decision cut into our guy social time.

I was still at the bottom of the barrel in the stack rankings at work, and I also was broke going into the holiday season. I was still paying off my credit card balance from the Brazil trip and paying for almost everything for Mari since she could barely make her rent and car payments. Living in Miami on a salary of $35,000 and a fat zero for incentive compensation took its toll on my finances.

My folks wanted me home for Christmas, but I told them I couldn't afford the plane ticket. It cost as much as what I had in my account at the time, and I wanted to be responsible by not adding plane fare to my credit card debt. My parents offered to pay for the flight home, and I obliged.

Though I was back together with Mari, my heart wasn't in it. I felt like I spent all my time trying to avoid confrontation. Therefore I never mentioned that I was going home for Christmas nor planning an Italy reunion.

One day sometime in November, Mari and I were on the couch, and as Dann passed by, he commented about Jen confirming her attendance to the reunion.

Mari promptly asked, "What reunion?"

I cautiously explained that Dann and I invited Rodrigo and Jen, close friends from our study abroad trip, to our apartment to stay and have a reunion.

Mari flared semi-rage from her eyes. She slammed down her Coke on the coffee table, splashing the black stickiness all over, and shouted, "What the fuck, Jac? You invited a girl to your apartment? And you don't tell me? I have to find out from Dann? When were you going to tell me?"

I looked over at Dann—he was silently loving this. I then looked back at Mari, "I'm sorry, it slipped my mind. We planned the reunion during the short time you and I were apart. I have been focused on other things since. Such as rebuilding our relationship and work."

Mari stood with one hand on her hip and asked, "Well, when are they coming?"

Dann replied, "They'll be here the weekend of December 17th. Then Jac and I leave a few days later to go home." If looks could kill, Dann would've been dead!

Mari took a second to process the second sentence. "What do you mean you then leave to go home?"

I knew I needed to take control of the conversation, so I spoke up before Dann could, "We are both visiting our families for Christmas. Dann is going to Virginia, and I am going to New Jersey."

Mari ran her hands through her thick hair, messing it up, making her look as crazy as she was acting. "What? You booked a flight home for Christmas? Without telling me? Without inviting me? What kind of relationship is this? Who does something like that? You don't want to spend Christmas with me?" After a pause, she continued, "Jacob! Answer me!"

I was speechless. I had no fight left. I couldn't grovel anymore.

"If you have nothing to say, then I have nothing to do here. And we have nothing together. I am leaving. You need to decide what you want in your life. Goodbye!"

Dann and I watched Mari gather her things and rush out the front door. Dann popped open a beer with a rapt grin as if he was watching a boxing match knockout.

Over the next few weeks, my anxiety about the Italy reunion kicked in. I felt certain that drama would crop up. Mari wanted back in my good graces and made it clear she expected to be invited to our weekend activities. I just couldn't come up with a valid excuse, so I told her she could join us when she wasn't working. I silently hoped it would be a busy weekend at the restaurant, so she'd be working a good portion of it.

Rodrigo decided to extend his stay due to the long flight. He showed up mid-week, and Mari and I picked him up from the airport, and the three of us went out to dinner. Rodrigo noticed that I was nervous, and he did a great job of calming my anxiety. He read people so well, especially women.

He interpreted Mari's body language and tone. He spoke to her like a gentleman, and he spoke highly of me, which made her feel better. Rodrigo left the swearing and crude remarks in Brazil and communicated like a professional, respectable man that I'd never really seen before.

When the bill came, Rodrigo scooped it right up. I was secretly fine with him paying as I was running low on cash, but I had to put up a fight for the check as he was my guest, and my girlfriend was with us. He whispered to me that he recently received a $10,000 bonus and dinner was his treat. I asked how he earned that type of bonus. He winked and told me we would talk about it later.

Jen came in on Thursday night. Fortunately, Mari had to work and did not join us. That night was the first time in a long time I felt relaxed and at ease. Being back within this comfortable group of friends felt like heaven with all the inside jokes, the sarcasm, and the endless laughs to be had. I wore a perma-smile the entire night. Dann, who didn't usually belly-laugh—he usually snickered—found himself laughing to tears a few times.

The next night, Mari was off from work, and I invited her to go with us to the Gryphon Nightclub, where thousands of crystals hung from the ceiling. Since Mari had to work a double shift on Saturday, she said she wouldn't be drinking much and offered to be the designated driver. I thought that was a nice gesture and would be an excellent way to introduce her to Jen.

However, the introduction of the two women at our apartment was tense and fake. When it was time to go, Mari said she didn't want to drive Dann's car, so all five of us squeezed into my G35 coupe. Mari occupied the driver seat, Rodrigo being the tallest, took the passenger seat. Dann, Jen, and I squished into the small coupe back seat.

Jen had a few more shots than she should've had at our apartment. She was already tipsy to slightly drunk when we squeezed our way into the car. Smashed between Dann and me, she was extremely flirty—something she had not been before; I would've welcomed it when we were in Italy! She kept grabbing my hand and made sure her hair flowed into my face, so I got a whiff of her fragrance. At times, she leaned in close and nuzzled my neck.

Mari's full attention was on the highway, and since it was dark outside, she didn't pick up on what was going on in the back seat. Rodrigo noticed the quiet commotion of drunken Jen and engaged Mari in conversation, using Spanish. I silently signaled a thank you to Rodrigo.

When we arrived at the club, Jen draped herself on me most of the night. I could tell Mari was getting annoyed, but Rodrigo had her ear most of the time to deflect her attention away from Jen. When I did peel Jen off of me, Rodrigo immediately started dancing with her so I could dance with Mari. Dann had a ball watching the drama play out like a soap opera.

Around three, Mari drove us all back to my apartment, and her Latina possessive nature displayed itself fully. Once we walked through the door, Mari grabbed my hand, dragged me to my bedroom, and immediately locked the door. She gave me a strip lap dance then rode me so hard the bed frame wobbled. She screamed so loudly she'd make porn stars jealous, ensuring the apartment's other occupants, as well as some of the other neighbors, knew what was happening.

My head was pounding the next morning when I awoke, but I decided to be a good host and run out before anyone else had awakened to grab some bagels for all. I returned to a catfight. Jen stood outside my bedroom door, obnoxiously knocking on it.

I asked, "What the heck are you doing?"

"Joey, your girlfriend is being rude. I need to get to my bag, and she has the door locked and won't let me enter."

Before I could respond, Mari rushed out of the bedroom, saying, "There, you can go in the room now. Jacob, I'm leaving." She jetted right through the apartment to the front door, not saying goodbye to anyone.

I followed her out to the hallway asking, "Wait, Mari. Wait. What happened?"

Mari turned around and stomped back to me. She angrily pouted, "That fucking bitch was pounding on the bedroom door. So rude. I was gonna let her in, but I was using the bathroom and told her to wait a couple minutes. She then said, 'I'll patiently wait while holding your Green Card.' What the fuck is that about? Everyone knows our business? Nothing can be private between us?"

I felt bad and didn't know what to say. I quietly responded, "I'm sorry. You're right; she's been acting like an asshole. You don't deserve that. Please come back to have breakfast."

"Look, I don't have the energy to fight with you right now. I have to work ten hours today. I'm not coming back until they all are gone. Call me later. If you want."

Mari gave me a peck on the lips and proceeded to the elevator. I slowly walked back into my apartment, wanting to throw shit around. *Serenity now.*

As soon as time permitted, I took Jen aside in my room and bitched her out about how disrespectful she was last night in the car and at the club. I then told her how shitty she was to throw the Green Card comment to Mari.

I paced back and forth in my room, and she sat on the end of the bed with her feet dangling off like a little innocent schoolgirl, except she wasn't a schoolgirl, and she sure as hell wasn't innocent.

"Joey! I mean Jacob. Whatever your name is...*I'm sorry*!" The after-effects of too much drinking prevented Jen's control over her emotions, and she started to sob. "I've never seen you with a woman before, and I guess I got jealous. I'm sorry!"

I took a seat beside her on the edge of my bed and put my arm around her. She hugged me, and her tears soaked my shirt. She looked up at me with her puffy eyes and innocently asked, "Can I sleep in your bed tonight? That couch is all sunken in. Must be from Dann's fat ass."

We both start chuckling. I said, "Sure, but just like before, clothes on! Oh, and you need to apologize to Mari. Just send her a text. Please."

"Ugh, do I really? Okay, okay. Just for you, Joey! Come over here and give me another hug, please?"

"Don't worry, Mari isn't coming by the rest of the weekend," I said.

"Thank God, man. I don't know how you put up with that shit—having to call her Princess? Does she think she's really a Princess? In that case, I'm a busty thin six-foot-tall Victoria's Secret runway model! I want you to call me Giselle from now on!"

That afternoon, Rodrigo and I hit the tennis court for a match. I then realized Tall Ward was probably hurting my tennis skills as Rodrigo smoked me that match. I also realized I needed to start working out regularly again and shed the post-college fifteen pounds I gained. After the game, when we were sitting at the mid-court bench, I remembered Rodrigo's bonus and realized it was the perfect time to bring it up to him again.

Rodrigo smiled and said, "Oh, you wanna know how to make some money, my friend?"

I lifted my eyebrows and shrugged.

"Remember how I told you how corrupt my country is? Well, I decided to make some money off of it. Now, I know what you're thinking; I mean, you are a Bubble Boy and all."

He took his towel and wiped the sweat off his forehead and arms, then took a long drink of water. "Ahhh, nothing like some cold refreshing water. Anyways, you know that PetroBrasil is a state-run oil company, right? No? Well, now you do.

"We have contractors bid on large projects. We are talking about multi-billion reais worth of contracts that executives at PetroBrasil need to place with the 'best' contractor and bid. I found out that these executives have all the contractors bid ten to twenty percent over what they normally would bid.

"This creates a price inflation that is presented to the government, who, in turn, funds the project to the contractors. All these Brazil executives have offshore accounts to accept the ten to twenty percent over-bid amount as a kickback.

"The executive I work for gave me a kickback as hush money because I am working on the project he is responsible for. These executives need options regarding these kickbacks. They need to move the money out of Brazilian banks, for if they're caught with the kickbacks, the government could seize the assets.

"I noticed they are building high-rise condos like crazy here in Miami. So I came up with an idea for the executives—they could buy these condos as a way to get the funds out of the country and own an asset that could appreciate. Do you think you can help with this?"

I hemmed and hawed for a few moments as what Rodrigo just explained sunk in. Before I could respond, he continued, "Actually, since we have DMNC Bank Brasil, and you work for DMNC Bank USA, you could open up U.S. dollar-denominated bank accounts for them so they can send the funds offshore. Do you get any credit for that?"

My eyes lit up like a Christmas tree. *Do I get credit for that?*

"Fuck yeah!" I exclaimed.

I then sat back and realized this would be some shady business, "But there are all these regulations at the bank with international clients. Some anti-money laundering shit, among other compliance nonsense."

Rodrigo furrowed his brow, "You're not doing anything illegal. You're opening accounts for Brazilian people. How they got the money is no concern of yours—I dunno, something to think about. We could charge them a 'convenience' fee for this service too. Remember, we always spoke about how to do business together?"

"Yeah, we did." My mind raced back and forth, trying to figure out if this was a valid proposition.

As we got up off the bench to walk off the court, Rodrigo turned to me. "Whatever you do, do not tell Dann. Our President, Lula, will find out in no time if Dann knows! One more thing, Joey. You can struggle and live the straight-edge way you have lived your entire life, or you could take a calculated risk with opportunity and be successful in your job and make some money as well. As I said, I only do this kind of business with people I trust. So you let me know."

"Okay. Let me think about it."

Rodrigo and I entered my apartment, and we found Dann and Jen hanging out on the couch watching football. I faintly overheard Dann talking about his job. Instead of going right into the shower, I told Rodrigo to take one first. I opened up the fridge and perused my beverage options while casually listening to Dann. I faintly heard him say something about "closing a loan for a guy that barely spoke English."

Jen said she didn't understand what he was getting at, and he explained the loan was a referral from a business consultant. He then laughed and said, "Believe it or not, I met the dude in a Wendy's because I don't even think he had an office!"

I popped open a Coors Light, turned towards the living room, and said, "Wait, are you talking about Pedro? You know the guy we met at that Wendy's where I got a bad feeling about his business and legitimacy?"

Dann's temperament quickly changed and started to backtrack a little, "Yeah, that's him, but one of Jerry's guys provided me with proof that his business was more than two years old, and underwriting looked at his credit. It went through our process the correct way."

I looked down at my Coors Light, took a sip, "Interesting. I'm gonna see if Rodrigo is done showering."

Before I knew it, the Italy reunion was over, Mari and I were exchanging Christmas gifts, and she was dropping me off at the airport for my trip home for Christmas, solo, again.

Sometime in the autumn of the previous year, I signed up for a social networking service called, Thefacebook. It was a way to stay in touch with other students at your university, and you needed a .edu email address to register. I still had my Jacob.Gilbert@bc.edu email, and I signed up and "friended" some of my old tennis buddies and a few other classmates. Apparently, within the past year, the social network made its way around the globe to sign up new universities at lightning speed.

One of the nights I was back home during the Christmas holiday was too cold to do anything fun. I decided to waste some time searching for more connections. I opened Thefacebook and was happily surprised to see a friend request from *Valeria D'Alessio,* including a little message saying, *Ciao Jacob. Buon Natale e anno novi! Baci, V.*

I grinned from ear to ear all night. I wrote her back asking how she was doing, and we became "friends" on that platform and started messaging every so often. Sometimes the best Christmas presents are the ones that cannot be purchased.

NINETEEN

A new year brings new beginnings. That's the saying, at least. I'm not sure how true it is if things become destroyed beyond reasonable resurrection. The past year had not been kind at work, financially, nor emotionally. But the start of the year meant reviewing the past year.

This is what Harry wanted to do, and he invited me into his office for a year-in-review meeting. I called around to The Banker Gang, and it seemed that I was the first one he chose to meet.

Lucky me.

I showed up at his office on the second Tuesday of the year after the branch closed. Harry greeted me like he always did. As he rose from his desk, his monotone voice said, "Hello, Jacob. Happy New Year. Please, take a seat. How are you?"

I pulled out a plush chair across from him, and in the process of sitting down, I replied, "Happy New Year as well. I'm good. I went home for the holidays, and it was nice to see family."

Harry began the conversation with a zinger. "How is everything with Mari? Did she go up north to meet your family?"

My eyes grew bigger, and I took a deep breath. "Mari is okay. She wasn't able to make the trip." I shrugged.

Man, I really need to stop that.

"I do feel bad for what happened to her, you know. But I am also concerned that her situation is taking a toll on you as well. That is something that cannot happen. I need you focused."

"I am focused, Sir."

Sir?

"Well, I am not so sure of that, Jac. If you were focused, we might have a different conversation than the one we are about to have. I chose to meet with you first for a reason. The reason is that you finished in the basement of the sales ranking for 2005. And, as the adage goes. Is it an adage, or—whatever it is, I like to start with the bad news then give the good news. What I am trying to say is, I met with you first because I have bad news, and I will meet with the top producers last to give them their good news."

I sat still, nodding my head slightly with pursed lips.

"I am just going to come out and say it because I don't like to sugar coat. Jacob, I am disappointed in your performance so far. You have not lived up to my expectations. As I mentioned in a previous meeting, to use tennis as a metaphor, you lost the first set 0-6, and you're down 0-4 in the second. Normally I'd give a ninety-day performance improvement write-up on someone I wanted to get rid of quickly.

"I believed in you when I hired you, and I want to give you a little extra time as I don't like to be wrong. So for that reason, I am giving you double that time to turn this ship around. I'm placing you on a formal performance warning, and if you do not hit your goal this first quarter, I'll place you on a final performance warning. If you have not hit your mid-year goal, you will need to look for employment elsewhere."

Harry stopped talking, and his office was dead silent. Many emotions zoomed through my nervous system. Sweat starting pooling under my arms. Chills traveled through my body, and my feet and hands became blocks of ice. I was paralyzed—at a loss for words.

Harry turned towards his computer and shuffled a few papers around. He then turned back towards me.

"Here's the document. You may read it over, but it basically states what I just explained. I need your signature at the bottom to prove you understand what is at stake. Oh, and one other thing, we will be having weekly one-on-one phone calls to discuss your weekly production and activities. When Sal is available for them, I will ask him to join as well. I feel as though you need to be micromanaged at this point in time. Do you have any ideas we can talk about to get your production higher at this point?"

I started scrambling in my head.

Jerry's guys stopped calling me when I turned down that shady deal. Ms. Li? Nope. Mr. Vacca? Hell no. Think, think, think! Bingo!

"I have a friend in Brazil. He works for the state-owned oil company, PetroBrasil, and offered me the opportunity to meet some of his bosses and encourage them to open DMNC Bank USA accounts."

Harry's eyes opened wide behind his Coke-bottle lenses, and he said, "Jacob, this is what I am talking about! Why did it take you this long to bring this to me?"

Well, because it's super shady, and I thought I had to abide by all those compliance regulations that Alex taught us. Oh yeah, you weren't there that whole week and probably don't even know what AML stands for.

"My friend just recently mentioned it, and I didn't really think it was a legitimate opportunity. But now that I know this is something that I can go after, I will try to see what I can do. I would need to fly to Brazil to meet these people. And I..."

I'm fuckin broke, and I cannot afford the damn flight!

Harry picked up my drift. "I understand. You need to fly there, and it's costly. Don't worry. I will have my assistant order you a corporate card, and you can purchase the flights, accommodation, and meals on the card."

"Thank you."

"Jacob, please understand that I am investing in you. You need to be certain that this will produce the business we need."

I nodded.

Harry continued, "Wait a minute. I just remembered something. There is this Banker in San Diego that has been killing it with international clients from Mexico. Let me find his name and contact information. I want you to speak with him before you do anything. Maybe he can give you the lay of the land on how to bring in international clients. Yeah, that's what I'm going to do. Let me get you his phone number, and I want you to call him. He might be busy, so I need you to be persistent in trying to speak with him. I will send him an email to let him know you'll be calling. Additionally, the Fed is going to continue to raise rates, so deposit accounts might earn more revenue than credit accounts this year at some point."

I edged forward in my seat and said, "Oh, and my friend, who was here about a month ago, noticed all the new condo high rises going up. He mentioned that the Brazilians might be interested in purchasing them. I heard that we have an international mortgage program as well. I guess I'll ask the San Diego Banker about that too?"

I could see the wheels spinning in Harry's head, and his body language was the most positive it was the entire meeting. He promptly ended our conversation with, "Jacob, I think you're finally on to something here."

I called Mari from my car ride home. I told her I was on a written performance improvement plan, and I had six months to get my numbers up high enough to keep my job. She expressed concern for me and invited me to meet her for dinner at a local Colombian restaurant. Her treat, she said.

Yeah right. On my credit card.

When I arrived at the restaurant, she was seated in a booth towards the back. She jumped out of her seat and greeted me at the door with a big hug and kiss. Although this dinner was on short notice, she still looked fantastic—one thing was always true of Mari, she knew how to dress.

She didn't wait long to open the conversation. "I am so sorry, babe. I know you must feel down. Tell me, is there anything I can do to make it better for you?"

Any remaining anxiety from my meeting with Harry subsided at that moment, and I felt a natural smile hit my face for the first time in hours. I said, "Thank you, Princess! I'm not sure there is anything you can do, but I do appreciate your support during this. You know, I am just so frustrated, and I feel this performance improvement plan is unjust.

"I feel as though other bankers have let their morals slide during their business dealings. I mean, I think I am just as smart as the other bankers, yet they are getting the good performance reviews and bonuses that I have missed out on.

"Like, I don't know if I told you, but Dann was bragging—yeah, I know, what else is new—but this time it was about a deal he closed where I met the customer. Do you remember me telling you about meeting a Hispanic guy at Wendy's? He hardly spoke English, and I dropped the deal because I felt it was shady. Well, I overheard Dann bragging about the fact he closed a $100,000 loan for the dude! Like, what the fuck is that about?"

Mari asked, "So, you think that there was some dishonesty with this?"

"I mean everything with Dann could be dishonest. But you know my mentor, Jeff, I think he's up to shady shit too. They are dealing with this Miami Business Consultants office that introduces them to customers. Fairly often, I see these paper applications faxed in for Jeff. That lazy fuck never leaves the office. When does he meet with loan applicants if he's always in the office? At dinner? Doubt it; he has a family and coaches all these sports teams. In the morning? Again I doubt it because he's in there before me usually and never mentions being anywhere else, like meeting with customers outside of the branch."

Mari replied, "Interesting."

"And I'm not done. You know the big dude, Pierre? Well, he works in one of the poorest branches in Little Haiti, and he has the most loan applications of anyone. I guess that shouldn't be a surprise, but his closing rate of the applications is pretty high and is always on the top of the stack rankings when it comes to credit. I can't put my finger on what is going on. But the crazy part is Harry could give two shits about any of these dealings. All he cares about is the numbers on the board."

Mari chuckled and said, "Harry! That little fucker only cares about getting promoted to a national executive position. And don't get me started on his super creepy hugs. He'll do whatever it takes to get there. I know it! So what are you going to do?"

Do I tell her about the Brazil business I proposed to Harry now? Nope, better not. It doesn't feel right.

I just shrugged.

She asked, "What do you think about Tim? Do you think he's doing shady business?"

I shook my head, "No. I mean, I am by no means stating that Tim is squeaky clean. But he knows what he can and cannot get away with. He likes to fly under the radar and never wants the spotlight on him. He'll make sure he's not on the very top or very bottom of the stack rankings. Steady Eddie; I guess that's how he sticks around. Maybe I should rethink working with the Miami Business Consultants?"

Mari shook her head and said, "Really? Aren't they shady? You should follow in Tim's footsteps. Enough about the bank. I think we should get the arroz con pollo!"

TWENTY

After countless email invitations and reminders, the big day was finally here—The Celebration of Achievement at the Hard Rock Hotel and Casino in Hollywood. It was the bank's annual prom. People dressed their best and looked forward to it all year. Everyone that has been with the bank for the entire prior calendar year was invited to attend. Often people told tales of things that happened at the celebration—things spoken of in hushed tones.

Sal gave me a little pep talk about it, saying, "Show up on time, don't drink too much, and act professional. You'd be surprised what some people do with an open bar at a casino."

I wasn't sure exactly what he meant by that but, I only could assume the booze encouraged some people to get jiggy in an unprofessional way. Anyway, the night was here, and although it was a black-tie event, I decided to save funds and wear my solid black suit with a white shirt and solid black tie. Since the Hard Rock was over a twenty-minute drive from downtown Miami, I offered to drive since I didn't plan to drink much, and I told Tim I'd pick him up on the way.

Tim, wearing a jacket for almost the first time, hopped in the back seat behind Dann, and we were on our way. He decided to be cost-conscious as well and wore a plain black suit.

Dann, in his flashy rented tux, babbled on about nonsense, but he stopped and asked Tim what he thought about this event, as he probably had been at a similar one with his previous bank.

Tim responded, "My other bank didn't put on an event quite like this. I did ask some of my branch teammates, and they told me that they close off an entire part of the casino for us where there is an open bar—"

Dann cut him off, saying, "Hell yeah, open bar! I'm ordering Grey Goose for sure! Stick it to those bastards."

Tim paused, then continued, "Anyway, I think they will bring around hors d'oeuvres, and the first hour is just gambling or bullshitting with other bank employees. Then, we will go to the performing arts theatre, where awards will go to the top people in the stack rankings among other corporate rah-rah shit. Afterward, some people go back to gamble, or I hear the clubs are pretty cool there, so some people hit them up. Apparently, tomorrow is the biggest sick or tardy day of the year for the whole staff!"

Dann interjected, "Yeah, the clubs are sick there. We went to Gryphon a little while back. Was off the hook! Also, Sarah told me you go on the 'bad boy' list if you call in sick tomorrow. So don't do it!"

Tim took a swing at the giant matzo ball Dann just left out there. "So you and Sarah have become pretty close, huh?"

Tim is the freaking best! I was grinning ear to ear.

Dann adjusted in his seat to turn and face Tim, then said, "Yeah, we talk. She gives me the 411."

Tim swung again, asking, "What do you have to do for that 411?"

Another zinger! I grinned even larger.

Dann scrunched his face and asked, "What do you mean? We are friends. She wants to help me out. That's all."

Tim decided to have the last word for once. "All I am saying is nothing is for free in this world. You are giving her something she wants."

I started chuckling aloud. Dann looked over at me and asked, "What are you laughing about, Joey?"

"Tim's got a point. I think there is something weird going on between you and Sarah as well. I mean, I hear you on the phone with her at the apartment. At night, on the weekends…I dunno…maybe she gets off to your voice."

Tim roared from the back of the car.

Dann smiled and shook his head, saying, "You guys are shitheads."

We rolled up to the valet and discovered a red carpet rolled out for us. Big signs out front read "DMNC Bank USA 2006 Celebration of Achievement." Arrows directed us on where to go within the Hard Rock Casino. Tim, Dann, and I strolled through the bright lights, jingling slot machine games, dealers' smiling faces to our private section of the establishment. A waitress in a tuxedo promptly greeted us and offered us some champagne.

Yes, please.

The three of us gulped them down, and we proceeded to the bar as we saw some familiar faces camped out there. Dann waddled in front of us.

I turned to Tim and patted him on the back, "I hope you took your Pepcid AC today. No one wants to see a tomato face lighting up the room!"

He started laughing, and I felt like it was going to be a good night.

The cocktail hour flew by—could've been that three Grey Goose and sodas plus a champagne made all the pain go away. Right before it was over, I noticed Rosie walk in wearing a red sequined dress. It was form-fitting, and what a sight it was. She may have broken the necks of some of the men who hadn't seen her in the flesh previously. She looked like a million bucks.

Liquid courage prompted me to sidle up to her like a new puppy dog. I think some eyebrows rose at how comfortable it was for me to walk right over and give the hottest woman in the place a hug. I complimented her looks, and she smiled brightly. She told me I looked good as well, but I think she was just being pleasant.

The liquid courage turned into liquid flames, and I talked way too much; this was definitely not the place to chat personal business. Luckily, I was saved by the bell. The alarm sounded for us all to congregate in the performance hall to take our seats.

Rosie appeared to be relieved the bell rang, and she quickly scurried away to find Naomi. I found Tim walking in.

Tim was with Pierre, who was with Steve and Don, who were with Dann, who was with Ward, who was with Naomi, who just found Rosie. So I ended up taking an end seat next to Rosie. I realized I ran my mouth a little too much the previous ten minutes.

I softly whispered, "Sorry, Rosie. The alcohol took over shy Jacob, and it sometimes consumes Jacob in total."

She smiled gently. I got a whiff of her aroma, and my mind went to that time in my bedroom for a quick minute. She offered me a flirtatious and seductive glance and told me, "Be the good boy I initially became attracted to. And pay attention!"

"Yes, ma'am."

Harry promptly took the stage in a full tuxedo, including a cummerbund, of course. The bright lights that previously lit up headline musicians now shone directly on Harry.

"Good evening to the best banking team in South Florida!" An enormous cheer erupted.

He continued from the stage, "This is my favorite night of the year. Why is that, you may ask? Well, because we are celebrating you and only you tonight! This past year has been tremendous for the Florida market. I am sure to receive nice accolades next month on the executives' trip to Hawaii; however, I need to make sure I acknowledge those who made that possible."

Rosie whispered to me, "Who in the audience do you think has sucked Harry's dick?"

My sudden choking laughter caused me to nearly spit out my Grey Goose. I put down the drink and tried to play it cool. I leaned towards Rosie and responded, "Whoa, Rosita! But, um, Sarah, for sure."

She rolled her eyes, "Obviously! Who else?"

I made a funny drunk face and whispered, "She sucked Dann's too, I'm sure."

"For sure! I think I told you how Harry gives these super long extended creepy hugs to certain females." Rosie then half-pointed to a middle-aged branch manager that I'd seen only a few times. "I think that woman has been on her knees in Harry's office too."

I shrugged. *This is a weird conversation.*

As Harry droned on and I leaned over to Rosie again, asking, "Why is Rosie being feisty tonight?"

"Don't you know Rosie is always feisty? And alcohol. Alcohol always keeps the shame at bay."

"You know I've heard some crazy stories of what happens at these events with an open bar for six hours."

"Oh my God, yes! Don't worry; I won't be one of those stories, and Jacob—don't you be either! I like good boy Jacob." She started to rummage her hand between the seats under my jacket coat to grab the side of my leg and buttocks.

I couldn't help think that Rosie was using me as her plaything. *Keep calm and chive on.*

Harry's assistant came on stage and rolled out a large display holding different-sized awards, all with the DMNC logo prominently displayed on their fronts.

I leaned over to Rosie again, asking, "Where has Alex been?"

"Where the hell have you been, Jac? Alex quit a couple months ago. Apparently, there was some big drama between her and Harry. Not surprised after what happened last year at the end of our training class."

"Interesting. She must have turned down his creepy hug or blow job proposition." I chuckled.

Harry started talking again, and now people were paying attention. Everyone hoped to collect a top banker or manager award to proudly display in their office for the years to come.

"Now, South Florida, this is my favorite part of my favorite night of the year—award ceremony time. When I call your name, I would like you to get up, come to the stage and collect your award, so everyone knows who you are.

"I am going to change things up this year. First, we are going to start with the rookie awards. These are the top bankers that had their first full year of production for 2005. When I observed the training classes that year, I had a good feeling these hires were going to be special. It wasn't until recently that I truly understand how special this team has been. I don't think a rookie class has produced like this one has in my entire thirty-year banking career! So without further ado, please take a look at the board.

Top Rookie for Credit: Pierre St. Paul
Top Rookie for Deposits: Donald Deeds
Top Rookie Banker for 2005: Steven Arnold

Our row roared. In unison, all of us shouted "YAOOO" at the top of our lungs. Confetti came down from the ceiling in the stage area, and our seating area vibrated like a prolonged thunderclap. I could barely hear myself think. I looked at Rosie, and we both raised our eyebrows. I caught eye contact with Tim, and he gave me the thumbs up.

I wanted to feel happy for my classmates, but I wasn't. I stood and clapped as the three of them walked down the central aisle to retrieve their awards and shake Harry's hand. But my applause was not in good faith. I felt empty inside; the alcohol that thoroughly warmed my insides just minutes ago froze over and became icy. I could tell Rosie was trying to brush up against me, but I just wasn't having it.

I wanted to run away and be alone. I actually wanted to run to Mari's arms. She'd know what to say to make me feel better during my time of need. But I couldn't; that wasn't me. I hadn't been a quitter in the past, and I sure as hell wasn't going to be a quitter now.

I think Rosie picked up on my subtle non-verbal signs. She put her arm around my waist, and I leaned down towards her as she whispered in my ear, "Don't worry, Jac, that will be us next year."

Maybe Rosie knows me better than I thought?

I smiled and shrugged.

She continued, "Don't let this ruin your night. I know you have it in you to be successful."

Why is she telling me this? Does she see something that I can't see right now? Was it that obvious that I severely underperformed last year? I don't want to be the top draft pick bust. I want to be successful. I need to be successful.

"Thank you, Rosie. That means a lot to me. I am confident you will be up there with me next year. I think we need to talk more about strategy and help each other out where we can. I miss talking to you."

It looked like her eyes were about to melt. She said, "Jacob—I, uh, yes. Let's help each other out." She quickly looked down and away.

What in the world is going through her mind? I sure miss talking with her.

I brought her back to my attention with a hand motion. "I am tired of seeing my name on the bottom of the stack rankings! I am tired of losing! I am going to win!"

She smiled, but I don't think she understood my intentions. I didn't want to tell her, but I wanted her to know I wasn't going to sit around like a wounded lamb while the aggressive dingoes were on display, winning all the prizes.

Between talking to Rosie, and my mind being elsewhere, I missed Harry handing the presentation over to Sarah. She spoke about credit goals and performances. She called Pierre back on stage to acknowledge he submitted the most credit applications out of all the bankers.

He received another standing ovation. Finally, she announced the winner of the top banker for credit transactions for 2005—Jeff Winder.

My shady mentor banker also won the most coveted award of the night, overall top banker. Being named the top banker almost makes you untouchable.

Dann shouted out, "Oh, what Jeff doesn't know is that I am taking over that trophy spot next year!" He started laughing.

Tim joined the laughter, then looked over to me and put his finger in his mouth as if to vomit. He then leaned over to Rosie and me and said, "Once this is over, let's head to Gryphon!"

We both nodded yes.

He leaned to the other side of the row and told them the same.

Fifteen minutes later, we all found ourselves filing out of the performance hall. We stopped at the open bar for some walking beverages. As Rosie sipped her stiff martini, her flirtation increased to the point that I completely forgot to call Mari to check in on her like I'd normally do if I weren't with her.

Rosie and I walked fast and broke away from the gang as we sucked down our drinks. She steered me down one of the side alleys right outside the casino on the way to the club.

"Jac, I want to apologize for everything that happened last year. I know it wasn't fair to you, and you didn't do anything wrong. The truth is that it's hard being married. I am still trying to cope with it. I miss that I can't choose my friends independently and do what I want without conferring with someone else."

I noticed she was starting to break down.

"Rosie, don't, no, don't cry! This is supposed to be a happy night! The Banker Gang is back together for the first time in a while."

Rosie looked up and tried to blot her tearful big brown eyes, so she didn't smudge her mascara. "Anyways, I think you are an amazing man. It hurt me to cut you off last year because the truth is, I still wanted to keep seeing you. But I felt like I didn't have a choice. I saw that same hurt in your eyes tonight—I know Harry wrote you up for your performance. He is such an asshole! But I know you have it in you to be successful, don't get caught up in everyone's bullshit!"

We looked right into each other's eyes. The kiss was waiting to happen—but it didn't.

Oh, God, I wish I was with Rosie, not Mari. She's so kind, so hot, and she gets me.

The gang was now drifting our way. Steve ran towards us, raising his Top Rookie Banker award above his head as if it was the World Cup trophy. "You guys are so cute. I think you should just fuck and get it over with!"

He hugged both of us. Within our three-way hug, I sucked up my jealousy for a minute and said, "Congratulations, Steve! We are all proud of you!"

The hug broke up, and Steve smiled, "Aw, Jac, that means a lot coming from you! Now let's get shitfaced! YAOOO!"

Rosie and I followed the gang with fake perma-smiles on our faces. Tim sidled alongside both of us, "And how are you two school kids doing? Damn, man, I'm fucking drunk!"

I laughed, saying, "Yes! Tim is finally drunk! And you do not have a tomato face in case you were worried. And enjoy Tim, I am the responsible one driving home tonight!"

With that, The Banker Gang entered the nightclub and danced the night away—well, we danced until midnight because it was a Thursday and we had to work the next day. Sarah found her way to the dance floor and spent a lot of time next to Dann, whose shuffle didn't quite qualify as dance.

As the clock approached midnight, I tried to gather Tim and Dann to head to the exits. Dann motioned that he didn't need a ride back. I didn't question it, but he indicated that he'd be the passenger in Sarah's vehicle.

I gave him the "naughty boy" eye, then grabbed drunken Tim's black tie as a leash and headed to the exit. On the way, I gave Rosie a big hug and sneaked in a grab of her voluptuous derriere.

That ride home with Tim is one that I will not forget as long as I live. It was the first time I'd seen him wasted, and he was in rare form.

"Jac, you know that tonight was complete fuckin' bullshit, right? I mean complete bullshit. Every one of those muthafuckers that got one of those piece of shit awards? They didn't earn them. I mean, do you know that?"

I nodded, trying to keep my eye on the highway but also trying to listen intently to Tim's cuss-ridden drunken confessions.

"Every fuckin' day, I wake up and ask myself why I followed Harry to this shithole bank! Every day! People are driven by two things in this world. Fear and greed. Nothing else. Fear and fuckin' greed. I chose fuckin' greed! I left my other bank because Harry promised me that I'd make more money and move up the ranks here. But I was a fuckin' moron. Do you know why I was a moron?"

"Uh, no."

"Because I actually thought this place would be fuckin' different! I mean, what, um, wait."

Tim made some abrupt drunken induced movements, and I was concerned he would vomit all over my ebony interior.

"Okay, I had to get that burp out. Ah, I feel so much better now. What was I saying? Oh, yeah. What is the definition of insane? Well, it's doing the same thing over and over and expecting different results. I'm literally fucking insane! I'm doing the same thing that I did at the previous bank with Harry. I expected different results."

Tim, get to the fucking point! I can't decode your metaphors and drive at the same time!

I finally interjected and asked, "Tim, what the hell is your point?"

"This entire bank in South Florida is a house of cards." Tim spoke so fast I hardly understood him.

"A house of cards? What the—"

He cut me off and said, "You know a house of cards is one where when the wind blows, it all comes tumbling down? There is no solid foundation. All those people that earned those awards are committing fraud. One hundred percent fucking fraud!"

"Woah, Tim. Let's walk that back a bit. That is a heavy accusation."

"Jac, I trust you, and whatever said in this car doesn't leave it. Do you understand?"

I nodded my head in agreement.

"So you met that shady fuck, Jerry, from Miami Business Consultants, right?

I nodded again.

"That guy is Harry's best friend! They started in banking thirty years ago. Jerry used to work with Harry at their first bank. Jerry is a fraud. His team is a fraud, and I am going to explain how the whole thing works.

"Jerry runs different teams of consultants—in Miami, Fort Lauderdale, and Palm Beach. They are all incorporated under different entities, so they look different. Jerry hires impressionable young guys that are wildly ambitious and want to make a ton of money. He hires loan brokers, realtors, accountants, etcetera.

"These foot soldiers help him find other impressionable ambitious guys to help with the fraud. In our case, it's finding bankers that Harry hired to be the loan officers on the loan files.

"I don't know your knowledge of what happens in there, but I am pretty sure they make fake tax returns and find old Sunbiz records, then pay the fee to re-incorporate them to show the company has been in business for longer than two years. I would even say many applicants don't even own a legitimate business, they just go to Jerry's place, and the guys coach them on obtaining different kinds of loans!

"Now, before we got here, Sarah was Jerry's favorite banker. She would do anything he asked. Who knows, she might have even blown him. Wouldn't surprise me."

"Is that why you were putting the heat on Dann on the way here about her?"

"Kind of, but I know he gives you a hard time, so I decided to give it back to him a little. But back to the fraud. In order for Harry to look good with the national executives of the bank, he had to promote Sarah even though many other bankers have more credit knowledge than she does. Have you asked her any credit-specific questions? If you did, you'd realize she doesn't know shit. She's just willing to bend the rules for Harry.

"Anyway, Harry came in here to hire 'his' people. He knows he can't come in and clean house of bankers that have been here over ten years and are average producers. So he needs to bring in easily corruptible people to be high producers and take over. Unfortunately, Jac, you are one of his people, and you didn't do what he was expecting—closing business no matter the means. He most likely wrote you up to get rid of you because you don't play ball his way. He made it known in my year-end review that he is not happy with me either, but I have done enough production to be safe for this year at least."

Still trying to absorb all of this, I asked, "What about Rosie and Naomi?"

"You mean why did he hire them? Because they are women. He couldn't hire an all-male team. Plus, especially Rosie, if she is just an average producer, he probably will promote her to manager as it looks good for him. And he'll try to get a blow job out of her too."

"You know he has sex with female staff?"

"Absolutely! At our previous bank, there was a huge human resource investigation. It uncovered that he received sexual favors for promoting different women when some males were more qualified for the job. That's the real reason he left the previous bank. He's made it clear he wants to become the bank's national leader. In that role, he'll make millions in stock option bonuses, among other compensation factors. He doesn't care what kind of business is being done. He just wants the numbers on the board for the corporate executive suite to see, so he gets his promotion."

"Why now? Why are you telling me all this now?"

"Because I wanted to see your integrity first. I had a good inclination of what it was before, but until I heard what happened with you and Jerry's team and now that you are on written notice, I thought it would be a good time to let you know."

"What do you think I should do now?"

"Either you give up, or you decide to compete. I don't see you being a quitter, Jac. But if you're going to compete, you need to develop a strategy and not conduct fraud like the rest of them. Because with what you're doing now, well, you'll be looking for a new job in a few months."

"I'm not going to give up. I never have in my life, and I don't plan on it now. I want to win. After seeing all those fuckers win those awards, I feel a burning desire to win!" I paused, then said, "What if I told you I do have a strategy? It's partnering with a good friend of mine who has connections to executives who do business with Brazil's government. They want U.S. banking services such as deposit accounts and possibly mortgages to buy vacation or investment properties."

"No way! That is awesome! Sounds like a gravy train to me if you can execute it."

"I am going back to Brazil next month to meet with my friend, and he is going to introduce me to his bosses."

Tim hollered out an alcohol-infused, "Fuck yeah!"

We pulled up at Tim's house moments later. He leaned over to my side of the car and hugged me. Then he drunkenly confessed, "I love you, man; I trust this conversation doesn't leave this car ride."

The following week, I received a forwarded email from Harry that contained the San Diego banker's contact information—Jose DeCastro. I emailed him and asked when was a good time that I could call him. He responded immediately, and I called him at the time that suited him.

After explaining the reason for my call, Jose realized I had no clue what I truly was getting myself into. He decided to cut the corporate jargon and shoot straight.

"I'm going to come clean with you. What I do, well, I don't brag about it. Those I deal with in Mexico can be some dangerous people, and they want their identities to remain private. This is why I help them create LLCs in Nevada or Delaware. I chose those two states because the actual owners of the LLCs are hidden from the general public. Usually, I work with an attorney to help them layer companies.

For example, an LLC might be the owner of a C-corp. This makes sure the identity of the owner is difficult to identify.

"When I open the accounts, we are supposed to run all the account signatories' names through the Office of Foreign Assets Control list. Well, a lot of Mexicans have middle names or have two last names. I play around with the names to ensure that nothing comes up. If their name doesn't pop up, I'm clear to open the account.

"If an alert comes up after the fact, I just make sure I clear it with a detailed explanation. So many alerts come up at this bank, there is no way someone sitting in a black hole cubicle can handle them. So don't stress if you receive alerts because you probably will. I have a don't ask, don't tell policy with my foreign clients. Don't ask where the money came from, and they won't tell you.

"Finally, I have created a nice network of professionals in San Diego to provide a robust menu of services for these clients. I work with real estate agents for the clients that want to purchase a house—these agents refer me to their other clients for loans and accounts. I work with accountants who help with the Mexican national's LLC's tax returns. And, as I mentioned before, I work with an attorney that is versed in corporate and international taxation, and I refer my Mexican clients to him."

Jose paused, and I took a moment to thank him for all the information. "Jose, this is incredible information! I really appreciate you taking time out of your busy day to explain all of this to me. What about non-resident mortgages? I heard we do that as well."

"Oh yes, if the individual is a DMNC Bank client in Mexico, or Brazil in your case, for at least a year and has a good standing, we can lend sixty percent loan to value on a mortgage for a second residence for them. Be creative in how you intend to show it as a second residence."

"Gotcha. Anything else I should know?"

"I think I gave you a good start. If you have specific questions later, please let me know. But if I can give you a piece of advice, don't approach them as though you will only help them open a U.S. bank account. Go to them and sell yourself as their American partner.

"As I mentioned, they are going to need more services here in the U.S.; if you can introduce them to people that you do business with and can help them, you will be an indispensable asset to them. From there, you can enrich yourself by obtaining referrals from them for their family and friends.

"I don't know if Harry told you, but I do not work in a bank branch anymore. I work in the office headquarters here in downtown San Diego. I make my own hours, have my own assistant to help with service and paperwork, and haven't made a cold call in two years. If you can create a niche like I did, your work-life balance will be pretty sweet in time—not to mention the hefty quarterly bonuses that come along the way."

Right after the call with Jose, I called Rodrigo. I told him I'd be booking my flight to São Paulo, and I wanted to confirm that I'd meet his boss.

TWENTY-ONE

When I informed Mariana about my banking trip to São Paulo, she was not thrilled. Oddly, she asked all these questions about why I was going and if I was working with the Miami Business Consultants.

While convincing her of the reasons I needed to go, I made a mistake. I mentioned some of the information Tim told me in the car ride back from the Celebration of Achievement night. I told her that it was a "known fact" that many bankers engaged in fraudulent activities to inflate their production numbers. My choices were to quit and lose, or dig deep, regroup, and try to find ways to manipulate the game to my advantage to win in the future.

My accidental slip about fraud deepened her disdain for Dann and The Banker Gang. She was pretty disgusted by what people would do to be successful in the eyes of others.

Mari was also disgusted in her life in general; she was still technically living in the United States as an illegal immigrant, working illegally, driving illegally, and waiting ever so patiently for our marriage interview at the immigration office so she could obtain a work authorization again. Apparently, there was a mix-up within immigration services between the Doral attorney submitting a petition on her old case and the new Fort Lauderdale attorney's petition for our marriage. But I couldn't be bothered to help sort it out; I had bigger fish to fry, and after agreeing to refund another couple of her checking account overdrafts and call her three times per day, I was on my way to Brazil.

After I retrieved my baggage, I found Rodrigo punctually waiting for me at the airport exit. Unlike the last time he picked me up, he was straight business. "Hey Joey, are you ready for this? Let's go over what services you can offer."

I spent the rest of the car ride back to his house relating the services DMNC Bank USA could offer the PetroBrasil executives. I mostly reiterated what the San Diego Banker, Jose, told me a couple of weeks prior. Rodrigo sounded impressed with how prepared I was. For every question he asked, I provided an answer.

Rodrigo showed me to my room in the guest house on his family's property, "Joey, I am super excited! We are going to make some dinero, my friend! Okay, you know we are going to charge them a fee for our services? I was thinking of settling at ten percent of the amount they want to send over to the U.S.—I think it is fair that five percent goes to you and five percent goes to me."

I stoically sat on the bed and processed this information, balancing it with figuring out ways not to get caught. Reluctantly I said, "That sounds good, but I don't know how I can accept those funds as I am financial securities licensed, and I have to submit my outside business dealings and brokerage account statements."

A sly smile widened across Rodrigo's face. "My friend, you seem to forget what we opened two years ago—the Swiss bank accounts."

Oh, how could I forget about the bank account that already had cost me $1,500 in fees! The bank account I had not used at all!

My eyes grew wide. "Oh yeah. I completely forgot about that! It would be nice to replenish all the funds lost to fees!"

"Replenish? The goal is to have six digits in there soon!"

"Six digits? Like a hundred thousand what? Pieces of rice?"

"You really don't understand how things work, do you? These executives receive millions of dollars worth of kickbacks from the contractors. They need a place to put their funds outside of Brazil with someone they can trust. We charge them a nice service fee that is wired directly to our Swiss bank accounts. Remember, those accounts are identified only by a number and not our names. Bingo."

Rodrigo had the whole thing planned out. All I needed to do was carry the ball from the one-yard line into the endzone without fumbling. He handed me the house cordless phone, "Oh, don't let me keep you. I am sure you need to call your Princess back home. Tell her I say hello."

The next morning we rose with the sun. We showered, dressed, ate, and headed out to Avenida Paulista to the São Paulo headquarters of PetroBrasil, where Rodrigo worked since the previous summer. I couldn't feel nervous about the meeting because, on the ride over, I was too busy grabbing onto the car's internal handles as Rodrigo played Frogger, weaving in and out of the heavy traffic through the robust city streets.

When we arrived in one piece, we took the elevator to the top floor of the building. Although the view wasn't as magnificent as the top of the Edificio Italia building, it was pretty sweet to see all the high-rise structures surrounding the downtown area.

Rodrigo was noticeably nervous, no joking on the ride over, and he was pure business when we walked into his office. He told me to wear jeans and a button-down as people like to handle business more casually in Brazil. He warned me not to discuss business right away, saying, "Brazilians like to bullshit first, maybe three-quarters of the meeting is pure bullshit, then the last quarter is where the business dealings get discussed. Keep a calm attitude, make sure you nod your head yes a lot, and look trustworthy."

Look trustworthy?

I wasn't sure what he meant by that, but I was cleanly shaven and wore exactly the attire he instructed. I also brought some DMNC Bank pens and pads to give away, and I had a notebook so that I could write down anything important.

Rodrigo left me in reception for a bit when we arrived, he then retrieved me, and while escorting me to his boss's office, he whispered to me, "Don't speak unless spoken to. Just think you are serving for the match, hit the shots you need to hit, don't take unnecessary risky shots."

As if my head wasn't already spinning.

Rodrigo's serious face brightened and plastered on a fake smile as he introduced me to his boss.

His boss shook my hand and said, "Jacob, very nice to meet you. I am Leonardo, but please call me Leo. Thank you so much for coming to visit with us. How was your trip? Rod tells me you live in Miami? Do you speak any Portuguese?"

I looked Leo right in the eye and firmly shook his hand. I replied, "Uh, yes, very nice to meet you. I do live in Miami. No, I don't speak Portuguese but learned some Italian previously. This is actually my second visit to Brazil." I paused.

What are you doing? Stop rambling about nonsense. Get to the point.

"Um, but yeah, I like it a lot here."

Leo proceeded to ask about my family, where I grew up, how Rodrigo and I met, and then wanted to know more about our tennis experiences. He asked all these questions about which racquet he should purchase, the string tension, the shoes. You name it, and he asked what he should do.

I tried to stay quiet and let Rodrigo answer the questions, but Leo asked me many questions directly. I really wanted to ask him some questions, but I followed Rodrigo's directive and didn't take unnecessary risky shots.

After about thirty minutes of seeming nonsense, Leo and Rodrigo started speaking in Portuguese. I sat still and tried to look as if I was listening intently.

Rodrigo turned to me and said, "Leo wants to start asking about your banking services. But he feels more comfortable speaking in Portuguese as it can be technical and wants to understand exactly. I'll translate."

After some back and forth between Rodrigo and Leo, I was asked how I could help. I said, "I understand that you want banking services in America; however, I am here to offer myself to be your American partner. My goal is to help you set up accounts in the United States through entities that make your identity private. I also want to offer you the opportunity to invest in real estate properties for investment purposes or as a vacation residence for you and your family or friends. I plan to find trustworthy Portuguese-speaking American partners that I can introduce you to as well. Ideally, you would have a suite of professionals working for you, a cross-border corporate attorney, an accountant, a real estate agent, and me, your personal banker."

Wow!

As that rolled off my tongue, I felt more confident with each and every word. Although I tried to practice my spiel in front of the mirror like Chicklet Don, I couldn't keep a straight face, so I went over what I wanted to say in my head. I have to admit it came out better than I could've imagined.

I looked over at Rodrigo, and he almost gave me a wink. I could tell we were in.

Leo had many more detailed questions about what I initially offered. But Rodrigo and I consistently answered all of Leo's questions, and we convinced him that we were trustworthy partners; we could help him move his funds offshore.

I suggested he open a DMNC Bank Brazil account so he could move funds back and forth between his accounts once I linked them up. He replied that he'd had an account there for some time. I then gave him details about our international mortgage program and suggested he'd qualify easily. He ate it all up and directed me to open the account immediately. I asked him how much he wanted to send for an initial deposit.

He said, "Um milhão."

"One million...dollars?" I asked, slightly shocked.

"Isso." He replied with a nod of his head.

Rodrigo then started talking to him in Portuguese. After a bit of back and forth, they stood up and shook hands. I followed suit and shook Leo's hand.

Leo informed me that if I did an excellent job with him, I could help many other executives throughout the company.

Rodrigo directed me to sit in the waiting area for a bit. Then after he chatted with Leo a bit longer, he ushered me toward the elevator and then to his car. "Holy shit, bro! That was amazing! Joey, you are one sweet talker. Where the hell did you learn all of that in such a professional tone? Whatever. Who cares where you learned it! We just made $25,000 each!"

"What!" I exclaimed in disbelief.

"Yeah, after you left, I negotiated our service fee. We settled at five percent, but I know I can get more in the future if this goes smoothly. Leo wants you to open a personal account. He also wants you to help him set up an LLC and open an account in that name as well. Then he wants you to find a condo in Miami for him to purchase. You can write the mortgage for him as well. How quickly can you get this done?"

Dumbfounded, I could barely think straight. I said, "Uh, I don't know."

Holy shit, I didn't even get his ID or any information to open the account! Shit! Shit! Shit!

"Um, I just realized I might have screwed up a little." I winced and said, "I forgot to get all the information from Leo that I need to get these all set up. Like his ID and contact information, among other compliance shit."

"Oh, that's not a problem. You tell me what you need from him, and I'll get it for you. I need to earn my half as well! One more thing, you're going to need to learn some Portuguese."

"What? Why? You already made me learn Italian."

"Oh yeah, and how did that go for you? You got to bang an Italiana hottie!"

He had a point. "Okay, fine. I'll find a tutor."

"Great! Oh, by the way, what did you tell Dann about coming here?"

I quickly replied, "I told him there was this amateur international tennis tournament that you invited me to."

"Nice one, I like that. You better have brought your racquet because I'm kicking your ass later. But for now, you know what this calls for? A sexy massage. Oh yeah!"

The rest of my visit was filled with early morning tennis sessions, eating too much with Rodrigo's family while he was at the office, and late-night dancing while drinking caipirinhas.

I pared my daily required calls to Mari from three to two. I told her I was on official bank business—I figured one hour a day counted.

When I returned to Miami, I immediately called the San Diego Banker, Jose. I went over what I was trying to do, and he gave me exact directions for what was vital to do to get it done properly. I sent him a $100 gift card for his help. He told me he appreciated the gesture and that he'd be around if I had to contact him again.

Rodrigo retrieved all the information required from Leo to get his personal account open. Once I opened Leo's account, I let him know I linked his DMNC Bank Brazil account so that he could transfer funds.

After that, Google was my best friend as I searched for local Brazilian accountants, attorneys, and real estate agents. Most of them were listed in the Deerfield Beach area. One afternoon, I told Sal I had official bank business to attend to. I made the near-hour drive north and met with a few people on the same day.

Initially, I wasn't clear about the reasons I inquired about their services; I wanted to wait to share details until after I interviewed and selected them for my new team. I had specific questions about their knowledge around corporation initiation law, international taxation, and international real estate buyers, among other topics.

It seemed most of these guys had a solid education here or in Brazil and set up a niche helping Brazilian immigrants navigate life here in America. I hired an attorney to set up a Delaware LLC for Leo. I hired a real estate agent to look for good investment condos, and I knew which accountant I would use when needed.

I reported my work back to Rodrigo. He was encouraged by my progress, and Leo was ecstatic at how quickly I made my promise a reality. Rodrigo, of course, didn't let me forget to sign up for Portuguese lessons. He dangled a carrot—when I could put a few sentences together, I could visit again, and he would introduce me to more executives.

I logged on to Craigslist and searched for a Portuguese tutor. I found an ad by a University of Miami student. I contacted her, and she asked if I could meet her at the university library the following week, one day after work. I obliged.

On the scheduled day, I hopped in my car, tossed my tie in my back seat, lowered the car windows, and blasted Shakira's "My Hips Don't Lie." I couldn't help think of Rosie's hips swaying back and forth.

After a few miles on US-1, I was in Coral Gables, entered the UM campus, and headed toward the library. My neck was on a swivel as I checked out all the attractive coeds gracing the campus. I walked into the library, noticing my hair was probably a mess from the car ride.

I was trying to flatten it down, and I heard, "Hi...Jacob?"

I turned to my right, and a young woman stood up from one of the tables. She took a few steps and greeted me, saying, "*Oi Jacob, prazer. Meu nome é Flavia. Tudo Bem?*"

I sort of knew what she was saying, so I responded in my Italian, "*Piacere Flavia. Si, mi chiamo Jacob. Come stai oggi?*"

She offered me a semi-surprised look and replied, "*Você falo Italiano*?"

"*Si*, I lived in Italy for nine months a couple years ago, and I took Italian lessons with a tutor."

Flavia's hair was a disaster. It was a mixture of two colors, put up in a bun so tangled that bees might have mistaken it for a hive if I put some honey on there. She wore an oversized t-shirt that did her no favors, and her sweat pants were baggy.

I think she has a nice derriere under those sweats. Isn't that what Brazilian women are known for?

She sat down and said, "So, Jacob, what makes you want to learn Portuguese?"

"I have a friend; actually, he's the one that had me learn Italian. But anyways, he's Brazilian and lives in São Paulo. We are trying to do some business together, and he told me it would be helpful to be able to put a few sentences together to gain credibility with some of his clients."

She smiled and replied, "That is pretty cool. I'm actually from São Paulo. Crazy city, huh?"

I noticed she had a cute smile, but I kept my gaze on her light brown eyes. I said, "Oh my, yes, the traffic is absolutely crazy. The city is ginormous! I don't know—I don't think I could live there. I'm surprised you're from there; you don't have an accent."

"Yeah, I've been here for the past twelve years and speak English ninety percent of the time. Almost all my friends are Americans, which I prefer, to be honest."

Interesting, should I ask why? Or is that too personal?

"Why is that?"

She said, "I just wanted to embrace the American culture and be successful here. Also, in my opinion, Brazilians can be shady. I just like to keep my distance. That's all." She sighed then asked, "So Jacob, tell me, how often do you want to meet? I think we can have you speaking decently in a couple of months if you already speak a little Italian. A number of the words are similar with a different pronunciation."

"I think once per week for an hour is good. Would you be able to meet me downtown at all? Not that it's a huge issue, but traffic can get ugly during rush hour trying to get here."

"Sure, I don't see a problem with that." Flavia opened up her Portuguese book, then she got up and moved her chair next to mine to start my first lesson.

Game on.

Initially, I didn't tell Mari I was signing up for Portuguese lessons.

What if the tutor was terrible, or I decided not to move forward with it? Why have that possibly difficult conversation if nothing came of it?

However, I was confident Flavia would be a good tutor for me, and I committed to seeing her right after work, once per week. The following week on the day of my tutoring session, I got into my car and called Mari. I told her I was meeting a Portuguese tutor for lessons now that my banking business included working with PetroBrasil executives. I left out the fact that my tutor was a UM female.

She was less than thrilled and said, "I don't think Portuguese is important. I can teach you Spanish. I can be your private tutor Jacob!" She paused, then said, "Anyways, I had some automatic debits come out of my account before I deposited my tip money. Can you refund the couple of overdrafts that hit my account the past week? I love you, Jacob!"

"Sure, Mari. I'll talk to you later."

This time I met Flavia at Bayfront Park. I barely recognized her when she approached me. She'd dyed her hair blonde and had it ironed straight, ending right past her jawline. She wore tight jeans that highlighted her sexy bubble butt and athletic legs. And she wore a white halter top that hugged her midsection. My face must have shown my surprise.

She greeted me by saying, "Hey Jacob. Oh, you didn't think I could clean up like this?"

She nailed it. I smiled widely and couldn't think of what to say for a few moments. I thought of Rodrigo and tried to think what he would say. I said, "Yeah, I am pleasantly surprised. You are looking good. I love what you did with your hair."

"Aw, that's too sweet, Jacob." She hugged me, and we headed over to a restaurant to sit down.

After the hour was up, we decided to walk over to a different bar and have a couple of drinks. She started asking questions about my life. I admitted that I had a Colombian girlfriend. She wished me luck with that and inferred Mari was probably a bit crazy. I didn't necessarily disagree. But she did make it known she was newly single and apparently ready to mingle.

TWENTY-TWO

I kept my head down as the next two months flew by. Besides working, spending time with Mari, and weekly tutoring with Flavia, I decided to join the local tennis league. I had matches at least two nights per week.

Noticing that I needed to increase my endurance level, I started running five miles a day, three days a week. I also drank less. I was on my way to losing the rookie fifteen pounds that I gained the previous year. Every week, I felt stronger and played better down the stretch.

In addition to feeling better physically, my professional life was improving. Leo from PetroBrasil decided to buy a condo and wire more funds into the account. I hired a Deerfield Beach real estate agent on Leo's behalf, and I provided a mortgage for the condo purchase. He was so satisfied with my service that he referred me to another executive, and I set up accounts for him with Rodrigo's help.

Due to the influx of Brazilian business, Harry took me off my written performance improvement plan. However, he also said that he'd put me right back on if I didn't keep this up, but with only three months' notice this time. He also canceled our weekly performance reporting call with Sal. That is what satisfied me most—no more questioning what I was doing every waking hour of the workday, and most importantly, no more weekly cold calling sessions, just monthly like everyone else.

Being so busy, I neglected my social life a bit. I still went out with Mari on the weekends when she wasn't working and, more often than not, had happy hour with Flavia after our session, but other than that, I hadn't even hung out with The Banker Gang or even Dann much recently.

But it was time for the monthly happy hour, and I felt that I should show my face since it had been so long. Or it could've been the fact that this happy hour was at the Clevelander pool bar on South Beach. I couldn't miss that one, right? I even convinced Tim to attend—he'd been more absent than me.

When I told Mari about the Clevelander happy hour, she was excited and, of course, practically invited herself. The plan was to have a true happy hour—without drama. But, of course, that would be too simple.

Dann and I went home after work, changed into some shorts, and took the causeway over the Biscayne Bay to South Beach. We were the first to show up and made our way around the bean-shaped pool in the middle of the outside patio area. We grabbed a seat at the bar facing Ocean Drive.

I was in the middle of texting Mari as YAO Steve and Chicklet Don showed up. "YAOOO," was now our standard greeting, as it sounded so appropriate. After the YAOOO hellos, Dann pumped out his narcissistic spiel. Yada, yada, yada. He pronounced that he was confident he'd be promoted out of the branch to be a business banker.

During his monologue, Mari entered the Clevelander, and we all greeted each other. After saying hi to Mari, Dann picked up where he left off, talking about the new pieces of business he already closed and was about to close soon.

Mari, overhearing Dann's bragging, rolled her eyes at me. I slowly closed my eyelids as if I was falling asleep. She shot me a sly look—a look I hadn't seen recently, and my stomach got really warm. Maybe it was the alcohol, or maybe it was my intuition telling me something was going to happen.

Mari cut Dann off mid-sentence, wiggled herself into the middle of us guys, and said, "Dann, isn't everyone sick of your shit talk?"

She looked around at all of us, and I froze like a mannequin.

She continued, "You know your shit stinks like everyone else here. Some humble pie would do you just fine! By the way, we all know you are getting fed some shady business, probably from your girlfriend, Sarah Stanley!"

Dann was stoic but shook his head in disgust. Dann loved to brag, but one thing he didn't like was a face-to-face verbal dispute. He backed down from the short fiery Colombian woman.

Mari quickly walked away and ran to hug Tim as he entered the establishment. I followed Mari over to Tim and greeted him.

Then I pulled Mari aside for a quick second and asked, "What are you doing? We both know what you said is true, but we are trying to have a good time without the drama! Why do you have to cause drama when it is unwarranted?"

"Jacob, I have to disagree with you here. This *is* warranted. He's never put in his place. He thinks he can talk shit wherever and to whomever. If no one else was going to speak up, I wanted everyone to know I would."

I rolled my eyes. The Latina fire was burning, and I didn't engage further. I didn't want to get burned.

A few minutes later, Pierre, Tall Ward, and Naomi showed up. Our crowd broke into two clumps. One group bragged about business, and the other group was Mari, Tim, Ward, Naomi, and me. It looked like the drama had blown over for the night, but I knew things wouldn't be easy at home for a while on the nights Mari stayed over.

MICHAEL G.

To: Jacob.Gilbert@aol.com; DannThaMann@aol.com; RGosta@hotmail.com
From: Jennifer.Russell@UF.edu
Date: Sunday, May 28, 2006; 10:24 AM
Subject: Patriotic Jax Reunion

Ciao Ragazzi,
Guess what? I just finished my second year of law school; only one more left! Anyways, I am spending this summer working an internship in Jacksonville, but will be staying in my parents' bungalow on Jax Beach. I want to invite you for the 4th of July weekend! I hope y'all can make it! Yay.

Baci, Jen

TWENTY-THREE

June flew by even faster than the prior months. I maintained the routine of work, tennis league, running, Portuguese lessons, and Mari sprinkled in whenever we both had time.

Our relationship wasn't great, but it wasn't terrible either. With a lump in my throat, I asked what she was doing for the 4th of July weekend. She said she was working.

Score!

When I thought the time was right, I let her know that Dann and I were invited to Jacksonville for the long weekend for another reunion. A major argument ensued, and we didn't speak much for the last week of June. I kept Dann in the dark about the fight.

Dann and I hadn't hung out in a while. I made it clear I didn't want to hear his feelings about Mari, and he told me that he started dating someone he met at one of the Coconut Grove bars.

Is this just a cover story to hide the fact that he's secretly sleeping with Sarah? But I don't have any proof. Still, I don't see Dann actually dating a chick he met at a Coconut Grove bar.

During the five-hour drive north on I-95 in Dann's Beamer, we didn't converse much. Mostly we listened to some chill music, getting ready for a few days on the sand with a beer in hand at all times. Unfortunately, Rodrigo couldn't make it, so the three of us shared a two-bedroom, one-bathroom bungalow a few steps from the beach.

We showed up mid-day on Saturday, July 1st. Jen was excited to see us and to express her patriotic feelings, she decorated the exterior of her bungalow with about fifty American flags. She greeted us both with a big hug and told us to get ready for some fun.

The next three days were filled with bike riding along Ocean Boulevard, beach time, house parties, and lots of drinking. My liver wasn't used to all the drinking as I prioritized being healthy the previous few months.

Right before heading out to see the fireworks that Tuesday, I went to Jen's room to retrieve something from my overnight bag. She snuck up behind me as I bent over and gave me a nice ole kick in the booty. She wasn't smiling. She shut her door. I was befuddled and gave her a look of confusion.

"Jacob, are you a fucking idiot? I mean, you always came across as a smart guy, but I have to think you are a fucking idiot! I know you're married to Mariana!"

My first reaction was a desire to vehemently deny, deny, deny. I considered doing that, but I didn't.

"Dann told you?" I asked.

"Yes, he told me awhile back, but I didn't believe him. Then when you were out for a run the other day, he went on my laptop and pulled up the public records in Dade County showing you married her a year ago. On Valentine's Day, too, you jackass! JACOB! Do you know how serious this is?"

"What do you mean? How serious is this? And why is Dann telling everyone?"

"I just took a class on immigration law. If you petition her to be your spouse, you are legally responsible for her for the next ten years! She cannot go on state aid, which means you will be financially responsible for her. What about the debts she accumulates while you are married? Well, you are responsible for that too—because I'm sure you didn't sign a prenuptial agreement!"

My heart stopped. I stared at the tiled floor at the foot of the bed. Jen's arms extended as wide as they could go.

She asked, "So what are you going to do?"

"I don't know. Probably kick the shit out of Dann for opening his big pie hole about this to everyone!" I stood up from the bed, towering over the 5'1 Jen.

She looked up at my face, right into my eyes, and said, "Jacob! Wrong answer. This is serious. Have you had your interview with immigration yet?"

"No." I broke the eye contact and looked away to my right.

"Before you sign anything else or go on that interview, make sure you call me first! I need to be your legal representation from now on. Ugh! Promise me." She grabbed my hands and pleaded, "Promise me you will, Jacob."

"I promise," I uttered with slight embarrassment.

TWENTY-FOUR

I made it through the rest of the Jacksonville trip, and the next few weeks passed relatively uneventfully.

One day as I walked out of my bedroom, Dann said, "I know why you're going to Brazil again." Dann sunk into the leather couch while he sipped his Pepsi and bit into his strawberry Pop-Tart.

I hadn't spoken to Dann too much over the past month as I couldn't decipher if he were genuinely untrustworthy or if he was trying to look out for me by forewarning me of the impending risk of marrying an illegal immigrant.

However, this comment completely caught me off guard. He knew I was getting a quick drink from the fridge and was heading out the door in seconds to go to work. His comment froze me while my head was in the fridge. After a deep breath, I slowly grabbed a bottle of water, closed the refrigerator door, and turned around to lean on the center island countertop in the kitchen.

"Oh yeah? What did you hear?" I responded after a few seconds.

"That you are opening big accounts from some executives in Brazil. I'm sure Rodrigo is introducing you," he said.

I pursed my lips and gently nodded. I was more angry than anything but felt a need to understand exactly who he'd it from. I asked, "Did Harry tell you something?"

Dann chuckled and said, "Nah, Sarah told me. Harry probably told her. I guess she noticed that you weren't on written performance warning anymore. I don't care what you are doing. I'm just glad you aren't going to get fired for poor production. Don't worry; I won't tell anyone. Get a sexy massage for me! Cheers." He lifted his Pepsi and took a chug. "Oh, and don't forget to call your Princess three times a day, Joey!" he said with a snicker.

As expected, Mari flew into a tantrum when I told her I was going back to Brazil, especially when I told her I'd only be able to call once or twice a day. However, she settled down when I again agreed to pay her overdrafts.

Rodrigo needed me in Brazil. Leo wanted to introduce me to his boss and a couple of other executives to help them with their U.S. banking needs. They also wanted to discuss pumping more money through the accounts to purchase more condos in Miami.

I knew the drill—Rodrigo picked me up, drove like a madman through the heavily traffic streets of São Paulo, and I was there to play my part. We met with three higher-level executives who wanted to send over $5 million in USD each within the next few months.

Although I didn't pay too much attention to the AML, BSA, KYC training, I knew this could become a compliance issue. I made a mental note to discuss it with Jose and Harry before I did anything.

Disregarding my concerns and lack of excitement, Rodrigo was calculating our service fee before we could even get back into his Peugeot. We also discussed their desire to purchase two or three investor condos—one would be coded as a secondary residence for mortgage purposes. Rodrigo asked me how much the current real estate agent earned on the two condos we already purchased for Leo and his friend.

After hearing my answer, he exclaimed, "That fucking realtor made $30,000 for basically doing nothing? You need to do something about that, Joey."

"What do you want me to do? I can't get a real estate license because I am in a regulated job, meaning I can't earn anything on those transactions. Basically, this agent owes me big time."

"Owes you? What? A blowjob? C'mon, man!" He paused, then said, "Wait a minute. How about having Mari get her real estate license and run it through her name?"

I took a deep breath and answered, "Mari is illegally living in the U.S."

"Oh yeah, you married her for her to stay." He started laughing.

As his laughter subsided, he smacked me in the arm while wearing a sly grin and asked, "What about your Portuguese tutor?"

I started semi nodding my head and replied, "*Isso. Eu acho que vai funcionar.*" I think this one can work.

"Well, it seems she's doing a good job teaching you Portuguese! Is she hot?"

"Yep. She's pretty good. Real nice ass."

"Oh yeah! Okay, get on that. I want her to get a real estate license to help these executives buy more condos. Then we can earn more service fees. Plus, wouldn't she be ecstatic to earn money for practically doing nothing! Oh yeah! Do you know what time it is, my friend?" He winked at me.

I arrived back in Miami around nine in the evening on a Thursday. Mari had class, so I took a taxi back to the apartment. My mind was spinning, but I was exhausted. I needed to contact San Diego Jose and Harry to let them know of the new business I was landing and clarify what I needed to do.

I called San Diego first thing in the morning California time, hoping that Jose would be in the office; he was. I told him about the prospective clients and my concerns about the amount of money they wanted to send over. I asked him about running their names through the OFAC list, documenting the source of funds, and how I could complete the KYC in a way that would satisfy the bank's compliance department.

Jose congratulated me for landing the business and began to assuage my anxiety. He said, "Jac, you have to understand that the bank is so vast that there is no way the compliance department can look at all of the new accounts. Just make sure that you document that you ran their names through the OFAC list. If they happen to pop up on the list, drop one of their last names, or use a period after a middle initial. Basically, change their name just slightly enough that you will get a clear search.

"Then make sure your account opening documentation is on point. As for stating the source of funds, that is your prerogative. I mostly list my clients' source as income from real estate investments in Mexico or income from a small business. Be creative, but make sure you don't put the same source of funds for every account you open, or that could be viewed as a trend."

I thanked Jose again for his time and sent him a thank you email later in the day as well.

I called Harry directly after hanging up with Jose. He wasn't available; however, he called me back later that evening around six. I was about to hit the tennis court, but I flipped open my phone and walked off the court to take his call.

I wasted no time and immediately gave Harry an update, saying, "Harry, as you know, I returned from Brazil yesterday. This time I met three more senior executives. They all want to bring over five million dollars and are interested in mortgages to purchase secondary residences in Miami.

"I ran their names on the OFAC list, and one of them had a hit. However, I spoke to Jose, and he advised me to change his name just slightly, such as add a period or drop a last name so that the name would go through.

"Also, to comply with AML guidelines, I am supposed to document the source of funds. Jose also advised me to be creative about what businesses they could own in Brazil. I don't want to cause any trouble. What do you think?"

"I think this is a fabulous opportunity, Jacob. Not to mention, this will earn you a hefty bonus check if all of this comes to fruition as we are earning about four percent on non-interest-bearing deposit accounts these days, thanks to the Fed raising rates.

"I think what Jose advised is what you need to do. We cannot afford to lose this type of business for the district. Don't worry; I will play my part to keep compliance off your back as best as I can. Remember how far you have come this year. You started on a written performance improvement plan. Do you want to go back to that?"

So there was my answer, I play their game, or I don't have a job. That's simple.

However, playing the game helped my bank accounts nicely. I gave the green light to Rodrigo, and he obtained all the information I needed to establish the accounts. I contacted my attorney, who helped set up LLCs, and the new clients were on their way to sending their kickback money to my bank, with my name listed as account officer. It was time to find out how trustworthy Flavia was and convince her to obtain her real estate broker license.

After the next tutoring session, I suggested we go to dinner, my treat. Flavia dressed up for the occasion, looking sexy yet professional. As soon as I saw her that night, I knew she would fit the visual part we needed to play. I also knew she would fit the intelligence part. I just needed to find out if she would fit the trustworthy part.

I planned to get her tipsy. I wanted to learn her true character a bit more, and as the adage goes, "Drunken confessions are sober thoughts." I needed her to confess some of her sober thoughts—her true beliefs—on certain issues. This was my night to do it.

We started at the Fontainebleau Hotel lounge for happy hour. She was impressed. I don't think anyone had taken her to the prestigious hotel that had been around for fifty years. After two martinis, she was loose with her words. She no longer wore the conservative facade she had shown when she was the teacher, and I was her student. She babbled incessantly about university issues, and I barely listened. My eyes drifted out the window to the co-eds in bikinis around the pool. Flavia must have noticed my limited interest and paused for a moment.

I returned my gaze to her light brown eyes and big smile.

Semi-sober, she asked, "So is this a date? I am a little confused about why you've brought me to such an awesome place."

I decided to flirt a little and replied, "Do you want this to be a date?"

She smiled even wider and gazed out the window I'd just looked through. Then she brought her eyes back to me and said, "I remember you telling me you had a girlfriend. I don't know what you think of me, but I am not one of those girls. I have never, and would never."

I pulled back from the thick flirtation to a more businesslike tone and said, "I would never proposition you like that. I think highly of you, and I have enjoyed our time together. I appreciate your dedication to helping me learn Portuguese. Even times when I get tired, you keep pushing me to learn more. I really admire that about you. To answer your question, this *is* a date. But think of it as a business date."

Flavia gave me a perplexed look and said, "*Não entendo.*"

"What if I had an opportunity for you? You'd be working with me, and I'd introduce you to my Brazilian clients. Your job is to represent them as their real estate agent. You'd earn commission, however—"

"However what?" Flavia sat on the edge of her chair, grasping her martini glass, eagerly awaiting my response.

"Well, just that we would be partners. For any business I refer to you, I would expect to split the commissions with you. You would collect the whole amount at closing and then send me my cut via wire transfer later. I am coming to you with this opportunity because I know you have the capacity for this type of work. I just want to make sure you are comfortable working with me."

"So I will need to get my Realtor's license? Can I still attend university to obtain my degree?"

"Of course! You would still go to school full time. Yes, you would need to get your Realtor's license and work part-time with it. You probably won't have time to tutor—other than me. Does that sound like something you'd be interested in?"

"Hell yeah! I'd love to make more money without having to deal with all the creepers I tutor. I swear some of these dudes just want to learn Portuguese to come flirt with me. It's so annoying."

"Well, I'd be happy to let you know you won't have to deal with any more creepers. Well, for tutoring, at least. By the way, the real estate agent I used for the last two transactions earned around $30,000. So expect to earn about half that for the first two for yourself."

Flavia quickly rose to her feet in heels, almost spilling the last bit of her martini, and gave me a giant firm hug. She said, "Oh Jacob, this is awesome! *Obrigada muito, muito, muito!*"

Then she pulled away from the hug, took the last gulp of her martini, and planted a big wet kiss on my lips.

The next day, I told Rodrigo that Flavia was on board to be our real estate connection. She needed thirty days to get through the licensing program and take the exam.

He told me that once she passed, he wanted us both to come to Brazil so he could introduce her to Leo and the other executives. I agreed that would be a good idea.

I was in such a groove that I didn't have much time to think. I was busy with work, tennis, running, tutoring, and Mari. My sleep was taking a hit.

One morning the week of Labor Day, I walked into my branch like I always did. This time, Sal jetted from across the lobby to intercept me before I entered my office.

He whispered, "Jacob, I don't want to alarm you, but two representatives from the Corporate Ethics Department are sitting at your desk. They didn't tell me what this visit is about. But I wanted to let you know so you can take a minute to collect yourself and prepare."

"Thank you for the heads up, Sal. This can't be good, huh?" I raised my eyebrows, appearing to be calm, but I really wanted to break down as that pit in my stomach immediately loomed deeper than it had all year.

They caught me. They saw the shady accounts I was opening. And Harry, that asshole, he said he was going to shield me. Some fucking shield!

I casually strolled behind the teller line to the break room. I took some deep breaths as I paced around the circular table multiple times. The tellers must have thought I was possessed or something, but I couldn't be bothered by their thoughts at that moment. I finally sucked it up and walked into my office as friendly and confidently as I could.

"Hello, Mr. Gilbert. We are from Corporate Ethics. If you are not familiar with our group, we are responsible for investigating any behaviors that go against our bank's code of conduct. If you don't remember, you signed that code of conduct on your hire date. I have brought a copy of it."

The ethics dude plopped the copy of the "DMNC Golden Rules" on my desk. I made them believe I was reading it when in reality, my mind was going a mile a minute.

What could this be about? What Brazilian account did I mess up on? Or all of them? Am I getting fired?

I looked up from the "DMNC Golden Rules" and gave them a forced blank stare.

The Ethics dude continued, "So you are probably wondering why we are visiting you today."

I nodded. *Bingo.*

"Whenever there are abnormalities in accounts, we receive alerts. One account flagged for an abnormality belongs to Mariana Rodriguez. Do you know this individual outside of the bank?"

"Yes, I do. Please, abnormalities?" I asked as I raised my arms with opened palms.

"Basically, certain transactions on accounts alert us. In this case, the alert came because of the number of overdrafts refunded on this account within the past eighteen months. It looks like fifty-one overdrafts have been refunded for the amount of $1,530. It also is reported that you are the one that has refunded every one of them. Please explain what has happened here."

This shit is monitored? What is the arbitrary cutoff of refunding overdrafts, so I won't ever be on this report again?

I replied, "This person lost her job and has had significant financial hardships this past year. I tried to help her out. I didn't realize that overdraft refunds were monitored as I refund multiple overdrafts daily here."

Tell me why this account was alerted!

"This was a lot of overdrafts to refund. Since you know this person, refunding this customer clouds your judgment. Therefore, this could possibly be unethical."

I put my hands over my face and felt some emotion coming over me.

Is this it? All the training, the meetings, the late-night call sessions, the clawing, the finagling, the BULLSHIT I had to deal with the last two years, to be fired over overdraft refunds—for my woman?

"Mr. Gilbert, I understand that this might be hard for you, but when you signed the code of ethics, this puts a tremendous amount of ethical judgment on your shoulders. We believe, in this situation, you did not use that judgment in good faith. Therefore, we have to document this situation, and it will be put in your human resources file."

They slid a document over to me that needed my signature at the bottom.

I asked, "If I sign this, does this mean my employment is terminated?"

"Oh, Mr. Gilbert, it's not our business to determine that. Your manager has been notified, and the decision is Mr. Goldman's to make."

Sort of good news, I guess!

I signed the document and sent them on their way.

I realized I left my phone in the car and ran out of the branch as quickly as I could to get it. Sal called after me, but I ignored him. I flipped open my phone, and I had a missed call from Harry. My heart and stomach sank concurrently. I immediately pressed callback. The time it took him to answer his phone felt like an eternity, and my anxiety was eating me up.

Harry answered, and with his customary monotone, said, "Jacob. Good morning."

"I assume you heard about my visit with the corporate ethics people. I can't take the suspense any longer. Am I getting terminated?"

If I get fired, it will be impossible to obtain financial employment with an ethics complaint on my file!

"I am quite disappointed that you used your judgment like that. But if you were getting terminated, I would've been there. Nice job on the three new accounts with over $15 million in deposits. Stop doing stupid shit and get back to work." Click.

I stood in the parking lot for what seemed like an hour, which in reality was ten minutes. My heart was still pounding. The Florida sun induced sweat on my forehead and under my arms.

I almost let Mariana get me fired. How could I let her stupidity in mismanaging her account lead to her manipulate me to help her? I helped her with the marriage. I helped her with buying her things. I helped her with refunding over $1,500. What else is she sucking me dry for? How much longer can I take this manipulation?

For as much as I resented Mari at that point, I realized that I could've said "no" anywhere along the line. But I also realized if I did say no, a disagreement would have ensued, which likely would have escalated into a full-on fight.

I could just picture her saying, "*Porque,* Jacob? Don't you want to help me in my time of need? I don't know If I could be with someone if they can't help me. I know I would do anything for you."

Well, you know what, Mari, I don't need you for anything now, and maybe not in the future either!

That night I had a movie night planned with Mari. I decided not to blow up at her for the morning's events. Ultimately, I was the one that refunded all her overdraft fees, and that onus was on me. But she knew me, and I couldn't hide my discontent too long.

I picked her up from her apartment, and we were on our way to the movie theater. I had already eaten dinner, and Mari harped on about being hungry. Did she not understand that we were going to a movie and not dinner?

She said, "Oh Jacob, you know what I am in the mood for? I want an order of loaded bacon cheese fries at the theater."

"Loaded bacon cheese fries? I don't want that caloric nightmare." I promptly replied.

"Um, it's not for you; I said I wanted them!"

"So, you expect me to sit next to you while you devour cheese fries, and I have to use all my self-control not to eat them while the aroma busts through my nostrils? You know I am still trying to lose weight and get in better shape. I just think it's shitty for you to order that when I am asking you not to."

Mari borderline yelled, "Jacob, I never tell you what to eat! Don't tell me what I can and cannot have."

I started to yell as well, "Oh really? You never tell me what to do? Fuck that! You tell me what to do all the time, and you know if I don't go along, you give me such shit that it's not always worth the fight, so I do it! I'm like your personal servant. I even married you for the wrong reason, BECAUSE OF YOU!"

Mari, taken aback, asked, "What are you talking about?"

"All your bullshit! I can't take it anymore! You almost got me fired today! And everything is about what *you* want me to do! And I'm going to Brazil again. I'm taking my FEMALE tutor, and I'm not calling you a thousand times like you want!"

I gripped the steering wheel hard, imagining it was her neck.

"I almost got you fired? What are you talking about? You are really going to Brazil again? WHAT THE FUCK?" she screamed.

"I knew that was going to be your reaction, and I can't take it anymore! I'm done. This is over. I need my freedom back—and space!"

Mari started screaming at me. Then she started hitting my arm while I drove. She became an unhinged mixture of violently yelling and crying.

I turned the car around, basically kicked her out, and drove straight home. I walked into the apartment, totally ignored Dann, who was sunken on the couch as usual, and slammed my bedroom door shut. I paced aggressively around my bed. Pulling on my hair, I mumbled to myself about how much of a selfish bitch she was and how much worse my life was since she'd been in it. She was like a drug, and the hallucinogens were starting to wear off. I was beginning to feel the negative after-effects.

After smashing a photo frame she'd given me, with a picture of both of us inside, I opened my laptop and started writing. I didn't even know what I was writing about at first, but then it turned out to be a three-page document on why this breakup should be for good—all the fights we had, the reasons why she was harmful to me, and how much better my life would be without her. I wanted to give myself written proof to reference whenever I felt lonely and wanted to get back together with her in the future.

When I finished writing, I did the only thing I could think to do; I called Tim. I told him about the fight, how I almost got fired, how Mari had taken away my freedom manipulated me for two years. He agreed and gave me friendly advice. He told me to "stay strong," and that time heals all wounds.

I knew the next week would be difficult, but I double-checked that Flavia was sitting for her real estate exam. I planned on booking her on my next trip to Brazil the following week. Rodrigo set up meetings in São Paulo, and then we planned to fly to Curitiba to meet some more executives in that city.

Everything went as planned. Flavia passed the test, and she was ecstatic to return to Brazil for the first time in over five years.

Although my heart hurt from the break-up with Mari, Flavia was kind and understanding. She helped me see that Mari was selfish and manipulative and that not all women were like that. Flavia was patient with me, and if she broached a topic I wasn't comfortable talking about, she changed the subject quickly and let me know it was normal to have the feelings I was having.

Although she was barely twenty-one, she'd been in a three-year relationship with a guy and told me she broke up with him only a few months before I met her. She said the first few weeks after the split were hard for her too. She shared her struggles, and we bonded over relationship woes.

She also showed me something that Mari hardly did. She was appreciative of the opportunity I presented her—I knew she would be successful at nearly anything I asked of her. Flavia grew up modestly, and I also knew she was racking up close to a six-figure debt attending the private and generally affluent University of Miami. It was a rich kid school, and that was something Flavia's family was not. The opportunity to join into partnership with Rodrigo and me was her golden ticket, and she didn't take it for granted.

I also warned her about Rodrigo and the personalities of the executives we'd meet. She listened intently, but these were "her people," and she had a good idea of what powerful Brazilian men could be like.

I typically slept the whole flight to Brazil. However, I slept very little on this one as Flavia and I talked and connected during the flight. She even forced me to speak Portuguese on the plane.

Rodrigo picked us up, and because we had a lady with us, I asked him to tone down his driving, but that fell on deaf ears. We went from the Guarulhos section of the city to the west end of Lapa, weaving in and out. I thought Flavia would freak out, but she was surprisingly calm.

Rodrigo tested her and was pleased I prepped her well. The conversation bounced between English and Portuguese, and I understood a portion of it. Rodrigo was particularly excited about meeting with the Curitiba executives. He felt a bit of anxiety, but it paled in comparison to his enthusiasm. He told me that they were the big fish, and if we gained their business, our Swiss bank accounts would become much fatter—which reminded me to check the balance; I hadn't kept track of any of the payments wired into that account.

He showed us to our separate rooms in his mother's guest house. Then he told us to get ready for a São Paulo city tour for the rest of the day. I looked at Flavia with tired eyes, but she was super excited about it. I didn't want to be the party pooper, so we were on Rodrigo's time.

The next day, Rodrigo introduced Flavia to Leo and the two other men from the office we had helped earlier. Flavia wore a professional business skirt suit that accentuated her curves. The men in the office took notice, and they were curious about the reason for her presence, which led to introductions to more people in the office.

Only good things. Meeting more people will only bring good things.

I knew the executives would ask Flavia about the real estate market in the greater Miami area, so I had her read up all the information she could find. I also asked her to approach other real estate agents and ask questions as if interested in working for their agencies. We tested her knowledge and practiced her presentation before we left and on the airplane.

Our main concern was that real estate values were tapering off and even falling slightly as interest rates kept rising. We needed to convince the executives that Miami real estate was still a wise investment and that they wouldn't get hurt by falling values if they planned on holding it as a long-term investment, or in some cases, as a second home.

The next day we took the early flight to Curitiba. Rodrigo suggested that he and I wear full suits and Flavia dress the best she could. He was super nervous as we were about to meet with PetroBrasil's top management of southern Brazil. He kept repeating the same things—say this; don't say that. I glanced at Flavia, and she was calm, relaxed, and collected.

I had a track record of helping five other executives and had the proof to show these new execs what our services could do for them. But Flavia was the unknown—especially since she did not yet have any real estate sales under her belt. Rodrigo added pressure because he figured that if we won these executives over, we could possibly gain an introduction to the C-suite executives of the entire company in Rio de Janeiro. He said those people would introduce us to government officials and told us that's where we'd earn the juiciest fees.

We walked into the downtown office building and took the elevator to the top floor—I had a heavy chest and was short of breath the whole walk in. Nothing was said on the elevator nor while sitting in the waiting room.

Our potential clients were late by a good bit, but that was expected as everything in Brazil is tardy. Once they arrived, Rodrigo opened the dialog by thanking them for their time and began asking personal questions trying to get to know them better. Eight men were in the room, and Rodrigo was a mastermind at creating instant rapport—always a struggle for me; I often thought small talk was just a nice way to refer to bullshitting. However, it was functional in business, especially when establishing trust. Now, more than ever, solid trust needed to be built.

After half an hour of polite discussion about each others' lives, it was time to talk business. Rodrigo began by telling them how he worked for their company in China, how he'd worked for Leo in São Paulo, and how he met me. Then he explained how we teamed up to provide PetroBrasil executives with U.S. banking servicing, including legal, accounting, and real estate needs.

They were impressed, and I showed them some of the work we did for others, such as setting up LLCs, finding investor condos, and providing a few mortgages as well.

Then it was Flavia's turn. These guys were really interested in setting up LLCs for the purpose of owning Miami real estate. She worked the room like magic. As she stood to talk, all the men's eyes focused on her tightly fitted business suit. She started writing on the whiteboard like she did when she tutored me at times. Then she put up the numbers—how many condos were being built in Miami, how many were vacant, the year-over-year change in value. Eventually, she discussed the possibility of a slowdown in the real estate market, and she persuasively presented that this would be an excellent time to negotiate asking prices from sellers. If this was an at-bat playing baseball, she hit a home run!

I was impressed, and Rodrigo had a perma-smile on his face from the moment she started talking. She was literally like a professor teaching students about the current state of the real estate market with an entire SWOT analysis attached to it. She did her homework, and it showed.

When her presentation was complete, and she sat down next to me, I put my hand on her thigh and whispered, "*Parabéns! Você foi incrível!*"

She smiled and whispered back, "Do you think I have a perfect GPA from not being prepared?"

The executives didn't state at that moment that they'd use our services. However, their reactions gave us a good indication. I really think Flavia sealed the deal—they liked that a sharp Brazilian woman was part of the team. I guess we built just the amount of rapport we needed.

The rest of the day, we wandered around the city and drank countless caipirinhas. I loved the freedom of not needing to find a payphone to call Mari. Flavia was easy company, going with the flow. When we checked into the hotel for the night, I told Rodrigo that Flavia and I would share a room.

"One or two beds?" the hotel concierge asked.

I looked at Flavia, and she gave me a partially drunk seductive smile. She said, "One bed, *por favor!*"

After we both brushed our teeth and changed, I was physically lying on the bed watching TV, but my mind was elsewhere. Flavia came out of the bathroom wearing only a sexy bra and panty set. She crawled on top of me, and we started making out. Not long after, her matching undergarments were on the floor.

Just as we were leaving for the airport for our flights back to Miami, Rodrigo received a phone call from the lead executive of the Curitiba PetroBrasil office. All eight of them wanted to use our services. Rodrigo was ecstatic. Flavia was happy even though she didn't quite know what the news meant. I was also pleased, but something in my gut told me that this wasn't exactly legit. However, I played along like everything was fine; hell, I was becoming wealthy quite quickly for doing my job.

We returned late in the day. Flavia took a taxi to Coral Gables, and I hopped into one headed to my apartment building. I walked in the door and found Dann sunken into the couch, as usual, holding a Coors Light. I greeted him and proceeded to my room. I noticed that someone had been in my room—papers on my desk were out of place, and my laptop was open. I was almost sure it was closed before I left. I walked out of the room to ask Dann if he had been using my desk.

He responded, "Nope. But Mari came by when you were gone."

A little baffled, I responded, "Why would you let her in? I told you we broke up."

"How many times did you break up previously? How was I to know it would stick?"

I slowly closed my eyes.

He continued, "She was here for less than ten minutes and stormed out the door. Is this time for good?"

Holy shit, holy shit, holy shit! Mari read my monologue about all the reasons she is bad for me and why I needed to end things finally! SHE READ IT!

"Why? What's with that face, Joey?" Dann asked.

I smiled and said, "Let's just say I have a solid reason to believe that this breakup is for good."

"Amen to that! Cheers!" Dann chugged the rest of his beer, then proceeded to let out a loud burp.

The final quarter of 2006 passed like a flash. Between onboarding the eight new Curitiba executives accounts, arranging new LLCs, and working with Flavia to find them two condos each, I spent my free time sleeping.

However, Mari was always in the back of my mind. Although we spoke a couple of times during those last few months, I was pretty confident that things were over between us. Flavia and I still exclusively slept together, but we didn't consider ourselves in a relationship.

After many calls to the Swiss bank where I opened the account three years ago, I finally obtained online access. I first logged into the account between Christmas and New Year's Day, and my eyes popped open. I froze in astonishment. The balance was $312,786!

I also qualified for two quarterly bonuses from the bank for $17,500 each—the maximum—and would likely receive an annual bonus in the $25,000 range as well. I was oblivious to the amount of money funneling to me for just doing my job. Flavia even made close to $60,000 for a solid three months of work representing the executives on the condo purchases. Rodrigo let me know that some of the executives were paying a flat "wrap" fee and others paid a percentage based on assets transferred. I didn't care much, either way; all I knew was my secret bank account was growing at a spectacularly fast rate. Things were as good as they could've been as 2007 rolled in.

Flavia and I even celebrated our new success at Mansion Nightclub in South Beach with a robust $700 tab, and for the first time in my life, I didn't flinch when paying the bill.

TWENTY-FIVE

A few days after the New Year's holiday, when we all returned to work, I received a voice message on my phone. It was from Mariana, and immigration was ready to see us for our marriage interview. My heart and stomach sank at the same time again.

I didn't know what to do or say. I called Jen immediately, as promised, and let her know of the situation. She told me not to do anything and that she would connect with the head immigration attorney from the law firm she interned with last summer to obtain some helpful information on what to expect and what my options were. Mari called me every day for a few days, and I made sure not to be home when I thought she could show up at my door as I waited patiently for Jen's call back.

Jen called me back a few days later, and I answered it on the first ring.

She said, "Okay, Jacob. I spoke with the partner at the law firm I interned for—he headed up our immigration legal department. He explained that this interview is to prove to the immigration officers that your marriage is real. Most likely, they will take you into separate rooms and ask you the same questions to see if your relationship is real or a sham—"

Antsy, I cut her off, saying, "Well, it was a real relationship, and as you know, now it is not."

"I was just going to say that during this individual discussion with the immigration officer, you can explain to him or her your recent breakup. Let the person you're speaking with know you would like to cancel your marriage petition for Mari."

I took a deep breath, then said, "Ahhh, I don't know. Will she find out I did that?"

"I'm not sure, but it's not your concern anymore if you withdraw. Jacob! Wake up! If you don't do this now, you will be financially responsible for her for ten years! Have you even thought about getting legally divorced yet? Does she know your financial situation? She can go after any assets you have earned since you've been married!"

"Holy shit!" I said as I started yanking my hair.

"What?"

"Let's just say I've made a lot of money recently."

"Really? At the bank that almost fired you?"

"Yes, I'll explain it another time. If I do what you recommend, can you help me get divorced? I really don't want another attorney dealing with this messy situation."

"Yeah. But not now. I'm not technically an attorney. I sit for the bar exam in May. Do you want to wait that long?"

I shook my head then replied, "I don't know what to do anymore. Fuck!"

"You know what you need to do, buddy. I'm here to help. Good luck."

I finally returned Mari's calls. She asked me nicely if I would show up to the immigration interview, and I said yes. She gave me the time and place, and I tried to put the whole situation in the back of my mind until the date came a few weeks later.

The day came, and I met Mari at the downtown Miami immigration office. We greeted each other at the front door and walked in together—we didn't speak more than a couple of words to each other.

Surprisingly, we hardly waited to be seen. We were escorted back to an office, and a middle-aged immigration officer sat across from us at his desk. He looked over our file and the picture booklet that Mari put together over the time we spent together—we'd heard that proving your relationship was real helped the situation. He asked us a few fact-based questions then asked me to leave the room for a bit. I paced back and forth in the hallway for a few minutes that seemed to be much longer. Then Mari was ushered out of the office, and I went back in.

The immigration officer caught me off guard as I waited for questions regarding our relationship. He said, "So I have good news and bad news for you. I believe that your relationship is real. However, your wife has had a deportation removal ordered against her for quite some time. For that reason, we have to detain her, and she will most likely be deported in a couple of weeks."

Someone pinch me. This cannot be real.

I didn't know what to say. I sat silent for seconds, possibly an entire minute.

He continued, "Mr. Gilbert, I know this can be extremely difficult to process for you. And trust me, I understand the emotions you must be going through at the moment. But know that I am doing my job, which is to uphold the immigration laws made by our country's legislative branch of government. You may not agree with them—heck, I may not agree with them at times—but it is my duty to enforce them."

As the frog left my throat, I finally asked some questions to figure out what was going on. "So what about my marriage petition for Mariana? Does that get denied?"

"As I said, I believe your marriage is real; however, I cannot make a judgment on that petition currently because she has a deportation order against her."

"So would Mariana have known about this deportation order? And when?"

"Of course. We sent multiple mailings to her address on file and to the attorney representing her. Um, let's see, looks like the deportation order was filed in December of 2004."

What? No way! I've been totally rooked! I can't believe how badly Mariana used me. That bitch!

"So, uh, she had this order on her before we got married? Wow. Most likely, she knew about this, huh? What if I do not want to move forward with the marriage petition? What happens, and what do I do?" I was more angry than sad at that moment.

"Well, right now, as I said, there is no hearing for your marriage petition. Most likely, what will happen after Ms. Rodriguez is deported is that she will have to make sure the USCIS in Colombia receives the marriage petition file, and they will work it from there."

"How does that work? I mean, if someone is deported, I read that they cannot re-enter the U.S. legally for ten years?"

The immigration officer shrugged. Then he said, "I don't know what will happen. All I know is Ms. Rodriguez is getting detained today and will most likely be deported soon. Do you want to see her before we take her away?"

I stared blankly at him, and in a flat voice, said, "Sure."

He walked me out into the hallway as petite Mari was being "guarded" by two six-foot-tall immigration brutes. Her arms were flailing, and she sobbed uncontrollably. She asked me what I did. I said nothing. I tried to hug her before they took her away, but she pulled away and said, "I don't believe you, Jacob! You did this! You ruined my life. Now I am going to ruin yours! Fuck you!"

I stood completely still as the guards walked her out of the building into a van that would take her to the immigration detention center. *What the fuck just happened?* In a dazed fog, I slowly walked out of the building to my car. I called Jen and left her a voicemail to let her know the situation and then went back to work at the bank.

TWENTY-SIX

Mariana was held captive at the immigration detention center for a few weeks before returning to Colombia. She wouldn't speak to me. I learned some of the details from the attorney that filed our marriage petition. I informed him that I would not be moving forward with my spousal petition. He didn't provide me with much information as he legally did not represent me, but he let me know that I would have to contact USCIS to withdraw my application formally. However, I didn't have time for that, at least not then.

February meant one thing for DMNC Bank staff—the annual Celebration of Achievement! Like the previous year, I skipped the tux and wore the same black suit, white shirt, and black tie. Like last year, Dann rented a tux. This time, he chose a baby blue vest and bowtie. The man had an unending need to be noticed.

I pretty much knew I would win an award for bringing in the most bank deposits due to my eleven Brazilian clients. Their cumulative average deposit balance was north of $25 million. I'd also opened other accounts for local branch clientele, so my totals approached $30 million—a number that I was almost sure no one in the district came close to.

Due to the Fed rate hike over the past couple of years, the deposits I'd made earned the bank a lot of revenue. Harry made it known that even though my credit numbers were just average, I was an integral part of his team because the deposit accounts I opened were earning approximately $1 million in revenue for the bank.

It was a night to feel free and strong, but I felt a bit queasy most days ever since Mari's deportation. I had a sour feeling in my stomach, like something wasn't right. I couldn't point to anything specific—other than the fact that my legal spouse was deported—but my intuition nagged me. I did my best to ignore it by staying busy.

Dann said he was picking up Sarah on his way to the Hard Rock for the Celebration. I wasn't really surprised as I knew he had been talking to her even more the past few months.

I told Tim I'd pick him up, and we made our way north to Hollywood. During the ride, I told him what happened to Mari. Since I had not seen him recently, he wanted details about the interview and what I thought Mari meant when she said she would ruin my life. Tim was the only person I mentioned that part of the conversation to, and when he brought it up in the car, the queasiness returned. I told him I didn't know how to interpret what she said.

He tried to make me feel better and said, "Yeah, I wouldn't worry about it. Lots of women say radical things in the heat of the moment when their emotions get the best of them. That was a traumatic moment for her, so I'm sure she said stuff she didn't mean."

I shrugged and quietly prayed everything would work out.

We entered the Hard Rock and headed straight to the open bar just like the previous year. Since I was excused from call nights the past few months due to my performance, I had not seen Rosie since mid-summer. I looked forward to seeing and flirting with her again, and I debated telling her what happened with Mari. Before I could look for Rosie, Tall Ward and Naomi drifted over to say hello to Tim and me. Ward proudly informed us that Naomi and he were officially dating. I asked the bartender for four shots to celebrate. We drank them; then, we all hugged each other.

More drinks followed the shots, and I was getting tipsy. I veered away from Tim as he was bullshitting with his branch staff, and I noticed Rosie walk in solo. She looked quite different from last year. Gone was her sexy dress, replaced by what looked like a loose-fitting muumuu. She came towards me and gave me a big smile. Her face was significantly rounder than it had been previously. She hugged me tight, and I felt a hard bump hit me in my lower waist. I backed up and gave her a look. She was pregnant! I was happy for her, but I couldn't help feeling a little sad about what could've been. I realized that I had not called her after Mari and I broke up because I had this secret hope that her marriage would fall apart and maybe sparks between us would flare again. But nope, we would just remain former lovers that were now only acquaintances.

"Jac, I know we haven't spoken for a while but have you heard?"

I shrugged cluelessly.

She continued, "That piece of shit, Harry! He changed my position as of this past month to branch manager! That's like a demotion. And although I cannot prove it, I believe it's because I'm pregnant. That mutha—"

I cut her off, saying, "Yeah, I did hear that. I agree he is a piece of work. But look on the bright side; you won't have the high pressure of unattainable sales goals!"

"Now I have the pressure of babysitting all these morons to make sure they do their job properly." Rosie rolled her eyes.

"When are you due?" I asked.

"May. C'mon, let's go into the auditorium to get a good seat." She grabbed my hand, and I followed like her future child would.

We ran into Sal as we shuffled into the theater, and he took the other seat next to me.

Shortly after we sat, Harry took the stage and began his spiel, saying, "Good evening to the best DMNC Bank staff! As I stated in previous years, this is still my favorite night of the year because we celebrate you. However, tonight might be a little different as we are celebrating everyone, even me." He paused to check the pulse of the audience.

I shrugged, then looked wide-eyed at Rosie and gave Sal a half-smile.

Harry continued, "Yes, we are celebrating you *and* me tonight. I would like to formally announce that I have accepted the position of National Director of DMNC Bank USA!"

The audience erupted in cheers, but as people were clapping, whispers flew around the room. I would've loved to hear all those comments.

"As your Florida market president, I would like to formally thank all of you for your fantastic production and performance over the past three years. Without you, there's no chance I would've earned the national director role. I know you may have mixed feelings because I am leaving the local market.

"But have no fear; your next Florida market leader is tremendous. I know because I have had the pleasure of working side by side with her for the past few years. She started as a customer service representative fifteen years ago. She then made her way up to banker, and she put up tremendous credit sales during her tenure as banker. A couple of years ago, I was happy to promote her to regional credit consultant. And now, I'd like to formally announce the promotion of Sarah Stanley to Florida Market President! Congratulations Sarah! Please come on up to accept the position." Harry was glistening and loving every second of his show.

Sal bumped into me as we were applauding, I looked over to him, and he looked at me timidly. I raise my brows.

He leaned over to me and whispered, "That fuckin' bitch is now our boss! I am fucked. She's had it in for me for years. Twenty-eight years at this shithole, and this is what I have to deal with?"

I didn't know how to respond. Sarah was a polarizing individual, and I'd kept my distance from her as best as I could. Although, she probably felt like she knew me pretty well because I'm sure Dann whispered about me in her ear.

I patted Sal on the back and murmured, "Don't worry, pal. You had my back this entire year. You were on my side for every one of those God-forsaken Harry calls! We are in this together, and I won't let Sarah treat you unjustly."

Sal, shaken, replied, "I don't know. We have had bad blood for years. I hope you're right."

Sarah then took the stage and bright lights shined down upon her. Her speech was canned and didn't state much of anything. But the fix was in, and we all knew that those who played along with Harry and Sarah's belief that sales performance over everything else would be rewarded. Those who didn't play along would be forced to bend to Sarah's will or be kicked out the door.

I'm not sure why the effects of the alcohol wore off so quickly, but by the end of Sarah's monologue, I felt stone-cold sober and ready for bed. But how could we all forget about the trophies—I mean awards—to be given out?

As Harry did last year, he started with the rookies, and I didn't pay much attention. Then it was time for the big boy awards. Like last year, Jeff snagged the top credit award—he continued pumping out unsecured loans all year long like he had been doing for the past few years.

I earned the top deposits award. Applause rang loudly from The Banker Gang. As I walked down the aisle, Steve, Don, and Pierre stood in my path, acting as if they would lift me up like a football coach whose team won the big game. I made it known I was not going to be embarrassed like that. The three of them gave me high-fives and congratulated me. My expressionless face transformed into a big smile as I entered the stage to greet Harry and Sarah to accept my award.

As I turned and walked back down the aisle to my seat, Harry addressed the crowd, "I have to say I am very proud of Jacob Gilbert. Last year he was an underperformer. But with the proper guidance and self-motivation, Jacob turned things around. He should be an example to each, and every one of you, proving what focus and determination to succeed can do! Congrats, Jacob!"

Sal greeted me with a big high five and a hug. Rosie gave me a little peck on the cheek for old times. As I admired my award, the time came to announce the big one—the top banker award for 2006. The selection of this person was entirely arbitrary. Management stated it was a combination of sales performance, leadership, and a consistent positive attitude. To me, it sounded like a nomination for high school homecoming court. The award was a glorified popularity contest of who was in the best graces of management.

Harry leaned into the mic again and said, "Without further ado... and I must say this is quite bittersweet as this is the last time I will be awarding the most prestigious Top Banker award…I cannot be prouder of a personal hire than of the man receiving the award tonight. Mr. Dann Frazier, come on up to the stage. You, my friend, are the 2006 DMNC Florida market Top Banker!"

I quickly looked over at Sal as we both stood to give our ovation. I mouthed to him, "Are you fuckin' kidding me?"

He whispered in my ear, "The fix is in. You wait and see what happens with Sarah! I'm telling you this isn't good. You better kiss Dann's big pear ass."

I watched Dann slowly rising from his seat with little emotion, excitement, or surprise. A smile plastered his face, but it was apparent he knew in advance he'd win the award. Sarah looked overjoyed.

I looked over to Rosie and whispered, "Look who just took over the reins of homecoming court!"

She gave me a scrunch of the nose—something smelled fishy.

TWENTY-SEVEN

An unassuming email was sent out from bank management a few weeks after the Celebration of Achievement. When I read it, nothing jumped out at me. Basically, it stated that some minor illiquidity existed in the secondary mortgage market and directed us to a webpage on the bank's internal site that I didn't bother opening. Essentially this meant that the mortgages originated by banks and independent mortgage companies were having more difficulty getting packaged up and sold to the mortgage-backed securities market on Wall Street. Due to this, the bank suspended all no income documentation loans.

Maybe no income documentation loans shouldn't have existed, to begin with. Who in their right mind came up with an idea to lend money to people without verifying their income source? There's no way to figure out how these people were going to pay the loans back.

Jeff took the email pretty hard. He ran into my office, which he rarely did. Breathless, he whispered, "Jac, did you see that email? They are fucking me! Almost all my business is no income documentation loans. How do they expect me to originate the amount of credit I had been doing previously if they take away those products?"

I shrugged and replied, "I don't know, Jeff."

He continued his low-voiced rant, "This bank doesn't care about all the hurdles they put in our way. They only care about one thing, sales production! Oh, I forgot to ask you, have you noticed that houses are taking a really long time to sell? I had a customer come to me stating he put his condo on the market six months ago and still has had no offers."

Indeed, this is something I knew about since Flavia provided me with weekly market updates. I replied, "Yes, the market is slowing down. I heard about a guy who picked up a condo at thirty percent less than the original asking price. Looks like it's a buyers' market."

Jeff didn't need to know that the guy who bought the discounted condo was my customer from Brazil.

"Interesting times ahead, bud." Jeff promptly turned around, exited my office, and returned to his.

Around this same time, Rodrigo planned to travel to Rio de Janeiro to attend PetroBrasil's annual meeting at their national headquarters. He wanted to wine and dine with some of the company's top executives. He told Flavia and me that he would mention how we have helped some of the local executives with their U.S. banking and investment real estate needs.

If he could win some of these executives as our clients, then it was almost guaranteed that we would be introduced to some senior government officials in Brasilia—which, according to Rodrigo, is where the real money was made. Rodrigo thought we could charge higher fee percentages as it was harder for these government officials to find a partner to assist them with their shady business dealings.

I had mixed feelings about the whole thing. I liked flying under the radar. If we landed senior government officials, I was certain I'd be pressing the edge of the bank's compliance guidelines with respect to OFAC, BSA, and AML policy.

Since I no longer had a formal girlfriend and Dann spent most of his free time with an unknown someone, I attended most social events I was invited to. Thus, in recent months I'd become a regular at The Banker Gang's monthly happy hour. The next happy hour was at Tarpon Bend in Fort Lauderdale. I convinced Tim to go, and we rode with Tall Ward and Naomi. While we were expecting to meet YAO Steve, Chicklet Don, and Pierre, no one heard from Dann regarding his attendance either way.

We settled in and ordered two-for-one happy hour drinks. Empty stomachs helped mainline the alcohol, and we were feeling no pain. Eventually, Dann waddled in. We welcomed him with a "YAOOO," and he made his rounds shaking hands.

Soon after, he flipped his phone open and texted feverishly for the next fifteen minutes or so. He paid so much attention to his phone that he forgot to brag—or drink for that matter. He put away his phone and quietly got up from his seat and left the establishment.

We all looked around and shrugged. It was Dann being Dann.

A few minutes later, he reentered the bar, and this time Sarah followed him closely. All of us did a double-take, and lots of secret eye rolls silently communicated what we were all thinking.

We welcomed Sarah to our happy hour, and the sucking up began. Our big boss was present at our favorite monthly social event! The conversation moved from being totally off-color to boring bullshit. The high energy that often marked these events moved to a slow crawl. We didn't want to say the wrong thing or act the wrong way in front of our market president.

Sarah stole the stage. She talked about everything from her nail color, to the new purse she bought, to business, and finally, she blurted out that the bank was sponsoring a golf event with Tiger Woods.

Everyone's ears perked at hearing Tiger Woods. Apparently, she opened her big mouth when she probably shouldn't have, as attendance was highly selective, and I know I hadn't received an invite.

Sarah backtracked a bit but then recovered. She slurred, "As you know, this event hosts our top executives, such as the bank's CFO, head of human resources, COO, along with the top clients of our bank. I think all of you sitting here are some of our top bankers, and I believe we have room for all of you to attend. What do you think?"

Everyone smiled and nodded their head in agreement that we wanted a free round of golf and to meet Tiger, not to mention a full day outside of the branch! I figured Dann was already invited to the event because he stayed quiet and didn't show a sign of surprise at what Sarah said.

Dann sat directly across from me at one end of the table, and for some reason, his smug look was annoying the crap out of me. Maybe it was because he was aligning his cart with the new market president or that he was so cocky about everything lately. His success wasn't about his skill or competency; it was ass-kissing the decision-makers. I believed his success was utterly unjust.

A quarter full glass of water stood between us on the table.

Oh, how I'd love to pick up that glass and splash the water in Dann's face! It'd serve him right. I've put up with his shit for over three years, and I'm sick of it. Should I do it? No. Really? No.

Suddenly my hand picked up the glass and threw the water on Dann.

Dann jumped up from his stool shouting, "Joey, what the hell? What is wrong with you?"

I froze, slightly embarrassed.

I've never acted so impulsively before. Why did I just do that?

Steve and Don winked at me and laughed. Dann got up and walked behind me to the bar to get some napkins to dry his face and shirt.

Before I knew it, something cool and wet splashed on my head—Dann poured an entire beer on my head. It ran down my face, over my shirt, and onto my lap.

Without thinking or looking, I took two beers from the table and sprayed them behind me. I mostly missed Dann but splashed multiple people sitting and standing along the bar.

Oops!

The bartender got sprayed too, which caused the bar's management to get involved, and I was a hair away from getting kicked out. Sarah intervened with the management on our behalf, and we stayed a bit longer.

I was slightly drunk but completely embarrassed by the situation. I paid my tab and made my way to Dicey Riley's; most of the gang followed, but we lost Dann and Sarah, and no one shed a tear about that.

TWENTY-EIGHT

The next day I sucked up my pride and called Sarah to apologize for what happened at happy hour. She laughed it off and thought that the whole thing was hilarious. She said she was pleased that Dann and I had that kind of friendship. I rolled my eyes and proceeded to ask her if I could still attend the golf event. She gave me an enthusiastic yes. I also apologized to Dann, and he played it off as it wasn't a big deal.

On the day of the golf event, Dann and I drove together to Doral National Golf Course, one of the country's toughest courses. Good thing Dann and I went to the driving range a whole two times in the weeks prior. Ultimately our practice sessions didn't matter; we both were terrible at hacking away at the ball. But who cared? I was there to enjoy the day and meet Tiger!

The bank went all out for the event. Valet service greeted us and motioned to the clubhouse as we entered. DMNC signage was everywhere. We met a smiling woman at the welcome desk, and she handed us a DMNC Bank branded golf polo shirt, hat, balls, tees, and towel.

I looked at my foursome and saw I was teamed up with Steve and two other people I didn't know.

Steve and I shared a cart that day. I'd picked up the idea he might have ADHD, but a four-hour day together in a cart confirmed it. The dude couldn't complete a thought. I wondered how he could conduct bank business properly without the ability to focus on a single topic for more than a couple of minutes.

Then it was our turn to play a hole with Tiger. The hole was one of those that has the green on an island. If you hit the ball too short, too long, or too far to either side, your ball plunks into the water. Steve was no better a golfer than I was. On many holes, we decided to quit playing. Instead, we'd visit the concession stands for a snack or drink, bullshitting about everything and everyone.

On the hole with Tiger, Steve approached the tee while Tiger and everyone else watched, including the photographer. He swung, and the ball landed on the edge of the island. He jumped up, trotted over to Tiger, and gave a high-five.

Then it was my turn. I stepped up and didn't think; I just swung. The ball went sky-high and eventually landed ten feet from the pin! I was in awe; I couldn't believe it. I don't think Tiger could either.

Tiger stepped up and swung, and his ball landed fifteen feet from the pin.

They say that the "money" is in the putting game in golf, and they sure were right. Even though Tiger's ball was further from the hole than mine, he sunk his first putt. It took me two putts to sink it for a par three. Tiger congratulated me and told me I was only the third person to par the hole that day—a nice consolation, I guess.

For the rest of the holes, Steve and I barely took our tee shots as we were more interested in finding the cute chicks providing beers to the players.

Before we knew it, the eighteen holes were over. Steve and I each had about six beers. Not bad for a Thursday where we were supposed to be locked in a bank branch all day.

After the play was over, the bank provided us with a delicious late afternoon meal at the clubhouse. At our table sat Rick, the bank's CFO, and we learned he golfed with Dann all day. Rick was in his late forties and seemed like a good guy, especially since he was willing to sit with a bunch of branch bankers.

Making polite conversation, he asked, "So, gentlemen, what does one do after a round of golf in sunny Florida?"

I wasn't touching that question with a ten-foot pole. But that's what Dann was there for.

Dann said, "Oh Rick, we have a nice place for you. Come ride in my car when this is over."

I knew exactly what Dann was referencing—Scarlett's Cabaret in Hallandale Beach. It was arguably the most popular strip club in South Florida. The Banker Gang had an agreement that whenever we were within a couple of miles from the fine gentleman's club, we'd go inside for one drink. The problem was that it was never just one drink. The place was open until eight in the morning, and I hate to admit it, but we closed it down a couple of times. However, it was a bit different from a typical strip club; it was popular with female patrons. Think of it as a dance club with the added bonus of naked women dancing solo on the pole.

That evening The Banker Gang consisted of Steve, Don, Tim, Ward, Pierre, Dann, CFO Rick, and me. When we showed up, CFO Rick was as happy as a pig in shit.

"Now, this is what I'm talking about, fellas! Let's have some fun!"

Once we walked in, I don't think I saw CFO Rick for the rest of the time we were there. He'd headed directly to the champagne room. I guess that's what a CFO salary can afford you.

The rest of us regular folk just took a seat around a table and proceeded to drink Red Bull and vodka. Something about mixing a stimulant with a depressant makes people act unpredictably.

Steve and I, sitting on opposite sides of our group circle, drank the most of anyone. It finally caught up with us. My vision blurred, and Steve was getting rowdier by the minute. As the seven of us watched the eye candy, a brave female tried to steal our attention. She seductively danced her way into the middle of all of us.

She danced in front of me then bent down to my eye level. Suddenly she let out a yelp right in my face. I opened my eyes wide and froze.

Everyone else laughed hysterically—to the point of tears—and it was all because of Steve. As the woman bent toward me, Steve darted his tongue into a place where the sun don't shine. The poor girl was totally shocked! In our drunken haze, all we could do was stare at Steve and crack up. The guy was indeed a maniac.

The next morning was rough as I was scheduled to attend an eight o'clock branch meeting. My head was pounding, and my vision hadn't yet returned to normal. Shortly after the meeting, I received a call from Sarah on my cell phone.

She started the call super friendly and bubbly, saying, "Hi Jacob, I just wanted to make sure you had a good time yesterday. Thank you for coming. It turned out to be an amazing event for the bank."

I stared out the window of my office into the parking lot. I was at a loss for meaningful words, so I replied, "Uh, yeah. It was great. Thank you for the invitation."

Sarah quickly changed the subject and asked, "So what did you boys do afterward?"

Why wouldn't she ask Dann this question as it's obvious they communicate regularly? What do I say? Think! Think! And fast!

I felt my head split open. I said, "We went to a bar. We had a really good time. Sorry, the effects of the drinks are still wearing off."

"I figured you guys partied! Dann hasn't answered his phone all morning. Where did you go? I'm surprised I wasn't invited."

Super uncomfortable situation. Dann, you piece of shit, not answering the phone on purpose today! I guess I'm the sucker, huh?

"Oh, Sarah, we totally would've invited you. Just that women normally don't like the place we went to."

Sarah continued to press and said, "You can tell me, Jacob. You're not going to get in trouble. We are friends."

I wanted the conversation to be over so badly. I broke down and said, "We went to Scarlett's."

Sarah's tone changed and became serious. "Oh, I see. Well, I bet you boys had a lot of fun. I just wanted to check-in. Have a good day. Call me if you need me. Bye."

Friday couldn't end quickly enough. All I wanted to do was go home and lie down and relax the rest of the night, as I had a meeting with Flavia the next day to discuss the latest developments with the real estate portfolio.

I entered the apartment, and Dann was already slumped onto the couch with a ratty tee shirt and his boxer shorts as if he was there all day. I nodded hello and turned right into the hallway.

Dann shouted, "Joey—what the fuck is wrong with you? You told Sarah we went to Scarlett's!"

I stopped in my tracks and clenched my jaw.

SHIT!

"Ah, I, uh, oops." I turned and put up both palms in supplication.

Emotionless, Dann continued, "Do you realize you just told our boss, the Florida market president, that all of us went to a strip club, including the CFO? Rick is pissed! Do not contact Rick. He wants to be as far away from you as possible."

Scrambling to make the situation better, I asked, "Aren't you buddies with Sarah? What is she going to do now that she knows? By the way, you took her to happy hour the other week; she knows what goes on."

Dann replied, more annoyed than angry, "Joey, happy hour is not the same as going to a strip club. I don't think she's going to do anything, but she's got dirt on all of us now. That's never a good thing. Shut your pie hole from now on, okay!"

We should talk about who has a big mouth! Dann told everyone something private about me when I specifically asked him not to, and now he dares to scold me for opening up my mouth?

I didn't engage in any more conversation and stayed in my room the rest of the night, falling asleep early.

TWENTY-NINE

May of 2007 meant it was time for Jen's graduation from law school. Dann and I decided to make the five-hour drive up the Florida Turnpike to Gainesville to celebrate with her.

What else were we going to do on an ordinary weekend in May?

We'd mended fences, and during the ride up, Dann talked more than usual. He bragged but also talked strategy—specifically his approach to obtaining a promotion to business banker.

I knew it was all bullshit. I assumed Sarah already agreed to promote him; it was just his way of showing me he was following a path to earn the promotion. He didn't fool me, but I listened anyway. Employees were beginning to notice Sarah and Dann's relationship, and anyone with smarts knew she'd grant him whatever he wanted.

Even though the drive was tiresome, I was glad we made the time to support Jen on her graduation. Other than her parents, we were her only guests. We stayed in Jen's apartment, where Jen and I slept platonically, as usual, and Dann crashed on the couch.

The next day, we attended Jen's ceremony and went to a nice dinner with her parents. The following day, Jen, Dann, and I headed to Ginnie Springs for an alcohol-infused raft ride. Once we were ashore, Dann took a phone call and walked away.

Jen and I now had a chance to discuss the Mari situation.

After Dann's call was over, his facial expression told us that he was not a happy camper. We all stayed silent until Dann decided to talk.

Eventually, Dann said, "That was Sarah. Apparently, there are whispers among the bank staff that she and I are having a secret sexual relationship."

About freaking time for this to come out in public!

"Sarah is not happy about it as it can jeopardize her position and career. She told me that the service banker at your branch, whom she worked with years ago, called to let her know things she had been hearing." Dann stared angrily at me.

I took a step back from our mini huddle and asked, "Are you inferring that I'm the one that told everyone you two are together?"

"Well, Joey, the person who informed Sarah is from your branch. Who else would she have heard this from?"

Oh, I don't know, Dann! Possibly the hundred people that saw you arrive and sit together at the Celebration of Achievement, or the people that were at the happy hour you invited Sarah to?

I decide to go on the offense, saying, "I can't believe you threw me under the bus to Sarah! So she now thinks I have been telling people that you and she are romantically involved? What horseshit!"

"You did open your big mouth and told her about the golf event afterparty. Didn't you?"

"Ugh, yes. I've apologized and told you that was a mistake. But I didn't tell anyone about you and Sarah. It could've been anyone. You have to admit you both have been brazen about being seen together outside of work!"

"What are you talking about? The person that told Sarah was from your branch, and you are the only one in that location that had seen us together outside of the office." Dann was agitated but kept his voice in a conversational tone.

"Fuck you, Dann! You opened your huge mouth to countless people about Mari and me after I specifically asked you not to. Many times! Don't come here and give me that shit!"

"You either need to find a new roommate, or you need to find a new place to live because when our lease is over in July, I'm out."

Jen sat on the sidelines and decided to intervene, "C'mon, guys. You're going to let your years of friendship end over this?"

Dann and I stared at each other, and we both knew the friendship was over. How could there be a friendship without trust on either side? The long ride home felt longer than ever as we didn't speak a word to each other. Conversation between us for the next two months occurred only when necessary. We didn't hang out again, and I mostly stayed in my room when he was on the couch.

At the end of June, the official announcement came out—Dann was promoted to business banker in the Fort Lauderdale market. He moved a half-hour north, and I only saw him a few more times at official bank meetings.

THIRTY

When Dann and I parted ways in July, I decided to buy my own condo, even though it wasn't in the best section of town. One-hundred percent loan-to-value mortgages were still available as long as I could prove my income.

I moved into my new place with only a couple thousand out of pocket for closing costs and nabbed it for twenty-five percent under the appraised value. Prices couldn't drop much further than that, right?

After I settled in, I called Jen, who'd recently passed the Florida and New York bar exams. She worked as a first-year associate at a prominent New York City law firm. I asked her if she could help me with filing for divorce from Mari. Jen already knew almost everything about my situation, and she was an attorney. Why not give her the work, and she could learn a little bit about family law in the process.

She informed me that the legal process of serving someone internationally could be an issue. We used the address I had for Mari's parents and put an advertisement in a legal publication stating that I was filing for dissolution of marriage. If I received no response within three months of publication, I could present my case to the judge, and they would most likely grant the divorce.

Within a few weeks, Jen informed me that a family attorney friend of one of Mari's brothers was representing her in the divorce, and it wasn't going to be a smooth ride. The attorney's name was Peter, and he represented Mari as a favor to her brother. Just what I needed.

Additionally, in July came a corporate communication stating that the bank suspended the foreign national mortgage program. I yelled at my computer screen for a few minutes. Sal heard the ruckus coming from my office and came over to ask what was going on. I let him know I had no idea how I would hit my credit goal now that the foreign national mortgage product was gone.

Sal was already beaten down. The branch lost out in the credit department due to Jeff's inability to obtain loans from Jerry's crew that met the new banking standards. Now I wasn't going to bring in the volume of deposits I did the prior year.

What I found peculiar was that Sarah canceled almost all of my one-on-one's with her. We'd had only two of them. She was nice but superficial during them, as if she was more scared of me than I should've been of her.

During the July call, which was also my third anniversary with the bank, she awarded me a $15,000, raise bringing my salary up to a sweet $50,000. I was pleasantly shocked, and she didn't mention any of my sales production. All she asked was if she could do anything to be of assistance. I thanked her, and she told me to keep up the good work and not to think about jumping ship.

Sal didn't have it so easy. Sarah had it in for him and microman-aged him to the max. She was doing to Sal what Harry did to me the year prior. I knew how it felt, and I tried to keep Sal's spirits up.

About a week after my pleasant raise, Rodrigo called. He told me about a huge meeting in Brasilia the following month. It was between the PetroBrasil executives and the government officials, and he wanted

Flavia and me to meet him there. He planned to host lavish dinners with drinks and discuss how we helped other executives. He wanted to sell our services to the big fish.

This sounded like a stressful situation to me, but I knew I had to play my part. I passed on the information to Flavia, and she was super excited about it.

Over the next couple of weeks, Flavia and I met often, to the point where she was sleeping in my bed more than she wasn't. We went over everything we had done with the prior executives, and then we came up with a revised servicing plan. The plan was to establish a real estate management company.

She would still represent the Brazilians as condo buyers, but this new company would manage everything from the moment they owned the property. This new management company would find qualified tenants, hire contractors to improve the units, and find handymen to fix any minor problems.

We thought this was clever and planned to present the idea to Rodrigo when we arrived. Flavia mentioned that she wanted to get a makeover before we left. Four hours later, as she walked out of the salon, she was a professional and classy-looking brunette.

My eyes popped wide, and I complimented her new look. I sensed her confidence growing exponentially ahead of our important meetings.

Neither Flavia nor I had ever been to Brasilia—Brazil's capital since 1960. It was a planned city which meant that the architecture was unique, and zones were established for government, education, housing, and entertainment. At only a sixth of São Paulo's population, it had a much different feel, which apparently excluded exciting nightlife.

When Flavia and I arrived, we took a taxi to the hotel that Rodrigo booked for us. The three of us went to dinner, and we presented him with our idea of managing the real estate for the executives. He loved it.

"This is fabulous!" he said. "I love the idea of earning a recurring revenue stream. Instead of one big fee, we can charge quarterly or annual fees."

I was glad he was on board because that is how I needed to accept fees moving forward since I'd no longer earn commissions from financing the properties for these clients.

He wasn't happy that we couldn't offer the mortgage service anymore. Still, he understood that a liquidity problem was hitting the U.S. capital markets. Property values started to plummet in 2007, and we wanted to show actual pictures of properties, their asking price, and what they sold for. Everyone likes a discount, especially on their investment.

Rodrigo worked his magic once more, and the three of us were invited to a private dinner for the PetroBrasil corporate executives along with over twenty government officials. The dinner was at a traditional Brazilian steakhouse that was closed down to everyone outside our party.

I wanted to taste everything. The waiters brought pieces of meat on a large steel rod—chicken hearts, lamb, sirloin, pork loin, and the best cut, picanha! I tried to people-watch as best I could but found it difficult while trying to flag down the waiter with the cuts of meat I wanted. Flavia even commented on everything I was eating. I told her it was a nervous habit.

I comprehended only about a quarter of the conversations, as my Portuguese was still elementary. Leo noticed my presence and came over to say hello. He was concerned about the real estate market in Florida. I let him know that Flavia was our real estate specialist, and we would meet with him individually to discuss what was happening with the market. I also mentioned the significant discounts available in the current market. That was music to his ears, and his eyes widened.

He said, "I like that! Jacob, come with me. I want to introduce you to a few of my associates from the Rio headquarters. Try to use some of the Portuguese you learned, you know, to impress them a little."

"*Tá bom Leo. Vamos.*"

He winked, and I followed him. I motioned to Flavia to come along.

Leo walked us into the other restaurant rooms, and we met various influential individuals within PetroBrasil and the Brazilian government. Leo introduced me as his favorite "*Banqueiro Americano*" and Flavia as his "*Brasileira-Americana*" real estate partner.

The men took a real liking to Flavia. She worked the room like a movie star, engaging in light, humorous small talk with the middle-aged power-driven men. She played them like a fiddle, making them smile and chuckle just as she wanted. She truly understood the Brazilian male persona and used it to our advantage.

Rodrigo met us in the room with the government officials and brought his sales pitch. He ended by saying that we'd be around for the next three days, and if anyone wanted to discuss their personal financial needs to send funds to the U.S., the three of us would be available at any time and any place to discuss. He passed out his business card and asked them to call or text his cell phone to set up meetings.

That night we went right back to our hotel room. I was so stuffed I couldn't move. No one indicated that they were interested in using our services, and I started to worry that this trip was a waste. I was also concerned that I would follow up a successful sales production in 2006 with a crappy 2007.

Flavia noticed my discomfort, and I blamed it on overeating. She knew that was a front. We lay in bed with the TV on, but neither of us was watching.

She turned to me and said, "Don't worry, Jac. We got this."

I closed my eyes, replying, "I hope you're right. Although I didn't understand a lot of the dialog tonight, I read their body language, and it didn't give me any indication that any of them were interested."

"Oh, you're a professional body language reader now? I thought you were a banker."

I smiled.

She continued, "Look, I never told you this, but my father was a city official in São Paulo when I was growing up. Some shit went down, and we were forced to move away, which is why we moved to South Florida when I was eight. I've been around these types of people. They put on this facade in public to make them seem almost non-human. But trust me, they are more flawed than anyone.

"I also read their body language today, and I would be shocked if we don't have at least a couple of meetings before we leave. These people are siphoning government money! They need people they can work with to send the money abroad. Did you see any European bankers in the room? I didn't."

I started chuckling as I realized how wise Flavia truly was. I was stressed over nothing.

"Yeah, you're probably right. I just can't shake this anxiety. Does it bother you that you know these funds are being almost stolen from the government?"

Flavia sighed and replied, "If you asked me that question a few years ago, I would've said absolutely. Now, honestly, I think, if it's not us, they'd use someone else. One person cannot stop this corruption; it's too embedded in this society. So why not profit from it? The whole world is corrupt. We aren't killing anyone or selling drugs or little girls for sex trafficking. So I'm okay doing a good job for them and lining our pockets."

She paused then continued, "Didn't you tell me your boss was a shady fuck? And that he allowed and encouraged his staff to do any and all types of business which catapulted him to a role where he would make over a million a year between compensation and stock options or whatever you call it?"

"Yeah, you make some valid points."

"Just think about it, Jac; if someone's bank account measured success, the most corrupt, step-on-anyone business people would be at the top of that list. Would you consider that successful? It's a rat race out there. I saw first-hand how much my parents struggled in America—from not speaking English to having to do shitty jobs. Meanwhile, I also watched spoiled rich kids complain about doing some stupid homework at UM."

I grinned and said, "You know something? You are so wise and pretty. How am I so lucky to have found you?"

"Oh, you wish to be so lucky to have me!" She laughed as we started kissing.

The next morning we woke up to the sound of pounding on our hotel door.

I opened it in my boxers, half asleep, eyes narrowly open, grumbling, "What the hell are you waking us up at seven-thirty for?"

Rodrigo, already fully dressed in jeans and a button-down, walked into our room. Flavia tucked herself completely under the covers.

"I have some good news, my friends. I have received over fifteen text messages from people we met last night that are interested in our services! But one of them is a top government official from the State of Bahia. He wants us to join him on his private jet to Salvador in two hours!"

What? Is this a dream? Do I need to smack myself to be sure?

I stuttered, "A private jet...to where? Salva—?"

Rodrigo cuts me off, saying, "Salvador, it's the capital of the State of Bahia. Get your asses ready. Meet me in the lobby, ready to go in an hour."

"How the hell are we getting back here then?"

"Bro, who cares? We are going on the private jet of one of the major government officials in the country!"

I looked at Flavia, who had the covers up to her chin as she was topless underneath. Her eyes were wide open. I shrugged at her.

She finally opened her mouth and said, "*Vamos!*"

The Falcon jet was a beauty. I'd never been on a private charter before, and I almost felt like royalty. It turned out three government officials were on the flight. An attendant waited on us hand and foot for the two-hour ride. Nearly all of the conversation was in Portuguese, so it was a bit difficult for me to understand what was transpiring. Flavia held her own, talking a decent amount about the specifics of our service in the U.S.; I mostly just sat there taking it all in.

At the airport, the officials needed to go but offered us a private car service to transport us to a hotel they'd booked for us for the night. In the car, Rodrigo let out a "Hellz yeah!" scream. I looked at him with awe and realized the conversation must have gone over really well.

I asked, "*Que foi?*"

Flavia, grinning from ear to ear, was about to speak, but Rodrigo beat her to it.

"We are in! They told us that they asked our previous PetroBrasil clients how they liked our services. Our existing clients gave us fantastic recommendations—we were trustworthy, and we didn't steal one dollar from them. In Brazil, that's about the best recommendation you can get!"

Oh, so they are stealing government money but do not like it when people steal from them. Makes a whole lot of sense.

I was happy but also anxious about how I was going to get this done. In terms of compliance, PetroBrasil executives were quite a bit different than officials of foreign governments.

"Do they know that the process is going to be a little different for them since they are government officials?"

Flavia replied, "Yes, I actually explained what we discussed previously. You know, how nothing can be listed in their personal names. I told them we'd establish Delaware LLCs, and the accounts and real estate would be owned in those entities."

I let out a deep sigh of relief. I realized that all the time I spent explaining banking to Flavia paid off.

I exclaimed, "*Parabéns amigos*! This calls for a celebration tonight. I hope the nightlife is better here than Brasilia."

Rodrigo said, "Oh yeah, my friend. A lot better. But we can't go out too late. We have to get back to Brasilia tomorrow to meet with a couple more people. And who knows, we might be invited on more private jets?"

"What? We're scheduled to leave in two days."

Rodrigo continued in his ultra-positive tone, saying, "Not if we can make more meetings, my friends. I'm sure everyone will understand."

Flavia and I both nodded in agreement.

Although we were not invited on another private jet, Flavia and I extended our trip another two days and met with fifteen more prospective clients. With every meeting, I watched Rodrigo's and Flavia's confidence grow. Almost all the people we met with asked our current clients about our performance. Nearly everyone gave glowing reviews of how we conducted our business in a trustworthy manner.

However, some mentioned that they believed they purchased condos at the height of the real estate market and would possibly lose money if they tried to sell them. Unfortunately, that was just part of the real estate market, and there wasn't much we could do. They were victims of poor timing.

Ultimately all the people we met were interested in using our services. We let them know that it would take time to onboard them and find suitable properties to buy as real estate negotiations took longer to complete these days. I also knew I couldn't open fifteen foreign national accounts over a short period without my lovely compliance folks visiting me.

I wasn't even sure if I had the "Harry shield" anymore, and Sarah's shield seemed to be very opaque to me. Brasilia turned out to be a phenomenal opportunity, and we all had our work cut out for us. I was delighted, but I also realized how much we had to accomplish over the rest of the year.

Since Flavia was technically in her last year at UM and was busy setting up the real estate management company in addition to finding appropriate real estate for our new clients, I had her use my spare bedroom as her office. This was easier for me as I could get daily updates on what she was doing. It also made it easier for her to move in unofficially.

She still went to her parents' house some weekends, but she brought almost all her things to my condo, so I guess she was my housemate as well. We both put our heads down the next couple of months, and unfortunately, my tennis and running were casualties of our success.

In the branch, Sal was crazed. His anxiety was through the roof, and nearly weekly, he had emotional melt-downs. To make things worse, he micromanaged me more than ever. Maybe Sarah was pressuring him to pressure me, so it didn't seem like she was directly micromanaging me. The stress level became so high that he had mandatory weekly bank meetings to discuss how we all were responsible for sales performance, even the tellers.

Mr. Vacca came into my office one day asking, "What are these sonz-a-bitches doing to your boy Sal? He looks like he's going to have a goddamn nervous breakdown. Tell them to lay off of him!"

I offered a sad chuckle and let him know that management had changed and our branch was not doing too well in the credit department this year. I shrugged.

Mr. Vacca reiterated for what seemed to be the fiftieth time, "I'm completely ecstatic that I don't have to deal with these corporate sonz-a-bitches anymore!"

Every time I entered the office, I felt my stress level rise. It was exhausting hearing a daily barrage of how important it was to hit our goals. Plus, I had to worry about compliance getting on my back about the foreign national accounts. Additionally, I had to find time to field progress calls from Flavia and Rodrigo. Some days I just felt I'd bitten off more than I could chew. Then, to our surprise, Jeff seemingly figured things out—for all of us.

One day in October, Jeff brought a new face into the branch. He asked Sal and me to join them in his office.

Sal now sported an eye patch due to the uncontrollable eye twitching caused by his high stress level. He thought it would be less upsetting to clients to see the eye patch than the involuntary twitching.

Jeff began his introduction, "Sal and Jacob, please meet Ronald McMillian. Ronald was introduced to me by Jerry from Miami Business Consultants. Ronald was in the residential mortgage business, and as you know, that business has imploded, so he pivoted to focus solely on small business lending.

"Don't worry; I already informed him that we would need these businesses to be well established and that we'd need two years of corporate tax returns to assess their cash flow."

I sat still, unenthused. But not Sal.

He jumped up from his chair and enthusiastically gushed, saying, "I'm thrilled we have a partner outside the bank that will assist us in originating much-needed credit accounts!"

Ronald told us that through his mortgage business, he had contacts who were small business owners. He'd target them, offering business loans. He also had mortgage offices in the Broward and Palm Beach areas as well, and he'd introduce his two partners to the bankers Jerry worked with in those markets.

I knew those bankers were going to be Dann, Steve, and Don. I kept quiet the whole time—my gut was telling me something wasn't right.

Maybe this whole thing is too good to be true. I learned a long time ago that when things are too good to be true, they are.

This conversation was none of my concern. All I cared about was servicing our new Brazilian clients, and raising no ethics eyebrows while doing it.

Jeff started putting loan applications on the system during the final quarter of 2007. However, Sarah didn't release the pressure on Sal.

I felt bad for the guy. She had it in for him, and there was nothing he could do. I figured there must be bad blood between them from years past, and she was settling an old score.

By the end of the year, I established accounts for eight new Brazilian clients. I had many more accounts waiting to get set up. They wired in over a total of $20 million.

Flavia worked day and night trying to find condos. Finding condos wasn't hard, as they were plentiful; the hard part was trying to figure out which ones weren't going to plummet in value due to the full-on real estate recession in South Florida.

Just as I did at the end of the previous year, I logged into my Swiss bank account—the balance was $868,885!

I spent the last two weeks of the year in New Jersey with my family as I realized I didn't spend enough time with them that year. It was nice to get away from everything and be spoiled as an only child again.

One night I took a ride into Manhattan and met with Jen. We had dinner at a traditional Korean restaurant in midtown, where dinner was barbecued right on our table. It reminded me that Jen was a crappy cook.

She told me that Mari's attorney, Peter, was a former United States Assistant District Attorney in the Southern District of Florida and that they had been chatting about legal business. Peter didn't care much for Mari and was dragging his feet—putting this case on the backburner—trying to waste time settling the dispute.

Jen advised me to offer Mari a $10,000 settlement.

I initially balked. I said, "Fuck that; Mari doesn't deserve one dime from me!"

Jen then told me that she'd have to charge me her firm's hourly rate of $300 and that my bill would rack up pretty fast if we didn't settle this. She made it known I could be screwed if this case went to a court trial.

After I made my way back to Miami, I called her to let her know that I agreed. We should just settle the case and make an offer to end it.

THIRTY-ONE

2008 started much like the prior year ended. Flavia and I still worked on coordinating the onboarding of nearly a dozen new Brazilian clients. And I listened to the stress level rising almost daily with Sal.

After his year-end review meeting with Sarah, Sal informed the whole branch staff he was on written warning and would be terminated if the branch didn't start meeting the sales metrics put forth by management.

I thought that was pretty shitty. Sal put his heart and soul into helping the branch clientele and was very popular among his peers for nearly thirty years at the same company.

During one of our weekly branch meetings, I got super annoyed and suggested that we all boycott this year's Celebration of Achievement due to Sal's mistreatment by management. My suggestion went over well, and as a group, we decided that no one from our branch would attend the festivities.

Sarah canceled my year-end review but sent me a report saying I was doing fine in the role and I would qualify for the maximum annual bonus of $25,000 again. I was just fine with our review cancellation, as I hadn't closed a loan for nearly six months.

Quietly, The Banker Gang's monthly happy hour was tabled, and I felt like I was doing my job in isolation the first half of 2008. I hadn't even spoken to Tim as much as I'd wanted. Practically all my interactions were with Flavia, Rodrigo, and every now and then with Jen.

During a lull in April, Flavia and I decided to take a week-long Caribbean cruise. It was nice just to relax while eating and drinking our faces off. Those voyages are dangerous for waistlines!

When we returned, I had a voice message from Jen. She had the good news that Mari accepted our offer. She said she'd started the negotiation at $5,000 and settled at $8,000. I still had to pay attorney fees of almost $7,000. The whole ordeal cost me a pretty penny, but it could've been much worse. About a month later, I was legally divorced and felt a little weight lifted off my shoulders.

Even though Flavia and I were not visiting Brazil for official bank business, Rodrigo still made the rounds. Any time he could finagle his way into a meeting with new executives, he would. He presented our services, and we onboarded a new client every couple of weeks. It was a steady flow, and no one in the bank questioned my sales performance.

Also, it turned out, Ronald, Jeff's new referral partner, was panning out. He introduced Jeff to numerous business owners, and in turn, Jeff assisted in opening credit and deposit accounts for the branch to the tune of a couple million. Sal couldn't have been happier. And since he wasn't in the "red level" of the branch stack rankings any longer, Sarah revoked his written performance improvement. Sal even lost the eye patch due to his reduced stress levels.

Ronald visited our branch more consistently than Mr. Vacca or Ms. Li. He was there multiple times per week, mostly going right into Jeff's office. One day, however, he intercepted me as I walked across the lobby. He casually asked me if I was interested in being introduced to a business client of his. He mentioned that they were Brazilian-American, and he had heard I had some success with Brazilian clients.

I politely brushed him off, mentioning I was pretty busy with the business I already had. In reality, I wanted nothing to do with anything of Jerry's business or his compadres. The brief conversion did pique my concern. I couldn't shake the fact that he knew about my Brazilian clientele.

What exactly did Jeff tell him? For that matter, what exactly did Jeff know? What did Sal tell Jeff?

I shrugged it off as paranoia, and the thought left my head over the next day or so.

For my 26th birthday in mid-July, Flavia surprised me with a hotel reservation in Orlando for a long weekend. We hit up the theme parks like a couple of adult kids. Something hit me during that trip, and I finally realized she was the woman I wanted to be in a committed relationship with. Neither of us dated other people, but we also didn't have an official relationship as she never introduced me to her parents or vice versa.

On the last night in Orlando, we sat next to each other, watching the Universal Studios' fireworks. I turned to her and told her for the first time that I loved her. I asked if she would make our relationship officially exclusive.

At first, her eyes watered with tears. I got super excited, thinking she'd accept, and then I realized they were tears of sadness. I was exasperated and speechless. I put my arm around her as I waited for her to speak.

After she rubbed the tears from her face, she looked up at me with her smeared mascara and said, "Jacob, I really want to tell you I love you, but I can't. I don't want to lie to you either and string you along. I think we are great business partners, and I have had a fabulous time with you. I am only twenty-two, and I don't want to commit myself to any man at this time. To avoid blurring lines, I think it's best that I find my own office for business and not work out of your condo anymore."

It was like I was hit with a gut punch and uppercut at the same time. I felt sick and got an immediate migraine from rapid blood flow to my brain. I rarely showed emotion, even when breaking down inside. But at that moment, I couldn't hold back. I was emotionally exhausted from the past four years—the sham marriage to Mari, the fallout with Dann, the stress of my job. The one person who had been my rock the past year and a half just told me they didn't love me back, and I was devastated.

I didn't say anything. I got up and walked out of the park quietly crying, trying to shield my face from the public. Flavia followed me, crying as well. She tried to console me, but it didn't mean anything.

Did I take Flavia for granted? Was I too scared from Mari to give Flavia the proper treatment I should've given her from the beginning? Did I show her that I wasn't a stable person? Why did she surprise me with a birthday trip?

I was so confused, but sometimes when emotions were involved, rational reasons don't exist. That night, we shared a bed, but my mind was elsewhere. I didn't get much sleep, and the three-hour ride back to Miami was quiet.

The following month was difficult for me. I felt like I'd lost a piece of my identity. Flavia kept her distance and even took all of her belongings out of my condo. We spoke regularly via phone, but conversations were purely about business. I had no desire to play tennis, run, or go out. I was a homebody for the whole month of August.

I called Tim regularly, and he tried to keep things positive. He even came over a few times to hang out with me, though I'm not sure if it was to keep me company or to get away from his wife, who he still complained about. Either way, I was glad to spend time with him. I felt all the emotions of a break-up, but we never had an official relationship—that phenomenon took quite some time to wrap my head around, and I moped around for weeks.

THIRTY-TWO

On the Tuesday after Labor Day, the staff opened the branch doors at nine in the morning like they did every day. I sat in my office going through email.

Sal walked in and asked me if I heard from Jeff. I told him I hadn't. Sal replied that he called Jeff's cell a few times that morning but never got an answer. Jeff was supposed to open the drive-thru with the teller at seven-forty-five and did not show up. Jeff had gone completely silent, which was totally out of character for him. This was the guy that taught me the art of texting on a flip phone. He was not one to ignore or blow off his job duties.

For the following two days, Jeff's office sat empty. Still no word from Jeff. Sal called human resources to report the situation, and they said there was not much they could do. Apparently, the person needs to be missing in action for a longer period of time before a job abandonment complaint could be filed.

On Friday, Jeff showed up at the branch in shorts and a t-shirt. He explained privately to Sal that his father was in the hospital in North Florida, and he had been there the past week. He apologized for not responding to Sal's messages. They contacted human resources and filed a family leave request. All Jeff had to do was provide HR with proof his father had indeed been admitted to the hospital.

After the HR call, Jeff came into my office, closed the door, and took a seat at my desk. His face, which was always smoothly shaven, was in full-on scruff mode, and he had circles under his eyes. I chalked it up to stress due to his father being in critical condition.

Jeff nervously asked, "Have you heard from Ronald or Jerry?"

I shook my head no, as if the question was outlandish. I asked, "Why do you ask?"

He quickly mumbled, "They left voicemails on my phone, and I was wondering if they had been in or called you."

I reiterated that they had not, and he got up from the seat across my desk, shook my hand, and scurried out the branch door.

I noticed his hands were incredibly sweaty. So sweaty that they left a mini puddle on the top of my desk where they previously laid. I took a Clorox wipe and cleaned my desktop, thinking the brief conversation was rather peculiar. Sal then came in and asked me what happened. I told him, and we both agreed something weird was going on, but neither of us knew what it could be, other than Jeff's father being sick.

That weekend's news cycle was horrific for those in the financial industry. There were multiple reports of a massive illiquidity problem in the financial markets. The reports stated that many significant institutions were on their way to bankruptcy due to the buildup of the mortgage meltdown that slowly began at the beginning of the prior year.

My eyes were glued to the television, and it appeared many backroom meetings were being held on Wall Street.

On the morning of Monday, September 8th, I received a frantic call from Jen. "Joey, where are you?" she asked.

Surprised and unaware of the meaning behind the question, I answered sarcastically, saying, "Oh, I'm just sipping champagne on a private yacht in St. Tropez."

"Joey, Jacob! Stop messing around. Where are you? Are you okay?" Jen screeched into the phone.

Realizing something bigger might be going on, I muted my sarcasm and replied, "I'm at work at my bank branch. What the hell is going on, Jen?"

Jen, speaking faster and breathing heavier, said, "Dann just got arrested! By the freaking FBI! I am worried that you are going to be arrested next!"

My jaw dropped. It was always easy for me to be at a loss for words, but I stood in absolute silence this time, looking out my office window into the parking lot.

"Joey! Are you there? Answer me, dammit!"

"Uh, yeah, I'm here..." my voice drifted.

I shook my head violently a few times to break my trance and said, "Sorry, I, uh, don't know—wait, what was he arrested for?"

Jen calmed down just a bit and said, "Apparently, it was for multiple counts of a few things. But I gather it's for bank fraud, conspiracy to commit money laundering, wire fraud, and some other things.

"I don't know a lot of details. Dann called me this morning asking if my firm could represent him. But before I represent him, I want to make sure you're not wrapped in this same bank fraud shit. I don't want to represent one of you and not the other because I cannot represent both of you under the same charges."

I didn't know what to say. I was freaking out inside. I wanted to tell Jen what I had been doing, but I couldn't over the phone. My mind bounced off the walls.

Before I could answer, Jen said, "Look, Joey, I am going to be in Florida first thing tomorrow morning to meet with Dann along with a senior criminal defense partner from my firm. I need to meet with you right afterward to figure out what shady shit you shady fucks have been doing in shadyville! Ugh! DO NOT tell anyone about this conversation or anything about what you may know. You got that? Make sure you are available to meet me when I tell you! Okay?"

"Okay, Jen, I understand. My mouth is shut until I see you tomorrow."

The rest of the day, I couldn't accomplish any meaningful work as I, along with Sal, was glued to the CNBC broadcast on the TV in the branch lobby. Sal worried that DMNC would be handed over to the Federal Deposit Insurance Company due to the illiquidity of all the non-performing mortgages on our balance sheet. I was freaking out inside for much different reasons.

The FBI arrested Dann. Was I next? I couldn't show anyone that I knew this. Tomorrow couldn't come soon enough.

The next day I stared anxiously at my cell phone. I willed it to ring in conjunction with Jen's name. Finally, at two in the afternoon, she called. She told me to drive to Fort Lauderdale to meet her at her hotel room on Las Olas Boulevard, near the Broward County Federal Courthouse.

I came up with an excuse to leave the branch early. Sal was less than thrilled. Jeff was gone, and I'd be out the rest of the day. But he saw in my eyes that this was something I needed to do. He gave me the okay to leave and told me to be on time the following day.

I drove like a madman via I-95 north. Rodrigo would have been jealous of the way I weaved in and out of cars, driving over one hundred miles per hour most of the way during the twenty-five-mile drive. I left my car with the hotel valet and briskly walked into the lobby. I was jittery and strung out on adrenaline. I greeted Jen with a professional handshake as she was with two other males.

She introduced one of them as the senior partner from her New York law firm, and the other was a guy named Peter, who just happened to be Mari's divorce attorney! She explained that she and Peter "connected on another level" while negotiating my divorce case, and since he was a former U.S. Assistant District Attorney, she thought he could help out.

He seemed to be a decent guy from a brief first impression. Jen then led me to the elevator while the other guys stayed in the lobby.

I gave Jen a quizzical look and, in a low voice, asked, "What's happening?"

We stepped into the elevator, and she said, "I need to talk to you alone first. Then the three of us will figure out how to handle this."

My heart was pounding as we exited the elevator and entered her room. "Take a seat, buddy!" she said as she plopped her bag on the desk and took off her suit jacket.

The room felt small. Jen sat in the desk chair, and I was on the mini-sofa next to the bed. My mouth was dry, and I thought my head would explode.

"Joey, I have good news for you!" she said. "We received the entire indictment today, and you are not part of it!"

I let out a deep breath and replied, "Oh my God! Thank the Lord!" I made prayer hands and looked up to the ceiling.

She continued, "Here is what is going to happen. You will sign a retainer agreement with my firm, and you are formally hiring us as your legal representative on retainer, as you don't have a current case against you. Doing this creates attorney-client privilege. This means I need you to tell me exactly what shady shit you have been doing. My job is to be out in front of any future wrath that you may encounter."

I signed the agreement.

Jen shook her head slightly. "This has got to be some freaking poetic justice or something," she said. "Do you know what I just learned downstairs from Mari's old attorney, Peter? That *Mari* was the one who tipped the FBI a year and a half ago. She suspected that fraudulent loans were being written from the Miami Business Consultants office!"

My eyes opened as wide as the ocean. I said, "What? No! You have got to be shitting me!"

"No joke, buddy. She told her attorney that she suspected *you* were involved, and since the guy was a former AUSA, he pointed her in the right direction of where to file the tip. They had three undercover agents working this case since the beginning of last year!"

I was utterly astounded. My body felt weightless as I sat on the uncomfortable sofa.

Poetic justice for sure.

Jen continued, "Apparently, she thought you were part of the fraud, but your name never showed up on any fraudulent loans, and you never engaged with the undercover officers."

I said, "Hey, was one of the undercover agents named Ronald McDonald, or something like that?"

"Ronald McDonald? Um, do you really think an FBI undercover officer would be named that? Why not just McLovin?" She let out a loud laugh.

I shook my head in disgust.

I can't believe she's making jokes right now!

"I don't know, but was the agent in charge of the Miami office called Ronald?"

She opened her bag and retrieved a file that contained the complete indictment. The room was quiet as she tried to find the correct section.

So many thoughts zipped through my head that I couldn't analyze any of them. A silent few minutes passed, broken only by the sound of shuffling papers.

"Ah, here it is. Yes! His pseudonym was Ronald McMillian. McDonald, you fool! Ha," she said playfully. Then she became more serious. "Wait. How do you know that?"

I took a deep breath as the dots started to connect in my head. "I was introduced to Ronald McMillian about a year ago at my bank branch," I said. "He had been working with my old mentor and current co-worker, Jeff Winder, and he mentioned that he worked with Jerry at that Miami Business Consultants office. I'm just trying to put the pieces of this puzzle together. Who else was arrested?"

"You know this is not public information yet, and you are not supposed to know any of this," Jen said in a very businesslike tone.

I smiled and shrugged. "Attorney-client privilege? Plus our five-year personal friendship."

"Joey, you need to promise me on everything you hold dear in your life that this entire conversation stays in this room until all this information is made public!" Jen's baby blue eyes bored a hole right through me.

I said, "I swear on my life, my parents' life, uhh—"

She cut me off, saying, "Okay, okay. Enough. I quickly read the whole indictment but need to read it a couple more times. It seems twenty-five people were arrested. The first two arrested were flipped by the FBI over a year ago, and they set up a lot of other people in exchange for a lighter sentence.

"I believe those first two were the ones that sat in the backroom of the Miami Business Consultant's office. The ones who created fake tax returns or other forged financial information used to fraudulently qualify for loans."

She opened up the binder again, perusing a few pages. "Here it is," she said. "It looks like fifteen bankers were arrested—four from your bank. Let's see, well, obviously Dann, along with Steven Arnold, Donald Deeds, and Jeff Winder. Do you know them all?"

I frowned and said, "Yep, unfortunately, I do. All of them. Do you have an idea what's going to happen to them?"

Jen looked out the hotel window, crossed her legs, then brought her attention back to me, saying, "Joey, they are all going to prison. The FBI doesn't arrest people if they don't have ironclad evidence against them. Well, at least they are not supposed to. I asked Peter—he read the indictment as well—and he concurred that they'd go to jail. It's our job to negotiate with the District Attorney to lessen the sentence and their monetary fines."

"Wow."

Jen's natural curiosity got the best of her. "Did you know Dann was doing this?" she asked. "Wait! Don't answer that. Again, between us, the FBI raided Dann's safe deposit box at his branch, and they found $78,000 in cash. Most likely, it was from illegal kickbacks from funding the fraudulent loans."

All this for $78K, what a sucker!

Jen continued, "Okay, enough about your old roomie Dann. Now, I need to know what you have been doing. The entire truth, buddy!"

I sighed and dragged the palms of my hands down the front of my face. "I'll start with the good news as well," I said. "I have not been involved in any fraudulent loans or any other type of fraudulent business."

Jen smiled, "Well, *that* is a good start!"

I continued, "Rodrigo—"

She promptly cut me off, saying, "Oh Lord, how did I know that he was involved somehow?"

"You know he's a sweet talker. Also, as you know, he has been working for PetroBrasil. A couple of years ago, he told me that many of the executives were receiving massive kickbacks from overbids by contractors. They were effectively fixing the bids, and since PetroBrasil is a State-owned company, the funds were coming directly from the government.

"These Executives didn't want to keep the kickbacks in Brazil as it would be easier for the government to find and freeze those assets in the future, so they looked for Swiss or other foreign bankers to help them hide the funds offshore. Rodrigo and I did a great job for Rodrigo's boss, which resulted in introductions to more of his peers, who then introduced us to Brazilian government officials." Jen asked, "Wait a minute. You opened bank accounts for these people with illegally obtained funds?"

I involuntarily shrugged. "I guess," I replied. "I didn't ask where exactly the funds came from. I found a corporate attorney who would set up Delaware LLCs to title some of the accounts, and then I worked with Flavia to represent them as their real estate agent. She found investment condos for them, so the funds weren't just sitting in a bank account. I also set them up with an accountant for doing the books and filing tax returns for the LLCs. You know, to show that they had a real LLC business with a tangible investment earning revenue."

Jen looked impressed. She said, "Joey, I have to say, this was a pretty impressive racket you and Rodrigo set up. One problem, it is totally illegal! You can't just take funds that you *know* were illicitly obtained! Have you ever heard of money laundering? Well, you are a major pin in it! Ugh. Please don't tell me you have a safety deposit box with cash in it or have personal bank accounts with kickback wires from Brazil coming in."

"I don't have a cash-filled safe deposit box or a U.S. bank account that shows any questionable activity. My local bank account shows only deposits from my salary from DMNC bank. One caveat, though—I do have a secret bank account in Switzerland. The account title is only numerical digits, and my identity isn't easily obtainable unless there is a warrant."

Jen shook her head in disbelief. "Who the heck thought of this?" she asked. "When did you fly to Switzerland to open the account?"

"Ingenious, huh? I'd like to take credit for it, but the Swiss accounts were Rodrigo's idea. Apparently, he had a vision, and the Christmas break after you left Italy, we went to Switzerland to open the accounts."

Jen rubbed her forehead. "How much is in this account?" she asked.

"Umm, actually, I'm not sure. Last time I checked was in December, and I had over three-quarters of a million. By now, probably double that or more."

"Holy shit, Joey!" Jen jumped up from her chair and started pacing the hotel room. "Okay, no more, I know enough now. You may go back to work now."

"Huh, what?" I asked, confused.

"I got this now. I need to meet with my partner and let him know we can accept the Dann case as his counsel. I also need to get ready to meet Peter for dinner. I'll call you tomorrow with updates. Bye, buddy."

"You're having dinner with Peter?"

"Yes, Joey! Don't worry, everything you said is between us. However, I am pretty sure I can gain more information from him regarding the whole situation. He has done the job of the person who is trying this indictment. And he's kind of cute too."

I shook my head as she ushered me to exit her hotel room door. In the hallway, I turned and asked, "What do I do now?"

"Exactly the same stuff you did before. Nothing changes. Okay, I'll call you tomorrow."

We hugged. I thanked her, and I was on my way back to Miami. In the car, I couldn't stop rehashing what she told me—Mariana tipped the FBI, and her tip most likely started a year and a half long undercover investigation that resulted in twenty-five arrests. I couldn't fathom that my old friend and roommate now faced federal prison time. Now Jeff's peculiar actions last week made sense.

I wanted to call Tim but knew that was entirely out of the question. I felt paranoid—what if Ronald McDonald McMillian knew something about my Brazilian clients?

What did Ronald know? Whatever he did know or suspect didn't result in an indictment for me, at least not for now.

And with that final thought on the drive back home, I was completely uneasy. I had a hard time relaxing for the rest of the night. My anxiety continued to spread as all the news outlets predicted the end of the world as the U.S. financial industry was almost up in flames.

The next day I wanted to speak with Rodrigo and Flavia to let them know what was going on. But then I thought of what facts I actually knew. All I knew for sure was that four co-workers got caught in lending fraud.

I wasn't part of that, and what was the ultimate point of meeting with Rodrigo and Flavia? To make them as paranoid as me? To make me feel better because I didn't have to bear this horrid news alone?

I tried re-thinking the reason for calling the meeting multiple times but always came to the same conclusion—keep my mouth shut and do as I had been doing.

Jen called me on Wednesday and let me know she was going to have a long meeting with Dann and his parents about the evidence against him and the strategy of her legal team. She let me know that Peter could drive her down to Miami Thursday afternoon, and she invited herself to stay at my condo until Sunday. She laughed and said she desperately needed some beach time.

I looked forward to her visit because I had plenty to discuss with her. Maybe she could calm my paranoia, somehow.

Jen didn't show up at my apartment until late on Thursday night, and we barely spoke since I was on my way to bed. However, she briefly mentioned hanging out drinking with Peter after the two day-long meetings with Dann and his parents.

The next day I sensed the financial world was ending. Still stressing about Jeff's situation, Sal barged into my office to let me know that Jeff still hadn't provided HR with proof of his father's hospitalization.

Because there was no proof.

Sal also was tense about what was happening in the financial markets. Multiple reports emerged that a couple of the largest and oldest financial institutions, Merrill Lynch and Lehman Brothers, were on the verge of bankruptcy. Additionally, the country's largest insurer, AIG, was in massive trouble as well.

DMNC Bank's name also had its share of time in the broadcast as well. Reports reflected that DMNC had taken on a lot of those negative amortization mortgages—the ones where the borrower pays only a portion of their actual monthly payment, and the rest of the payment gets tacked on to the balance of the loan, so the mortgage balance actually grows, not decreases.

That's a recipe for financial disaster. I'd like to meet the genius that came up with that financial engineering.

The news reported that DMNC didn't sell these atomic ticking time bomb mortgages because someone in some corporate office thought it was a good idea to keep these mortgages on the bank's balance sheet instead of selling them on to the secondary market as most mortgage originators had done. The financial world was on the edge of a credit freeze, which meant a possible seizure of DMNC by the Federal Deposit Insurance Company or FDIC.

Sal was petrified that this might happen. He had been scraping by for thirty years at DMNC, and the last thing he wanted was to have his last few years be a disastrous acquisition where he'd have to learn a new culture and systems, or worse, be laid off due to the acquisition.

I called Rodrigo to let him know that DMNC was likely going to be in the news. If he received any calls from our clients, he should let them know he talked to me. He should tell them that there was a good chance DMNC would just be bought by another bank and that their accounts were safe—hopefully.

When I arrived home from work, Jen was hanging out on my balcony. We were both so emotionally drained from the week that we barely said anything. I asked her if she wanted to order-in some pizza, she agreed. We popped open a couple of beers which quickly multiplied to a twelve-pack and an early night to sleep.

The next day when our slight hangover wore off, I took Jen to Surfside Beach—much tamer than the southern part of Miami Beach. We set up our chairs on the sand and faced the beautiful, calm, turquoise water.

As we sat peacefully, I quietly said, "I never asked about Dann or his parents."

Without breaking her stare into the water, Jen somberly responded, "Joey, this was such a difficult week for all of us. Dann is embarrassed and scared. I've never seen him with his tail between his legs—you know he's always so proud.

"His parents are super cool but made it known they were extremely disappointed. They let us know that they would pay for his entire legal defense and agreed that having Peter as an attorney on our team would help. They agreed to pay his legal bill moving forward as well.

"As for me, I was trying to learn as much as I could from the partner from my firm and stay positive for Dann, not to mention freaking out over your possible issues as well. My partner is really good, and I guess the silver lining for me is that I'll gain a ton of experience from this case. But it's still incredibly sad to see a friend go through this."

She turned to me, gazed into my eyes, and said, "I still cannot believe that two of my best friends, friends I thought were smart and successful, actually ended up being so greedy and careless."

I took a deep breath and replied, "Well, they say that people are motivated mostly by fear or greed. I think Dann has had a severe inferiority complex his whole life and tried to overcome it through accumulating wealth. He was motivated by greed. I mean, what person in his right mind would brag as much as he did? I, on the other hand, realize I was most likely motivated by fear."

Jen asked, "What the hell have you been scared of, Joey?"

"Failure." I felt my eyes start to tear up and was glad I was wearing sunglasses. I continued, "After the first year in my job, I was at the very bottom of my peers. I was pretty close to being fired. What was I going to do? Go back to New Jersey to sell freaking cars and live with my parents again? How would I find another solid job when I'd been fired for poor performance? I was so scared to fail that I took the lesser of two evils, I guess.

"The worst evil was what Dann got involved in, which was pure bank fraud. I could've followed his path as I had the opportunity multiple times. But Rodrigo had an idea that I vetted with my narcissistic manager at the time. My then boss told me that if I didn't do it—or change my production level somehow—I was out. What was I supposed to do?"

Jen nodded, not that she agreed with me but that she understood.

I continued, "You know where that fuck—I mean my previous manager—is now? He's the freakin' National Director of DMNC Bank! Even if DMNC gets acquired and fires the guy, he'll get a golden parachute worth millions. He'll demand millions if he goes to work for another financial institution.

"These are the people the FBI should be going after. They create this culture where they make it known non-performance is unacceptable and promote anyone who plays their game of bringing in any kind of business. They look the other way. I mean, management had to know there was a good chance that the accounts I opened were with laundered money. But instead of warnings, I received a pat on the back, awards, a raise, maximum bonuses, and the message to keep up the good work."

Jen's eyebrows raised in surprise. Until now, she didn't understand the corrupt, crony corporate environment that we'd been working in for the past four years.

She said, "I do understand your point, Joey. I also know you were raised properly with parents that taught you integrity—you know the thing where you do the right thing, no matter who is looking. I think you and Dann lost all the integrity you had down here. You both got caught up in the rat race, and *you* are lucky!" She pointed right at me.

"I say you are lucky because you have done illegal stuff and didn't get caught. Which brings me to my next point, what are your plans?"

She caught me off guard with the question. Bewildered, I asked, "Huh, what plans? You told me to do the same things I was doing before."

I noticed through her sunglasses that Jen rolled her eyes. She said, "Do I have to teach you everything! Yes, you need to do the same things right now, meaning in the short term. But long term, you need to start planning."

She took a deep breath then continued, "Okay. You're winning the game as of now, but that could change in the future. I know for a fact that the FBI is subpoenaing DMNC Bank branch records, starting with the four guys that got caught. Well, one of the guys is from *your* branch.

"What if, during this bank record review, they notice something suspicious on an account you opened. They might look at more of the accounts you opened. Then they might see the pattern that you opened all these large accounts for Brazilian nationals. They'll run background checks on them and find out they all work for PetroBrasil. In this scenario, the best case is you get fired from DMNC, and the worst case is you get indicted for money laundering. Why take the chance?"

"So what do you suggest I do? Keep in mind I currently have at least another ten Brazilian prospects lined up to onboard."

"You need to resign and leave on your terms. I am not telling you to quit tomorrow as the scenario I just gave would take months to complete. But, you want to be out in front of any problems you might incur. Here's an idea, you onboard a few more accounts over the next few weeks. If the bank gets acquired by another bank, that would give you a reason to quit—maybe you don't like the new culture or whatever. Just have a plan, and that plan has to be getting out of your current job soon, like by the end of this year!"

All I could do was gaze out into the pristine water as I analyzed what Jen was trying to tell me.

"Okay, buddy, I'm taking a dip. You coming?"

"Yep!"

If everyone thought the financial news from the week of September 8th was head-spinning, they had another thing coming the week of September 15, 2008.

The entire financial industry was in seismic upheaval. There was a severe illiquidity problem due to the previous careless mortgage market, and the massive under-reported credit default swaps loomed large. I'd never heard of a credit default swap before those few weeks, and these financial instruments are ultimately what made some institutions fail.

I tried to keep my head down and work that week, but my eyes remained glued to the branch TV. I spent most of my days trying to calm clients' nerves when they asked if their deposits were safe if DMNC failed. I learned more about the FDIC in that one week than I did the previous four years!

Rodrigo called, and I told him business was as usual. I also said we needed to discuss the future soon. After that call, I started to picture my future.

What was I going to do? My whole life, all I'd ever known is tennis and banking. The world was massive, and yet I only took time to learn two things. Can I do something else with what I already know?

One morning, after a restless night, I had an epiphany. I knew I wanted to give back, and suddenly it hit me that I could become a tennis coach or instructor. I wanted to teach value and integrity to impressionable young kids—teach them that lessons learned on the tennis court can translate to lessons in life. For the next few days, I daydreamed about how I could be a positive force in someone else's life. Focusing on this dream made it easier to get through the days and gave me a reason to get up in the morning.

Two weeks later, the news I had been expecting for days happened—DMNC Bank USA was being acquired by one of the largest banks in the country for something like fifteen billion dollars.

When numbers get that big, it feels like they are discussing monopoly money.

On the day of the announcement, Sal was noticeably shaking. I realized he'd been motivated by yet lived in fear his whole life.

Watching him those weeks made me realize I didn't want to live motivated by fear any longer. And since I had a decent amount of money in the bank, I didn't want to be motivated by greed either. My motivation had to come from within. The dream to become a tennis coach or instructor gained traction from within me and was something I was finally ready to announce.

One day, at the beginning of October, I took a day off work and told Flavia to come to my condo. I told Rodrigo to buy a burner phone and email me the number. I bought a burner flip phone as well. I wanted to make sure no one—meaning the FBI—was listening to our call. Paranoid, maybe. Cautious, definitely.

I welcomed Flavia into my condo with a pleasant handshake rather than a deep kiss. I asked how she had been. She told me good, and I didn't want to know more. We went right into my spare room office and called Rodrigo.

He answered immediately and asked, "What is happening, my friends?"

Flavia looked at me, and I said, "As you may have heard, DMNC Bank has been acquired by another large bank here. I suspect the new bank will have a higher level of compliance. The good news is that it will take a year or longer to integrate the two banks. Everyone in DMNC, from the top of the house to us within the branch, will be entirely distracted."

Flavia looked at me, and her eyes reflected fear. I motioned with my hands to calm down.

I continued, "The FBI has indicted Dann for bank fraud. This is *not* public information yet, so you cannot tell anyone. Jen's New York law firm is his legal defense counsel, which is how I found out. She said that the FBI would subpoena bank records. My branch is one they're looking at closely, because believe it or not, another banker, who was my original mentor, has also been indicted for bank fraud.

"I am not part of this indictment in any way. However, if the FBI pokes around in my branch records long enough, they might notice a pattern that I had been opening substantial accounts for many Brazilian nationals.

"Jen tells me if they notice that these accounts are from PetroBrasil executives, or worse, government officials, the best-case scenario is I get fired, and worst case is I get indicted for money laundering or assisting with it."

Rodrigo, who'd remained quiet—the longest silence from him I'd ever experienced—spoke up, saying, "Oh man! Dann got arrested?"

"Yes, and Jen is positive he is going to prison. Her job is to negotiate the least amount of time. Anyways, I have decided to resign from the bank by the end of the year, which is a little less than three months from now."

Flavia put her hands up and frantically said, "Jacob! No! Why? What are you going to do? What are we going to do without you?"

I continued, "Here is what I suggest. Rodrigo, tell the remaining interested prospects that things have changed due to the financial disaster of this past month, and the cost of our fees has doubled, ah fuck it, tripled. See who still wants our services, and I will work round the clock to get them onboarded. Get maximum revenue out of them. As I mentioned before, everyone in the bank will be distracted, so I think I can open quite a few accounts without anyone noticing too much.

"Flavia, you continue what you have been doing—finding new condos to buy and managing the real estate management company. I want out of the real estate management company by the end of the year. We can talk about what is fair regarding a settlement.

"Basically, I do not want any wire transfers hitting my Swiss account after a few months, when I plan to fly there and close it down. I haven't thought of what to do with the funds after that, though."

Rodrigo knew me well, and hearing the tone of my voice, noticed that I'd not stuttered or hesitated once on this call. Quietly he said, "So this is it, huh? What are you going to do, Joey?"

"You know, I have thought a lot about that the past couple weeks. I don't want to be a cog in the corporate rat race anymore. I want to be a positive figure in young kids' lives and teach them about integrity. I am leaning towards being a tennis coach or an instructor. Not sure where, but that is pretty much what I am seriously considering."

Rodrigo, rolling with change as quickly as he always did, promptly said, "You know what your problem is, Joey? You always have good ideas, but you think too small. You need to think big. You have a lot of money in the bank. Why go work for someone else when you can work for yourself?"

I looked over at a highly focused Flavia. She shrugged.

Rodrigo continued, "What about opening up a tennis academy? I attended one for years in Florida. I know what it takes to create a successful one. With the number of hours we have played tennis, we know what coaches to hire and how to spot talent for players. If we aren't going to have this little business anymore, I don't want to work for this corrupt company. For that matter, I don't want to live in this corrupt country anymore."

Flavia finally chimed in, asking, "So you both are leaving me?"

I replied, "I wouldn't look at it as we are leaving you. Consider it this way—you get to run your already successful real estate business solo from now on."

Rodrigo became more confident in his idea. He said, "You know, I have Portuguese citizenship from my grandfather. I think we should look at opening the academy in Europe and possibly attach it to a boarding school."

Things that take me literally weeks to think through, Rodrigo sees in minutes. Maybe he was more of a risk-taker than I was, but he also knew how to take advantage of opportunities too. I asked Rodrigo to fly up to Miami within the next month to discuss these plans in more detail.

Rodrigo flew up during Thanksgiving week, and our entire discussion from the moment I picked him up to when I dropped him off was about starting the tennis academy. He was passionate about it, and it was something I wanted to do as well.

At one point, I commented that I felt guilty for having all that money in my Swiss bank account and rhetorically asked how I could pay it forward.

Rodrigo brought up a great point and said, "You know the money sitting in our Swiss accounts came indirectly from the Brazilian Government. How do you give back to a super corrupt government? The answer is that you don't.

"But let's think about who gets screwed the most by the corrupt politicians. It's those poor kids growing up in poverty in the favelas. You saw it for yourself. Some of these kids don't even have shoes to wear!

"Here is what I suggest, and this will be our way of giving back; we issue a certain percentage of tennis scholarships to Brazilian kids from the favelas. I think that is truly giving back."

I agreed.

In a moment of downtime during his visit, I logged on to Facebook and had a generic Happy Thanksgiving message from Valeria. I showed it to Rodrigo.

He exclaimed, "Get her phone number and let's call her immediately!"

I knew exactly why he wanted to speak to her. However, I felt a bit awkward about the situation as I had not spoken to her verbally in four and a half years. But as always, I took Rodrigo's directive and messaged her right back, asking for her phone number.

She responded within hours. I took out my international calling card, dialed the number, and she picked up promptly, "*Ciao Jacob. Come stai amore?*"

Things can only be positive when you are referred to as love, right?

"*Molto bene*, now that I am finally speaking to you again! Oh, before you say anything super confidential, I need to tell you that Rodrigo is sitting with me here in Miami, and you are on speakerphone."

Rodrigo chimed in from across my living room, shouting, "*Ciao Valeria!*"

Valeria's voice became even more lively, and she responded, "Oh, um, *Ciao Rodrigo! Come stai?*"

I didn't let Rodrigo answer. I cut in, saying, "It's so good to hear your voice. I must say your accent is much better than the Latin women down here."

She giggled.

I continued, "So Rodrigo and I have been in a partnership the past couple of years, mostly helping Brazilian nationals with American real estate. As you may have seen on the news, the financial industry has been imploding recently, and I decided to leave my banking job by the end of the year.

"Rodrigo and I have seriously discussed the idea of opening a tennis academy in Europe, possibly Italy. Are you able to point us in any direction of who to contact or how to go about starting this type of business there?"

"*Bravo, ragazzi!* This is amazing, Jacob! I would love to help you guys. As you may remember, my father is in engineering and has contacts within the government. It will take some time and convincing, but I think we can point you in the right direction. Are you going to need to find investors to fund the construction of this?"

"Probably not. We have done pretty well in our side business. *Come va, Valeria?*"

Her tone softened, "Eh, I'm okay. I lost my job a few weeks ago, due to that financial crisis you mentioned before. I was in the real estate business as well, but unfortunately, I did not have success like you boys."

Rodrigo got up from the other couch, sat next to me, and began to talk into my phone. "Aw, Valeria. I am sorry to hear that," he said. "What if you work with us on this business? Maybe you can help us gain the proper approval and help us hire contractors to get this thing built. We can compensate you for your time and efforts. And who knows, maybe you'll want to work for us when we get this thing open?"

Valeria, sounding slightly surprised, asked, "*È Vero?* You are serious about this, aren't you?"

"Yes, we are," I said. "We have been discussing this for over a month, and Rodrigo came to visit me this week to go over this plan in more detail. If you remember, as a teen, Rodrigo attended a prestigious tennis academy in another area of Florida, and we want to open one that is more affordable to European phenoms."

"You know this is going to be expensive, right?" Valeria asked nervously.

Rodrigo replied, "Of course we do. That is why we are trying to plan this properly. We will take care of you however we can if you are able to assist us with the government and find us a place, then construction workers. Or, perhaps you can find us an already built apartment complex that we can build state-of-the-art tennis courts and facilities next to."

I interjected, "That might be the best idea."

Valeria replied, "You know, if you don't mind getting your hands dirty, I can possibly provide a place for you to say for a month or so. It's a condo in a little town on Lago di Como. My father has been renting it out for years, but he wants to fix it up a bit so it will be ready for him to stay there this coming summer. Of course, I have to ask him if this is okay. But what do you think?"

Rodrigo and I looked at each other with wide eyes and broad smiles. I shrugged, of course. I answered, "That sounds great! Please let me know what your father says."

"Of course I will. Soon! And since I don't have a job, I could come as well! Let me talk to my Dad and see if he will allow this."

"*Va bene!* Talk soon Valeria. *Grazie!*"

Rodrigo needed to return to Brazil. When he left, we both felt we were on to something big that would direct us into the next phase of our lives.

As I waited to hear from Valeria regarding a place to stay in Italy, the big news publicly emerged. I walked into my bank branch one morning in early December, and Sal made a beeline over to me.

"Can you fuckin' believe this shit, Jac?" he asked. He showed me the Miami Herald newspaper.

The headline read: "FBI breaks alleged Miami, Broward, Palm Beach bank loan scam." As I perused the article, I remembered I had to act super surprised. The story reported that federal authorities charged twenty-five local residents with bank fraud, bribery, money laundering, among other offenses. Dann, Jeff, Steve, and Don's names were all mentioned with their age and city of residence.

It was surreal. I'd known for months this was happening, but reading it in an official publication proved this shit was real. It also triggered my paranoia, and I realized I needed to get out of the bank soon.

I tried my best to act shocked. Sal and I discussed how Jeff's bullshit excuse of his father being ill was a complete fabrication and that he was under arrest this whole time. On the day the news broke, Sal finally convinced HR to terminate Jeff officially.

The rest of the day, my phone rang off the hook, Tim, Ward, Pierre, and even Rosie called to discuss the big news. Every time I looked down and realized it was one of them, I had to put on my surprised act. Eventually, I moved back into reality and realized I didn't have time to bother with that; I needed to onboard the last Brazilian accounts before making my grand exit; on my terms.

A few days later, I received a call from Valeria. Her voice conveyed excitement, and I had a good feeling. She said her father would allow Rodrigo and me to stay in his condo loft in Menaggio from mid-January until the end of March. There was one caveat, of course, her old man wanted to meet us at some point. I didn't see that as being a problem. She also reiterated that in exchange for free housing, we needed to assist with renovations of the place. Although Rodrigo and I had minimal experience with manual labor, I blindly agreed to it.

After our call ended, it finally hit me that my life was about to undergo a major change. I needed to put together a complete list of all the things I needed to take care of before I moved—including telling my parents I planned to move to Italy again. However, I had to plan the conversation carefully, as I'm sure they'd ask how Rodrigo and I would fund our grand plans for a tennis academy. They couldn't learn about the millions we had stashed in our Swiss bank accounts. But my list had more important items, such as finishing up my work at the bank, figuring out what to do with my condo, and what to do with Flavia's real estate business.

On Friday, December 19th, one day before my flight up to New Jersey for Christmas break, I formally advised Sal and Sarah of my resignation via email. Sarah called me immediately, and although she made it sound like she was upset over my resignation, I sensed her phony facade.

Her tone had changed from the last time I spoke to her, before the FBI indictment news. Now she sounded far less sure of herself. Though she didn't ask what she could do to encourage me to stay, she said that I would always be welcomed back to DMNC or the new bank that took over DMNC. The call lasted three minutes, and I knew that would be the last time I'd ever speak to Sarah.

Sal took the news a lot harder. He came into my office and wanted to know why. I wanted to tell him the whole truth. I thought he deserved more than a canned response, so I told him as much as possible. I let him know that I genuinely enjoyed working for him for the past four and a half years. I told him that he was a man of high integrity in a place where integrity was a rare trait. I also said that these years had changed me into someone I didn't want to be anymore. I didn't want to feel like a pawn for an almighty and powerful central regime that controlled everything from compensation, to call-nights, to mental psyche.

I also mentioned that I believed the client's desires rarely matched up with bank management's desires. I felt that I was the cog in the system, lying to both sides to create false harmony. I didn't want to be that cog in a system that was too big for anyone to stop. I wanted to be proud of what I offered in life, and moving forward, I was going to provide a positive force in the lives of young people. I finally let him know of my plan to open a tennis academy.

For the first time almost ever, Sal was practically speechless. He was the man who honed the small talk to a fine art. He had something to say in every situation. But now, he just stared at me in silence. I think for the first time in his thirty-year banking career—always working for the all-powerful machine—he could look back at the younger version of himself and realize I was correct.

Although Sal lived a comfortable lifestyle all these years, deep down, he wasn't satisfied. Maybe he sold his soul to live that comfortable lifestyle. Perhaps he was a little jealous that I could escape the monster of corporate America at a young age and not be stuck there decade after decade.

Sal finally broke his silence and said, "I admire you, Jacob. I wish when I was younger, I had the guts to do what you're doing. I wish you luck in your endeavors and appreciate everything you have done for this branch."

He got up, walked around my desk, then I got up, and he hugged me. I told him that once I was settled in Italy, he was more than welcome to visit. I also winked and asked him to stand up for me if any compliance issues drifted my way. He knew what I meant and nodded his head in agreement. He also asked me to come back after Christmas for two weeks to train the new guy for Jeff's old position. I said I would.

He ended our meeting by saying, "You know what, Jac? I'm gonna try and stick it to these sonz-a-bitches. I had a doctor's appointment regarding my eye issue. It turns out I have something called blepharitis. I think I'm going to plead my case to those HR bastards and get on some kind of disability."

Sounded like a bunch of baloney to me!

I responded, "That's good, Sal. You deserve it after all these years. Stick it to those sonz-a-bitches!"

It was hard to get into the Christmas mood. I was stressed and had so much on my plate, including telling my parents my plans. I treated my parents kind of like Sal, but I included how I could've easily made the wrong decision, like Dann, who would be sitting in federal prison for almost four years. They were grateful I escaped my banking career unscathed and didn't question me too much on the tennis academy plans. I think they were just relieved I was not going to prison.

I squeezed in a trip to Manhattan to meet up with Jen. I met her at her upper west side apartment. She was glowing, and it was a good look on her. We walked a couple of blocks in the frigid cold to a small Italian restaurant tucked into the basement of a brownstone building.

As soon as we took our coats off and sat down at the table, Jen said, "I have some exciting news! You remember Peter? Well, we have been talking regularly, and he has come up to visit me a couple of times. I guess you can say we are officially dating. Due to my performance as Dann's counsel, he got me an interview with the District Attorney of Southern Florida. I will be interviewing for the Assistant District Attorney position!"

I wanted to be happy for her, but I was kind of sad that she would be moving to Miami at the very same time I'd be leaving. I explained that to her, and she understood.

"Nonetheless, I'll be rooting for your career success!" I said.

During the middle of the meal, she brought up an interesting scenario. She said, "Joey, I'm curious. If the FBI caught you and you knew that Dann was doing illegal shit, would you have ratted him out?"

I'd honestly never thought about this and needed a few minutes to process her question. I hadn't even formed a complete answer, nor words to convey it before she interrupted my thoughts.

She said, "I know you wouldn't have. Who can live with themselves when they rat out someone else for no reason, right?"

I remembered my vocabulary again. "Yeah, right. What makes you ask this?"

As was often the case, a couple of glasses of wine into the meal, Jen became a little loose with her words. She said, "Oh, just that Dann came to me. He wanted to try to help himself by ratting you out to the FBI."

Shocked, I lunged forward onto the small table. Quietly but fiercely, I said, "What! What did you say? What happened?"

"Relax, Joey. I told him that would be the worst thing someone could do. And if he did it, I would fire him as our client. He'd be sent to the wolves and be in prison for a maximum sentence. He got scared, and I told him he would still have a life after he gets out. I said that this experience might be good for him, and he could focus on making himself a better person."

"Jen, I can't thank you enough for what you have done for me. And I'll even thank you on behalf of Dann because I've never heard the dude say those words before."

"Aw, Joey, you don't have to thank me. I know you would've done the same thing if the roles were reversed. Although you had a serious slip in judgment, I still believe you have a lot of integrity. I know you will live life on the straight edge from now on. By the way, I want to be the first visitor for you and Rodrigo in Italy! That's my only demand, for now." She laughed as she brought the wine glass to her lips for a final sip down the hatch.

I chuckled and nodded in agreement. I said, "You know, I hope you get this AUSA job. You will do shady Miami well, buddy."

"I know. You want me to get the job so I can tank any possible money laundering charges against you."

She let out a loud drunken laugh that disrupted the relatively quiet, quaint restaurant.

I shrugged.

I helped her out of her chair and gave her a big hug, saying, "I'm going to miss you, my quirky blondie."

"Oh Joey, me too," she said as her big light blue eyes started to tear.

When I returned to Florida to work the last two weeks at the bank, I met up with Flavia. We agreed to take my name off of the real estate management business and that it would be hers to own wholly. I negotiated a discounted current value lump sum payment to be wired to my Swiss account.

Additionally, we agreed that she would live in my condo and use it as her office. Since the real estate market had taken a drastic turn south, I was underwater in the condo, and didn't want to sell at a loss. In exchange for living there, I told her to cover all expenses and sell it the minute I could make a profit. She agreed and thanked me for the opportunity.

Through working with Rodrigo and me, Flavia gained financial independence and a portfolio of clients to manage moving forward.

Before we adjourned the meeting at my condo, Flavia said, "I've always loved you, Jacob. Your situation with Mari turned you into a wounded duck for a long time. Look, Jac, it took you such a long time to tell me you loved me. I feel that if you truly loved me and I was the one for you, you wouldn't have waited two years to tell me.

"The past five months have been hard without you in my personal life, but it was something that needed to be done. I honestly don't think I am the woman you are madly in love with. I was there for you in your time of need, and we turned out to be excellent business partners. We had a lot of good times. But in terms of someone to spend the rest of your life with? I don't think I am or was that person for you."

All I could do was sadly nod in agreement. My eyes watered, and I realized that Flavia was correct. I used her as a rebound to fill a hole dug by Mari. If I really wanted to be with her, I shouldn't have waited all that time to tell her that I loved her or wanted to be exclusive with her.

We ended our meeting on a somber note, but I know we were both grateful to have met each other, and I had to accept that this might be the last time I would ever see her again—another tough pill to swallow.

On my last day of work, I sold my beloved Infiniti, withdrew $10,000 in cash, closed all my DMNC bank accounts, and walked away with a cashier's check.

The Banker Gang demanded that we have one last happy hour, at the Ale House, of course. I let them know that it had to be an early night as I was leaving the next day. Everyone from our training showed up, well, except those on the verge of being incarcerated.

Tall Ward and Naomi were still together and said that they both accepted roles at different banks. We all congratulated them.

Pierre got bitten by the ethics police and was terminated a couple of weeks back for numerous loan customer complaints. Tall Ward offered to help him obtain an interview at a new bank.

Rosie even showed up, pregnant again, with baby number two. She said she told management that after giving birth in the spring, she would not return to work. Her wish was to be a stay-at-home mom. I congratulated her on following through with what she yearned for. She looked relieved to be out of the rat race.

As for Tim? Harry tapped him on the shoulder yet again. This time he'd be responsible for the Florida market bank metamorphosis program. Tim would run the integration that transformed DMNC into the new giant bank that would plaster their names on all buildings and letterhead in the coming months. I congratulated Tim on his promotion out of the branch and said I saw this as a giant opportunity for his career. He was sort of satisfied.

I also let him know how much I appreciated his genuine friendship over the last four and a half years and how I would miss him. He was happy for me. I invited him to visit whenever he wanted. Though I doubted he would take me up on the offer, I knew Tim would be a friend for life, even if we didn't see or speak to each other for months or even years. We fought a metaphoric war together, we became battle brothers, and I would never turn my back on him. I am pretty sure he wouldn't turn his on me either.

And for Harry, well, he kept his National Director position, and you can say it was a promotion now that he would oversee more employees. His stock options exploded in value due to the bank acquisition, and I'm sure he was happier than a pig in shit. Harry was like Teflon Don of the banking world. Go figure. His buddy Jerry didn't get to share Harry's good fortunes as he would spend the next eight years locked in a federal penitentiary. As for Dann, Steve, Don, and Jeff, they're counting down until 2013, which will be the next time they are free men.

After happy hour, I went into deep reflection mode. I don't think any of us in The Banker Gang—or very many DMNC employees for that matter—ever set out to become bankers. We got sucked in for a plethora of different reasons. We started competing because that's what we'd been conditioned to do throughout our lives. We maintained and honed that sense of competition while working in corporate America.

We chased after what everyone else chased after, regardless of whether or not we actually cared about the work. Irrespective of the consequences, we all wanted to win. With the game of life, people sometimes win, sometimes lose, some quit before the end, and some decide not to compete at all.

Let me make this clear; competition is not bad. However, toxic competition is unhealthy and is the undoing of many teams. I realized we needed to care about our teammates and not see them solely as competition on a stack ranking. Yet, in some cases, healthy rivalry doesn't advance certain people's career aspirations.

Until this problem is fixed, I imagine countless corporations—whose employee motivation is based on detrimental competition where "winners" step on anyone to get ahead—will be rewarded in the end. All you have to do is look at Harry and Sarah.

That night, I finished packing my entire life into two suitcases and a tennis bag. The next day, I ordered a taxi to the Miami airport and daydreamed about my future life during the entire flight to Milan.

When I landed, Valeria met me with open arms, and she planted a gentle kiss right on my lips. It was the first time the immense pressure that I'd harbored in my chest for months dissipated. Immediately, I felt we made the right decision. Although I never admitted it to Valeria, she was my first true love, and I was ecstatic to be reunited with her. I also promised myself that I wouldn't wait years or even months to express my love towards her.

For the next two hours, as we waited for Rodrigo's flight to land, we sat at the airport talking about everything and anything—mostly about where our lives had taken us the previous five years.

After we greeted Rodrigo, we promptly hopped on a train for a two-hour ride to the idyllic village of Menaggio on the western edge of Lake Como. It was dark when we arrived; we were tired and called it an early night.

When I awoke the next morning, a chill was in the air. I opened the balcony doors and was greeted by a beautiful view of the blue lake at the bottom of the cliff; mountains rose in the background. It reminded me of looking down at the Biscayne Bay from the DMNC Tower, but here I saw no highways, no hustle, no bustle—just a tiny, quaint, quiet lakeside village in Northern Italy.

I sat alone on the balcony while Valeria and Rodrigo were inside. A thought popped in my head that I couldn't easily dismiss, *what is success*? After a crazy few years, I developed a new definition. Success doesn't rely on external validation. Success isn't being listed on top of a corporate stank—I mean stack—ranking that starts at zero every month, quarter, or year. Success isn't trying to please your family, your boss, your significant other, or your friends. Success isn't measured by how many zeros show up in your net worth, how large your house is, or how fast your car is.

Success comes from within. It's feeling a sense of accomplishment for trying your best and being proud within your own skin. Success is a personal positive state of mind that no one can erase with nasty words or a negative performance write-up. For the first time in my life, I felt success in my gut. I knew I'd never let my internal moral code be corrupted again. Yes, I may be a previously flawed individual, but I've started over—living in a foreign country. I now knew my self-worth and happiness came from within.

I also realized that luck comes to those who work hard. And boy, do we have a lot of work to do now, metaphorically and literally, but I am confident that we'll put our heads together and work hard day after day, year after year, and the luck will come.

Valeria came out to the balcony and greeted me with a morning kiss. She said Rodrigo ran out to grab some breakfast and coffee for us. We stood in our sweatshirts overlooking the magnificent Lake Como. Valeria stood in front of me, and I hugged her back to my chest. I leaned down, reacquainting myself with her scent. I squeezed her a little tighter, and she looked up at me, reminding me of the first time she gave me that look almost exactly five years earlier.

Rodrigo arrived and broke up our moment. He exclaimed, "Breakfast is here, my friends!"

We sat around the little wooden table on the balcony. Even though it was quite chilly, the three of us were just happy to be together and hopeful for what the future had in store for us.

I lifted my coffee and offered a toast, "I'd like to dedicate this delicious *caffe* to the best friend I could ask for and to the reunion with my first love."

They both stared at me.

I continued, "To our lives, our liberty, and our future happiness! Cheers!"

Rodrigo raised his coffee. "*Saúde, meu amigo*!"

Valeria got up, hugged me then sat on my lap, saying, "*Salute, mi amore*!"

I couldn't help but grin. I looked at Rodrigo and said, "Now it's time to get to work, my friend."

Rodrigo smiled back and looked at both of us, then asked with a wink, "Hey, you know if they have sexy massages here?"

Made in the USA
Las Vegas, NV
22 July 2021

26887979R00184